Dark Days

Book 2 of
The Albatar Chronicles

Leonie Rogers

DARK DAYS

Book 2 of *The Albatar Chronicles*

The moral rights of Leonie Rogers to be identified as the author of this work have been asserted.

Copyright 2022

Hague Publishing

PO Box 451

Bassendean, Western AUSTRALIA 6934

Email: contact@haguepublishing.com

Web: www.haguepublishing.com

ISBN 978-0-6488346-4-9

Cover: Dark Days by Jade Zivanovic

http://www.steampowerstudios.com.au/

Typeset Garamond 11½ /12½

Acknowledgment

In loving memory of my father, Desmond Casey.

A man who loved greatly, and was greatly loved.

Chapter One:
Haunted

Kazari bent over, gasping and dry-retching. Her heart thumped wildly in her chest, as she braced herself against the cold stone pillar outside the gate into the Abbey's grove. She'd taken to running around the entire Abbey grounds, hoping to tire herself out in order to sleep soundly enough to drown out the echoes of the gorgone's voice. A voice that still haunted her dreams and stalked her meditations.

Each morning she ran, but whether she was trying to chase the words away or run from them, she wasn't sure. At least for the minutes when she pumped her legs and arms, pushing her body to its limits, the voice was held at bay.

Now, as she leaned on the cool stone, fighting the urge to vomit from the effort, she wished with all her heart that the physical act of throwing up could rid her of the memories of that hateful voice. But of course, it wouldn't.

A stench, as if the smoke from a fire had swept across a decaying corpse, struck her nostrils, and Kazari spun in place, heart pounding anew. Nothing. She sniffed, despite her heightened nausea, as her limbs quivered and phantom pains tingled through the scar on her face. Again, nothing.

She drew a deep breath through her nose once more. Was she mistaken? Had there really been the smell of gorgone on the wind, or was her imagination playing tricks on her? She took a few steps away from the pillar, eyes travelling over the trees and bushes that surrounded the Abbey.

The chilly light of dawn played muted colours across the landscape, and the surrounding vegetation was indistinct without the brightness of the sunlight to delineate branch and leaf. Kazari's pounding heart was so loud in her own ears that she wondered if she'd be able to hear anything nearby anyway. Once again she drew in a breath, trying to sustain the inhalation while her body fought the slowness, still starved of oxygen from her run. Still nothing.

She turned away, convinced her memory was playing tricks. But then, from the corner of her eye, something moved. She spun back again, automatically going to a half crouch, weight centred, both hands seeking the knives at her belt, while the memory of the enormous gorgone that had assailed the Abbey all those months before sent a fresh surge of adrenalin surging through her veins.

Nothing moved. Nothing stank. The first tremulous rays of sunlight dragged themselves above the horizon to her left, and second by second the leaves and branches came into clear focus. The evergreens stood out starkly against the bare branches of their deciduous neighbours, and Kazari forced herself to relax, muscle by muscle. She crouched there for a few more minutes, half convinced there was a threat to the Abbey while the other part of her told her off for being hypersensitive, still traumatised by Suborden. Finally, after another indrawn breath that smelled only of fresh air, Kazari turned back to the gate in the stone wall and entered the grove.

The back of her neck continued to prickle, however, and her shoulder blades twitched.

Now, as always, the grove breathed a little serenity into Kazari's turmoil. She eased herself to the ground near the tree at the centre, and sat cross-legged in the faint dawn light, allowing herself to breathe deeply of the chilly air. Slowly, she sank into slow, measured breaths, as Andiss had taught her. She allowed the process to calm her racing heart and still her quivering limbs, until she was ready to examine the nightmare images that stalked her, and the sounds that seemed burned into her mind.

Lady, why? She prayed. *Why?* The Lady's voice was silent, but the calmness of the grove spoke deeply of her care, even though Kazari wished desperately for answers that never seemed to come. Night after night she'd awoken, mind in turmoil and full of images of fire and death. Andiss and Javon called them flashbacks and had told her it wasn't uncommon for a Hunter to be haunted by images of the gorgones they'd faced. They'd encouraged her to speak of the fears they dredged from her soul. Both had listened to her describe her nightmares with compassion – not condemnation. And, of course, they'd all heard the voice of the greater gorgone, so Kazari knew they understood – at least a little.

She used the moments of stillness to work through her sudden panic outside the grove, trying to sift the sensations dispassionately, and to focus only on what she knew. Mind you, she thought to herself, that meant pretty much everything left her disquieted right now.

Life in the Abbey went on as normal, but there was a hovering angst that had begun to colour each moment. Messengers came and went more and more often. Kazari's fellow initiate, Abel, a Navigator, had been in and out of the Abbey frequently. When she'd asked him what he was up to, he'd shrugged and said it was just normal training – but he hadn't met her eyes. And she knew from Javon and Andiss, that every sept had increased the rate at which the new initiates were being trained, and from her own experience in Suborden, she knew that the learning went well beyond what a new initiate would have otherwise been exposed to. The events she'd been involved in at Suborden had changed the feel of the Abbey from one of comforting routine to one of routine under-pinned with an air of unspoken urgency.

Images of the fire gorgone seared her closed eyes, and once again, she heard its master's words echo in her mind. 'You think you've won? Because you defeated a fledgling infestation?

Think all you like. This war is just beginning, and Albatar will fall.' The remembered words chilled the sweat on her body. The snake woman, the hoofed woman, the searing pain she'd felt at their hands, and the fear she'd seen in Sendar's eyes, flooded her mind once again. And then the fight with the flaming monster, won only because of Sendar's cleverness, and because she'd been relatively whole.

She pressed her palms against her eyes, trying to blot out the images, but her hand touched the puckered line of scar that now marred her skin, and once again, the remembered threats against her family echoed like distant thunder inside her skull. 'I see your family. I hear their fears. And I will come for them. And you will not save them, because this day, you die.'

But of course she hadn't died, and the words had shown themselves lies. But after weeks of Kazari's recurring nightmares, the Abbot had sent a messenger to Athos to check on her family. They were safe, and the local incumbents were maintaining a covert watch on them – and indeed the entire village. Her family was safe. She *knew* they were safe, but still the gorgone's words continued to haunt her.

She traced the scar with a fingertip. The wound no longer hurt, and the scar was fading, but it was still very obvious and pulled at the corner of her mouth whenever she smiled or frowned. Even now, she was still shocked each time she looked in the mirror. Her fingertip paused at the corner of her mouth, and wetness slid down her cheek, touching her fingertip. She knew it was silly to mourn the loss of her smooth skin when the villagers of Suborden had lost so much more. But she did, and she hadn't been able to stop.

She wished she'd heard *from* her family, not just *of* them. She hadn't seen them for months – not since she'd left to become one of the Lady's servants. In fact, she hadn't heard from them once. Her parents hadn't wanted her to devote her life to the Abbey and had actively campaigned against her choice. But in the end they hadn't stopped her. The thought gave her hope, even if it was only a tiny one. They hadn't stopped her, but they hadn't made her choice easy.

Unlike most initiates, Kazari had no warm memories of her parents proudly waving her off to the Abbey. All she had were memories of the lonely walk to the village square. No mother, no father, no brothers, just little Jaden at the last moment. Jaden had come by himself and had probably gotten into trouble because he had.

Dari, her best friend, had supported her, as had Dari's family, but they weren't *her* parents. And now, if she perished fighting gorgones, all she'd have as a last memory of them was a furious argument.

Despite her meditations, even the memory of Dari didn't warm her. Dari's regular letters had trickled off. Early in her training, she'd had regular letters, and even before Suborden, there'd been a letter every few weeks. Now, she couldn't recall a new one since she'd returned. Perhaps they'd gotten lost on the way. She shelved the thought and tried to resume her measured breaths, but her mind wandered back to the last argument with her parents again. Her mother's words still haunting her. *"Some of those who pledge to the Lady die, Kazari – they die, or fall into darkness!"*

Well, she hadn't died, not quite. And she hadn't fallen into darkness, although sometimes it seemed as if the darkness was walling her in, pressing down upon her like some vast weight. When she and Sendar were trapped in the room at the mercy of the 'changed', the darkness had indeed surrounded them, but even then, it hadn't taken them and they had escaped. Death had continued to stalk them, and when she thought back to the fight with the fire gorgone, she knew just how close they'd come to it.

She took another breath, drawing the grove's cool air deep into her lungs before releasing it. Each breath a prayer, each moment an entreaty to take the dreams from her nights and the words from her mind. One day she hoped she'd wake refreshed and clear-headed again. Slowly, Kazari regained her equilibrium, until, as the sun sent its rays slanting through the trees, she felt steady enough to open her eyes and embrace its warmth. Around her neck, the amethyst on its leather thong caught and held the light, glowing momentarily, and even warming slightly on her chest.

Startled, Kazari gripped it tightly, and a few of the knots within her mind and body released, allowing her thoughts to move more freely, much as her blood had when Sendar had loosened the too-tight knots that had bound her hands in the dark cell beneath the mayor's house. Perhaps this time, the Lady had answered her entreaties with a yes. Perhaps tonight she might sleep undisturbed.

A quiet footfall disturbed her reverie, and she looked up, startled. Sendar stood there, looking awkward.

"Sorry, Kaz. Didn't mean to disturb you. Dreams again?"

She nodded mutely, miserably. When they'd first returned from Suborden, Sendar's nights had also been troubled, but after a few weeks, his dreams had seemed to settle. He crouched beside her and tucked an arm around her shoulders.

"They'll go eventually, don't worry."

Kazari made a face. "I hope so," she managed. "How's your leg?"

Sendar was scarred as well, but his wound had been much more serious than hers. With her self-healing gift, hers had become mostly cosmetic, making her guilt even worse. Sendar's leg, despite both Kazari's and Andiss' help, had taken longer to heal. Even now, he still exhibited a slight limp, despite returning to the care of the Abbey's Healer's Sept. In the end, even the Abbey's most gifted Healers had shaken their heads over the wound.

The Healers had told both of them that wounds were some of the easiest things for a Healer to work with – and generally resulted in unscarred skin. But neither Kazari nor Sendar's wounds had responded in the normal fashion, and in the end the Healers had shaken their heads, puzzled. Each injury had occurred at the exact moment a greater gorgone had spoken directly to their minds. Kazari had somehow managed some kind of extra healing in Suborden, but none of the Healers had been able to shed light on what she'd done. In the end, they'd decided that perhaps the Lady had intervened when Kazari had been trying to heal Sendar, as there appeared to be no other explanation.

As it was, Sendar was still building the strength in his leg, and only time would tell if he would ever recover completely.

"You haven't answered my question – how's your leg?" Kazari asked, ashamed of her thoughts, when her own wound was so much less than his.

"Improving, slowly," he replied at last. "It doesn't hurt as much as it did, and it *is* getting stronger. In fact, I'm allowed to spar again today. I thought perhaps we might try a kata together, before breakfast. Fourth kata?"

Touched, Kazari nodded, and stood. They separated slightly, allowing each other space, and then at Sendar's count, began.

The 'kata' with its gliding movements, often performed with a partner, underlay a Hunter's training. The fourth kata started slowly, all the movements controlled, but gradually gained pace, until the pair performing it were moving quickly, mirroring each other's movements, as if dancing to silent music. Kazari allowed herself to fall into the rhythm of the movements, stepping from stance to stance, and allowing her arms and legs to flow from defence to offence, without breaking the measured pacing.

The grass of the grove bent softly under their feet, almost caressingly, as they moved through the forms in the prescribed pattern. The first time Kazari had seen a pair of Hunters performing a paired kata, she'd been awed, amazed by their serene, yet deadly grace. She'd never imagined she could show that same grace, but as she and Sendar moved together through the steps she at last recognised how deeply her body and soul had absorbed her Hunter's training.

The kata's measured pace spoke of the Lady's love, paired with Kazari's own fierce desire to protect her people from the threat Kazari knew all too well, and strangely, this time it both soothed her and calmed her fears. As one, the two of them moved faster and faster. The numbered katas were performed without the use of a Hunter's Gifts, so each Hunter stood on an equal footing with the others as a mark of unity. There were others, each one designed to *use* a Hunter's Gifts, but they were taught only after the Hunter was comfortable with their Gifts, and only in order to allow the Hunter to adapt their Gifts to enhance already hard-won skills. Those, they performed with others who had the same Gifts.

As they reached the midpoint of the kata, their limbs moved with almost blurring speed. Yet each movement remained precisely planned, each movement precisely executed, so that even with the height difference between them, Kazari and Sendar looked perfectly matched. A warm glow enveloped Kazari, and her dark mood lifted, the last dregs of the dreams blown to tatters by the flowing movements. At last, they stopped, poised in perfect balance, and the tension drained from Kazari in a rush, leaving her relaxed and supple.

"Perfect!" breathed Sendar, "That was perfect." He relaxed his stance and wrapped a warm arm around Kazari. She hugged him back.

"Your leg had no trouble, Sendar! None at all!" She was so pleased for him, so relieved that he was whole again.

"No, not even a twinge." He smiled, and she could hear the relief in his tone. "Come on, let's go to breakfast." He squeezed her warmly again, and she smiled up at him, her own troubles forgotten momentarily as she shared his joy.

One last squeeze, and Kazari was suddenly aware he'd released her just before the hugging became awkward. She sort of wished he hadn't, because the warmth of human contact was one thing that kept the dream images at bay, and because she enjoyed his infrequent hugs. They'd become close because of their shared experiences, but continuously hugging her fellow Hunters wasn't really appropriate behaviour, whether or not it helped her nightmares. She almost blushed.

He punched her lightly on the arm. "Come on, I'm starving." She smiled and followed him towards the breakfast hall, warmed inside and out.

Chapter Two: Revelations

After breakfast, Kazari spent several hours lifting weights and practicing on the agility course with Javon. She was much tougher than she had been, leaner yet more muscled. When she'd joined the Hunters sept, she'd been short and stocky, with luxurious curly hair. Now, she was still short, but her stockiness had begun to give way to firm muscling, and she'd found unexpected strengths within her compact frame. Her long locks were now short, tightly curling, trimmed as they were to the prescribed neatness of the Order, and while her skin was the same olive tone it always had been, it was now marred by the scar on her face.

Things that had been completely beyond her six months ago were now easy, and Javon had begun to concentrate on Kazari's specific strengths. She had become proficient with her knives in close combat fighting and throwing, but a Hunter learned many weapons, not just one, and she had yet to favour one type over another.

"I think we'll keep on working with a variety of weaponry at this stage, Kaz," Javon suggested. "You're flexible, fast, and getting stronger, but being a bit on the short side does limit your reach. It might take you a while to figure out what suits you best. In the meantime we'll continue to teach you the basics in everything."

Kazari nodded and took aim with the bow. She was still figuring out exactly how much elevation she needed for each target's distance. But, as Javon constantly reminded her, practice made perfect. Still, her arms were trembling with exhaustion as she steadied herself for the draw. She rolled her eyes as the arrow hit the edge of the target once again.

"Well, perhaps you can bludgeon them to death with your bow, Kaz, if you can't get the arrow reliably into the target," Javon said, smiling at Kazari's expression.

Later, as they stretched slowly together, Kazari found her thoughts wandering back to her morning kata with Sendar. Her face warmed slightly as she relived his hug, and she turned her body away, pretending to stretch her back, hoping that Javon wouldn't ask why she was blushing. She was being fanciful, reading more into that casual moment of happiness than was there, perhaps, and turned her attention back to the business at hand.

Once again her thoughts wandered. How was Dari? How were her parents? And her brothers? And what had happened to Dari's letters? Every time she thought about any of them, the hurt seemed to freshen. She sat up and began to stretch her hamstrings, enjoying the sensation of tightness running down the back of her legs. It was early spring, still cold here at the Abbey, but it would be milder in her home village. They'd be preparing for the spring celebration, a time when the whole village came together to display their wares, eat good food, celebrate, and thank the Lady for her care and for leading their ancestors to Albatar.

Homesickness struck like a rockslide, and to her embarrassment, she felt her bottom lip tremble. She masked it by changing to another stretch, and gritted her teeth deliberately, once again focusing on her breathing.

"Don't forget the class this afternoon, Kaz," said Javon.

Kazari breathed out and nodded, still not trusting her voice. When a novice joined a sept, the sept took care of the first six months of training – understanding what your sept did in the Order was of utmost importance. Like many others new to the Lady's service, Kazari had imagined being part of several septs, but not the one she'd ended up in. And the Gifts that she now knew the Lady had placed within each of Her servants were unique to each sept. To get to know *who* you were in the Lady's service was something that took time to even begin to understand. Letting go of your preconceived ideas about your sept was even harder. Kazari sometimes felt that she still didn't know exactly who, or even what, she was now.

Andiss and Javon had explained that every initiate had the same doubts and fears, but not always the same experiences in the first six or so months. Sendar was almost a year ahead of her in the Hunters. He'd had much more time to learn who he was and to develop his skills, but their shared experiences had still nearly undone them both. Even so, once the initial six months were over, each initiate was expected to work with others also new to the Lady's service. There were many things to learn in common – rules, laws and history, and the ways that the septs were bound together within the Order. Bound together but still separate in their roles within greater Albatar.

And now, with the threat of gorgone incursion more real than ever before in living memory, working together would be even more important. She'd seen hints of what the other septs could do when the greater gorgone had climbed over the Abbey wall several months before. She still wondered why it had done so, and where it had come from. It seemed so futile, and it must have known it would be defeated and killed. The thought nagged at her – usually in the dim hours of the night. Why *had* it come to the Abbey? And then she remembered that hint of stench in the dim light of the morning. Had she *really* imagined it?

Several hours later, clean and fed, Kazari took a seat in the large classroom set aside for the new initiates. A moment later, she saw the dark head of Charla, the only Adviser initiate, peer around the door frame. She patted the seat next to her, and the girl hurried over, relief evident in every line.

"So glad you're here, Kaz. Everyone else will come with someone, and it seems so long since I've seen any of the others."

Kazari nodded. She'd been training hard since her initiation into the Hunters, and then there'd been Suborden. She stopped that line of thought dead in its tracks. "I know, apart from you and Abel, it's not like I really got to know anyone else much, either. Except for the people we came in with, of course," she said, thinking back to the day of her own choosing. She'd not thought about Quisil for months, she realised, embarrassed. The older woman had made her decision to choose the Lady at the same time as Kazari, but as she'd been initiated into the Growers sept, they'd taken very different paths. Kazari looked around curiously, wondering if the woman was already in the room.

It was filling up quickly, and the room was buzzing with quiet conversation as people took seats with friends.

"Did you join with anyone, Charla?" Kazari asked.

"There were five of us. But I didn't know anyone particularly well, and most of them were older than me." She shrugged. "And like you, I'm the only newcomer to my sept." She turned sideways in her seat, taking one of Kazari's hands. "You'll always be my friend, won't you, Kaz?" she entreated. "The other Advisers are nice, but I'm the first in three years, so everyone's older than me by far. I know you're out and about a lot, but at least you understand. I mean – you understand what it's like to be the different one."

A little shock ran through Kazari. She'd been so caught up in her own troubles that it had never occurred to her that Charla could be feeling lost and alone as well, sequestered as she was within the Abbey. She looked around the room again. Clumps of green jerkins sat in rows, emeralds gleaming on silver chains. A gaggle of blue robed Judicars clutched tidy folders to their chests, sapphires gleaming in copper settings. White robed Intercessors entered in a flurry, and a small group of red garbed Healers clustered together over by the door. She and Charla sat together like stripes on a bumblebee, one all black, the other all gold. Then three Navigators entered together, Abel's long skinny body towering above the other two. He dragged the others over to Kazari and Charla, smiling a welcome even as the Abbot and all the Sept Leaders entered and arrayed themselves at the front of the room.

Like Kazari, the Navigators wore clothing in a different colour from their gems – in their case, aquamarines in silver glimmered over clothing similar to that worn by the Hunters, but multihued in earthy and green tones.

'Designed to blend in,' Andiss had said, when Kazari asked about it. 'They've got several different sets, depending on the season.' Mind you, Kazari reminded herself, even the Navigators wore bright blue robes for ceremonial occasions, while her own sept wore only black. She'd never thought to ask why. She filed that thought for later.

"Welcome," said the Abbot, stepping forward to the lectern. The chatter came to a sudden stop. The tall woman in her unrelieved black was flanked by the Sept Leaders in their rainbow of robes. Andiss, her second within the Hunters, stood just behind her.

"Times have changed since the day of your initiation. Then, we were at peace, and now we stand on the edge of a full blown gorgone incursion; the first for over a hundred years." She swept her eyes over the room, the blackness of her robes making the amethyst at her chest stand out as if lit from within. Kazari looked at her – really looked. Accustomed now to Hunter training, she could see past the black robes and the amethyst, to a woman whose every gesture spoke of the potential for sudden movement. Yet her voice and her robes softened the effect, as if she were an edged weapon in a velvet box.

The Abbot paused, and the silence in the room was absolute, as if time itself had suddenly stopped. "Learning to work together, learning our histories, serving the Lady – these things are even more important than you can imagine. Each one of you will have a role to play in the days ahead. Some of you will play those parts here in the Abbey, while others will range further afield. And only the Lady knows how and where you will serve. But heed my words. We know that gorgones are abroad in Albatar. They have penetrated our borders in numbers greater than at any time in the last hundred years. When they will show their hand is unknown, but your time here together is more precious than you can ever imagine. Use it wisely, learn quickly, and work together, because Dark Days lie ahead, and the Lady calls all of us to serve in the war against evil."

'Dark Days' wore its capitals again, and now the Abbot had spoken the words openly in public for the first time. Shock rippled around the room, and Charla's hand clenched hers, her fingers pressing tightly into Kazari's.

"War!" she said, turning her eyes on Kazari. "But . . ."

"Yes, war," said the Abbot, as if she'd heard Charla. "War is coming, and we must prepare. But before war comes, you must learn all you can in the time you have left before its wave rolls over us. You have just begun your journey as the Lady's servants, and normally this is a time of nurture and growth. Growth it will still be, but forced rather than nurtured. Your Gifts must be honed, your minds even more, and your trust in the Lady must be absolute. Heed the words of your tutors, of your Sept Leaders and your fellow servants. There is more evil afoot in Albatar than you could possibly imagine. The Lady be with you all."

She bowed her head briefly, and then nodded to them, and left the room, striding with the strong grace of a Hunter – the weapon momentarily unsheathed before them.

Kazari shook her head, almost dazed, as a gold robed Adviser stepped forward to the lectern, and she felt Charla stiffen slightly beside her, sitting more erect.

"Hear now of the heresy that stalks Albatar," the Adviser said. Once again, a frisson ran through the room, rippling through the novices as if her words were a rock dropped into a pond. "There are patterns we can see spreading throughout our land. Listen and learn, and then you will hear how other incursions have also been heralded by a turning away of our people from the Lady's truths."

***

Kazari stepped out into the chilly air with a sense of relief. Hours of lectures later, her head felt thick and woolly, her thoughts chasing themselves around like butterflies in her skull.

The Adviser had spent the first hour speaking of previous incursions and the signs that had hinted at their onset, and the next two hours on facts and figures demonstrating that those same signs were now visible.

"Do you think she's right?" Abel asked.

"Right?" said Charla. "Of course she's right. Haven't you seen such things in your own home town? Kaz?"

Kazari shook her head. "Athos is really small. If there had been those signs surely everyone would have noticed? I mean, questioning the whole idea that the Lady exists? Or that the gorgone threat isn't real? Or that it was, but isn't anymore?"

"My town was small too," replied Abel. "And no, not in my town. Well, I don't think so, at least." He shrugged.

Charla huddled more deeply into her robes, tucking her hands, in their voluminous sleeves, under her armpits.

"I came from a large town – well, closer to a city, perhaps – maybe it's more obvious there."

"What do you mean?" asked Kazari, as the other girl shrugged.

"It's fashionable to . . . um . . ." Charla paused. "Look, I'm not sure how to put this. But people sort of . . . talk about the Lady as if . . . as if she isn't real." The last words came out in a rush.

"*Isn't real?*" said Kazari incredulously. "But our histories, Albatar's founding, *suckers* for the Lady's sake!"

"Well, *I've* never seen a sucker," said Abel. "But Kaz is right, Charla, we have our histories, and we – us – the Lady's servants I mean. Healers – they're out and about doing stuff that others can't do. How can people discount that?"

Charla drew them both down to sit on one of the steps. The chill stone bit into Kazari's buttocks even through her Hunter's trousers, almost as cold as the import of her friend's words.

"We all saw that . . . thing . . . that crawled over the Abbey wall, but everyone else? They haven't actually seen anything like that – although I suspect Kaz has." She touched the scar on Kazari's face lightly with one fingertip, and Kazari flinched away slightly. She nodded, just a tiny inclination of her head, but the others knew what she meant. "You Hunters do a good job of protecting Albatar. So good that the number of people who've actually seen a gorgone is tiny and scattered. In fashionable circles, people have talked themselves into a sense of complacency. They say things like: 'Even if it did happen, that was long ago, and it'll never happen again. Let's move on.' Or: 'Those stories are for children. And for the Order to maintain their grip on things in Albatar. It's time we threw off their yoke.'"

Charla drew her knees up to her chest and stared unhappily into the distance, and for a time Kazari had no idea what to say. On Charla's other side, Abel was looking similarly dumbstruck.

"I had no idea," said Kazari, eventually. She tucked an arm around her friend.

"Me neither," said Abel. "But that can't be the majority, surely. I mean, you're here, and your parents were proud – you said so." He waved his hand to emphasise his point.

Charla smiled at him, but it was a wintery sort of smile, and wobbly around the edges.

"They are, but . . . it's also hard for them. Their friends are where I heard those things. You can imagine what their friends said when I chose. And *my* friends."

Kazari sighed heavily and propped her chin on her hands. She'd had no idea that things were so different in other parts of Albatar. Or that someone could be . . . denigrated for choosing to become one of the Lady's servants. Her parents hadn't agreed with her choice, but it hadn't been because they didn't believe in the Lady, or doubted the Writings. It seemed she had even more to learn than she'd thought.

Chapter Three:
Doubts

Several days later Kazari watched the arrow she'd just shot at the target, skitter across the dry dirt to one side of the boss, completely missing it.

"Concentrate, Kaz," Javon said, as Kazari brushed the sweat out of her eyes, and fumbled with another arrow. "You can do this. You *have* done this." Javon was right. Kazari had shot arrows very effectively – on occasion. But now everything she'd learned seemed to have deserted her, just because Javon had decided she needed to try some different sized and weighted arrows.

Kazari drew and released again, trying to put every ounce of her understanding of technique into the shot, but although the arrow struck the target this time, it was on the edge, and it bounced off to join its fellows lying in the dirt. Frustrated, she reached out for another one to try again, but Javon's hand forestalled her.

"What's up, Kaz?"

She brushed a hand through the tight curls on her head and frowned up at Javon.

"I don't know. I just can't seem to do it!" The words came out with more force than she'd meant them to. "Sorry." She looked down at the ground, scuffing at it with one of her boots.

"Is it the dreams again?'

"Maybe, maybe not. I just don't *know*, Javon!" The words burst from her in a spatter of sound.

Javon motioned to the arrows scattered all over the practice ground, and Kazari ground her teeth and went to collect them. Dust marred the arrowheads, and she brushed them off on her trousers, leaving dirty smears on the black fabric. She brushed at her legs irritably, and somehow dropped the arrows. With an exclamation of frustration, she bent to collect them again, feeling tears prick her eyes. Nothing seemed to be going right.

Each class with the others seemed to provide her with more doubts, and more uneasiness. Each lesson with a Hunter seemed to demonstrate just how poorly her Hunter skills were progressing. And the coming war seemed to be rushing towards her and she knew she wouldn't be ready.

She deposited the arrows on the table with the others, and began to wipe the dust off again, this time with a rag. Then she dusted herself off as well, flicking the polishing rag across her legs to brush away the marks that marred the fabric.

"Stop, Kazari."

It was the first time Javon had used her full name in weeks, and Kazari was shocked to stillness. She put the rag down and looked up, not wanting to meet Javon's eyes.

"You're not the only one feeling the tension, Kaz," said the older woman. "We all do. None of us expected a gorgone incursion in our lifetimes, but then, I suspect that no-one ever does. Yet we are the Lady's servants, and she will not abandon us."

Kazari felt a hot tear slide down her face, tremble on the corner of her lip, and then drip off. She scrubbed a hand across her face, remembering belatedly that her hands were filthy, and looked at the ground again, gripping her hands together. To her shame, she realised that her bottom lip was, once again, trembling. She tried to stop the trembling by force of will alone, but it increased, and then she was sobbing. Great heaving sobs that shook her body, and a torrent of tears that flooded her face and turned the dust on her hands to mud. Embarrassment fought with an emotion she couldn't identify, and she dropped into a ball of misery, huddled on the ground.

A warm arm wrapped itself around her shoulders, and she kept on sobbing, unable to articulate what was wrong, what she was feeling, or even why she was crying so ridiculously dramatically. Eventually, she sobbed herself out, and sat there on the ground, drained and dirty, suddenly blank of any emotion. Javon squeezed her shoulders, and eventually Kazari gathered enough of herself together to speak.

"I . . . I'm sorry, Javon."

The other woman drew back slightly, and turned Kazari towards her, looking deeply into her eyes.

"I know, Kaz."

"And, I'm . . . I'm afraid. That I won't be ready, or that I won't be good enough, or that there's other stuff going on that we don't know about." She broke off, looking down at the ground.

"Kaz, we're *all* afraid," said Javon. Kazari looked up, surprised as Javon continued. "Not one of us has experienced an incursion. Not one of us knows more than what our records tell us. But we *are* the Lady's servants, and no matter what, she walks with us for all time. If I should perish, or you, or any of us, we are *hers* forever. Hold onto that, at least."

"But what if I don't, I mean if I can't, if I . . . I don't know, if I *fail* her?"

"Kazari," said Javon, using her full name once more. "Can you promise me something?"

Doubts arose within Kazari's heart. What could she promise Javon? She nodded hesitantly, uncertainly.

"Promise me that you won't stop *trying* to do the right thing?" said Javon.

"I . . . yes, I think so, but how does that help?" Kazari asked.

"Because the Lady asks nothing more than we do that. That we try to do as she wants us to, and never to cease trying."

Realisation broke over Kazari like a wave. "You mean, that if I'm trying, even if it all goes wrong, then it's still all right?"

"It's still all right," reaffirmed Javon. "Look, if it all goes wrong, it won't *feel* all right, but you're human, and I'm human, and our best is the one thing we can offer the Lady, and the one thing she requires. If we give her that, and it still goes wrong, then we have done everything asked of us."

"But how will I know if I'm doing my best?" Kazari asked.

"Kaz!" said Javon. "If you think you're doing everything you can do, then you just have to accept that you are. Stop second guessing yourself!"

"But . . ."

"And stop 'butting' – at least for a moment or two. There's nothing wrong with asking questions, but sometimes you have to stop for a while in order to get stuff done." Javon rolled her eyes.

Kazari blushed, and nodded. *Javon* was afraid? She didn't look afraid, in fact, she looked serene.

"Stop thinking so much, Kaz, and pick up those arrows and shoot again."

It was as if Javon was reading her mind. Kazari shelved her thoughts with an effort of will, and bent to collect the arrows. Then, as Javon had directed, she stopped trying to 'but' and applied herself to the purely physical actions her teacher required of her. To her surprise, she was able to strike the target with the pointy end at least two times out of three by the end of the lesson.

When they'd put the last arrow away, Javon clapped Kazari on the shoulder, and told her to go and get clean before lunch.

"You've smeared dirt all over your face."

Later, clean, dressed in another set of Hunter's blacks, and seated next to Charla, she bent to shovel a spoonful of soup into her mouth. She was hungrier than she had been for weeks. Strangely, her emotional outburst seemed to have relieved some of the pressure that had been building inside her. She didn't really have any answers to her questions except for 'try your hardest to do the right thing,' but somehow everything seemed a bit better. Perhaps it was knowing that in her doubts and fears, she was not alone.

Abel dropped into the seat beside her, his aquamarine gleaming on his chest. It contrasted quite oddly with his multi-hued clothing, but so did her own amethyst, she realised. The other septs matched their clothing to their gems, but both the Hunters and the Navigators did not. Then she nearly inhaled her soup as the improbable image of purple leather-clad Hunters battling gorgones popped into her mind. She coughed, and Abel pounded her on the back.

"What's up, Kaz?"

She shook her head, sniggering slightly until he asked again.

"I was just imagining me, dressed in purple, trying to fight a gorgone. I mean, clearly the colour of the clothes doesn't matter, but the picture looked really weird."

Abel looked at her and rolled his eyes.

"Yes, and me sneaking through the undergrowth in bright blue, pretending I'm what – a blue wren or something?"

Kazari burst out laughing at the improbable image of her lanky friend imitating a tiny bird.

"Our colours are definitely more practical for our jobs, aren't they?" she replied, still amused.

"Whereas Charla's golden robes, with the golden gem on the golden chain, definitely work better in her context," said Abel.

"Implying the eminent wisdom and integrity I currently fail to possess?" said Charla. She sighed and propped her chin on her hand, stirring her soup idly with the other.

"You've got heaps," said Abel. He waved his own spoon at Charla.

"Ha! You should have heard me *not* demonstrating that to Feruna this morning," she replied, and then sighed and stirred her soup again.

The long table held mostly new initiates, eating before their afternoon classes, and Kazari looked around at the multihued robes dotting its wooden length. Most of them looked sombre, and here and there, she could see red eyes and puffy faces. So she wasn't the only newcomer feeling overwhelmed by the thought of an incursion. Except, perhaps, Abel. His face seemed unworried, and he was eating enthusiastically.

"Abel, aren't you even a little bit worried?" Kazari asked.

Her friend barely paused in his eating.

"Of course I am," he said, nodding his head, and spooning in another mouthful of soup, "but since I can't do anything about it right now, I'm just going to work hard and learn as much as possible. Besides, there's so much to learn, I haven't got time to agonise over it." He dunked a piece of bread into his soup, and went on between bites. "And I'm sure it's the same for both of you too."

"But aren't you curious?" asked Kazari. "Like, why did a gorgone try and attack the Abbey? Why is it happening now? And how are they getting into Albatar?"

She'd been wondering that for a long time, but now, with some of the edge taken off her anxiety, she felt comfortable enough to voice the words that had been rumbling around the back of her skull for months.

Abel shrugged.

"Of course I am, and I'm sure there's a reason, but that reason won't make any difference if I can't navigate without getting lost, or shoot straight when it really matters." He returned his attention to the bowl in front of him, waving his spoon. "And time's limited, so we need to make the best use of it."

Kazari nodded. He was right, and she should probably heed his advice. But gorgones were the province of Hunters in particular, and she knew there had to be some reason behind the monster's willingness to sacrifice itself, and reveal that greater gorgones had penetrated this deep into Albatar.

Later, as early spring thunder echoed around the Abbey, she wondered if she might perhaps broach the subject to Sendar. He often had insights that she found helpful. Perhaps he was privy to more information than she was, having been a Hunter a bit longer. Besides, it had been several days since she'd had a proper chance to sit and chat with him. In fact, she realised, he'd been leaving their shared quarters early, and getting back late every day. She wondered why.

Chapter Four:
Hints

Kazari tucked her cloak more tightly around her body, shivering as the wind gusted down the walkway outside her quarters. Javon had given her the afternoon off. Storm clouds scudded across the sky, chasing each other in serried ranks, and thunder echoed off the stone buildings, rolling and rumbling like the thud of a bass drum.

Perching herself on the sheltered side of the low stone verge that ran on either side of the walkway, she looked out across the Abbey grounds, hoping to see Sendar's familiar form striding across the grass. Despite Abel's blithe words, she hadn't been able to stop wondering about the gorgone that had assailed the Abbey. She ran the images of gorgones she'd studied through her mind. Viper gorgones, fire gorgones, corruptors, revilers, suckers – the list was extensive, yet the thing that had crawled over the wall didn't match any of those descriptions.

It had had multiple limbs, and limbs designed to cut, claw and rend, and it had breathed a dark fog. Or had it? Suddenly Kazari wasn't certain whether the fog she remembered seeing was real or imagined. She pulled her notebook from beneath her cloak and began to sketch, trying to get the basic details down on paper. She wondered why she hadn't thought to do so much earlier. But then, it was the first greater gorgone she'd ever seen, and she hadn't really been thinking coherently at the time.

Accustomed to designing decorative leatherwork, Kazari had a sure touch on her pencil, and as she sketched, the feel of the gorgone's presence solidified inside her mind. The cold, the gloom, the despair and desperation. The hate, the darkness that seethed and roiled like fog that penetrated the mind and body, and the unrelenting evil. It was so vivid that her pencil paused for a moment and her breath caught, until she was able to drive the lead across the paper once again, pouring the emotion onto the page, and notating the sensations and her impressions in neat letters beside the picture.

When she was done, she was able to sit back and look more dispassionately at the picture. Even on the page, the pencil drawing was terrifying. But somehow, by putting pencil to paper, she'd put a tiny bit of her fear to rest. Without thinking about it, she'd put in the tiny figures of the Abbot and the two Hunters who'd faced the beast down. The perspective provided by the human figures only served to emphasise the immensity of the beast and the darkness that it drove with its will.

Boots echoed on the flagstones, and she nearly dropped the notepad in surprise as Sendar rounded the corner. She looked up at him, noting the fatigue and weariness in his movements.

"Kaz? What are you doing out here?" he said.

"Waiting for you."

"Me?"

"And sketching this." She proffered the notepad.

"That's the gorgone that climbed over the Abbey wall," he said, frowning as he stared at the paper.

"And you know what?" asked Kazari.

"All right, I'll bite, what?"

"I can't find it in any of the books I've studied."

"You can't?"

"No."

He took a seat beside her, and she realised he was wet through, and shivering.

"This can wait, Sendar. You're wet."

He shook his head absently, still studying the sketch, so she settled back and waited for him to speak again. Eventually he frowned.

"Have you asked Javon or Andiss?"

She shook her head.

"Why not?"

"I haven't seen Andiss much lately, and . . ." she broke off, slightly embarrassed, remembering her disintegration moment, then hurried on. "Javon's been working me so hard there hasn't really been the right moment." She blushed and looked out across the grass again as the rain began to pelt down.

"Well then, let's go and ask, shall we?" He handed the sketch back and stood up.

"Just like that?" she said, surprised.

"Well, why not?" said Sendar. "I mean, it's clearly bothering you, and I'm curious too – I don't recognise it from the bestiaries either."

He pulled her to her feet with a hand, and pushed open the door into their quarters. Warm air and light spilled out, and suddenly Kazari was happy to be inside, away from the cold and wet.

"Javon's not here," she said as they entered. "Nor Andiss."

Sendar smiled. "But since I'm meeting Andiss in the practice room when I'm dry, we can ask him then. You're finished for the day?"

Kazari nodded.

"He won't mind if you join us. There's a couple of things I'd like to try, and you can be my assistant. I'd like Andiss to see what I mean."

He vanished into the bathroom, and Kazari was left wondering what 'assistant' meant. The practice room meant that Sendar would be working with his Gifts. Since his were Anticipation and Ascension, she would probably either be sparring with him, or being lifted by him. Suddenly she wondered if he meant her to be his target. Since Suborden,

Sendar had taken to throwing things around with his Gift quite enthusiastically.

When they reached the practice room – that same tiered area in which Kazari had first seen other Hunters demonstrate their Gifts – Andiss was waiting, perched on a seat in the front row reading, with a stack of books at his feet and a chest containing a variety of throwing weapons to one side. As they approached, Andiss lowered his book and looked up.

"Kazari?" he said, puzzled.

"I asked her to come," said Sendar. "For two reasons: I need someone else to practice with, and secondly, she has a question to ask." He urged her forward.

Embarrassed, Kazari proffered her notepad. "Andiss, what type of gorgone is this? I've been through the bestiaries, and I can't find it. And I don't understand why it would attack the Abbey. It's been puzzling me for days."

The older Hunter regarded her steadily for a few moments, then very deliberately put his book down and waved them over to the seats beside him. He looked tired, she realised, and for the first time she could remember, frustrated.

"And that is the question, isn't it?" He waved a hand at the books on the ground. She recognised one towards the bottom of the stack. It was the bestiary kept in every Hunter's quarters – a listing of gorgones that categorised them by type and subtype. She read the spines of the others as best she could from her seat. Cracked bindings and worn leather spoke of age and long use, and the book Andiss had placed on the seat beside him was even older. In fact, now that she was looking at it properly, she realised it was barely holding together, and that the drawings within it were covered in almost transparent leaves of some kind of protective paper.

"You mean you don't know?" Kazari shivered, icy prickles of fear crawling up and down her spine.

"This is not common knowledge," said Andiss. "Most of the other septs don't routinely record or teach gorgone types beyond the basics. We, who fight them for the Lady, *need* to know everything we can. This one's an enigma. Since our return from Suborden, I've been trying to track it down. I'm down to the last few books in the archives." He shrugged. "And if I can't find a record, then this is a new type of gorgone, not seen before in Albatar. And then we have to ask ourselves more questions. Where did it come from? Did it come from beyond our borders. Or was it summoned by someone within the bounds of Albatar itself? Or has something occurred in the outside world that we, sequestered here in our haven, are unaware of?"

Kazari shivered, cold suddenly striking deep into her being. The questions Andiss had posed were terrifying. That he had no answers to speak of, even more so. He'd always been so certain, so strong and steadfast that his presence had been like an anchor within Kazari's world – unseen, yet keeping her moored in safety despite the winds and waves that rode in turmoil around her. Now, for the first time, she saw uncertainty. Not fear – that would have cut her to her core – but uncertainty that troubled her almost as deeply. Andiss was a man of decisive action, not a man who prevaricated or wobbled, yet now, here, he'd laid himself bare and posed questions that he knew would trouble both the young Hunters before him.

"You are Hunters, even though you are our newest. You deserve to understand what we might be facing."

All at once Kazari felt both frightened and yet determined – two emotions that warred with each other, but somehow complimented each other. Even understanding what might lie before her, Kazari suddenly knew that to stand between the people of Albatar and evil was not only the Lady's choice, but her own. And knowing that, despite her fears of failure and her terror at the unknown, and even knowing that Andiss was uncertain, she knew that this was right, in a way that she somehow hadn't known only a moment ago.

"And we will strive to be worthy of your trust," replied Sendar.

Kazari nodded, not trusting her voice, so strong were her emotions.

"In that case, Kaz, might I take this sketch? It can only aid me in my search. Javon has also drawn pictures, but every extra detail is helpful. You know she contributes to the bestiaries?" At Kazari's nod, Andiss went on. "And I think you'll also be a good contributor. This is fine work."

Kazari ducked her head, pleased but embarrassed.

"And now that I've scared the living daylights out of you both, how about we work a little of that off with some training?" he said. "Sendar, you said you have something to show me?"

"Kaz, you remember when we fought the fire gorgone? And I gave you the really cold stuff?"

She nodded.

"Well, I've been experimenting, Andiss. The cold stuff was a bit of air that I sort of . . . compressed. And it turns out that there's all kinds of things I can do if I extrapolate from there. We've mostly just lifted people and things with Ascension. But if you think about it, lifting's really just sort of pushing – but up. And compressing things is just pushing them from all directions at once. And once you start thinking like that there's all kinds of possibilities that occur to you. In fact, I got really wet today compressing water in the air – I accidentally made it rain on me."

Kazari guffawed. He'd been *very* wet, but *before* it had been raining. Sendar rolled his eyes at her. Then she began to worry slightly. Perhaps he was planning on compressing *her*.

"And just where is this going?" asked Andiss, patiently.

"I think it's best if I show you," said Sendar. "Kaz, can you throw stuff at me? But properly. With . . . intent."

Kazari raised her eyebrows, shot a look at Andiss, who nodded, and then bent to rummage in the chest. She selected a variety of throwing knives, and as an afterthought, she added a stack of throwing stars. She'd only practiced with them a few times, but the technique had seemed to come naturally to her, and she liked the feel of them in her hand. She tucked everything away in her Hunter's gear, and then waited for Sendar's call.

"No 'dancing', Kaz, just throw them. But try and move around at the same time a bit. Ready? Go."

She threw the first knife, somewhat hesitantly, and watched astounded as bounced off something just before it was going to hit Sendar. Something that was there, and then not there, puffing away into a vapour.

"Come on, Kaz, again. Faster this time."

She threw again, and then again, almost unable to believe what was happening. Somehow, Sendar was putting a barrier between the knives and himself. She began to move around the practice area, firing off the knives until she had none left. She pulled the first throwing star, and sent it towards him. It spun through his barrier, but was deflected to one side. She sent the rest of the stars in quick succession, feeling certain of her aim in a way she hadn't for days, and one by one they broke the barrier, but bounced off in a myriad of directions.

When she finally stopped, puffing slightly, Sendar was looking happy, relieved, and proud, and Andiss was crouched behind the first row of seats, several throwing stars embedded in the seat backs in front of him. Kazari noted that Andiss had not stopped the demonstration, despite his need to take cover from the ricocheting stars.

"Sorry, Andiss," she said, contritely.

Andiss lifted his head above the seat backs as she levered the first star from it. It left a notch in the wood, scarring what had once been a polished surface.

"That was . . . interesting," Andiss said. "Definitely . . . interesting," he repeated, thoughtfully. He strode to face Sendar. "And if I attempt to punch you?" He raised an eyebrow at Sendar.

"Try it?"

Andiss flicked a punch towards Sendar without any warning, and Kazari gasped, but Andiss' fist stopped as if it had hit a wall, and there was a cracking noise from his knuckles, and Kazari saw blood appear on two. Andiss drew in a hasty breath but didn't exclaim in pain, instead he turned his eyes towards his hand.

Kazari watched as Andiss' Gift of Healing activated, and the skin closed, leaving dried blood on the surface.

"That hurt," he said. "But you're fast, Sendar. Next question, how long can you keep it up?"

Several hours later, they'd established that Sendar could keep blocking for quite some time. But they'd also discovered that whatever he was doing with his Gift wasn't foolproof. Using blunted sticks they'd managed to establish that he could block things he knew were coming, and even manage to set up a sort of shield around himself and hold it, but that holding it for any length of time tired him quite rapidly. And once he was tired, stuff got through, though with reduced impact – as a result Sendar was now sporting some multicoloured bruises.

Later, when they were eating the evening meal, Kazari mused on the gorgone. Andiss didn't know what it was, or where it had come from. Javon didn't know. And more troubling than anything else, no-one else seemed to know either.

Chapter Five: Letters

Kazari leafed through the pile of letters from Dari. She'd tucked them away tied with a string in her personal shelving. Initially, there'd been one a week, but slowly their frequency had decreased. The last one had come only a week or two before they'd left for Suborden. She'd replied immediately, speaking in general terms about life in the Abbey, and her gradually increasing fitness.

She unfolded Dari's last letter. It had been written in Dari's familiar style, on a thick piece of paper that looked like it had been torn from a larger piece. In fact, as she smoothed the creases with her hands, a faint odour of honey wafted from the folds, and Kazari realised it had most likely been part of a piece used to wrap the candles bought from the chandler in Athos.

Homesickness struck like a hammer, and Kazari felt her breath catch in her throat. That smell. It spoke of familiarity, warmth, and cold nights by the fire at home with the scent of beeswax filling the air from the candle lanterns around the room. It spoke of Dari's bedroom on her farm, where the two of them had spent hours talking, playing with Dari's sheepdogs, and dreaming of their futures. She inhaled deeply, drawing in the familiar scent, almost unable to read the words through the tears that blurred her vision.

She breathed out again, closing her eyes and blinking the tears away, and then shook the page again to flatten it.

Hello, Kaz, (read the letter).

Hope it's all going well for you. It's been a bit busy here. I suppose it's like that when we're all following our dreams – things to do, stuff to learn, people to meet. Sounds like you don't have much time on your hands, but I suppose that's what's expected at the Abbey. Enda said there was heaps to learn when she went, and she still says that now, even when she visits.

Enda was Dari's sister, and one of the Healer sept – Kazari read on.

And I've got heaps more to learn too, apparently, even if I'm not at the Abbey. Mum and Dad have had a tutor here for me from Seraph. An expert in wool and clothes and other stuff. They said they want Settler's Run to grow, so they wanted to make sure I've got even more learning, and also connections. We're looking at fine wool growing to supply some of the cloth-iers in the city. Anyway, you know what I think about that kind of stuff. Got to go.

Missing you. Dari.

Kazari folded the letter again, and tucked it between her hands, then inhaled the scent of beeswax once again. It had been several months since the letter. She wondered what might have kept Dari from sending another. She'd sent several herself since her return from Suborden. Perhaps Dari'd been overly busy, or perhaps she and Dari were 'growing apart' as her parents had said they might as they got older. Or perhaps Kazari's letters had been boring, or preachy, or . . . something . . . and she'd offended her friend.

She shook her head slowly, took another breath and placed the letter back on top of the pile. Then she heaved a heavy sigh and pulled out a fresh piece of paper and a pencil.

She needed to do what she'd put off since she'd returned from Suborden. She needed to write to her parents.

She'd imagined writing to them. She'd started a dozen letters and then stopped. She'd thought up hundreds of beginnings, and middles, and ends for this letter. She'd imagined her parents' faces multiple times. Sadly, in every imagined scenario, her parents had crumpled the letter without reading it. Still, each day she woke with a feeling that something wasn't right, and for weeks she'd known what it was.

She'd left home under a cloud, and a tiny corner of resentment had been festering away inside her, and some days, it seemed to bubble up until she wanted to scream and rant and shout to the winds that *it wasn't fair* and that *it wasn't her fault.* Which in both cases was true. Mostly. Suborden had put a new perspective on things. The reality of gorgone hunting had shown Kazari that she wasn't immortal, and she didn't want her parents' last memory of her to be an angry one. If things all went wrong during the days ahead, she wanted to know that she'd done everything – short of leaving the Lady's service – that she could to put things right between them.

She smoothed the already smooth paper unnecessarily, and then furrowed her brow and began to write.

Dear Mum and Dad (and Jayden and Piddy of course),

When I left, it wasn't how I wanted it to be. I should have understood more about how you were feeling. I should have understood that you only ever wanted the very best for me, and that even though what I wanted and what you thought was best for me are very different things, that it was always love that drove your words.

By now you'll know that I am, and will be forever, the Lady's Hunter. And I know that it's probably your worst nightmare. To be fair, I never expected to become a Hunter, but that is where the Lady wants me to serve, and I will do so to the best of my ability. It's a hard road. It's a dangerous road. More than I ever understood or imagined, but I do know that I am in the right place, even when it isn't easy.

No matter what happens, please know that I am content with the Lady's choice for my service. I love you all, and wanted to tell you that. Please forgive me for my angry words. I should have spoken more gently.

Once again, I love you all, no matter whether you're still angry with me or not.

Kazari.

She re-read it, frowning over her inept words, hoping with all her heart that the letter would be read, and that it would convey to her parents just how much she loved them. She almost crumpled it up several times, but then thought better of it. Finally, she folded the paper, addressed it, sealed it with a dob of purple wax, and tied a string around it, and took it to the dining hall to be placed with the Abbey's other correspondence, knowing that it would eventually find its way to her parents.

It was late afternoon, and for once, she had nothing scheduled. No training, no classes, and no study, so on the spur of the moment, she begged some bread and cheese from the kitchen staff and set off to wander the Abbey grounds. After so many months, most of the Abbey was familiar ground. She strolled aimlessly for some time, wandering through the grove, walking through the huge colonnaded walkways that lined the walls, until eventually she found herself pacing up and down near the wall where the gorgone had invaded. She shivered, realising that her apparently aimless wanderings hadn't been quite so aimless.

The wall showed no sign that a monster had climbed it. There was no sign of the battle they'd fought – not even a scar in the grass. Kazari got up and examined the wall, walking close enough to run her hand across its rough stones. There was nothing to see, nothing to feel, and nothing to sense.

Still, there was an itch inside her mind about the beast, and eventually, still feeling stupid, and slightly embarrassed that she couldn't let this go, she exited the Abbey via a side gate and began to walk the wall outside.

The moment she began to pace the wall, the hair on the back of her neck rose. She sniffed, drawing the air in slowly through her nostrils, stretching for any scent of gorgone. Nothing. Unscarred trees and early spring growth seemed to make a mockery of her fears. She paced back and forth as her skin crawled.

How had a gorgone even approached the Abbey? There was nothing close by. No villages, no borders. Nothing but thick bush full of towering trees and undergrowth that leaned from beneath the trees in search of sunlight. Where on earth had the thing come from? And how had no-one seen it?

Straightening her shoulders and taking a deep breath, Kazari set off around the Abbey, following the running track, and taking the time to sense. When she'd completed the full circuit, she'd seen and sensed nothing. She wondered what secrets the bush might hold.

All at once she shivered violently. She must have been out there for hours. Squinting at the sun, she realised that she had only half an hour or so of daylight left, so she began to cast back and forth across the bordering vegetation, not knowing what, if anything, she was looking for. At last, when the sun had begun to touch the horizon, Kazari gave up with a sigh and went back inside the Abbey grounds, unsatisfied, with more questions than answers, and anxiety gnawing at her.

It didn't help that she felt as if unseen eyes were watching her every move. Even though she was unable to sense anything, she couldn't help glancing behind her towards the vegetation before she opened the side gate and took herself back inside the Abbey.

Chapter Six:
Lead In

Kazari woke before dawn. Once again, the nightmare of the gorgone's voice drove her from her sleep. Not wanting her restless tossing to disturb her companions, she tiptoed out of her quarters, and made her way through the chilly, predawn darkness to the dining hall.

It was mostly dark, but warm lamplight came from the big kitchen. Kazari peered through the doorway, and when one of the green-clad Growers smiled at her, ducked into its bustling warmth. Loaves of bread sat cooling on racks, and pots steamed on the stove top above the ovens. Before she could open her mouth, she was handed a hot mug of tea and a plate of warm bread, butter, and honey. The Grower, whose name she thought was Piper, waved her over to a side bench. Another figure was already sitting there, hands tucked around a steaming mug of her own, and Kazari had taken her seat before she realised it was the Abbot.

She slid off her stool, blushing, and stammering. "I . . . I'm sorry, *Ailani,* I didn't realise. I'll move somewhere else."

The Abbot waved a hand. "Kazari, please, sit and join me. It's not often I have company at this hour of the morning." The woman smiled and took a sip from her mug, and then raised her own bread and honey and took an appreciative bite. "I'm very fond of warm bread, and Piper indulges me all too often."

Slightly hesitantly, Kazari sat down again, and took a sip of her tea to cover her embarrassment. She burned her tongue, and nearly spat her mouthful out on the Abbot. She managed to swallow it down instead, feeling her throat tingle from the heat, and took a deep, cooling breath to cool her mouth and throat.

"It's quite fortuitous you're here this morning, Kazari, as I've been meaning to talk to you," said the Abbot. "Would you mind if we took our food and drink outside?"

Talk to her? And now? The Abbot wanted to talk to *her*? Before Suborden, Kazari had been having lessons with the Abbot. Like Kazari, the Abbot was a Dancer. They had yet to resume, and Kazari had wondered why, before reasoning that the Abbot was probably too busy – and with an imminent incursion on her mind that made complete sense.

Still, she couldn't help wondering if she'd done something wrong, or whether Javon and Andiss had taken their concerns about her nightmares to the Abbot, and it had made her hesitant to continue working with her. She picked up her plate and mug, and followed the Abbot.

Instead of taking a seat at one of the dining tables, the Abbot led Kazari to a stone bench tucked away in a corner of the Abbey grounds. Dawn had come, and the little bench was bathed in early morning light. Kazari sat at the Abbot's gesture, and joined her as she closed her eyes, breathed deeply, and faced the rising sun, enjoying the play of gentle warmth on her face.

"You're still having nightmares, aren't you, Kaz?"

Kazari's eyes flew open. They *had* spoken to her. Dread settled in her stomach, and she nodded mutely.

"There's a Servant I'd like you to meet, Kaz, and going to visit him will serve one of several purposes."

"Visit?" Kazari said.

"Alexando's in Chator," replied the Abbot.

"Chator?" said Kazari, realising belatedly that she was repeating the Abbot's words again. Still, for some reason, Chator sounded familiar.

"Yes, Chator. Sendar's home town. I'd like both of you to spend some time with Alexando, and it will be good for Sendar to see his family. You'll visit Athos as well. I'd like you to see that your family is well."

Tears pricked Kazari's eyes. To see her family – that would be wonderful! Or would it? She'd sent her letter, but would it really be good to see them? What if they didn't want to see *her*?

"I know your leaving was complicated, Kaz, but I think you need to see them with your own eyes." The Abbot paused and sipped from her cup again.

Kazari played scenario after scenario inside her head – then something clicked. "I'll be travelling with Sendar?"

"And Javon and Andiss as well. There is more than one task to accomplish during this journey. I've spoken to both Javon and Andiss, and I'll be speaking to Sendar later today. Clearly, the Lady had a purpose when she brought you into the kitchens this morning. Perhaps you have questions you'd like to ask of me?"

"Why did you stop teaching me to Dance?" Kazari blurted before she could stop herself. The Abbot looked pensive for a moment.

"Time, Kazari. Nothing to do with you, simply the demands on my time. It's something I regret. But your foundations in the basics are strong, and much of dance comes from the instincts gained by a Hunter learning her katas. There's only three Dancers in the sept including you, and I wish I'd had more time with you, but we can only do so much."

"And the Outer World," said Kazari, despite her mind exclaiming: *three?* She'd thought there were only two. "What is it really like? I mean, I can imagine, but . . . there are traders. And they aren't gorgones, or changed, or . . ." she shrugged.

"It's complicated," began the Abbot. She ate the last piece of her bread and honey, dusted her hands, and sat back, staring at the brightening sky. "I suspect that like many in Albatar, you've spent your life imagining lands peopled by horrors?"

Kazari nodded.

"And now your rational mind has realised that there are contradictions in that?"

She nodded again.

"In some lands, gorgones rule openly, Kaz. But in many places, the Outer World appears like Albatar – at least on the surface. And how do I know this, you ask?" She shrugged. "I was part of a team to the Outer World. As you know, the Order sends teams at times. Members of every sept go, some to assist, some to survey, and on occasion, some to stay."

"To stay?" asked Kazari.

"The Lady hasn't abandoned the Outer World, Kaz, although sequestered here in Albatar, it might seem as if she has. Even now, some of Her servants still labour against the foe under much more difficult circumstances than any you would find within Albatar's borders. And perhaps, one day, you'll travel there yourself as part of a team from the Abbey. For now, remember that the gorgone threat takes many forms. Where subterfuge is required, they use it, and where an overt presence is required, they provide that also. There's a lot more to this world of ours than what you see within Albatar's borders. And even within Alabatar's borders, more happens than you yet know."

Then the Abbot's face softened, and she smiled. "And although things look dark at times, the Lady watches over us. Remember that Kaz." The Abbot rose, collected her cup and plate, and left before Kazari could say anything more.

She sat there, in the early dawn light, eating the last of her warm bread, sipping from her mug, and pondering. There was a lot more to the world around her than she'd realised. But even so, there was comfort in what the Abbot had told her. Still, she did wonder who the sept's third Dancer was, and why she hadn't been told of them. In fact, now she thought about it, it seemed as if the information had been deliberately kept from her. She wondered why.

Chapter Seven:
Chator

As Kazari turned Stumpy's head away from the Abbey and towards Chator, thoughts chased themselves around her mind like kittens around a ball of wool. She absent-mindedly patted her horse on his warm neck. She'd grown fond of Stumpy. He was sure and steady, and she'd learned to trust him. It was a far cry from the first time she'd ridden him all those months ago. Then, she'd struggled against the pain of muscles unaccustomed to riding. Now, she sat his saddle easily, lulled by his rhythmic strides as he stepped along steadily behind Andiss' much larger horse.

When her training was complete, and she was a fully-fledged Hunter, she'd be able to choose her own mount, but at this point, Stumpy was everything she wanted or needed in a horse. He was responsive, steady, and reliable; and she'd come to consider him a friend. Despite her niggling worry about seeing her family again, the spring sunlight warmed her, and Stumpy's strides lulled her, giving her some much needed respite from the air of urgency that had permeated the Abbey.

She realised that she was gently stroking the amethyst on its black leather thong around her neck. It was warm to touch, comforting, a reminder that the Lady was ever-present, watching over her Hunters. Kazari looked sideways at Sendar, riding beside her as usual. He'd been quieter than he usually was since the announcement that they'd be travelling to Chator and Athos. They'd been busy readying themselves for the journey, and during such a task, Sendar normally enlivened it with quips and conversation; this time he'd been unaccustomedly morose. When she'd asked him about his family, he'd simply shrugged and said: "My family is poor." She wondered what 'my family is poor' really meant, and what filled his thoughts so full he'd abandoned his sense of humour.

She was also curious about this 'Alexando', whoever he was. Apart from mentioning his name, neither the Abbot, nor Javon or Andiss had spoken of him again. Kazari wondered why the Abbot thought he could help. Mentally, she shrugged, and turned her thoughts to other things – undoubtedly she'd find out in time.

She wondered if she'd meet Sendar's family, and then began to worry again about meeting her own. At least there were five days solid riding before they arrived in Chator, and it would be longer still until they finally reached Athos. Perhaps she'd have stopped thinking about it by then. Her fingers drifted to the scar on her face. The image of her mother's expression hovered before her, and her stomach churned. *Some of those who pledge to the Lady die, Kazari – they die . . ..* The remembered words echoed in her skull once again, and she pulled her hand guiltily from the scar.

"Keep your wits about you, you two!" called Javon. Kazari started, disturbing Stumpy so that he snorted and bobbed his head. "Keep your eyes peeled, and Kaz, let us know if you sense anything odd."

"Yes Javon," Kazari replied, hearing Sendar echo her words. She drew in a deep breath, testing, but there was nothing. They were only just outside the Abbey – of course there was nothing. But then the memory of the monster that had crawled over the Abbey wall only a few months ago slithered through her mind on scaly feet, and a chill ran down her spine. It had come close without any of the Lady's servants detecting it, and they still didn't know how, or why. Or even what it was. She shivered and took a quick glance around.

The land was greening in the early spring. The previous day's storm had washed everything clean, and the fresh scent of growing things lent a richness to the air. Green-robed Growers worked the fields to the north of the Abbey, occasionally raising a hand in greeting as the four black-garbed Hunters rode by. For a moment, Kazari found herself envying them as they laughed and talked together, all the while nurturing the crops they grew. She'd once thought to join them herself. But then reality asserted itself. Even knowing what she now knew, even having suffered through more physical and emotional hardship than she'd thought possible, she knew in her bones that being the Lady's Hunter satisfied her in ways she hadn't even known existed.

Even the puffing and gasping and the aching muscles, were nothing compared to the satisfaction she felt after dispatching a gorgone. Not, during, she qualified, but after. It was one less monster to threaten her people. Still, she was only human, and for a moment, the peaceful fulfilment in the Growers she saw before her generated a sense of longing. Intellectually Kazari knew that even the Growers, nurturing their crops, must feel the anxiety that pervaded the Abbey, but their fight was not usually on the frontlines against the gorgone foes as hers was.

But even her own sept had had secrets she'd only just become privy to – the Gifts that now manifested themselves within her. Clearly the Healers and Intercessors had similar skills, and although she didn't know the details, she'd seen some of their Gifts at work – and known of them for many years, now that she thought about it. As they rode, Kazari mused on what Gifts the other septs might have tucked away. She supposed that some, like Healing, were supportive, rather than offensive in the fight against evil, but as she thought upon the subject, she speculated that the Navigators must have some Gifts similar to the Hunters, given their roles. The memory of their blazing arrows was still etched in her memory.

Three days later, Kazari dismounted and stretched, running her hand down Stumpy's warm neck. She led him to a small creek to drink and then began to remove his tack and rub him down. He snorted, and tickled the back of her neck with his whiskery nose as she picked up his legs one by one to check his hooves.

"Silly horse," she laughed, patting him, and then hobbled him and left him to graze, as she carried her gear over to the campfire Javon had started in a small hollow.

Andiss set water to boil as Sendar dragged up a log to use as a seat. The four Hunters ate quietly, watching the play of flames in the fire, enjoying themselves, camping in the freshness of the spring evening away from the busyness of the Abbey. In two days, they'd arrive in Chator, where they would be accommodated at the chapel with the local incumbent.

Kazari remembered Enda's joyous homecoming two years previously. Dari's sister hadn't seemed nervous at all. Like the others who'd returned for visits, she'd stayed with the incumbents – a pair of Intercessors – but her visits to her family's home had been celebrations, and there hadn't been any hint of awkwardness that Kazari had seen. And she was sure she would have, because she'd been there so frequently as Dari's guest.

"Have you been home, Sendar?" she asked.

"Yes," he replied, and a hint of discomfort entered his voice. "Not long before you joined the sept."

"Was it all right?"

There was a long silence, and just as Kazari was about to repeat her question, Sendar spoke.

"In the end, yes it was, but it was difficult at the beginning." He stood and stirred the coals of the fire, sending a gout of sparks into the air. He busied himself for a moment, setting the water to boil for more tea, and then turned and looked at Kazari, silhouetted against the brightness of the fire so she couldn't read his face. "I told you my family was poor?"

She nodded.

"The hardest bit was going back and seeing my family's poverty. I'd go back to the chapel each day knowing that I'd be eating better than they were, and wearing good, well-made clothing, while they struggled to make sure everyone was warm."

Kazari felt a lump form in her throat.

"Why is it like that?" she asked, uncomfortably aware that the lump had changed the tone of her voice. "Why do some have so much and others so little? Don't the Writings tell us that we should take care of each other? Athos isn't like that."

Athos, her own village, was a fairly prosperous place. Some definitely had more than others, but she didn't know of anyone who wasn't adequately fed, or decently clothed. But then, perhaps she just hadn't noticed. Now, after many months away, she wasn't as certain she knew as much about her home town as she'd thought she had when left.

Andiss nodded, the warm light from the fire casting shadows over the planes of his face.

"They do. The Writings tell us very clearly that those of us who have more, should take care of those who have less. It is the Lady's will." He hesitated and then went on. "This is one of the hardest things for anyone to understand, Kazari. What the Writings *say* is very clear. What humanity does in response is not so simple. As Her servants, we help wherever we are able, but we are only so many, and we can't do everything that is needful, so the balance falls to those who lead Albatar – the secular authorities."

"And those secular authorities are only normal human beings, with all the failings and strengths of all of us," went on Javon. "Some are seduced by greed, others by petty jealousies, and others by selfishness. The end result is that sometimes they place themselves above others, and sometimes those others suffer."

Javon turned to Sendar. "As your family has. And mine, and many others. Much as we of Albatar would like to believe otherwise, we must recognise that despite resisting the gorgone incursions and the chaos of the Outer World, we are not perfect, and that evil finds a foothold wherever it can."

There was silence while the fire crackled and glowed. Sendar stood motionless, face hidden in the darkness, and Kazari pondered on what Javon and Andiss had said. *Why, Lady?* she asked silently. But she already knew, deep inside her own self. She wasn't perfect – no human being was. Within Kazari lurked the potential for evil, despite her pledge to the Lady and to Albatar. In her insecurities, her fears, and her moments of disbelief, lay the potential for wrongdoing.

She wondered if that was how the first gorgone incursion had really begun – in the second king's weaknesses? In his vanities? She felt vulnerable then. Vulnerable, frightened, and fearful. If a man so respected for his good deeds had still been corrupted by his inner desires, then how did 'normal' human beings *ever* resist? The Writings seemed so clear when she read them, but the doing of what the Writings demanded? Not so much.

Finally, Sendar spoke again.

"Things have improved for my family. Not completely, but somewhat. Alexando from the chapel keeps an eye on them for me. They may not eat like kings and queens, but nowadays they always eat."

Kazari let out a breath she hadn't realised she was holding. Some of the warmth had come back into Sendar's voice – a warmth that had been missing for several days.

"They work hard, and their vegetable garden is productive most years, but sometimes the taxes are higher than other years, or there is little rain, and in those years they need to hunt to make sure the family is fed. And hunting is . . . difficult. It requires trespass on the Lord Juster's hunting preserve."

"You mean the crown land adjacent to Chator," Javon corrected.

"That's not how Lord Juster sees it," replied Sendar, "or how he treats it."

Kazari saw Javon open her mouth to reply, but then shook her head slightly and remained silent.

Sendar swung back to the fire and busied himself with the tea. A few moments later, he handed the refilled mugs around. Kazari sipped hers reflectively, staring into the fire as Sendar perched himself on the log next to her again. His posture was more relaxed than it had been, but the mood around the fire was more thoughtful than the other evenings. When she climbed into her bedding an hour later, her thoughts churned inside her head. This Alexando was most likely an Intercessor then; as an incumbent, it made sense, and she knew from Androvar's comments that some Intercessors specialised in the care of the mind. Still, she wondered why the Abbot thought he might be able to help her more than the other Intercessors. Even so, it took her a long time to sleep, and even then her dreams were ominous and she spent the night turning restlessly from side to side, trying not to disturb the others.

Chapter Eight:
Viper

The next morning, Kazari, scratchy eyed and yawning, tightened Stumpy's girth. He turned his head and nosed her gently, as if he could sense her fatigue. His warm breath was comforting, and he smelled of horse, a smell she'd come to associate with all the good things about being a Hunter. Resting her forehead against his shoulder, she felt her tension ease.

The discussion of the night before had unnerved her. Knowing she wasn't perfect or knowing that her friends weren't perfect was one thing, but understanding that some of Albatar's rulers weren't – it unsettled her more than she could have believed. No-one could be perfect, she knew, but the rulers of her land were meant to be *better*. Brought up by her parents to obey the laws of Albatar and to believe that the rulers above her had the best interests of their people at heart, the idea that some of them didn't take care for the people they ruled, seemed at such odds with what she'd learned as a child. And what if some of them were even worse than neglectful?

She rode beside Javon in silence for some time, pondering. Hunters always worked in pairs, and she'd begun to wonder how they ended up in those pairs. She'd never asked, and so far it hadn't been covered during her training. Of course, that had been somewhat reorganised since her ability to sense had been discovered and the possibility of a gorgone incursion had raised its head. Perhaps they just fell into partnerships, or maybe there was some other method of determining who would work with whom? She opened her mouth to ask, when the acrid smell of gorgone flickered on the breeze.

She drew Stumpy to an abrupt halt and raised her head, sniffing the wind. It was clean and fresh again. Confused, she turned her head from side to side, and then rode in a circle around the others who'd also stopped and were waiting for her.

"Kaz?" asked Andiss.

"Thought I smelled gorgones," she replied absently, still sniffing the air.

"But?"

"It seems to have gone now. Perhaps I was wrong?"

Andiss drew up beside her, and Javon and Sendar fanned out to either side. Kazari could read the tension in their postures.

"It's gone now," she repeated, "it was there, and then not there."

A little further along, they paused in a hamlet, where a small, overall-clad urchin approached Kazari, where she was watering the horses at the well while the others purchased lunch at a nearby inn.

"Are you a Hunter?" asked the urchin.

Kazari smiled.

"I am, or at least, I'm learning to be one."

The urchin scuttled forward and held out a somewhat wilted yellow flower, clutched in a grubby paw.

"This is for you. My Mum says that Hunters are the Lady's special servants, and says we should thank Her for your service." The words were oddly phrased, almost archaic, but Kazari recognised them from an old form of the Writings she'd studied in the meditation grove. Dredging back into her memory, she drew out the correct reply.

"This Hunter thanks you for your thanks to the Lady."

Kazari took the flower and tucked it into her top buttonhole as the urchin smiled back at her. "What's your name, little one?"

"I'm Freda, Hunter." The words came out in a rush, and then Freda jiggled on the spot, and rushed away.

"Nice flower," commented Javon when the others rejoined her. Kazari related the story of the urchin, and Javon nodded. "It's a tradition in some parts, mostly the smaller parts, of Albatar. An old tradition, but a nice one. Some of the larger places could learn from places like this."

Later in the day, Kazari's anxiety had reached an almost intolerable peak. There had been hints of gorgone on the wind every hour. Never strong, but definitely there. Every time she signalled a halt, and then all of them would cast about, looking for physical signs of gorgones. They saw none. Kazari began to wonder if her Gift of Sensing was working properly or whether she was just imagining things – or even if she had it at all. But then she'd remember Suborden, and the horrors she'd seen there would refuel her determination. They passed through hamlets and villages, and each time, people came out into the streets to look at The Lady's Hunters.

The reactions of the people varied widely. In one town, Kazari was given a bouquet of wildflowers by a tiny boy, barely old enough to leave his mother's side. He'd waved vigorously at her as they rode through. In another, the people had stared, but they had been silent, and Kazari had the feeling that despite the legends, had they stayed there, they would not have been welcomed warmly. She wondered at it, puzzled, opening her mouth to ask Andiss a question as they rode out, but he'd shaken his head at her, and mouthed *'Not now'.'*

At last, at least a kilometre down the road, he nodded.

"Ask now, Kaz."

"What's with the people in that village?" She burst out. "I mean, *everyone* looks at Hunters, but they . . . didn't seem to want us there?"

"They probably didn't," Andiss said. "There has been . . . a . . . falling away, in some places."

"A falling away?" She remembered with a sinking feeling in her gut, what Charla had said.

For a moment or two, there was nothing but the sounds of spring, and their horses' hoofbeats on the roadway.

"There are places in Albatar where the truth of the Lady is . . . doubted," said Javon.

"Places like that last town, or Seraph, for example," said Andiss slowly. "Places where people believe that the stories of gorgone incursions are just that – stories, myths, tales to frighten children."

"But they're history!"

"You come from a town where things haven't changed much for decades, Kaz," Andiss said. "Your parents may have had reservations about you taking up service with the Order, but their core beliefs, and those of the rest of your town still march in step with the Order's teachings. Some of the larger towns do not see things in the same way."

Kazari's mind reeled. There were people who didn't believe their own history? It . . . it was *history!*

"But the Writings, the Order, the laws of Albatar! They're our history. How can people *not* see this?" she asked. Charla had said it, and she'd heard it at the Abbey, but this was Andiss. And she knew him, trusted him. And for some reason to hear the same words from Andiss seemed somehow different.

"You asked about poverty a few days ago," Sendar said. "You get poverty when the Ruler of your region pays only lip service to the laws of Albatar, and doesn't live them." His tone was sad.

"But . . ." said Kazari.

Andiss looked at Kazari, and spoke again, sadness tinged with a hint of frustration in each word. "The Order and the Abbot cannot force people to believe, Kaz. People will believe what they want to, and despite the obvious – to us at least – presence of minor gorgones like suckers, some choose to believe a sucker is only an animal, not an embodiment of evil. But then again, most people have never encountered even a sucker. You see, we've been so effective, that for most people gorgones are just a myth – not reality. It seems that the Order, in some ways, has been its own worst enemy."

"But our Healers, our Growers, their Gifts are obvious!"

"Human beings can explain away anything they want to if they – or I should probably say we – try hard enough," replied Javon drily.

"I've been really naive, haven't I?" asked Kazari, shame-facedly. She felt as if her world had indeed been tiny before she joined the Order.

Andiss laughed, but it wasn't a nasty sound.

"Naive – perhaps. It's hard to be anything else if you're from a place like Athos, Kaz. But you see the Lady so clearly as a result that it's almost a Gift in itself. Don't be hard on yourself, but do understand that you'll meet people who don't think like you do. Try and understand them, or at least under-stand why they think as they do."

Kazari nodded, sobered. Things had seemed so simple back in Athos. She'd never met anyone who'd thought that the Lady was a myth, or that gorgones weren't real. Then she was honest with herself. Perhaps she had and hadn't realised because it had never occurred to her to ask. Perhaps she'd been too naive to read between the lines. She rode on, disturbed to her core, wondering how much more she didn't know about life, and her own people of Albatar.

Spring had come in a warm flush, and the fertile paddocks around the farming villages were covered in the fresh green of growing crops. If there hadn't been the ever more frequent smell of gorgone on the wind, Kazari felt as if she could have dozed in the warmth and the sunlight as she rode along.

This part of Albatar was flat, low lying, and well wooded. Small farming towns sat at the centre of paddocks that radiated away from them like petals on a flower, their rich fields burgeoning with produce. Thickly forested stretches ran between the towns, their trees ensuring that wood for carpentry and warmth was widely available, and providing habitats for the abundant wildlife now stretching its legs in joy, as spring sprung into life around them.

Kazari rode Stumpy along the roads, intermittently casting glances at the towering trees that hemmed them in on either side. They made her vaguely uneasy, and she wasn't sure why, except that she was a child of the rolling hills. Trees this large were new to her, and they concealed the sky when she was among them. Perhaps that was it.

Again, the scent of gorgone wafted on the breeze, and she pulled Stumpy to an abrupt halt. It was faint, yet the acridity was unmistakable. The other three joined her, automatically bracketing her and Stumpy in a three petalled flower, their horses facing outwards, each covering a third of the imaginary circle drawn around Kazari.

She sniffed, tilting her head, heart hammering as always, trying desperately to discover from which direction the scent originated. She pressed her leg into Stumpy's side, and he obediently turned his haunches, pivoting on his front legs. The smell grew stronger as the breeze strengthened from the east, and Kazari pointed. "That way!"

She wanted to be off at a gallop in her relief at finding a clear direction, but Andiss stopped her with a quick head shake.

"Steady, Kaz, lead on, but slowly."

Kazari took the lead, with Andiss and Javon flanking her, and Sendar directly behind, as they moved off the roadway and into the trees. She sniffed again.

The scent grew stronger, and Kazari almost rubbed her nose. Her nostrils felt as if they were about to catch fire.

"Getting close," she said, voice just loud enough to be heard over the soft sound of horses, and the quiet thud of their hooves on the forest floor. "So strong . . ."

"Leave the horses," said Javon, drawing hers to a halt and dropping its reins on its neck. Kazari slid off Stumpy, leaving him to do as he wished. Abbey horses were trained not to stray, so if all went well, even without hobbles, the horses would be waiting for them on their return.

"Quietly," said Andiss, "Kaz, this way?"

Kazari nodded as he pointed deeper into the trees, rubbing at her nose. The stench was becoming unbearable. "It's really strong."

"Stronger than at the Abbey?" asked Sendar. Cold struck deep into Kazari's bones – the creature at the Abbey had been enormous, and it had taken many of them to bring it down. She hesitated, drawing the stench deep into her nostrils, trying not to dry retch, and then shook her head.

"Not quite. Strong, but different." Sendar made a face, and both Javon and Andiss drew in quick breaths.

"We look then, but we don't fight unless we know what we're up against," Andiss said. He motioned for the others to follow.

Kazari checked her knives compulsively, and touched her amethyst briefly. The stench intensified, and Kazari placed a warning hand on Andiss' back. He slowed, gliding around the tree trunks slowly and cautiously, and parting thicker bushes gently with his gloved hands before stepping through. Then he held up one hand. In the green dimness, surrounded by the cheerful colours of spring, Kazari felt as if she was inside a dream. Suborden's icy environs seemed a more fitting place to find a gorgone, not the fertile lands of central Albatar.

Andiss signalled again, and they crept forward to join him, peering around the bole of a forest giant. Kazari cupped her hand over her nose and mouth, but the action was futile; no matter if she felt as if she smelled the gorgone with her actual nose, blocking it never made any difference at all. The rough bark of the tree scraped Kazari's cheek as she inched her head around it, but the mild discomfort felt good, grounding her.

And then she saw what she'd sensed.

A scaled monster sat coiled in a tiny clearing, its two heads resting over a collection of wicker baskets. It was almost as if the baskets contained eggs and the gorgone was a backyard hen, guarding its nest.

"A viper gorgone," whispered Javon. "Just as well we're downwind. They've got a good sense of smell."

Viper gorgones were poisonous, Kazari knew, and fast. With their two heads, they had the ability to see in all directions. She'd always wondered how that worked – were there two brains to make the decisions, or were the brains, if they had two, even located inside the heads? Or was there one brain, somewhere else? The bestiaries were unclear. Kazari had read the margin comments in one. "*Almost impossible to kill and leave a body intact for dissection,*" read one, and "*It is an advantage to have an archer or two with you, should you encounter a viper gorgone,*" read another.

Well, they had no archer. They all carried bows, but they were cumbersome to carry in dense bush, and were consequently still on their saddles.

Still, they all had their Gifts, and Javon and Andiss were highly skilled. Javon tapped Andiss on the shoulder, an eyebrow raised. He looked back and shook his head, and then made several hand gestures. Kazari only knew one of them. 'Wait.' The others she had yet to learn. She almost sighed. She still had so much to learn before she'd be a fully-fledged Hunter.

Javon dropped to her belly and wriggled forward carefully. Kazari realised she was trying to see what the gorgone guarded so carefully. For several long moments, the three watched Javon until she slithered backward and crouched behind the tree again. "Couldn't get close enough."

Andiss grimaced, frustrated.

"Can we take it?" Javon whispered, shooting a look at Kazari and Sendar.

"Maybe," replied Andiss. He touched the hilt of his long knife, and looked at the two trainees, frowning.

The sharp sound of a twig breaking rang through the air. Kazari crouched again and cold sweat broke out on her forehead, convinced the gorgone knew where they were. Nothing was visible, but the monster's heads had jerked up, and it was now fixated upon something coming towards it from the other side of the clearing. Kazari felt her breath come more quickly, and readied herself, poised on a hair trigger. She could feel her fellow Hunters tensing, alert to any threat. If someone out walking or hunting stumbled upon this monster, they would have no choice but to intervene.

The gorgone's noses sniffed the air, and it coiled itself more tightly around the wickerwork it guarded, rising on its coils as both tongues flickered and fluttered in the now steady breeze. The sounds of more twigs breaking came clearly on the air, and then four people appeared in the bushes on the other side of the clearing. Kazari prepared herself to leap out of cover to protect them, but Javon's hand restrained her. She turned her head to whisper a furious question, but Javon held her finger to her lips, and then motioned to Kazari to watch.

The people were there by intent, not accident. There were two men, and two women, dressed in the normal, everyday clothing common to most regions of Albatar. It was difficult to make out their faces in the dappled light slanting through the trees, no matter how Kazari squinted. They approached the gorgone, seemingly unafraid, and abased themselves.

Bile rose in her throat as she watched – human beings, bowing down to the viper gorgone. How could they debase themselves like that? she wondered, and found her hand reflexively gripping her amethyst. *Lady, why?* Chills ran down her back, and then the hand in her other one, forgotten for the moment, gripped more strongly, almost crushing her fingers, and she turned her head to see Sendar, his face mirroring her revulsion.

She leaned forward keeping her head low and shielded by the leaves of the copse just in front of her, craning to see what was occurring on the other side of the glade. There appeared to be some kind of conversation, but they were too far away to hear what was being said, even if the wind was in the right direction. A few moments later, the gorgone hissed loudly and uncoiled itself. The baskets were now exposed, and the four crawled forward and then scrabbled backward, clutching them.

Kazari noted the wary glances they gave the creature before them. They might have approached confidently and abased themselves, yet they were still fearful of it when they were close.

"Kaz, go back and get the bows," whispered Javon. "Sendar, follow the ones with the baskets while we deal with this monster. Follow them, find out where they go, and then meet us in Chator. You know where."

Sendar let Kazari's hand go, nodded, and began to work his way silently around the clearing.

Kazari left as quietly as she knew how, wincing as leaves crackled softly underneath her boots. She was forced to pause each time to make sure she hadn't alerted the creature to their presence.

It was much harder to move silently knowing that a gorgone with acute hearing was close by. The horses were all moving restlessly when she reached them, as if they knew exactly what might be waiting just through the trees. Perhaps they did, Kazari thought. She soothed Stumpy absently with one hand as she grabbed her bow case and quiver off her saddle, and then collected the other two. It was much harder to move quietly through the thick growth encumbered with the three bow cases and quivers.

She was sweating heavily by the time she rejoined the other two. The viper was still alone in the clearing. Javon gestured vigorously to her, and she handed the two bow cases over and began to open her own. Javon shook her head and motioned Kazari closer.

"You're the distraction, Kaz," she whispered. "To get a good shot, we need its neck exposed, so you're going to 'dance' with it."

Kazari nearly screeched *What?* out aloud, but remembered just in time to stay silent, taking a deep breath and then letting it out through her mouth, struggling to keep her breathing even.

Dance? With a viper gorgone? The things didn't just bite, they spat poison, which was why killing them with a bow was a much better idea than getting in close.

Andiss and Javon strung their bows in silence and set their quivers at their hips. Javon placed Kazari's between them so the arrows it contained were within easy reach of both. Each held an arrow nocked, and then Andiss nodded at Kazari.

Kazari slid two of her knives into her hands, her long one and a throwing knife, checked her stash of throwing stars, and prepared herself to Dance, all time trying to stop herself shaking her head in disbelief at what she was about to do. She could feel her hands trembling.

They crept forward while Kazari tried to calm herself with deep, slow breaths. This was much more difficult than reacting to an attack. She'd fought suckers, and the fire gorgone, but this time, she was to be the bait, a distraction for the others. Still, she had to trust that Javon and Andiss knew what they were doing, so she thought a quick prayer to the Lady, and at Javon's gesture, stepped from the cover of the greenery feeling incredibly exposed.

"Hey, snakey boy!!" she shouted, then began to dance.

The thing was fast – much faster than the suckers or the monster that had assailed the Abbey, and much, much faster than the fire gorgone at Suborden. She ducked and wove around it, staying just ahead of the thing's darting movements, trying to get it to lift its throat. The sheer speed of the thing was incredible.

It hissed and sent a jet of poison arcing through the air towards her. She accelerated even more, relying on instinct rather than planning, and avoided the jet, but then almost ran into a second one. The two heads made the thing dangerous, even for a Dancer. She ducked under the deadly stream, and it sluiced into a shrub, turning the leaves black and dead, smoke spiralling into the air.

As always, when she danced, Kazari felt as if her opponent's movements were predictable, but it still took concentration, and the viper gorgone's two heads moved independently from a branching point a metre below their skulls. Fleetingly, she wondered again which one drove the body, before she dodged once more, trying to figure out how to get the thing to rise up far enough to expose its vulnerable parts.

Another jet of poison hissed into the vegetation just behind her, and once again, she nearly ran into the second. She circled back slightly, giving herself a bit more space, while trying to keep the thing far enough from Javon and Andiss. The clearing was a small hollow, set slightly lower than the surrounding area, enhancing the nest-like ambience she'd noted earlier.

As well as the venom, the thing spewed hatred into the air. Hatred that scalded and burned the mind, just as its venom burned the vegetation around it. It *seethed* with hatred, and Kazari wondered how one creature could possibly hoard so much hatred as it poured out from the monster in waves, buffeting her. It was like a physical force, trying to throw her off balance.

She ducked and wove, anticipating the creature's every move and countering it, trying to stay just far enough ahead to keep the gorgone's attention. Instinct was one thing, but as the Abbot had said during one of her lessons, instinct was a guide, but Kazari's brain still needed to be involved.

It was the first time she'd really danced with deliberation, rather than reaction, and with a conscious goal – other than staying alive, that was – in mind. Twice she left her move almost too late, acrid fumes from the gorgone's venom stinging her nostrils as she bent away from it, waiting for her chance to drive it into a mistaken move towards the spot where Javon and Andiss were concealed. She could only imagine what might happen should she inhale a full breath tainted by the monster. Then the thing struck, and distracted, it nearly had her. It was only by a sudden convulsive leap that she was able to throw her body out of the way of the beast's fangs.

Sweating, her breath coming faster, Kazari ducked and wove, keeping the attention of the beast's two heads. Slowly, she began to see a pattern. One head would strike, and then the other would follow up from a different angle. The gorgone was trying to trap her between the two heads so that she would have no option but to end up facing one of them close up.

But where there was a pattern, there was also a weakness. Or at least she hoped there was. She also hoped that the endurance that Javon had so patiently instilled in her would hold out long enough for her to use the monster's weakness against it. Sticks crackled under her boots as she ducked and wove, and once, a small rock turned beneath her foot, nearly spilling her onto the ground. With an effort, she pulled her legs back under her and then ducked beneath the viper's left-hand head, narrowly missing yet another stream of venom.

Two huge rocks sat on the edge of the bowl just in front of where Andiss and Javon waited, concealed in the scrub. Concentrating fiercely, Kazari drew the gorgone closer and closer to them. Sweat tracked down her forehead, and stung her eyes. Dancing with intent, rather than instinct, was harder. It required more discipline, and Kazari's mind almost had too much time to think. She faltered as sweat trickled into the scar on her face, distracting her with images of fire and snow, and the creature nearly had her again and she was forced to abort her first run. She gritted her teeth, pushed the thought of the greater gorgone away, and deliberately slowed herself again, enticing the beast towards the rocks.

It turned, and the moment hung before her. She leaped from the ground onto the lower of the two boulders, sheathing her knives as she did so, and then flung herself onto the uppermost one. She saw Javon begin to rise from her crouch, bow fully drawn as she moved, and Kazari threw herself into the air to grasp a tree branch directly above the rock. She let her momentum swing her forward, and flipped one leg up and around the branch as the gorgone lifted its snouts towards her.

Rough bark stung her hands, but she levered herself onto the branch, and scrabbled towards the trunk of the tree, just as four arrows took the thing in the throat. Two were sheathed in aquamarine light. And as the viper thrashed, another two glowing arrows struck it from either side of the hollow, and both Andiss and Javon fired again, their mundane arrows sinking deeply into monster's flesh. The beast hissed, gurgling, and then spasmed once more, before sprawling lifeless onto the leaf litter at the bottom of the hollow.

Kazari realised she was trembling as she slid down the tree trunk. The grazes on her hands stung once more, and then healed, and she turned her head bemusedly as Elliam and Abel appeared out of the bush from either side of the bowl.

Chapter Nine:
Alexando

"Our thanks, Navigators," said Andiss, striding forward towards the old Navigator. Elliam lowered his bow, and Kazari saw that Elliam's aquamarine pendant on its silver chain flickered with starry glints. The arrows in their sheath at his hip were limned in bright blue, very clear against the mottled browns and greens of his clothing. The colours blended into the vegetation and broke his outline, making it much harder to see him than it was to see Andiss.

"You are most welcome," replied Elliam, "Abel, good shooting." Kazari's friend blushed and smiled, ducking his head. She hadn't seen him for some time, and she wondered when Elliam had joined him. Last she'd heard, Abel was off 'field training,' but she'd seen Elliam just before she'd left the Abbey, so clearly he hadn't been with Abel the whole time. Abel darted a look at her, and Kazari realised that he'd seen her dancing, and was itching to ask her about it.

Of course, she'd also noticed that his arrow had been outlined in blue fire, as had the arrows of the Navigators when the greater gorgone had assailed the Abbey. She looked at his quiver curiously. Here and there she could still see hints of blue, sparking briefly in the fading sunlight. She wondered whether it was something he did, or something special with the arrows.

In turn, Abel was looking equally curiously at the variety of knives slung from her belt.

She turned her attention back to Elliam, Andiss and Javon, who were talking quietly.

"How did you come to be in this neck of the woods, Elliam?" asked Javon. "Not that we're unhappy about it, of course."

Elliam shrugged. "I came out to work with this one here," he jerked his head at Abel, "But with directions to keep my eyes open. The Abbot mentioned you might be around." He shrugged. "We followed the crowd from Seraph to this place as practice. The viper gorgone was a bonus."

"A bonus?" burst out Abel. "A bonus? I nearly wet myself!"

All heads turned to the young man, and Elliam made a curt hand signal, paired with an eye roll. Abel blushed again, and prevaricated.

"I mean, it was horrible, frightening, and not what I expected." At least he'd kept his voice down this time.

Kazari tried not to snigger. Almost wet himself! As if he would have. Mind you, she reminded herself, she hadn't exactly covered herself with glory at her first gorgone encounter. She recalled her clumsy knife strikes with some embarrassment. She'd been terrified. And it had only been one sucker, not a viper gorgone.

Elliam frowned at Abel.

"'I nearly wet myself,' while descriptive, is a little emotive, Abel. As one of the Lady's servants, you should remember to think before you speak." He sighed. "I see we have a long way to go in your education."

Javon smiled kindly at Abel.

"But you kept your head and your arrows flew true, Abel. We are most grateful. It must have been very difficult to encounter a viper gorgone so early in your training."

Abel blushed again. "I'm sorry, I spoke hastily. But —" he turned towards Kazari, and she knew he was about to ask what she'd been doing.

"That's enough for the moment, Abel," broke in Elliam smoothly. "We'll discuss all of this later. I'm sure you have many questions." He sighed. "You usually do." He shook his head wryly but not without amusement. "But there are more important things afoot." He turned back to Andiss and Javon. "I believe there were four of you?"

"Sendar is following the 'crowd' as you so quaintly put it, Elliam. He'll meet us in Chator. Will you join us there?"

There was a moment of silence while Elliam considered.

"I think we will, Andiss. We have Navigators roaming all across Albatar right now, and there are several groups in this area. Most will check-in at Chator within the next two weeks. It will suit us to meet you there. I have a report of my own to send."

Both Andiss and Javon nodded, and Kazari was struck by a thought.

Why Chator? Why did the Navigators all 'check-in' at Chator? What made Chator so important?

She opened her mouth to ask, and then shut it again, catching another wry look from Elliam. This was not the time. Right now, they needed to get to Chator themselves – but what about the gorgone corpse? Something as large as a viper gorgone would decay and attract scavengers. Another question raised its head. Did scavengers eat gorgones?

There were too many questions wandering around inside her brain, so she rolled her eyes at herself and shut them down, then watched Abel and Elliam fade into the vegetation. She'd thought Hunters were stealthy, but Elliam made them seem positively noisy.

"Kaz?" It was Javon. She beckoned to Kazari.

"What do we do about that?" asked Kazari as she hurried over to the woman, waving a hand at the gorgone corpse.

"We leave it here – as a warning," Andiss said grimly. "If there are more who've fallen under the spell of the gorgones, then this will remind them there are consequences. And if those who have fallen away encounter it, then perhaps they'll reconsider. It's a pity we haven't the time to dissect it. There are many questions this corpse could answer."

Kazari nodded uncertainly. Dissect the corpse? Would she have to do that one day? Every time she thought she was beginning to understand things, another question popped up. She resolved to ask about some of them once they arrived in Chator.

As if she'd spoken one of her questions, Javon responded. "If we concealed it, and it simply vanished, our quarry would be even more likely to conceal their tracks. The four of us have been travelling openly, and the sudden death of a gorgone, known to its *worshippers*," she almost spat the tone with distaste, "will be attributed to the normal duties of Hunters."

Kazari nodded, understanding at last. They'd been travelling openly. Of course they'd kill a gorgone if they encountered one.

The ride to Chator was quiet. Javon led Sendar's horse behind hers, and Kazari rode ahead with Andiss. As they rode the country began to change from farming land to rolling ground covered in tall trees. There was an abundance of wildlife, evident in the tracks of wallaby and deer that meandered across the road.

Kazari rode deep in thought, wondering how Sendar was getting on, and how far he'd trailed the people they'd seen. And if they'd split up, how would he have decided who to follow? She sighed, and Stumpy snorted gently. She ran a hand down his neck, relishing the warm smell of horse that rose from his coat. He was shedding heavily now that spring had arrived, and a cloud of horsehair rose into the air as she thumped him gently. Thoughts of Navigators, Gifts and gorgones vanished as her stomach rumbled.

Just as the sun touched the trees ahead, the smells of smoke heralded another village. Kazari sniffed, searching for hints of more than smoke, but the air was otherwise clear, and she relaxed and wriggled slightly in her saddle, thankful that Stumpy chose not to interpret her wriggles as signals.

"Not far now," said Andiss. "We'll be staying with Alexando tonight."

"He's an Intercessor?" asked Kazari, curiously.

Andiss smiled and turned his head towards Kazari. "No, he's a Hunter."

"A Hunter?" Kazari was surprised. She'd thought that Hunters were usually on the move, patrolling or searching out signs of gorgones, not staying in one place as an incumbent.

"He was injured some time ago, and was unable to keep roving like the rest of us, so the Abbot established him here about five years ago. He's a source of information now, and provides a place for Hunters and Navigators to drop by."

An injured Hunter – one injured so badly he was unable to continue roving? The thought was sobering, and Kazari was shocked at how deeply it affected her. She frowned, feeling her own scar pulling against the movement. She wondered what Alexando's injuries were, but Javon didn't elaborate.

"Ten minutes and we're there," called Javon. "I can see the stables." Kazari looked ahead as they rounded a bend. A long avenue of trees leaned inward, forming a green tunnel that would be cool and inviting in the summer, and at the end a red tiled roof was visible. "That roof is the stables, Kaz. Our horses will be comfortable tonight."

And indeed they were. Kazari marvelled at the stables which rivalled the Abbey's for equine comfort as she brushed Stumpy down. Clouds of horsehair enveloped her, and she sneezed, wondering whether Stumpy might be bald after he'd finished shedding. He leaned into the brush, clearly enjoying the attention, but it was hard on Kazari's arms.

"Shove over, horse," she murmured. "I'll get to all the itchy bits better if you don't lean on me." She drove the brush over his rump, and more hair floated away, glinting in the last gleams of evening sunlight.

Finally finished, she turned Stumpy into a large stall, made sure he had a good biscuit of hay and a small amount of hard feed, and that his water bucket was full. He blew into her hand as she gave him a farewell pat, admiring the shine on his coat.

"Finished, Kaz?" called Javon. "Come and help me with Jumper." Kazari joined Javon who was rubbing down Sendar's horse. More horsehair fountained into the air as they applied themselves vigorously. They worked in silence for a few moments, before Javon spoke. "You're wondering why Alexando hasn't appeared yet?"

"Well, yes, actually," replied Kazari. Everywhere else they'd been, the incumbent had appeared to welcome them. Here, they'd just walked in and helped themselves to the stables.

"Alexando lost a leg to a gorgone. He's on a crutch, and he gets around pretty well, but there are things he's unable to do. Try not to stare when you meet him."

Kazari nodded silently.

"He may decide to tell you the story, or not, but if he does, it'll be in his own time."

Kazari nodded again and filled the water bucket for Jumper.

"Andiss has gone up to the house already to speak with him. We'll be housed all together in one room while we're here. Hopefully Sendar will be along shortly, with something to report. Elliam and Abel will turn up when Elliam decides." She smiled drolly, and Kazari had the feeling that this was not unexpected.

As with many chapels, this one was set on a small knoll overlooking the town. Chator was a largish town, bordered on one side by thick bush. True forest giants towered along the border, packed in by undergrowth that grew thickly between their mighty boles.

Most of the houses were tile roofed, and in various states of repair. Those that stood closest to the tree line appeared run down and smaller than most of the others, and there were signs that the edge of the town also housed the more unpleasant detritus of local industry. Kazari wondered if Sendar's family was down there somewhere. Apparently, in Chator, poverty lived on the edge of town. In contrast, the centre of the town appeared well kept and prosperous. From the knoll, Kazari could see tidy gardens, and even one large house set apart from its neighbours by a manicured lawn that surrounded it on all sides.

Athos had few lawns. Most of its residents grew vegetables in tiny patches, or had the occasional flowering bush on either side of the front gate. Lawns were things of leisure and money, and the vast majority of Athos' inhabitants had little of the former, even if they didn't lack for too much of the latter. Maybe things were different in Chator, she mused. Chator was much larger than her home, which now seemed humble, and rather pedestrian, compared to some of the things she'd seen since joining the Order.

"Coming Kaz?" Javon prompted.

Kazari started, realising that she'd paused while she'd been thinking.

"Sorry. Wool-gathering. It's . . . big." She waved at Chator, spread out below.

Javon smiled at her. "I suppose it is, compared to Athos."

The older Hunter paused at the front door of the residence – it was, as Javon had said, a large house, double storied and blocky – and knocked briefly before pushing the door open. The hallway inside was of well-worn wood. It was polished and smooth, and the faint smell of eucalyptus oil and beeswax lingered in the air. It was a welcoming place, full of warm wooden colours and Kazari was enchanted. She'd never seen wooden panelling before, and like the floor it was polished to a gleaming sheen. A selection of cleverly carved crutches sat in a rack at the door, each one depicting a different theme. They were padded on top, and the gloss on the wood matched that on the walls and floor.

"Boots off in here, Kaz," said Javon, bending to untie her own laces. She added her boots to a neat line of other footwear. Kazari was sure one of the battered pairs belonged to Sendar, and felt a warm rush of relief as she bent to remove her own.

Walking slightly awkwardly in her socks, and trying not to slide on the polished floor, she followed Javon down the hallway and into a large sitting room. It was well lit, but as they entered, she was transfixed by the spectacular view of the sunset through the broad windows, and almost overlooked the man seated in one corner talking quietly to Sendar and Andiss.

"Welcome, Javon – and you must be Kazari. It is a most delightful sunset tonight, isn't it?" His warm tones matched the glow of the wood that surrounded them, but Kazari blushed, embarrassed to have been so entranced by the view she'd ignored the people.

"It's very good to see you again, Alexando," replied Javon, bending to clasp the man's hands. "And yes, this is Kazari – Kaz to her friends." She waved Kazari forward.

"I hope you'll allow me to be counted among them, then, Kaz," he said, as Kazari bent in turn to take the man's hands. She felt awkward until he waved a hand at what should have been his right leg. "I'm afraid that by this time of day, I'm a bit worn. The remaining leg's been working hard all day and deserves its rest."

She tried not to stare, but then gathered her thoughts. "I'd be honoured, Alexando. Sendar has spoken very well of you."

"Nicely said," he replied, "I believe dinner will be on the table momentarily," and wiggled his eyebrows at her.

His eyes were warm under their dark bushy brows, and his weathered skin was olive, and well darkened by the sun. Despite his missing leg, he clearly still spent many hours outside and the rest of his body appeared well muscled and trim. She felt welcome, and a load seemed to lift itself off her shoulders. Despite the gorgone encounter, despite the worry and the fear that Albatar was under siege, and despite the many questions still bumping around her skull, Alexando exuded a sense of peace in an otherwise turbulent world.

"One of the villagers – a lay brother – cooks for Alexando," Andiss said, then laughed at Kazari's surprise. "He was never a good cook, even when he had a proper kitchen to play in."

"And you think you were better?" Alexando asked.

"At least my cooking was edible," retorted Andiss. "Your efforts?" He made a face and mimed sticking two fingers down his throat. Sendar let loose a snort of laughter, hastily stifled, and Kazari was hard put to keep her own face straight. Andiss, normally so serious, was *teasing* Alexando? Disbelief warred with amusement inside her, until the amusement won, and her mouth stretched itself into a smile. Andiss was an excellent cook, with a fine touch with the spices he carried in his pack.

"What is for dinner anyway?" he asked.

"Still just as focused on your belly as I remember," said Alexando.

He took his leg off the hassock it had been resting on, and climbed agilely out of his chair, pulling yet another elaborately carved crutch from behind it. "We'll go and find out, shall we?" He swung along easily with the crutch, using it to push a door open, and led them into a dining room. It contained several tables, but only one, placed in the middle of the room, was set for dinner. Kazari counted seven places. "Elliam and Abel will be with us shortly, according to their signal. They said not to wait."

"Ever organised," said Javon drily.

"Of course," replied Alexando. He pulled a chair out, and patted it. "Sit beside me, Kaz, and we'll get to know one another."

Kazari smiled at him, liking the man more each moment, and sat down.

After the blessing, they ate from large tureens delivered efficiently by a young man wearing neat livery. Although not officially a Servant of the Lady, his tunic bore an elaborate badge surrounded by tiny gems in the colours of each of the septs. Kazari asked what the badge meant – she'd never seen one before – and Alexando explained that Mendis was a lay brother, one who'd abstained, but had wished to spend his period of abstention serving the Lady's servants. She'd heard of such people and had always wondered why they didn't just choose and become part of a sept.

"They have a deep devotion to the Lady," Alexando explained, "but are uncertain that they should take formal orders. Serving as a lay brother or sister allows them to consider their choice, and decide if joining our ranks is truly the path the Lady would have them take. Besides," he leaned over and lowered his voice, "he's an excellent cook and assistant, and I have no idea what I'd do without him. You may speak freely before him."

Kazari nodded. The food was delicious, and she was ravenous, so she sat and listened, and answered Alexando's questions. Before she realised it, she'd told him all about Suborden, only belatedly considering that maybe she should have omitted a few things. But neither Javon nor Andiss had interrupted, so she assumed Alexando (and Mendis by extension) was privy to all the information already. When he touched her face gently, and asked about her scar, she discovered that she was able to tell him about it quite easily. More easily in fact, than she'd been able to tell anyone else about it.

When she stopped talking, he nodded, put his knife and fork down, and traced the line of it gently with one fingertip.

"I know of such things. Those who heal, do so very well, usually. But a greater gorgone . . . " His face and voice were grim, and he shook his head. "We have much to discuss when our Navigators arrive. We need to consider what a viper gorgone so far into Albatar means in the context of all the happenings these last months." He looked around the table at all of them, face serious. "For now, please: rest, eat, and take time to think. We'll meet after dinner when you've all settled in and the others have arrived. And Kazari and Sendar, you two and I have much to discuss."

Kazari rather nervously wondered what Alexando could want with two trainees.

Chapter Ten: Plans

Kazari washed in the warm water in the communal bathroom, absently towelling herself dry as she stared at her face in the mirror. The scar had faded slightly, or perhaps Kazari's deepening tan was beginning to conceal it. Never fair skinned, her skin was now a rich brown, and the constant exposure to the sunlight seemed to deepen the tint each time she looked in a mirror. The scar was beginning to feel less tight, but it still shocked her each time she saw her reflection. There was a small crack in the bottom corner of the mirror, marring its otherwise clean silver surface. It was a bit like herself, she mused, mostly whole, but slightly battered on a corner.

She wondered what it was that Alexando wanted to talk about. He'd mentioned it immediately after looking at her scar. Her stomach twisted with anxiety, unsettling the meal she'd consumed, and for a moment she felt as if her dinner was about to leave her. He'd said he'd heard of such things. Well, if he had, then perhaps what he knew might be helpful. She forced herself to relax, and slowly felt her stomach settle. She splashed more water on her face, and tried to distract herself by wondering where Sendar had followed the gorgone worshippers to. He'd been very quiet at dinner.

There was a knock at the door.

"I'll just be a moment." She hurriedly scrubbed the damp ends of her curling hair with the towel, and, after pulling on her clothes as fast as she could, opened the door. "I'm just finishing up."

"You took long enough," said Sendar, smiling.

She smiled back him, wondering how he seemed to turn up every time she was thinking about him. Or maybe she'd just been thinking about Sendar a lot. She blushed. Of course she hadn't been. It was just that he'd been so quiet.

"Sorry," she replied, trying to cover the blush by pretending to dry her hair again. Although it was short, the ends curled, and rubbing it with the towel had probably made them stick up. She was too far from the mirror to check, so she sighed and kept her eyes down as she exited quickly.

"Tell Andiss and Javon I won't be long," he said, shutting the door behind him.

She hung her towel over the end of her bed and ran her hands through her hair, trying to calm the ends, twisting around to plonk herself on the quilted coverlet. What was up with her? Blushing? It was ridiculous. And then Sendar's lean form ran through her mind, his dark skin sliding smoothly over his muscles. She'd seen a fair bit of him one way or another over the last few months and she knew the shape of him well. His ready smile and intelligent eyes had become a constant in her life, but today, suddenly something was different. More. She puzzled, trying to figure out what had changed.

"Ready, Kaz?" Andiss' asked from the door, startling her out of her reverie, and to her horror, she blushed again.

"Oh. Yes. Almost. And Sendar said he won't be long."

"Come down as soon as you're ready."

Kazari pushed herself to her feet and followed him down the stairs to Alexando's comfortable study. It was festooned with maps, some marked with pins, and others covered in pencilled annotations. Several of them detailed the same area, but were in a range of different scales.

A pot of tea steamed on a side table, surrounded by pottery cups, with a dark blue milk jug set to one side. Alexando reclined on a large chair, foot up again, a tabby cat purring contentedly in his lap. Javon, Abel and Elliam were already there, holding mugs and chatting. Abel held a half-full dinner plate somewhat awkwardly in his lap, and an empty one sat on a side table near Elliam.

"Sendar won't be long," said Kazari.

Andiss nodded and bent to pour a cup of tea for himself. "Tea, Kaz?"

"Yes please," she replied, and then made herself walk over to Abel, trying to banish the image of Sendar's smile from her mind. She made small talk, trying to put her friend at ease, realising that he'd probably never been part of a discussion like this one, and that he was just as curious as she was about what he'd seen. Then she giggled. "How's the bladder, Abel?"

He poked her in the ribs. "Kaz!"

"His bladder?" queried Alexando, looking puzzled. "I gather there's a story?"

Kazari told the story, as Abel interjected indignantly.

"I didn't mean to say it like that, I mean, it just popped out . . ."

Alexando laughed heartily, disturbing the cat on his lap, who gave him a disgusted look. He soothed her with his hand, scratching the cat's cheek until she subsided into a purring puddle of stripy, grey fur.

A few moments later, Sendar entered, and Elliam took great delight in telling the story all over again to Abel's discomfort, as a kind of introduction to Sendar. Abel ducked his head, embarrassed, but he was also more relaxed, and Kazari noted the satisfied look on Elliam's face as he regarded his young charge. She nudged Abel with her elbow, and he made a face at her.

Alexando called the group to order, and they took seats around the room. He motioned to Sendar, and the young Hunter explained what had happened when he'd followed the people who'd come to take the baskets. They'd travelled together on foot for some kilometres, then separated at a crossroads, the two men taking the road to Seraph, and the two women the one towards Chator. Sendar hadn't recognised either of them. He'd followed them to the outskirts of the village, but they'd separated again in the market square, and he'd had to decide which one to follow.

The woman he'd chosen had taken a circuitous route through the market, carrying her basket openly. He'd tried to see if she was taking anything out at any of the stalls she'd visited, but instead, she'd seemed to be purchasing various items and then storing them inside the basket. He'd then followed her to a merchant's house in one of the more prosperous parts of Chator, entering via the front door, which suggested that she was a resident, rather than someone who worked in the house.

"The thing is," Sendar said, "that house used to belong to Shenny the wool merchant when I lived here, but I know all of her family, and most of the staff, and I didn't recognise that woman at all."

Alexando nodded.

"Shenny passed away about a year ago, Sendar, and the house was sold to a merchant family from Seraph – I believe they trade in both metal goods and fruits."

Sendar sipped from his mug, hands wrapped around it as if they were cold, nodding. "That'd make sense then. But who was the woman? She wasn't overly tall, just normal height, braided hair and the kind of working clothes you see everywhere. Middle-aged, but fit. She moved along at a fair clip."

"Sounds like the wife. Ira, I think her name is. Thin looking woman, but she usually dresses up, not down, if you get my meaning."

Sendar nodded. "That's her then, I'd guess. Maybe the clothes were so she didn't stand out?"

The others nodded. It made sense. But what was a merchant doing worshipping a gorgone? What was *anyone* doing worshipping a gorgone?

"Let's talk about Seraph," said Elliam. "We came from there, following some odd rumours. Lord Juster seems to have decided to interpret some of the laws relating to land and property in a rather creative fashion."

"Is it only the property and land laws Lord Juster has re-interpreted?" Javon asked curiously.

Elliam shook his head. "His Adviser has sent a number of notes to the Abbot in the last few weeks. He's requested the services of a legist from the Judicial sept – one skilled in the breadth of Albatar's laws – and also an additional assistant for himself, as he's aging and unwell. Apparently Juster disagrees with his Adviser's advice, and I understand the Adviser's had some difficulties."

Elliam frowned. "And it might be a good idea to ask the Abbot to send a Healer too. Seraph Cathedral's Healers aren't bad, but I think Adviser Eriad needs a maven's healing. Anyway, we saw those two leaving Seraph just ahead of us and they didn't seem . . . right, so we followed them." He shrugged. "And you know the rest."

Javon stood and looked at the maps. "Where's the house, Sendar?"

Sendar studied one of the maps then tapped it and Javon placed a pin in it.

Javon frowned at it thoughtfully. "There's a lot we're not seeing. Is there anything more you have to add, Alexando?"

"At this point – no. But I think we need to ask people who might know a little more than we do."

"And they are?" asked Javon.

Alexando waved a hand at Sendar. "Ask him."

All eyes turned to Sendar.

Sendar grimaced. "I'll drop in on my family tomorrow. I'd be doing it anyway, and if *we* ask around, anyone with something to hide will know. I'm sure the family'll help, and there's a few old friends I can call on, too."

"Kaz, you go with him. Javon and I will do as we're expected to – call upon the Mayor, and chat to the notables. Elliam, would you and Abel have a look around as well?"

"Of course," Elliam said.

Kazari sat back in her chair, glad she hadn't been called on to comment. The day had been long, and busy, and difficult.

She yawned, exhaustedly, wondering how she could be so tired yet at the same time have her mind galloping all over the place. There was a hint of excitement at being off by herself with Sendar, and some regret that her reunion with Abel was to be only momentary. There was fear about the future and the uncertainty of the gorgone threat, and curiosity about a one-legged Hunter who seemed to know more about the wound on her face than he was saying up front.

"Keeping you up, Kaz?" Sendar asked, just as a lull occurred in the conversation.

Suddenly Kazari was aware of everyone's eyes upon her. Sendar looked slightly embarrassed, and she was mortified until Alexando spoke into the sudden silence.

"I'm also tired. Until more information comes to hand, there is nothing else to plan. Perhaps we should take the opportunity to follow Kazari's example, and rest?"

Andiss looked slightly surprised, but then nodded his agreement. "You're right. We need more information. We've got fragments, but nothing cohesive. We could talk all night and get no further."

Kazari yawned again, involuntarily, and stood up and stretched. She was bone weary, even more tired than she'd first thought she was. It was a quiet group that made its way up the stairs to the shared room. Abel waved a good night to her, as he and Elliam opened the door opposite and vanished inside.

The house at Chator was comforting even in the bedrooms, and Kazari slept better than she had for weeks. Even her nightmares were subdued. She'd fallen into a sleep so deep that when she eventually woke, she felt as if she was climbing out of a deep pit.

Outside dawn was just breaking, the sun hoisting itself towards the sky with fingers of pale gold reaching for the clouds above. She stretched luxuriously, yawning, but she was completely awake now, so rather than disturbing the others, and feeling the need to remind herself of the Lady's words, she picked up her Book of Hunters and The Writings, and took herself into the chapel on the knoll to greet the day in the Lady's presence.

She opened her Book, and began to meditate as Andiss had shown her, eyes closed and breathing relaxed. With her body rested, she felt the need to refresh her spirit. Slowly, the turmoil of the previous day settled as she worked through her memories of it. The hiss as the viper gorgone's venom struck the vegetation became an image without sound, and the beating of her heart began to settle until she could step through her actions during the fight, analysing them dispassionately. It was a thing of Hunters, akin to the katas she performed daily, and for the first time she really understood how important it was.

Almost without thought, she arose, and began to step through one of the basic katas. It took her meditation to another level. She moved slowly, breathing evenly, placing each limb with care, making each movement precise. When she'd first begun to learn it, her movements had been jerky, disconnected, as if she were a puppet, moved by an inept puppeteer. Now, she danced, not as she danced with her Gift, but in the strength and grace of her body alone.

Her spirit lifted, buoyed by the rest she'd had, and the simple act of devotion. Her amethyst stayed cool, but she could still feel the Lady's presence, and her pleasure in Kazari's act of worship. At last the kata finished, and Kazari came to a stop, facing the stained glass window at the front of the chapel. She took one last breath out, and lowered her arms, relaxing, feeling refreshed in body, mind and spirit.

"Very well done, Kaz." Alexando's voice was loud in the silence of the chapel and she spun, startled.

"I'm sorry, I shouldn't have done that in here," she said, slightly embarrassed that he'd been watching.

"Kazari, this is the Lady's place, and you are one of her servants. An Intercessor might have sung the morning worship in the chapel, but we are Hunters, and our acts of worship are more than just song." He smiled. "Your acts just now were right and fitting, and done with a heart seeking the Lady." He shrugged. "Would anything else have been more pleasing to her, or better for you?"

Kazari smiled back at him. His words made sense. Despite her initial struggles with the physicality demanded of a Hunter, she now knew that her body was very capable. And by extension, the kata, normally performed outside, or in a training room, had meaning in every movement. That those same movements could be a meditation as well as the foundations of her ability to destroy a gorgone was not contradictory. Every gorgone she destroyed was the destruction of one of the Lady's enemies. That too could be construed as an act of worship.

She liked Alexando. He seemed to know what she was thinking almost before she'd thought it, and his presence was calming, comfortable, and despite only knowing him for half a day, she was more relaxed in his presence than she would have believed possible with a near stranger.

He was leaning on his crutch, fully dressed in Hunter garb, and his missing leg looked particularly incongruous. From surreptitious glances, Kazari had been able to see that there was a tiny piece of thigh left to him, and that his Hunter blacks had been tailored around it. Her basic studies of human anatomy told her that he must have been very lucky to have survived the injury, given the major arteries in the leg. He must have seen her glance, because he looked down at his thigh as well, and then back up at her.

"Might tell you about that. When the time's right." Once again Kazari blushed, but he wasn't offended, just smiling faintly. "Fancy a cup of tea instead?"

"Yes, thank you," she replied, and followed him back to the kitchen.

She carried the cups of tea Alexando made to the large table in the middle of the kitchen. It was quiet, but a pot of porridge was simmering on the back of the stove, and the comforting smell of warm bread permeated the air.

"Mendis also makes good bread," said Alexando when she was unable to prevent herself from taking a deep appreciative breath. "Another of his many worthy skills – much like his discretion."

"Do you think he'll declare for the Lady?" asked Kazari, and sipped her tea. It was delicious, quite unlike any of the other teas she'd drunk. "What is this?"

"Mendis? The Lady knows, not you, nor I. And this tea comes from the hills north of here. There's a variation in the soil there that produces this particular flavour, and the villagers use some kind of fermentation process. I've asked about it many times, but they refuse to tell anyone exactly what they do to produce it. Consequently, it's one of the most sought after teas in Albatar – and commands a price that reflects it."

His admonishment was gentle, and Kazari coloured slightly again, but he talked to her easily after the mild rebuke, and eventually she began to enjoy the discussion about different types of tea. She'd always enjoyed tea, but her experiences were limited. For Alexando, it was a passion, and he was full of information, not only of the tea, but of the places the different teas had come from. Like all Hunters, before his injury he'd travelled extensively throughout Albatar, and he had many anecdotes to tell.

She found herself becoming more and more curious about his injury, and just how it had happened, and it was becoming harder for her to avoid looking at the space where his leg should have been. At one point, he lifted a hand and scratched the air where his knee would have been, and at last she couldn't contain herself any longer.

"What were you scratching just then, Alexando?"

"It's my leg," he explained, "It still itches a bit."

"But it's not there!" she blurted.

"No, but it really does still itch," he replied, and scratched the air again. "Talking about it makes it more itchy."

"But . . ." stammered Kazari, completely out of her depth.

"It's a phantom limb," explained Alexando, patiently. "Happens all the time when people lose a body part. Your brain still thinks it's there. Or perhaps it's still there, but only in your brain." He tapped a finger on his jaw, thoughtfully. "I've been thinking about it for years, and corresponding with a couple of the Healers, but we're still trying to figure it out. Used to hurt too, but that's settled down in the last few years."

Curiosity overcame reticence, and she leaned forward and tapped the air where he'd been scratching.

"Can you feel that?"

He shook his head. "Nope. But if you were to scratch it when I'm itchy, it'd still help."

"That's just weird," she replied, sitting back and picking up her cup again.

He chuckled. "It is, but it doesn't change the fact that that's what happens."

"Does it happen to everyone who loses a limb?"

"No, but it does happen more frequently than you'd think. Now, how's that scar this morning?"

The question came out of nowhere, and Kazari was shocked to silence. Few people mentioned her scar, but it was always painful when they did. Not that her face was painful, but rather her heart hurt, particularly because her mother's face arose before her each time someone commented on it. Without volition, her hand rose and she fingered it gently.

"It's . . . there," she said. "Always there."

He nodded sympathetically, and she felt her eyes fill with tears that threatened to spill over and pour down her cheeks. Self-pity warred with practicality, but she fought the pity back down to a manageable level as his warm hand covered hers.

"If you need to talk, Kaz, feel free. I know what it is to lose something."

Then she felt pathetic. He'd lost his leg, and all she had was a little scar – perhaps not so little, but it didn't impair her ability to move, or think, or feel. Still, the hot tears welled again, and her throat tightened convulsively. She took a few breaths, slowly, trying to ease the tightness before it strangled her, and let out a shuddering breath.

"You know, it is all right to mourn, Kaz. You've had a momentous start to your life as a Hunter. Your face is on display to the whole world, and now it's not the face you've always known. It's normal to have a period of grieving."

She was almost undone by his kindness, and was reduced to nodding, taking shuddering breaths. At last the tension eased, and she felt limp, wrung out.

Finally, she was able to speak. "Thank you." Somehow Alexando's understanding made it all seem a bit better.

Chapter Eleven:
Sendar

As she saddled Stumpy, Kazari shot a curious look at Sendar. His head was down as he picked out his horse's feet. He'd been quiet all through breakfast, much as he had been on the road. Stumpy snorted softly, and she returned her attention to where it belonged – with him. Still, she was unable to stop herself sneaking looks at Sendar. He'd placed his saddle on Jumper's back, and was tightening the girth, and his forearm muscles tightened and flexed as he drew it up another notch. Then she realised she was staring again. Stumpy poked her with his nose as if to admonish her for her lack of focus, and she rubbed his neck contritely, drawing in a deep breath of warm horse.

Chator was larger than Athos, and far less rural. As they rode through it, Kazari noticed gutters running with greyish water, and people bustling back and forth on errands, always in a hurry. Its busyness was intimidating, yet at the same time exciting. Still, even here the people looked at the two of them in the way Kazari had begun to associate with 'Oh look! Hunters!'

The smells on the air spoke of concentrated humanity, and Kazari couldn't help feeling slightly claustrophobic, despite the hive of activity around them. Athos was a rural town, bounded by farms and wilderness, and there had been plenty of space for Kazari and Dari to roam as they grew up. Even the Order's

Abbey was surrounded by paddocks full of growing things on two sides, with forested lands on the other two.

"Sendar, are you all right?" she asked abruptly. The words popped out of her mouth without volition, but her companion's continuing silence was so contrary to his normal easy-going nature, that her concern had eclipsed her reticence.

He turned his head towards her, eyebrows raised, and opened his mouth to speak and then shut it again, shaking his head.

"Sort of, Kaz." He turned his head forward again, and patted Jumper's neck. They rode for a few more minutes, while Kazari cursed herself silently for her words. She was uncomfortable, feeling as if she'd crossed a line she hadn't known had existed. But then he spoke again, almost too quietly for her to head. "It's this town. I always . . . always feel as if it's . . . suffocating me."

"But your family? They're here."

"Oh, it's not them, Kaz. It's the place." He broke off again. "It's – I don't really know. There aren't many good memories here for me."

"I'm sorry, Sendar. I-I didn't realise," she replied. He shrugged, looking into the distance.

They rode in awkward silence again. Kazari still didn't really understand what he was trying to say about Chator. She knew he'd grown up in poverty – something she was still struggling to grasp – and that he'd had to hunt and work hard to help his family survive. She remembered something he'd said on the trip to Suborden. *"I thought that when I entered the Abbey I'd never be so exhausted from work that it hurt to sleep, and that I'd never have another sleepless night."*

So exhausted from work that it hurt to sleep? How hard *had* Sendar's life before the Abbey really been? And how difficult was his family's life now? She realised that they'd spent a lot of time talking about *her* former life, and not a lot talking about his. She counted Sendar as one of her closest friends in the Abbey, so how could she have been so insensitive?

"Sendar," she began again, intending to begin remedying that.

"Not now, Kaz. I promise I'll explain later, but I just can't go there right now."

Abashed, she nodded, and wished she'd never opened her mouth. They rode on silently until they turned into a narrow alleyway.

"Not too far now. Down here, and then out the other side and along the riverbank."

The buildings were jammed together, with no gaps to allow either light or air flow, and the smell of effluent rose from open drains on either side of the cobbled road. Kazari fought a desire to cover her nose with her hand as Stumpy tossed his head and slid slightly on the slimy cobblestones. She grabbed reflexively with her legs, and then tried to relax and trust her horse to do the hard work of remaining upright.

Athos had nothing like this. Its streets were open, airy, and its houses had flourishing gardens full of vegetables. The townsfolk prided themselves on order, and trees lined most streets. Here, there was a maze of winding streets, jammed in on each other, with no room for gardens anywhere. Instead, the houses had doors that opened immediately onto the squalid streets.

The alleyway narrowed again, until there was barely enough room for even one horse. Here, Sendar dismounted and began to lead Jumper on a short rein.

Kazari eyed off the open gutters but followed suit. Stumpy's snort could almost have been a sigh of relief.

Despite her care she almost ended up in the slimy, green algae covered gutter, when her boot slipped on some grease. She made a wild grab for Stumpy's neck, and he snorted in resignation. Now with a firm grip on Stumpy's mane, she followed Sendar around a corner and out of the alley. Fresh air drove the lingering smell of human waste away for a second or two, before it was replaced by the smell of something nastier, and Kazari saw the discolouration in the river.

"What's that smell?" she asked.

"The Guild of Dyers. The run-off enters the river up there." He pointed to a canal not far upstream, where muddy coloured water could be seen trickling slowly into the river. "They use all kinds of stuff to make the colours. Some of it stinks."

"You're not kidding," replied Kazari, feeling slightly nauseous, as the reek assaulted her nostrils. She followed Sendar towards a small bridge built over the canal. Its stonework was sturdy, supporting them easily, but Kazari's mouth twisted with distaste as her boots slid momentarily on something slippery staining the grey stones.

About five minutes later, Sendar stopped in front of a tumbledown cottage not far from the river, bounded on all sides by racks full of drying plants. He tied Jumper to a post near the front door, and Kazari followed suit, looking around at the racks with interest.

"What are these?"

"My family collects and grows plants and other things used by the dyers," Sendar replied. "Some of them need to be dried to be usable."

She followed as he took a deep breath and tapped at the door, seemingly bracing himself. A harried voice called from inside.

"If that's you, Dunkley, leave it on the front step."

"Mum? It's me," Sendar called.

Hasty footsteps sounded, and the door was flung open.

"Sendar? You didn't send word!" A brown figure threw itself at Sendar.

Sendar had clearly braced for the impact, because he didn't stagger, but simply closed his arms around the small figure. "It was a last minute trip, Mum."

The small woman unclasped herself and leaned back, looking upwards into Sendar's face, revealing grey hair, brown eyes and a smiling mouth. Wrinkles around the mouth and eyes told of good humour and fatigue, but also softened its angles.

"And who is this then?" she asked, waving a hand at Kazari.

"This is Kazari, Mum, she joined the sept at the last intake."

The woman was truly tiny, Kazari thought as her hands were clasped by the warm, stained ones of Sendar's mother.

"And of course he hasn't told you my name, has he?" she said. "I'm Wanda."

"I'm pleased to meet you, Wanda," said Kazari, smiling at the woman. Her enthusiasm and warmth were infectious, and Kazari liked her immediately.

"Well, come on in, then, will you," said Wanda. She gestured towards the door. "The others are out, but your father will be home shortly, Sendar. You'll have to bring us up to date on all your news." They followed her in, down a narrow hallway to the kitchen. It was a tiny room, spotlessly clean, but containing only a stove, a wooden table and half-a-dozen chairs tucked around the walls. Wanda stirred the fire up and pulled the kettle from the back of the stove onto the heat.

She bustled around, asking Sendar what he'd been doing over the last year. Fortunately, most of her questions were answerable with a yes or no, but Sendar wasn't able to conceal that something important had brought him home unexpectedly.

"You'll be wanting your father and the others, then?" asked Wanda. "I can see you've something to say, and not just to me."

Sendar looked slightly embarrassed as Wanda placed rough pottery mugs on the table in front of the two of them. They steamed, and the smell was fragrant, helping to erase the stench that seemed to have followed Kazari in from the canal. She picked hers up and sipped.

"That's delicious!" she exclaimed. "What is it?"

Wanda laughed. "Just a little of this, and a little of that."

"Does Alexando know about it?" asked Kazari, "He loves tea!"

"Oh yes," smiled Wanda. "I trade it to him for flour, and the occasional bag of spices. The Abbey supplies him well, and he's always on the lookout for someone to help. He's a good man, Kazari." Kazari nodded, smiling as Wanda sat down and pinned Sendar to the wall with her eyes. "Now, come clean, young man!"

Sendar sighed and put his mug carefully back on the table. "Yes, I do want to talk to you all, and probably a few others. We need some information – mostly about the people who've moved into Shenny's old place."

Wanda pulled a chair out for herself, and sat down, wrapping her hands around her mug. "Because?"

"Because things are on edge, and there may be gorgones, Mum."

"Gorgones?" she exclaimed. "Here?"

"Possibly," Sendar qualified, "But if they are, they're not here openly."

Wanda nodded, taking a deep breath. "In that case, you'll need the others to help. And I think we already have some of the information you need." Her face was troubled, and she refused to say anymore, just shook her head and told Sendar he'd have to wait until the others came home.

Then she beckoned to Kazari, and leaving Sendar in the kitchen, began to show her around outside, where the drying racks held the foraged plants. Kazari was fascinated by her deep knowledge.

She'd had no idea that dyeing clothing could be so complicated. Or that there were whole families involved in obtaining the colouring ingredients, let alone whole districts in towns that did the dyeing. Or that they could be paid so poorly. Despite the volume of drying plants spread across the drying racks, the tiny house with its minimal furnishings spoke eloquently of Sendar's family's finances.

Kazari knew how much her parents earned from their leather goods. Slightly ashamed, she felt her face heat as she remembered how much her last belt had sold for. She supposed that a decorative belt was something that could be considered a luxury, but then she recalled the utilitarian leather goods that her parents turned out in bulk. They weren't expensive, but they sold continuously because people needed them. The elaborate pieces were works of art in their own right, and Kazari knew her family provided custom made pieces regularly for out-of-towners, some of which they sent on consignment with traders.

She'd never thought much about who bought them, despite knowing something of the prices her parents charged. As her own leather carving skills had developed, she'd taken it as a given that people would ask for her work – and be prepared to pay for it.

Athos was relatively wealthy. Suborden was definitely prosperous. But on this trip, she'd seen that some of the towns they'd passed through were tiny, and the houses less well kept than she'd expected, and now here, in Chator, she was seeing poverty that she'd never suspected existed within Albatar's borders.

Why didn't the local Lord – Juster – see it and recognise it? Or more, what was Lord Juster's Adviser telling him? Surely a Servant of the Lady would speak out against this type of poverty? The Adviser had asked for help. Perhaps this Lord didn't listen to his Adviser – that was what Elliam had implied – but the thought was anathema, astounding. She frowned as she followed Wanda down yet another row of drying racks. These ones held familiar smelling plants. She searched her memory, trying to track down the elusive scent. She inhaled again, wrinkling her forehead. Wanda chuckled. The sound seemed happier than it should have, given the poverty of her life, and Kazari looked up, surprised, to find the woman wagging a finger at her.

"You know the smell, don't you?" she asked, amusement written all over her face.

"I do," replied Kazari. She sniffed again. "I know I've smelled it before, but I can't think where."

Wanda beckoned, and led her into a tumbledown shed at the end of the row. Neat hanks of rope hung from pegs on beams that were stronger than the outside of the shed suggested. New, pristine strands in varying diameters hanging in the dim light.

"Rope?" exclaimed Kazari. "Of course!" She inhaled again, taking in the scent deeply. "You make rope too? Sendar didn't say anything about that."

Wanda smiled. "Sendar doesn't know anything about it. This is only our second batch. Alexando arranged for Sendar's younger sister to be apprenticed to a rope maker in Seraph. Each time Jalax comes home she teaches us something new. So in a way, the whole family are now apprentice rope makers. Her maven doesn't object, because we're supplying him with what he needs to make the finest rope available. Our first lot went to Calimo for sale – very quietly, I might add – Lord Juster doesn't like his crofters sending their wares anywhere else for sale, but the prices are much better in Calimo. Go and fetch Sendar, will you Kaz? I may call you Kaz, mayn't I?" Wanda smiled again, and Kazari felt warmed by the smile.

She nodded and ducked out of the shed. Sendar would be pleased. His preoccupation had been worrying. Then she thought about Wanda's words. She'd said that Lord Juster didn't like his crofters taking their wares anywhere but Seraph. Surely they should be able to send the work of their own hands wherever they wanted? She frowned again, and went into the kitchen to find Sendar.

Sendar was sitting at the table, staring into his mug, slumped on his elbows. His face was unguarded, open, but full of sadness, and she hesitated to open her mouth, but she must have made an involuntary sound, because he started and looked up, looking embarrassed.

"Kaz?"

Deciding not to say anything, she tilted her head towards the door and forced a smile onto her face.

"Your Mum has something to show you."

As they walked through the drying racks, she heard his footsteps pause and turned around to see him fingering the drying fronds on one of the racks.

"What's this?" he asked. "It's new."

Kazari said nothing, just smiled and waved him towards the shed. He lifted an eyebrow, but opened the door and went in. Kazari paused at the door, not wanting to intrude on Wanda's moment, but still wanting to see Sendar's face when he realised what his family had accomplished in his absence.

"Mum!" Sendar came to an abrupt halt, and Kazari saw his head move rapidly as he took in the rows of ropes. "But how?"

"Jalax," replied Wanda simply. "Alexando arranged an apprenticeship for her, and she's been teaching us everything she learns. Of course, we had the racks and the knowledge of plants required, so it's just the drying, the preparation and the weaving we've needed to learn. Her maven is a generous man who's very happy with her progress, and has no problems with her passing on the knowledge at home, because he is now being supplied with quality raw supplies, prepared just as he wishes." She shrugged her shoulders. "Your choice has been a blessing to us in more ways than one."

Kazari smiled as she saw Sendar's shoulder lift, as if he were setting down a burden he hadn't realised he was carrying. Wanda hurried towards him, as Kazari saw his shoulders lift again, and realised that he was almost crying. She withdrew quietly, leaving him alone with his mother, and went back to the house to put the kettle on again.

Chapter Twelve:
Thinking

Alexando smiled at Sendar, patting him on the shoulder. "It was nothing, Sendar. Only a thing that anyone might do for a friend. And be certain, Sendar, your family *are* my friends, and they deserve better than they've had. It seemed like a perfect match – Jalax has always been good with her hands, and your parents have the plant knowledge required to match Roper Dudgeon's exacting standards." He shrugged, leaning on his crutch, and cocked his head. "And one day they'll have a better income. Small steps, but steady ones. That's the way."

They'd found Alexando in the chapel gardens, swinging along on his crutch. Due to their late arrival, they hadn't had a chance to look around the day before, and Kazari was surprised at the extent of the grounds. A flat grassed area sat behind a high hedge, with a tall spreading tree standing in one corner, spilling shade in a deep pool around itself. There were carved wooden seats set around the edges, made of weathered wood.

The seat under the tree was more decorative, with elaborate carving on the backrest, and a well-worn cushion on the solid wooden seat.

"We call this the outdoor chapel," Alexando said quietly, as Kazari looked distractedly around the area. "And of course, visiting Hunters are welcome to use this area to train." He smiled at them both. "It always reminds me of the Grove at the Abbey. I've spent many hours here in meditation and contemplation, and in working the forms. So, now, I'd like the two of you to show me where you're up to in your training. And I will critique." He waved a crutch expressively, and Kazari's eyes suddenly blurred. She enjoyed her training – most of the time – and she had a small inkling of the loss that Alexando must feel every day.

"It would be our pleasure, Alexando," replied Sendar. "Kaz, shall we step through from the beginning?"

"The beginning?" she blurted. Did Sendar mean that they would work through all of training katas from the beginning to the end? She didn't know them all yet, but the number that she did know would take several hours at least. She could feel her knees quivering with exhaustion before they even began.

"The beginning," said Sendar firmly. "Andiss told me that Alexando was one of our most skilled before his injury. It will be an honour to have his feedback. We'll stop when you run out of things you know."

An honour it may have been, thought Kazari wryly, several hours later as she staggered to a halt, her ears ringing with Alexando's comments, but it had been a very sweaty honour. She wiped her hand across her brow, feeling thirsty, and wishing she'd thought to drink more earlier in the day.

"Here, both of you, sit on the grass and stretch. Mendis will bring us drinks," said Alexando said. He turned and pulled a rope dangling from the tree above his seat.

Kazari heaved a sigh of relief and let herself down onto the ground to stretch. The sweat dried slowly, leaving her feeling sticky, and thirstier by the second. A Hunter was meant to meditate while she stretched, using the slow movements to focus her thoughts, but this time Kazari's thoughts were scattered. Alexando's critiques had been to the point, and more exacting than even Javon's or the Abbot's. She was exhausted. He'd had her tighten her forms a fair bit, adjusting hands and feet at his urging – by what seemed like millimetres – until he was satisfied with her stance and her balance.

He had a point, she was forced to concede, but she'd really thought she'd mastered at least the beginner's katas. Even Sendar came in for his fair share of criticism. Apparently, he had a lazy arm. Unfortunately, it seemed Kazari had two of them.

She changed her position, guiltily trying to place her focus on the Lady, where it belonged. *Sorry, Lady,* she thought as she leaned forward a little further. *I'm just feeling tired and scatterbrained.* Her amethyst warmed briefly, and she nearly let go of her ankles in surprise. She had the brief impression of amusement, and then the feeling passed, and she looked up and repositioned herself properly, meeting Alexando's smile.

"The Lady reminds us of her presence when we least expect it, Kaz."

She realised he must have seen the glow of her amethyst and smiled back at him, blushing.

"While you stretch, meditate on this: The Lady's Hunters hear her voice in the darkness. They hear and do not give in, for she walks by their side for all time."

Kazari moved smoothly to another position and tried to keep her attention on the words he'd quoted. They came from The Book of Hunters. She'd now read it from cover to cover several times, but much of its meaning still escaped her. She rolled the words through her mind repeatedly, committing them to memory, and then realised with some embarrassment that she'd have to ask for the reference when they'd finished.

Peace sank deep into her bones as the stretching continued in the shade of the tree, and just as they finished, Mendis arrived with a wooden tray on which sat a tall jug and three cups. She was so thirsty that her hand almost trembled as she took the cup he offered her. The first sip felt as if it was evaporating before it even hit her stomach. The taste was tart, and sweet, and more refreshing than anything Kazari ever remembered drinking.

"It's a cold tea, mixed with juice from the lemons behind the house," said Alexando as she sipped. "Now, let's get down to business. You both have some very good skills, but Sendar, that arm!" He waved a finger at the young man, who ducked his head and made a face, "And both of yours Kaz! Let's work on the finer points one by one."

As he began to talk, Kazari found herself able to focus on his words, understanding them all the better for having heard him say the same things while she moved. But this time, he elaborated on why it was so important. And all the while Kazari wondered why a man with Alexando's obvious talents in instruction was mouldering away in Chator. Surely there were others less skilled in teaching who could be spared from the Abbey? It seemed that the day was a day of questions, but she sighed inwardly, and tucked them away to ponder on later, and applied herself to understanding what Alexando was saying right now. If she were one day to rove as half of a Hunter pair, she needed to be better than she was now – much better.

She heaved a real sigh, as Alexando worked his way through another kata's issues, and he raised an eyebrow.

"Kaz?"

"Sorry. I was just wondering how . . . how long it might take me to become useful, if I have so many flaws? Like, how long does it usually take?" She realised as she said it that she really had no idea how long it took to train a Hunter.

"Was I that hard on you?" he asked.

"No, not really, it's just . . ." She faltered and then recovered. "I've just never really known how long training will be – actually I don't think I've ever asked. Or maybe no-one's told me."

Sendar laughed, and the sound was freer than Kazari had heard for some time.

"Kaz, training finishes when it finishes. It takes most of us years. And Javon once told me that she's still learning new things."

Alexando nodded. "Exactly, Sendar. Your training will finish when you're ready. But you're still useful when you're training, of course. Think about Suborden, Kaz. You both did well there – in fact, it was due to the two of you that we've discovered this incursion as early as we have." His face darkened. "Although we still have to repel it somehow. And that's what our work here is about. Wherever a Hunter is, he or she is the Abbot's eyes and ears. Of course, the Lady knows what we're about, and we are, above all, her avenging sword."

Kazari had never really heard anyone else speak like Alexando did. Her avenging sword? The Book of Hunters did mention the term once or twice, but she'd always just skipped over it, because it seemed a bit dramatic. Perhaps she should go back and have another look – read through the relevant texts, and see what the context was. She wondered a bit though – the Lady saw everything, knew everything – why didn't she just intervene? She'd had the thought previously, but had buried it as too hard to think about or answer.

She opened her mouth to ask, but Alexando held up another hand and went on.

"And your next question, Kaz, is about the Lady, isn't it? Why doesn't she just put paid to the gorgone threat and be done with it?"

She nodded mutely. How did he know what was going on inside her head? Was there a Gift no-one had mentioned?

"Kaz, every novice asks those questions. If you didn't, you wouldn't be worth having in the sept. A Hunter needs to question, needs to think, and to strive to understand the harder questions." He paused for a moment, and took a sip from his glass. Belatedly, Kazari realised that she'd stopped stretching, and moved into the next position as Alexando spoke again. "Tell, me, either of you – would you be a puppet?"

A puppet? Kazari's mind sprouted a picture of herself, wooden, and with strings attached to each limb, moving and bouncing as her handler twitched. What did Alexando mean? And then understanding dawned, just as Sendar spoke.

"I wouldn't want to be a puppet. But what does that have to do with this discussion?"

"Kazari?" asked Alexando.

"I wouldn't want to be one either, but you're talking about how much or how little the Lady chooses to intervene in our affairs, aren't you?"

Alexando nodded. "It's one of the hardest things to comprehend. This world could be perfect, if the Lady chose to use her power to make us do as she wishes. She isn't lacking in power, but she allows humanity to take its own path, because not one of us would choose to be a puppet. Of course, that means that those who court evil, are allowed to take their own paths too. And those of us who declare for the Lady must then oppose them. Not without help, of course. Still, the cost is high."

Kazari looked at his leg, or rather where his leg used to be. "Do you regret it, Alexando?" she whispered into the sudden silence.

"Regret losing it?" he asked, waving a hand at his missing leg. "Of course – I'm human, and like anyone else would, I miss my leg. When I watched the two of you, I could feel it twitching." And at their raised eyebrows, he went on. "Remember how I told you about my phantom limb, Kaz, and how it itches? But regret doing the Lady's work? Never. I told you yesterday that one day I might tell you the story of what happened . . . but now is not that day." Then he smiled at them mischievously. "I'm saving it up for the right moment."

Kazari swallowed her disappointment. Knowing why Alexando thought it was worthwhile to lose a leg for the Lady might help her to understand things a bit better, but Javon had said she was to be patient, and Alexando wasn't going to tell her until he wanted to, so she finished her last stretch, silently admonishing herself to be quiet.

A few moments later, Sendar voiced another query. "If we're not puppets – none of us – then why do some choose to follow evil? I mean, why *would* you?" The topic seemed to be a recurring one in their conversations, Kazari thought.

"There are many reasons, Sendar. Some are about greed, others selfishness, and yet others because they're feeling envious, or because they feel they've been slighted in some way.

You might as well ask yourself why you're petty, or mean, or even silly sometimes. The answers might surprise you if you're honest with yourself." He wriggled on the bench seat. "And now it's time for me to be gone. I have things to do. As have the two of you. Go and wash, and be ready to report back this evening."

He unfolded himself, arranged his crutches to his liking, and swung off towards the chapel. Kazari looked at Sendar. Sweat still glistened on his dark skin as he sat cross-legged on the grass. His expression was contemplative, dark eyes looking off into the distance. She wriggled a bit, and then pushed herself onto her feet.

"Want to share them?" she asked.

"Share what?" he replied.

"Whatever those thoughts are that you're chasing around inside that skull of yours," said Kazari.

"I was just thinking over the stuff Alexando said. I suppose it'll take me a while to sort it all out. Sometimes it seems as if everything I think I know I don't know. You know?"

Kazari laughed.

"Exactly!"

She held out a hand to pull him off the ground. "Make sure you grab with the good arm."

"But you don't have a good arm – what if you let go?" he asked mock seriously.

"Ha!"

But he grasped her hand, and she pulled him up, momentarily forgetting that he was much taller and heavier, so that she was pulled into him as he rose. She ended up with her face buried in his chest. It was sweaty, but he smelled nice in a funny kind of way, and her momentum made them both stagger, so that Sendar was forced to put his free arm around her, holding her close as they both struggled not to fall over.

"Sorry," she managed at last. He was still holding her close, and suddenly, Kazari was aware of just how close. She blushed. "Sorry," she said again. For a moment, he left his arm around her, and for another moment, she wished he'd leave it there forever. Then it was gone, and Sendar was laughing down at her. He was still holding her hand.

"What was it that Alexando was saying about arms? *I* reckon there's an issue with your legs too."

He let go of her hand and turned away from her, leaving her feeling warm and very aware of him. They'd trained together for months, in close physical contact much of the time, so why was she feeling like this now? Confused, she followed him back to the house to clean up, still trying to understand what had just changed inside her.

Chapter Thirteen:
Uneasy

Kazari woke gasping. The nightmare was slow to release her, and she felt as if it were trying to drag her back down into its terrifying grasp. Once again, the gorgone's voice echoed in her dreams, threatening her family. She was sweating, shaking, and trying desperately not to sob as she slid quietly out of her bed, and found her way to the bathroom.

As she splashed cold water onto her face, her breathing calmed, but her mind spun into turmoil again. She squeezed her eyelids shut, trying to still her racing thoughts, but the images of her family dying in the grip of a gorgone threatened to overwhelm her. This time the dream had been slightly different. This time, the viper gorgone had been a part of it.

She clenched her fists on the basin as her memory replayed the image of Jaden, held in the coils of the monster while it sprayed a fine mist of venom towards him. She'd woken just as he'd begun to scream, with the memory of the gorgone's words splattered across her mind. *'And I will come for them. And you will not save them.'* She straightened, trying to blot out the image by replacing it with her own in the mirror above the basin, but it was still too early in the morning for her to be able to see her reflection.

She splashed another handful of water on her face and then dabbed it off with the rough towel hung to one side. The chill of the water centred her a bit, and she let a shuddering breath ease its way past her lips. When she'd regained some composure, she crept back to her bed and slipped under the covers again.

For an hour she lay unsleeping. At last she gave up and crept out of bed again, slipping into her clothing, and making her way down the hallway to the stairs. It was almost dawn, and Kazari could see a faint lightening on the horizon through the windows of the stairwell. Her socked feet made no noise on the wooden stairs. Crouching to put on her boots, she decided to go to the outdoor chapel and try to meditate her way to calmness.

It was cool outside, which felt good on her too-warm face. Taking deep breaths, she walked through the gardens and sat herself on the chair under the tree and watched the dawn light creep over the horizon. In her mind, she repeated the phrase Alexando had encouraged her to meditate upon the day before.

"The Lady's Hunters hear her voice in the darkness. They hear and do not give in, for she walks by their side for all time." She spoke the phrase quietly in the semidarkness, repeating it again and again until she could hear herself saying it with conviction. Then, feeling more in control, she began to work through the first kata again, paying careful attention to her arm placement. Her muscles hurt, but as she moved, she realised that the changes Alexando had made heightened her precision.

Already confident in the movements, she moved more smoothly than she could ever have imagined, and she almost felt as if she were dancing her way through the forms. She paused and checked – she wasn't. It was at last the total control that comes with perfection. She felt lighter than she ever had before, placing her arms and legs precisely where they should be, each tiny movement perfectly controlled. When at last she finished, along with sweat she found release and relaxation.

The images of the nightmare still lingered, but Kazari felt as if she were able to step away from them, at least for now and function in the waking world. She stretched, and then decided to walk down to the town.

Chator had different sounds to the Abbey, and even Athos. The Abbey woke with a combination of daytime activity sounds and music, and Athos greeted the day with the cheery sounds of traders and birdsong. Chator, with a base more in industry than agriculture, rumbled. Carts and wagons rolled on the cobbled streets, and the sounds of the early morning sellers sounded harshly on the air.

It was, at once, more raucous and more energetic than the other two. Kazari walked quietly, keeping to the shadows. Not hiding, just trying to minimise her presence as a Hunter, and the stares that now seemed to follow her wherever she went. Eventually she turned into a market square. Unlike her home town of Athos, she knew that Chator had several such markets. This one was a conglomeration of all kinds of things. She perched herself on a handy box, sandwiched between a store selling bric-a-brac and a towering stack of cut wood.

People were people regardless of where they lived, and Kazari found watching them fascinating. Across the road, a tinsmith opened her shutters with a clang, while the feed merchant next door stacked bales of hay in a pyramid, his quiet rustling a complete contrast to his noisy neighbour. Perhaps people took on the persona of their wares, Kazari thought. She smiled as a cart trundled past, cages of complaining ducks quacking indignantly. They sounded aggrieved to be on the back of a cart and not waddling along on their own feet.

The smell of the freshly cut wood was a pleasant contrast to some of the other more unpleasant smells that Chator had to offer. Kazari wondered if perhaps she'd find something in the market to take back to the chapel to share. Fruit maybe, she thought as a wagon full of fruit and vegetables rumbled past.

A furtive movement caught her eye, and she leaned forward on her box, wondering what had made her notice it. It was the tinsmith's shop. A dark figure was peering out through the service counter towards her. Something about the figure bothered her, but the angle of the sun was making it difficult for

Kazari to see into the darker interior. A moment later, the figure was gone.

Kazari rubbed her eyes, wondering if she'd even seen it to begin with. The sense of disorder persisted, though and she frowned, running the memory back. She sat for a further few moments, but as the minutes passed, more people began to look at her curiously, so eventually she gave up and took herself off to the fruit and vegetable stall.

As she sifted through the mounds of fruit, unseen eyes made the back of her neck prickle. She turned swiftly – nothing. She shook her head, mentally castigating herself for jumping at shadows, and turned back to the cherries she'd been considering. Dark and luscious looking, they made her mouth water.

"Ten dins for the bucket," said the merchant. "And only because you're a Hunter. Or it'd be twelve." He smiled to take the sting from his words. "Tell Alexando they came from Jono."

"Are they as good as they look?" she asked, and he grinned and dropped one into her outstretched hand. Brown eyes crinkled at the corners as she popped it into her mouth, nodding and smiling as the sweetness burst on her tongue. "They are," she managed, spitting the stone out and dropping it into the bucket full of scraps by the table. She dug in one of her pockets and counted out the requisite coins and then turned and began her trek back to the chapel, swinging the bucket by her side.

She sniffed the air. Nothing. Not even a tiny hint of gorgone. She sighed and kept walking, still mildly uneasy. Several times she spun, checking behind her, but there was nothing and no-one following. Still faintly concerned, she walked quickly, shrugging her sleeves feeling for the comforting weight of her concealed knives.

By the time she'd arrived back at the chapel, her sense of unease had escalated. There was a constant feeling of unseen eyes, and the memory of the half-seen figure in the tinsmith's shop loomed large. There was no hint of gorgone, no real reason for her to think there was anything there to worry about or to be concerned about. Perhaps she was becoming paranoid.

The feeling eased as she walked the last few metres to the residence. Alexando sat at the kitchen table with a cup of tea. She waved the bucket of cherries at him and tipped some into a bowl, placing it on the table.

"Out early, Kaz?" he asked, pouring a cup of tea for her.

"I woke early, so I thought I'd spend some time in the outdoor chapel. Then I went for a walk." She took a sip of the tea. It was the special one again, and she smiled her thanks over the rim of her cup.

"You were up early indeed, if you've been to the chapel and the market already," he said, raising an eyebrow. He didn't say anything more, but Kazari knew what he meant. She sat, sipping her tea, undecided whether she should tell him about the change in her nightmares. At last, when her cup was half drunk, and he hadn't pressed her or demanded any further information, she put the cup carefully on the table and looked at him.

"I had the nightmares again last night. But this time it was different."

He nodded encouragingly, but didn't speak, so she went on.

"This time the viper gorgone was in it. And my brother. The viper was . . ." she struggled to speak the words, and to her horror, realised she was close to bursting into tears. A warm hand covered hers.

"Was doing something dreadful to your brother?" She nodded mutely, throat tight with emotion. The dream had seemed so real. The voice had seemed so real. As if he'd read her mind, Alexando asked: "Did it speak?" Surprised, she looked up at him.

"No, not the viper, but the other one. The one from Suborden. It said the same thing it said then." She looked down but then frowned. "No, not quite the same – just part of it. A phrase. *'And I will come for them. And you will not save them.'*"

"So not the whole sentence this time, just a part of it?" he asked.

"Yes, just that bit."

Alexando was nodding, to her confusion, as if he'd expected something like this.

"Is it important?"

He sighed and stretched his leg, absently scratching the air where the other one would have been. "Possibly." He pulled a note from his pocket. "This came from the Abbot." He pushed it across the table to her.

She took it uncertainly, and unfolded it. It was short and to the point.

Alexando,

We finally have the information you requested. Maricon has dedicated himself to tracking down the fragments one by one, and will continue to do so. Piecing together the references has proved time consuming and difficult. Please correspond with him directly. As you know, archival records of Marking are few and far between, but Maricon found this reference only a day ago among an old stack. It's an account that appears to have been handed down verbally and then transcribed:

Several hundred years ago, there were four 'marked' by a gorgone. Marking occurred prior to the Fourth Incursion, when all four fought and defeated a greater gorgone on the northern border. A margin-note in the records said that each was spoken to during the fight. They described the voice as threatening and terrifying. All the marked experienced nightmares in the aftermath. The dreams repeated themselves regularly. Changes in the dreams heralded an increased threat during the Incursion. The dream changes are often subtle, so such marked should be made aware of this, and report anything slightly different.

Please send priority messages via pigeon, addressed to myself and Maricon.

The Lady's Blessings be upon you.

Injani

Kazari looked at Alexando, mouth hanging open.

"What does 'marked' mean? Do you think *we're* 'marked?'" she asked.

Alexando deliberated before replying. Then he looked at her with an intensity that she found abruptly disturbing.

"Only as marked as I am," he replied.

Chapter Fourteen:
Marked

The note dropped from Kazari's suddenly nerve-less hand.

"*You're* marked?" she asked, stunned. "But –"

Alexando picked the teapot up and poured another cup. "I told you that I might tell you about my injury one day." He paused and took a sip of his tea, looking reflectively at the ceiling. "It seems today is that day. But not yet. Not until Sendar is with us."

He added milk to her cup, while question after question raced through Kazari's mind. She didn't know where to start, except that it didn't seem fair of him to show her the letter and make his point, and then still not tell her everything immediately. He looked reprovingly at her. "He is also marked, Kaz. Even though his nightmares haven't been as intense as yours, it doesn't mean he doesn't have them or that they don't bother him. Some people are just better at hiding things from those they care for."

Still slightly resentful, Kazari made herself nod. Sendar was still having nightmares? He hadn't said anything to her – surely he'd know she was the one person who'd understand how awful it was? She frowned down at her cup of tea.

"Kaz – what's the matter?" Alexando pushed.

For a moment, Kazari wanted to retort like a spoiled child, but she swallowed the comment and instead prevaricated.

"I'm just not sure what I should be thinking right now." It wasn't quite the truth, but it touched on it. She put her cup down. "I think I'll go and wash." She got up without a further word and left the kitchen, her anger growing. Why hadn't Sendar said anything? Why had he suffered alone, knowing she might be able to help him?

By the time she'd returned to their quarters, she was gritting her teeth, all the relaxation of the morning gone to irritation at herself for being petty, She was angry at Alexando for not telling her what she wanted desperately to know right now, and at Sendar for not sharing what she felt he should have. She was angry at the Abbot because she'd obviously had at least some of the information at her fingertips, even before they'd left on this journey. And then she realised that there had been no date on the letter. How long had Alexando known all of that? When had the Abbot sent it? And why hadn't the Abbot told them about Alexando? Why hadn't Javon or Andiss? Part of her knew she was being irrational, but another part of her was relishing wallowing in the self-pity, resentfulness and irritation that were coursing through her. She hadn't had enough sleep, and now people she cared about were hiding things from her.

Perhaps this 'Maricon,' who she vaguely remembered as an Archivist wearing Intercessor's robes in the library at the Abbey, had found this information for Alexando *years* ago.

Not normally someone who struggled to control her temper, Kazari wanted to kick something – hard! She stomped up the stairs to the shared room and threw herself down on the bed, staring sightlessly at the ceiling. Her fingertips traced her scar. She was marked – whatever that meant – and the letter had mentioned dreams and nightmares as if they were ongoing – and as if the source of the Marking and the apparent portents within the dreams might come from a dubious source.

She sat up again and went to the window, looking out across the spring kissed garden, still fuming. It was lushly green, and flowers were beginning to blossom. Her anger felt out of place – as if her emotions were at odds with the season, and for some reason that infuriated her even more. She began to pace, and with each step, her anger grew. Why hadn't anyone told her? Why?

The door opened, and Sendar strode in, dropping a small sack onto his bed.

"Hi Kaz!" he said cheerily, and then stopped in mid-step as he saw her face.

He was there and he was handy, and her anger, irrational though it was, overflowed.

"Why didn't you tell me you were still having nightmares?" she hissed.

He looked taken aback. "Why would I, Kaz? You were having enough trouble coping with your own."

"But I would have understood!" She bit off each word.

"Kaz, calm down."

"You're marked, I'm marked, and now apparently Alexando's marked, and everyone's known about it except me!"

"What are you going on about, Kaz?" Sendar asked, perplexed.

"Our scars," she snarled. "Alexando has one too, and it's called being marked. Alexando and the Abbot knew about it and didn't tell us."

He took her shoulders, forcing her to stop pacing, and she wriggled angrily under his grip. "Let me go, Sendar!"

"Kaz, calm down!"

As soon as the words were out of Sendar's mouth, Kazari felt the anger start to drain away, to be replaced with a combination of guilt and weary exhaustion. She was so tired. She felt as if the morning had lasted for hours, and all she wanted to do was to curl up on her bed and cry. She took a shuddering breath as Sendar's hands tightened on her shoulders. His grip was strong, and the pressure of his fingers was firm, but it steadied her a little, and then he drew her in, tightening his arms around her.

For a moment she resisted, the embers of her anger fanning to flame for just a moment, but then the comfort of human contact was too much to resist, and she snaked her own arms around Sendar's waist and hugged him tightly.

"You know, I still don't know what that was all about," he murmured, "but this is nice."

Kazari drew back slightly, feeling awkward all of a sudden, but Sendar's arms tugged her towards him again.

"Do you mind this, Kaz?" he asked, uncertainty in his voice.

"M-mind?" she asked, slightly confused.

"This," he said, and tucked her back in. Warmth flooded her, replacing the anger with embarrassed amazement. Sendar felt like *that* about her? The whole idea warmed her. But then she began to worry. Did she feel like that about him? Had she given him the wrong idea? Or did she have the wrong idea? Was she even old enough to think she might care for someone like she thought she might care for Sendar?

"Kaz, stop thinking, and just answer."

Sendar's voice startled her, and she looked up at him in surprise, astounded that her emotions could seesaw backward and forward like this.

And how had her anger transformed so suddenly into . . . whatever she was feeling now.

"Um . . ." She had no idea what to say, and he loosened his arms, giving her room to move, should she so wish.

"Kaz?"

"I – think so. I mean, I don't *mind*, I just . . . I don't know what I think about it all. Everything. This, the other stuff, everything."

He shook his head and laughed, but didn't let go of her completely. "And what that meant, I have no idea, but it was definitely a Kaz comment," he said.

She blushed, but didn't retreat, feeling more comfortable in his embrace by the moment, despite her conflicted emotions. She lifted her head to speak again, but was interrupted by Alexando's voice.

"Kaz! Please, come on out, and we can talk about this properly."

They broke apart as Alexando's firm knock sounded on the door, and Sendar went quickly to the door and opened it. Kazari took a couple of steps back, trying to regain her composure, feeling confused all over again. In fact, she was so confused, and so conflicted, that she was tempted to climb out the window and run away from her own bad behaviour, Alexando's explanations, and the turmoil that Sendar's unexpected actions and comments had aroused within her.

Unfortunately, climbing out the window without anyone noticing was completely impossible, and as Sendar opened the door, she tried to compose her face into some semblance of normality. It was a futile effort, because she knew that her face was red, and her thoughts remained scattered like leaves on the wind.

Alexando peered cautiously into the room.

"Kaz, Sendar? There are things we need to talk about."

"There certainly are," replied Sendar, shooting a look at Kazari.

She felt her face heat again and looked down uncomfortably.

"Kaz?" asked Alexando again, and Kazari nodded without speaking. She didn't know what might come out of her mouth if she spoke – whether she'd cry or shout. Emotions tumbled and twirled inside her head as she followed the two men out of the house and down into the garden.

They walked in silence until they reached the tree they'd sat under the day before. Alexando hopped over to the wooden seat, and sat with a sigh, propping his crutches beside it and waving at two more chairs that had been placed nearby. Kazari assumed that Mendis, ever efficient, had placed them there. There was even a tray of tea, toasted bread spread with butter and honey, and some of the cherries Kazari had purchased from the market, all set neatly on a folding table.

Alexando poured as the other two sat in silence. Kazari sat staring at her hands clasped in her lap, worrying at a rough edge on a thumbnail, determined not to look at Alexando or Sendar.

She was hungry, and the smell of the hot buttered toast set her stomach to rumbling despite the turmoil inside.

"Eat Kaz, Sendar. Kaz, I can hear your stomach rumbling from here, and by the look on your face, an empty stomach's only going to make things more difficult."

Insulted, Kazari almost spoke a retort, but then she realised he was right and she was hungry. She helped herself to toast and honey and a few of the cherries, and sat back with her plate on her lap and took the first bite. The toast had just the right amount of crunch, and the richness of the butter and honey soothed the growling in her stomach, which, oddly, seemed to allow reason to begin to creep back into her mind.

As her stomach filled, she found herself growing more and more ashamed of her behaviour. *Lady, how could I?* She ran the words through her head, feeling her face heat. She kept her eyes on her plate as she finished the first piece of toast and licked her fingers. Picking up the second slice, she kept her eyes down, thoughts flittering and floating like twigs bobbing on a flowing creek.

"Read this, Sendar," said Alexando, and Kazari lifted her face long enough to see him hand over the message from the Abbot. "And before we go any further, let me make it quite clear that neither Andiss nor Javon knew about this. This information has been kept strictly between the Abbot, myself, and Maricon. Until recently, we didn't really understand the significance of it all."

Kazari swallowed the last of her toast and washed it down with a swig of her tea. If Andiss and Javon hadn't known, then it would be unjust of her to hold it against them. Still, letting go of even that tiny bit of irritation was difficult. She wanted to hold onto it and allow it to fuel her sense of resentment. But that was juvenile – the action of a sulky child rather than one of the Lady's servants.

"What does it all mean, Alexando?" asked Sendar, shakily.

The older man sighed. "We don't really know – not exactly."

"And what did Kaz mean when she said you were marked?"

There was silence, and Kazari fiddled with her cherries uneasily, rolling them around on her plate.

"As I told Kaz this morning, this is the time to tell you how I was injured." He sipped from his own cup, and then took a bite of his toast, chewing slowly.

Kazari wished he'd just get on with it, but then shoved her irritation back down again. She'd already behaved poorly enough for one day.

"Injani was my partner."

For a moment, Kazari wasn't certain who he meant, and then she remembered the signature at the bottom of the letter. He meant the Abbot. Injani was her name.

"We roved for years, mainly on the northern borders, coming back to the Abbey at intervals as all Hunters do. But right from the beginning, it was clear that Injani was destined for higher duties. Even then, her wisdom was remarkable, and her insight . . ." He shook his head. "She'd see right to the heart of things." His eyes were distant, and for a few moments he was lost in his own thoughts, and Kazari thought he'd decided not to continue telling his story, but then he gave himself a little shake and took another bite of toast.

"Injani became the head of the Hunter Sept about ten years ago. It didn't stop us roving, but it did mean that we roved for shorter periods, returning to the Abbey frequently. Our last trip took us right to the northern border – to the pass below Banchon, escorting a team to head out into the wider world. When we'd farewelled the team, Injani decided to follow them covertly for a little while. She felt that the pass was too quiet – normally we'd have encountered at least a few roving thylafex, but there were none."

"Thylafex?" asked Kazari, curiously.

"Yes, I know they haven't been seen in wider Albatar for many years, but they're actually fairly common on the northern border, and there's always a Hunter, or Navigator presence up there as a result," said Alexando. "They're dangerous, yes, but they also protect our borders. The Lady's creatures have their own place in the world, even if sometimes it conflicts with what we see as ours . . ."

"Anyway, we stayed behind the team for two days. It's a pretty hazardous pass – steep in most places, and with many dangerous drops. It was quiet the whole time. Not one thylafex; not even much of the normal wildlife. And then, just as the team left the pass, a greater gorgone appeared. And there was only Injani, myself, and the two Hunters on the team. Of course, the other septs have skills to assist, as I'm sure you're aware?"

He looked at Kazari and Sendar, and they both nodded, although Kazari made a mental note to ask exactly what other skills each sept might have. She knew about the Navigator's arrows, obviously, and she'd heard the Intercessors sing, but the Healers? The Growers? And what type of martial skills might the Advisers or the Judiciary have to add to a fight with a gorgone?

"Kazari," Alexando continued, "you've seen Injani Dance – you've even danced with her. She's remarkable, and so will you be, once you approach her skills with your body and your weapons. I have the Gift of Vigour, and once upon a time, I could Dance almost as well as Injani. The other two Hunters had Suppression and Ascension, but even so, we were extremely hard pressed."

Kazari noticed that he said 'had' in regard to the other Hunters. Had they died that day, she wondered? And Alexando was the other Dancer of the Sept. Her heart fell – with the loss of his leg, the freedom of being able to Dance must have been lost. She understood why the Abbot hadn't mentioned it.

"Our Intercessors sang. Our Navigators shot their arrows. Our Grower made the plants surrounding us grow vines around the gorgone's limbs, but the beast was huge, and it fought back." His voice grew distant again, and Kazari could hear the echoes of pain in its tones.

"Kane went first. Her Gift of Suppression failed as she died, and the gorgone's words pierced my heart," whispered Alexando, and his voice tore at Kazari's own heart.

"What did it say?" asked Sendar, his own voice rough.

"It said: *One by one I will kill you. I will take your lives and your loves. Albatar will fall to me. This, I assure you.*" The words fell like stones into the silence. "At that moment, it struck, and I was still too stunned by Kane's fall to Dance. It was too late for me to move, and its barbed arm struck my thigh and left seven of the barbs embedded. I fell, and it prepared itself to strike again, as I lay there, unable to move, or even to roll away."

"And then Injani was there. She was everywhere and nowhere. She was standing over me when it struck, and her blade took it in the side of the neck. It roared, spewing despair, but she stood above me, holding it off with the strength of her body alone, until our Navigators could fill it with arrows. Even as it died, it took Caris, and the Intercessor from the team. By the time it was dead, the team was half gone, and only Injani remained unharmed."

His eyes were moist with emotion, while Kazari's mind was filled with the image of the Abbot standing above him, fighting the gorgone, almost alone. The Abbot had faced down a greater gorgone like the one at the Abbey, almost by herself!

"Even as it died, I nearly joined it," Alexando went on. "The barbs were poisoned, as many are, and they were embedded deep in my flesh. Fortunately, the Healers always send their most skilled into the Outer World. Without him, I would have died. As it was, I lost my leg, and the scar remains angry to this day. And since that day, I, too, suffer the nightmares of the marked."

There was silence under the tree. A silence at odds with the beauty of the spring morning around them. Kazari's mind was full of questions – so many of them she didn't know which one to ask first. At last Sendar spoke.

"How . . . how long have you known about the connections mentioned in the letter?" His voice was quiet, but Kazari could hear echoes of her own anger in its overtones.

Alexando sighed.

"Not long. The Abbot did have the information when you left the Abbey, but she hadn't decided what to do with it. She was concerned that the two of you weren't ready to deal with all the ramifications, so she left it to me to decide when to talk to you about it. Believe me. Injani would *never* wish to hurt you by withholding vital information, but there are concerns about the origins of the dreams, and their long-term effects. She felt that alerting you too early might increase your anxiety beyond what you could bear. Or that it might compromise you."

"Compromise? In what way?" asked Kazari.

"You're only new Hunters, not fully trained, despite your early accomplishments, and you both have far to go. You are also young, and the young are vulnerable, despite the Lady's favour. In fact, we're all vulnerable, and older heads than yours would struggle to deal with the nightmares of the marked – I know this too well. It's our duty as seniors to protect you as much as we can until you're ready to stand completely on your own, requiring no support but the Lady's." He paused, and deliberately refilled his teacup, letting his eyes rest upon Kazari first, and then Sendar.

"Your reaction this morning, Kaz, no matter how you feel now, showed me that it was right to delay."

For a moment, Kazari wanted to retort hotly, but then she subsided, ashamed again.

"If Injani had told you back at the Abbey, without me to explain a few things – like how to cope with the dreams for instance – you would have been left in great doubt and fear, and perhaps the viper gorgone might have prevailed. You already know how they prey on our fears and failures."

"But it wasn't just Kaz," said Sendar, and there was a hint of resentment in his voice.

"Very true, Sendar, but would you have been able to keep your own counsel? Knowing about Kazari's nightmares and struggles?" His eyes were intent, focused directly on Sendar, and Kazari had a feeling that he'd said something else to Sendar, only without using words, and that Sendar had understood.

Sendar frowned, rubbing his brown hands on his thighs. He looked at Alexando, nodding reluctantly. "So, how *do* we deal with the dreams then?" he asked.

Alexando grimaced. "With time and practice. I write them down when I awake. All the particulars, or as much as I can remember. It seems that once I've written them down, they lose some of their power to disturb."

Kazari noticed he'd said 'some,' not 'all,' but she nodded as he went on. "And then I meditate – I'm sure you've been taught how to meditate on the Lady's words?"

They both nodded.

"But I meditate on the dreams."

Chapter Fifteen:
Dreams

"On the dreams?" exclaimed Kazari. "But . . ."

"The dreams," replied Alexando firmly. "Sometimes I gain insight into my own fears. Sometimes there's nothing, but usually there's something I can pick out as different, or something I'm able to learn from. It's about accepting the dreams as part of me, and then dealing with them."

Again, there was a moment of silence, while around them the birds sang on unconcerned, and the sun shone down upon the green grass and hedged borders of the outdoor chapel. Kazari grappled with the idea of meditating on her nightmares. They were filled with fear and edged with dread, and she had no wish to relive the gorgone's words deliberately. As she glanced at Sendar, she could see that he, too, was troubled. There was a tightness to his mouth, and he was sitting motionless, eyes fixed on Alexando, a slight frown on his face.

"But surely meditating on the dreams would increase their power?" he asked slowly.

Alexando shook his head.

"Meditating on them lessens their hold. You see, as I said before, it's about acceptance. We are marked. Our physical scars are part of us, and we have no choice but to accept them as part of our bodies – unchanging and unchangeable. I try to think of the dreams as a kind of mental scar. When I think of it like that, I can see the logic in embracing them as part of me. The encounter with the greater gorgone shook me for a long time. I had the loss of my leg to deal with – that was the most evident thing – but what haunted me most were the deaths of the other Hunters – Caris and Kane – and the Intercessor. She had the most beautiful voice."

Again his eyes grew distant, and Kazari could see hints of moisture gathering in their corners. Even now, Alexando's sorrow was very evident. She gave him a few moments to gather himself before she asked the obvious question.

"But why, Alexando? You couldn't have done anything more than you did."

He sighed.

"I know, Kaz, but even now my mind says that perhaps if I hadn't been stunned when Kane died, I'd still have my leg, and the others would have their lives. I was a Dancer almost as accomplished as Injani. *Objectively*, I know that's just wishful thinking. That thing almost killed us all. We were fortunate to escape without more dead. *Subjectively*, it's all much harder to deal with."

He reached above his head and pulled the bell rope.

"It took a long time for me to come to terms with it all, and even now, in my weaker moments, I'm still haunted by the deaths and the words. Still, I have found within me the ability to embrace even those darkest thoughts, to look at them in the light of day, and accept that the experiences will always remain a part of me. In a moment, Mendis will bring each of you a small journal and a pencil. Each night, when you wake, you'll write in it immediately, and then use what you've written as a focus for your meditation." He held up a hand as Kazari opened her mouth to protest the instructions.

"And Javon and Andiss will be moving to another room for the next three nights so you won't be disturbing them – our discussion here is with their full knowledge and support, even if they don't yet know the gist of it. In addition, if you wake with a nightmare you are to wake the other as well, and talk it over with them as you write it down. It'll mean sacrificing some sleep, but that can't be helped. Your dream could provide us with clues about the Incursion. Each morning, you'll meet here with me for breakfast, we'll train, and then we'll go over your notes in detail, and I'll compare them to mine."

Mendis appeared with more tea, toast, and the journals, and then Alexando had them step through the katas with him once again. By midday, Kazari was wringing wet with sweat again, and her apprehension about the coming night had begun to rise. When Alexando had lunch brought to them, along with a selection of weapons, Kazari began to suspect that Alexando was exhausting the two of them deliberately. She looked over at Sendar, and edged slightly closer while Alexando fussed with the lunch tray.

"Do you think he's wearing us out to make us sleep?" she whispered.

Sendar looked back and nodded. "Yes. And I'm glad of it. There's too much happening inside my head right now for me to sleep unless I'm exhausted." He shrugged. "But he's the best instructor I've ever had, so let's not waste the time." He gave her arm a little squeeze, and stood up to help himself to bread and cheese. Kazari felt her face warm at the touch of his hand and pretended to check her knives to allow it to cool down.

Again, Alexando worked them hard, and again, Kazari found herself improving her technique exponentially. She was amazed to discover what a slight position change could do to her ability to react quickly. By the time the afternoon had worn to a close, she was wrung out both physically and mentally, but the throwing stars were feeling more and more a weapon that fitted *her*. Sendar had also shown his new abilities to deflect thrown objects, to Alexando's intense interest.

"Your innovations remind me that we should all be encouraged to explore our Gifts more deeply," said Alexando as they finished stretching. "But for now, go and get clean."

Kazari sluiced sweat from her body, and rubbed the rough flannel over her face and limbs. The soap smelled faintly of lavender, and the hot water was soothing. It would have been relaxing had her mind been less active. She feared confronting her dreams. She felt as if confronting them would somehow allow the gorgone access to her inner self. It wasn't as if she'd actually heard it speak again, except in her dreams, but the fear that thinking about the dreams – something she'd been trying *not* to do – might make things worse niggled away at the back of her skull.

She relaxed in the bath, forcing her limbs to float in the warmth, willing them to loosen their tightness. But even as she tried to force her muscles to relax, Kazari's mind tied itself in knots. The day's events were many and varied, and they were jostling each other in her mind, as if they were people, pushing their way to the front of a queue. Sendar's face and warmth wriggled to the forefront, and for a moment, she dwelled on the warmth of his arms around her with a feeling akin to taking a deep relaxing breath.

Eventually, clean, dry, and reclothed, she joined the others for dinner, uncomfortably aware that everyone knew what she and Sendar were about to do. The normal chit chat after dinner seemed stilted. Javon and Andiss were planning to follow Elliam and Abel as they scouted the area between Chator and Seraph. Elliam suggested leaving very early the next morning to make the most of the daylight.

Despite her inner turmoil, Kazari was unable to suppress a snicker when she saw Abel's face fall at the mention of 'very early.' She felt Sendar's elbow in her ribs, but Abel's slightly hurt expression across the table only made her giggle more.

"Sorry," she said between snickers. "Just – your face, Abel!"

"So much sympathy, Kaz," he replied, wagging his finger, "just be glad it's not you!" She returned his smile, feeling her mood lighten slightly, and drained the dregs of her cup. Tiredness washed over her all of a sudden, and she decided she might be able to sleep after all if she went straight to bed, so she excused herself and left the table. A moment later, Sendar caught up with her as she climbed the stairs.

"I have mixed feelings about this," he said as they reached the top.

"You and me both," replied Kazari. Then she yawned, surprising herself. "But at least I'm tired. And maybe we won't dream tonight."

"Ha!" His voice was sceptical.

At least the night was cool, thought Kazari as she snuggled down into her bed. If it had been hot she was sure she'd have struggled just to close her eyes. She yawned again as Sendar extinguished the lamp. As she drifted off, she was surprised how easy it was.

She slept. Dreams, normal ones, came and went. Somewhere, even in her dream mind, Kazari was reassured. Perhaps tonight she could just drift in the security of normality. But then the dreams changed again, and she was swept away into the horror of the gorgone's words. Her family's faces flashed before her one by one, followed rapidly by a montage of her friends and teachers. Dari's family's faces appeared, then her teachers, and the incumbents of Athos. All her teachers at the Abbey appeared, and her mentors within the Hunter Sept. At last, the Abbot appeared, and then the gorgone spoke again. *'I see your family. I hear their fears. And I will come for them. And you will not save them, because this day, you die.'*

The dream deviated then, to a montage of the gorgones in whose demise she'd participated. Images of multiple suckers appeared, along with the changed from Suborden, then the viper gorgone appeared and they circled around her, paths crossing and overlapping in a mesmerising mirage until the monster that had climbed over the Abbey wall appeared behind them, looming threateningly.

In her dream, her legs refused to carry her away from the beasts. It was as if she was mired in deep clay, or a snow drift that trapped her legs. The words repeated over and over *'And I will come for them.'* It was as if the words were spears, or arrows, penetrating deep into her heart, wounding her over and over.

She clawed her way to consciousness, deliberately dragging herself out of the dream, and awoke sweating and fearful, tangled in her blankets. Next to her, Sendar was moving restlessly, tossing from side to side. Still shaking from the force of the gorgone's words, she stumbled over to him in the darkness and shook his shoulder gently, and then more firmly.

He woke with a gasp, eyes wild, whites gleaming, and was out of bed, his arms wrapping around her so fast he had her in a choke hold before she could even gasp his name. As his arm tightened around her throat, Kazari tugged at it frantically, trying to dig her chin into her chest so she could breathe. His arms loosened almost as quickly as they'd tightened, and he spun her, holding her away from him, his eyes so tragic in the dimness, that Kazari felt tears start involuntarily to her own eyes.

"Sorry, I'm sorry, Kaz!" he panted. "They were attacking, and I was trying to defend you. And I thought you were a gorgone when you woke me." He dropped his hands from her shoulders, letting them hang listlessly, still looking horrified. "I could have killed you!"

"But you didn't," she replied quietly, despite the pounding of her own heart. "You let go as soon as you realised it was really me."

He nodded but didn't seem convinced. She stepped towards him, and put a hand on his arm, feeling the firm muscles there. He relaxed slightly.

"It seems we were both having nightmares," she said.

He nodded, silent, and she turned back to her own bed, picking up her journal and pencil.

"We'd better do as Alexando said." She bent and lit the lamp on the bedside table, and for a moment, as the wick caught, the shadows springing up on the walls reminded her of the gorgones in her dreams. Her breath caught in her throat and she made herself exhale slowly, before sitting herself cross-legged on the bed.

As she wrote, the nightmare replayed itself vividly inside her head and her pencil quivered on the page. She steadied her hand with some effort, and continued writing, forming the letters and words deliberately. At last, she finished, and sat quietly, listening to Sendar's pencil scratching. When he finished, she cleared her throat and began to read what she'd written, aloud.

She didn't dare look at Sendar as she read. One by one, the words tumbled from her lips and when at last she was silent, she felt as if she'd run miles. A moment later, Sendar spoke, reading from his journal.

"It begins as it always does, with pain. There's pain in my leg, searing deeply, as if someone is sawing my leg off. Then the voices – repeating the same words, over and over. *You think you defeat us? The Abbey will fall to me. And you, and she, will die here today. The Abbey will fall. The Abbey will fall.* The words resound over and over and over, thundering in my mind. Then there are faces – they whirl around me, some zooming towards me, fading to nothing as they approach. The faces are my family, friends and teachers. They're all people I care about. I see the Abbey, wreathed in fire and smoke, and I see Chator in ruins, buildings tumbled, and bodies in the streets.

"Then I see you. Surrounded by suckers, with only a knife in your hand. In the forest a fire gorgone stalks, setting trees alight. I try to run to you, but I can't move my legs. They're mired in snow – deep snow. So deep, the cold burns them, setting them afire with more pain. I try to shout, but the noise of the suckers drowns me out, and my voice is deadened by the snow, sucking the sound from it, and at last I fall silent, helpless, only to watch the fire gorgone sweep towards you. Then I awake, and my leg throbs still."

He cleared his throat, as Kazari stared at him, eyes filled with tears. His stark description stood out in her mind as if he'd painted it in pictures. They stared at each other, eyes wide. And then Kazari took a deep breath and forced her tight muscles to relax. Sendar followed suit, and then he smiled tremulously.

"I feel better? I think?" he said uncertainly.

Kazari searched her feelings, probing cautiously, and pursed her lips as she nodded.

"So do I – a little. Not as overwhelmed, maybe?"

"Yes, not overwhelmed." He fell on the phrase eagerly. "That's it exactly."

He settled into a cross-legged meditation pose on his bed, hands resting palm up on his knees, eyes closed and breathing even. With a sigh, Kazari mirrored him, reluctantly sending her mind back through the dream images and breathing a prayer to the Lady for help. Although the images were still disturbing, Kazari found that actively engaging with them did somehow deprive them of some of their power. She focused on the words once again, and ran Sendar's description through her mind.

There were similarities between their two recounts, she realised. Threats to family, friends, and the Abbey. And her. The end of his dream was about her, and his inability to get to her to help her. In both of their dreams, she was surrounded by gorgones, and under threat. It struck a cold shiver through her, and she struggled to reorient her attention. Meditating was about being in the moment rather than speculating on the future, or so she'd been taught. She breathed to her belly, relaxing her muscles, until exhaustion began to make itself felt again.

A little while later, she snuffed the lamp and snuggled down under her bed clothes with a sigh of relief and closed her eyes. For the first time in days, she slept soundly for the rest of the night.

Chapter Sixteen:
Slow Developments

The next three days and nights were exhausting, harrowing, and relieving in turns. Kazari's brain scarcely felt as if it knew which way was up. She battled nightmares, disturbed sleep, and flash backs, with exercise, meditation, and the strangely cathartic exercise of writing it all down. She was torn between bettering her inner demons, and the knowledge that neither she nor Sendar were contributing to the efforts to track down rumours or gorgones.

She saw Elliam and Abel come and go daily, sometimes leaving before the Hunters rose, and once, coming in late, when she and Sendar were meditating in the aftermath of one of Sendar's nightmares. She was struck by how much he'd kept hidden from her. He'd confessed that he'd been afraid to burden her with his own dreams in case they'd made hers worse.

After the first night, he'd apologised, and so had she. Knowing that someone else was sharing the same experience was strangely comforting.

On the morning of the fourth day, Kazari sat yawning over her breakfast. She propped her chin in her hand, spooning up the porridge Mendis had placed in front of her, eating it slowly. She yawned again, trying to hide it behind one hand. Sendar poked her in the ribs.

"Keeping you up, are we?" He looked just as tired as she did, but at least he wasn't yawning. She grunted and took another spoonful of porridge as he helped himself to the teapot.

"We'll be moving on tomorrow," Javon said, pushing her mug across to Sendar.

"Tomorrow?" asked Kazari, startled.

"We've done as much as we can here, for the moment," Javon said. "And you need to see your family, Kaz."

Joy and fear warred in Kazari's mind. Her mother. The last time she'd seen her family they'd fought, and Kazari had left for the Abbey without their blessings or their farewells. Instead, her best friend Dari and her family had stood in their stead, waving her off.

She looked down at her porridge and stirred it, and then took another spoonful, giving herself time to think as she swallowed it down. Seeing her family seemed such a small thing in the scheme of things, but it loomed large in her mind, as if it was a mountain obscuring her view.

"Kaz," said Alexando. "Seeing your family will go a long way to helping you come to terms with the nightmares."

She nodded noncommittally; perhaps it might. Or perhaps not. Maybe they wouldn't want to see her. Her mother's shouted words echoed loudly in her mind. *Some of those who pledge to the Lady die, Kazari – they die, or fall into darkness.*

The rest of the line ran through Kazari's mind. 'And though My path may lead you into darkness, and your very life become forfeit, I will walk beside you always. Those who lose their lives in My service will walk with me all the days of eternity.' It didn't say that the Lady's servants could fall into darkness, as her mother had said, but that her path might lead her servants into darkness. And she'd already been led into darkness, both literally and figuratively, in Suborden. She ran through other texts, quotes from both The Writings and The Book of Hunters, mustering her theological arguments. Then she stopped herself. All the theological arguments in the world wouldn't help if her parents wouldn't see her.

A warm hand rested on her shoulder, and she jerked upright, knocking over her mug of tea, and sending her porridge plate skittering across the table, where Sendar fielded it and set it securely back on the table.

"Sorry!" she began to get up, but the warm hand – Andiss' – she realised, pressed her back into her chair.

"It's all right, Kaz. Mendis will get a cloth. And I'm sorry I startled you. You were very deep in thought, and you looked . . . lost."

In her confusion, all Kazari could manage was a somewhat wobbly smile for his thoughtfulness.

"Still, Alexando's right, you do need to see your family, and we need to be on the road. We mustn't lose sight of the bigger picture." He frowned. "Although which bits are part of the bigger picture remain to be seen." He gave her shoulder a gentle shake. "And we're all here for you, Kaz. You're a Hunter, and one of the Lady's servants, and her hands hold us all together."

Suddenly overwhelmed, Kazari nodded mutely, and as Mendis mopped up the spilled tea, she managed to thank him in a quiet voice, and began to spoon her porridge into her mouth again.

Alexando spent one more session correcting their technique, and then sent them off to visit Sendar's family. Ashamed of her own self focus once again, Kazari realised that this might be the last time he saw them for a long while. As they neared the tumbledown house, she reminded herself that even if her family didn't want to see her, she could still see them, make sure they were safe, and at least go and see Dari and her parents. Warmth rose in her as she thought about her best friend, despite the recent lack of letters. Still, she'd been on the road for a while with the Hunters. It was entirely possible that there was a pile of letters waiting for her back at the Abbey.

After leaving their horses tied at the water trough, they joined Wanda near the drying racks. She was carefully loading a box with dried leaves. Kazari sniffed appreciatively. The leaves smelled delicious – fragrant and almost energetic – if energetic was a smell.

"Morning, Mum!" said Sendar. His mother put her last sheaf of leaves into the box and rushed over, clasping her arms around her son.

"Just in time," she said, smiling up at him. "You can carry the box to the shed, and then we'll have tea. Wait till you try basitea, Kaz, I'm sure you've drunk it before, but this'll blow your socks off."

Kazari smiled at Sendar, who nodded enthusiastically.

"We're fed well at the Abbey, but I do miss fresh basitea," he said. "Just wait Kaz. You'll love it!"

Once they were seated around the kitchen table, she toyed with her mug as Sendar poured hot water over the freshly crushed leaves, and popped the lid on the teapot. Fragrant steam wafted from the spout as he lifted it to pour.

"We'll be off tomorrow, Mum. Is there anything else you've heard that might be of use?" He tipped the pot over Kazari's mug, and she inhaled appreciatively as he filled it.

Wanda wrinkled her forehead.

"Not a lot. Mostly rumours, and nothing concrete. Jalax is keeping her ears out in Seraph, and the boys too, when they're out and about, and your father's made a few cautious enquiries. The merchant's wife seems to be keeping a low profile, and of course we can't ask openly in case we raise suspicions. Jalax reckons there's something up in Seraph, but she isn't sure what it might be. She'll be home for a few weeks tomorrow. It's a pity you'll miss her. Drink your tea, both of you."

The tea was every bit as good as advertised, and the sweet aroma and warm fruitiness slid comfortingly down her throat. It warmed her all the way to her toes, and even seemed to lift her fatigue a little.

"It's just as good as you said!" she exclaimed.

"Don't sound so surprised, Kaz," said Sendar, as Wanda laughed.

"And before you ask, I've a box ready for you to take to Alexando, and another for yourselves," she said.

Eventually, it was time for them to leave. Wanda was unable to tell them when Asadir might be home, so with some reluctance, Sendar stood to leave, while Wanda bustled around and handed three boxes of tea to Kazari. She thanked Wanda, and hurried out to the horses, so Sendar could say a private farewell to his mother.

Stumpy greeted her with a gentle snort, and stood stoically while she secured the boxes in a saddle bag, idly resting one hind leg, his eyes half closed against the afternoon sun.

The front door creaked open, and she turned to see Sendar hugging his mother. The tiny woman was almost lost next to Sendar's muscular frame, but the smiles on both faces were the same.

As they rode through Chator, they passed the market square, and Kazari suddenly remembered the furtive figure at the tinsmith's. She rode up beside Sendar and related what she'd seen. He frowned in thought, but then shrugged his shoulders.

"It's not much to go on."

"I know," she replied, "But I'd totally forgotten until we rode past the market. I was a bit distracted."

They rode on in silence then, each wrapped in their own thoughts. Kazari's were on her family – and the reunion that might or might not come. Trying to ignore her doubts, she turned her mind to seeing Dari again. Dari of the long golden hair and scruffy clothing. Her friend loved sheep farming, and wore clothes that were comfortable and practical, despite her mother's best efforts. At least she could look forward to seeing her friend, and introducing her to Sendar and the others.

They left just after dawn the next day. Neither Abel nor Elliam had appeared the night before, and Kazari regretted not being able to farewell her friend. Still, whatever they were doing was probably just as important as their own mission. The ride from Chator to Athos took them through meandering hills and into open farmland peppered with small villages.

Kazari gained a new appreciation for the comforts of a medium sized village like Athos. Some of the tiny villages had barely any houses, and she wondered what it might be like to live so isolated.

As the day wore on, though, Kazari began to see some familiar sights – places she remembered from her trip to the Abbey. At midday they rode past their first campsite after she'd chosen the Lady, and Kazari recalled the exhaustion and excru-ciating muscle soreness that had assailed her the next morning. She now had a new appreciation for just how gently they'd travelled, and how kind the Abbot and her servants had been to all of the new novices.

Her physical fitness now, was astounding in comparison. That exhausting, painful ride, was something she could now toss off in a morning. Andiss saw her looking at the campsite.

"There've been a few changes, haven't there, Kaz?" he said.

Kazari nodded, and patted Stumpy's neck. He'd been her mount on that trip too. More and more she appreciated the stocky little beast. He might not be as big as the horses ridden by the others, but he was kind and reliable, and she counted him among her friends. He flicked an ear back towards her as if acknowledging her thanks.

"You must have felt as if you were crawling along," she replied.

"We try to be gentle on that trip," he replied, smiling. "Imagine if we'd moved at this pace!" His eyes twinkled.

"I actually fell off on my novice trip," said Javon. "I had dreadful balance, and I'd never walked farther than the market square at home. I was so sore I had to be helped off my horse!"

Kazari was surprised. Javon was the epitome of a Hunter. Tall, weathered face, brown eyed, strong and limber, with her weapon sheaths well-worn and well oiled. Trying to imagine her falling off a horse was difficult.

"You fell off?"

"I did. Several times. Despite riding the kindest, most placid horse in the Abbey. I was a dreadful rider in the beginning. I thought I'd never learn." She smiled reminiscently. "I think I told you I wanted to be an artist? I had grand dreams of entering the Intercessors, or perhaps the Judiciary. My hands had never done a hard day's work in their life. I had blisters from the reins, and scrapes and scratches and bruises all over me. I thought I was going to die. And then, on the second morning at the Abbey, I woke up a Hunter!"

Andiss laughed. "I was a few years ahead in training, and I remember that day well." He pulled his horse in on Kazari's other side and leaned towards her in his saddle. "It was the talk of the sept! She woke up and looked at her gem, and yelled blue murder until everyone else was awake. Mazil, who was our leader at the time, was horrified."

Kazari felt her jaw drop. Javon? It didn't seem possible.

"I had a lot to learn," replied Javon, drily. "A lot of it was painful."

Kazari couldn't help laughing, remembering her own aches and pains. And she at least came from a village where she walked a lot and had helped on Dari's family's farm regularly. As they crested the hill and began to ride down to Athos, Kazari felt her stomach lurch. Compared to all the gorgones she'd already faced, returning home to her family now seemed more frightening a task.

From the hillside, Athos was beautiful. Neat houses clumped together around the town square and the market square. From their elevated position, Kazari could appreciate the care with which the town had been laid out. Paddocks and pastures radiated out from the town like spokes on a wheel, interspersed with barriers of native bush. Here and there across the countryside, small farmhouses dotted the landscape. She squinted, looking to the north of the village where Dari's farm was. She could just make out the roof of the homestead. She breathed deeply, filling her lungs with the familiar scents of home. The smells were like old friends, speaking warmly of companionship and the love of family.

Family. Her heart clenched in her chest, and she was suddenly drowned in apprehension. What if they didn't want to see her? The feelings of dread followed her all the way down the hill and into the village like a trail of dust. As they rode through the streets, familiar faces turned to wave, their awe at seeing a group of Hunters, turning into surprised recognition when Kazari's features registered. There were even a few cheers, to Kazari's horrified embarrassment. None of it served to ease her worry, and it was with very mixed feelings that she turned with the others into the chapel grounds.

Dismounting outside the stables, she rested her head on Stumpy's warm flank for a moment. A warm hand on her shoulder, and Sendar's quiet voice startled her.

"It'll be all right, Kaz. No matter what happens, you have us, and you have the Lady."

She drew in a ragged breath and forced herself to smile back at him.

"Welcome, Hunters! And Kazari, welcome back!" It was Jenex, short, round, dark slanting eyes, and brown skin. His well remembered smile wrapped Kazari in warmth. "A bird from Alexando arrived a few hours ago, so your rooms are ready, and Zarchess and I are delighted to have you with us!"

Chapter Seventeen: Meeting Them Again

Kazari walked with Javon towards her family's home as the spring sun slowly drifted towards the horizon, her Hunter's boots making unfamiliar sounds on the homely cobblestones. The air was soft, scented with the warm smell of growing things, and each twist and turn along the road set off a new memory like a fountain of sparks inside Kazari's mind.

She knew her parents and her brothers would be at home, because Andiss had sent a message to them only an hour ago. They'd sent one back confirming they'd be in and ready to see them. He'd shown it to Kazari, and the familiar loops and curls of her mother's handwriting had almost undone her.

Now, she found her breath quickening, her hands trembling, and her jaw locked. She undid her facial muscles by deliberately wriggling her jaw, and then discovered she was clenching her hands instead of her teeth. Frustrated, she uncurled her fingers one by one as they turned into her family's street.

The leatherwork shop, its double story housing both the shop and her family's dwelling, sat in its familiar spot several houses from the corner. Smoke drifted from the chimney, and the windows were lighted against the dusk. Kazari's breath caught in her throat, and she stumbled to a stop, heart hammering, hand tracing the scar down her face to the corner of her mouth. She took several breaths to try and steady herself.

"Kaz, it *will* be all right, one way or the other," said Javon. The other woman tucked an arm around Kazari's shoulders.

"The Lady will be with you. Remember that." A faint warmth tickled Kazari's chest, and she dragged her hand from her scar to rest it on the amethyst, now glowing faintly, that hung around her neck.

Kazari nodded mutely, taking strength from that reminder of the Lady's presence.

"Are you ready?" Javon asked.

Kazari nodded again, wishing she could shake her head, and took a deep breath. "I think so."

"Then come; the sooner you see your family, the better." Javon urged her forward, and Kazari drove her legs into action, trying to match the other Hunter's firm pace. She focused on Javon's feet, letting the rhythm of her steps drive her forward. Javon's long legs covered the ground too quickly for Kazari's comfort, and before she was ready, they were at the entrance to the shop, and Javon was tapping politely on the door.

Footsteps sounded, and as Kazari recognised her father's firm tread, she nearly broke and ran. What would he say when he saw her face? What would her mother say? But the desire to see them in the flesh, still safe, alive, and unharmed, kept her feet still, despite the tremble in her limbs.

The sound of the latch being lifted set her heart thudding again, and then the door opened, and Kazari could see her father's familiar frame silhouetted against the light pouring from inside. The brightness behind him hid the expression on his face, and for a moment no-one said anything. Finally, Javon spoke.

"Francon? Might we enter?"

Francon cleared his throat uncomfortably, and then he took two swift steps forward past Javon and gathered Kazari into a bear hug. Slightly stunned, Kazari found her eyes tearing, and as her father's familiar scent of leather mixed with soap washed over her, wrapped her own arms around him, and hugged him back as tightly as she could. A moment later, two small forms cannoned into her legs and she nearly fell over as Jaden and Piddy, her brothers, joined Francon.

For several long moments, all Kazari could do was hug her brothers and her father. Jaden had grown, she thought, as she finally stepped back, and even little Piddy was taller than she remembered. Her father was unchanged, tall and comforting, and in the faint light, Kazari could see the familiar smile crinkling the corners of his eyelids.

"Please, come on in, Kazari and Hunter . . .?" he trailed off.

"Dad, this is Javon," said Kazari.

"Welcome, Hunter Javon." Francon gestured towards the lighted doorway.

"Just Javon is fine, Francon."

Despite her father's warm welcome, Kazari's stomach twisted with worry again. Her mother hadn't come to the door. With a little brother attached to each hand, she walked through the leather shop and into the family's living area. The familiar rooms tugged at her heart. Flames flickered on the hearth, and she could smell roast chicken and vegetables. Her father led them into the kitchen, where Liselt, Kazari's mother, had just lowered the kettle onto the stove.

Kazari's heart caught in her mouth as her mother slowly turned around. The woman's diminutive frame didn't reduce the force of her personality one bit. Brown eyes found their way unerringly to Kazari's face, and she had to fight to keep her hands from covering her scar. There was silence thick enough to cut with a knife, and Kazari found that she was holding her breath again.

Hands on her hips, Liselt jerked her head at Kazari's brothers, who scampered immediately up the stairs at the back of the kitchen. Then she deliberately dried her hands on her apron, removed it, revealing her normal working clothes beneath, then folded her arms on her chest. Kazari regarded her mother nervously, trying to calm her breathing.

She couldn't take her eyes off her as her mother's words rolled around and around inside her head. *"Some of those who pledge to the Lady die, Kazari – they die, or fall into darkness!"* She resisted the urge to cover her scar, but felt her lips begin to tremble, and pressed them together firmly.

"Liselt," began Francon, but she waved him silent with a hand. Her face, normally lively and full of expression, was unreadable. Kazari had never seen her mother like this. Even the night before the Day of the Choosing when she'd defied her parents, her mother had been full of fire – her normal, forthright, plain-speaking parent – the one who never left her in doubt of how she was feeling, or what she thought.

The person standing before her seemed a stranger, and all of a sudden, Kazari felt as if she was an intruder in her own home. *Lady,* she whispered silently, *what's happened, where is my mother?* As she prayed the words, she realised that was what she was feeling – it was as if her mother had gone away somewhere and this woman standing before her was an imposter of some kind.

The silence stretched endlessly, and Kazari could feel the tension like a taut string in the room – a string that connected them all, but was pulled to breaking point between her mother and herself. She found herself doubting her convictions. Had her departure torn her family apart? Clearly, her father had no reservations about her actions, and her brothers seemed just the same as ever, but her mother? Had her relationship with her husband broken? Had she shut herself away from her other children? And was it all Kazari's fault?

Behind her, Kazari could feel Javon's tension. Accustomed to living and travelling with the experienced Hunter for months now, Kazari could feel her coiled caution. She had the feeling that Javon was holding her breath, waiting to see whether either Kazari or Liselt might snap. She stood still, reluctant to be the one who provided the catalyst for disaster. In her mind's eye, she could see her family disintegrate in front of her. The moments drew out, one by one, until Kazari felt as if she was ready to snap as well.

Still, Liselt didn't move. Statue-like, she stared at Kazari, blinking only occasionally, as second by second, Kazari's hopes that her mother might have forgiven her, faded. She wrestled with her emotions, hanging desperately onto the promises of the Lady's love. She sought the warming of her amethyst, but this time, when she felt she needed it most, the stone stayed cool against her chest.

She tried to rationalise. She was one of the Lady's servants, with a home at the Abbey forever. She had companions who cared for her – Javon, standing like a shield at her back, and Andiss and Sendar, still with Jenex and Zarchess in the residence at the chapel. She knew they stood with her, no matter what happened with her family.

But the imminent loss of something so dear struck her to her heart. The gorgone's words rang in her mind. *I see your family. I hear their fears. And I will come for them. And you will not save them, because this day, you die.*

Well, she hadn't died, but at that moment, she could see her family's fears – or at least her mother's – and she began to wonder if the gorgone's words were words she should not have taken literally, as she had at the time and ever since, but rather, figuratively. Maybe there had been more to them. Perhaps the monster's words meant that it had heard her mother's fears and somehow infected her – much as the villagers of Suborden had been infected and changed by the malmetal.

The thought made her knees tremble, and she began to feel faint. The idea of her family under the sway of a gorgone was her most dreadful nightmare. It left her feeling desolate and alone, despite Javon's sturdy presence at her back.

Then Liselt took a step forward, raising a hand. Kazari flinched back involuntarily, and Liselt's face paled and her hand trembled.

"No, Kazari – you mistake me," said Liselt. She raised her other hand, took a swift step forward, and cradled Kazari's face in her hands. Kazari was horrified to see that her mother was crying. "Darling, I'm sorry."

"S..sorry?" Kazari stammered.

"Oh, Kaz . . . you left by yourself. We weren't there. And now . . ." Liselt broke off, and swept her daughter into her arms.

Kazari felt her mother's warm body tremble against her own as she wrapped her own arms around Liselt, tightening them until her mother's sobs rocked them both and she realised that they were both crying, and that tears were pouring down her own face. She couldn't speak, couldn't see, couldn't feel anything but the warmth of her mother's body and the strength of her mother's arms around her.

The stresses of the last months found relief in a fountain of emotion so strong that Kazari had never felt its like. She realised, while still clinging to her mother, that the lack of farewells had gnawed at her constantly, no matter what kind of brave face she'd put on it at the time. The love so evident in her mother's arms, and her father's face – now peering slightly anxiously at the pair of them – was like a warm blanket tucked around her.

At last, Kazari was able to step back slightly as her mother's weeping began to subside. Liselt's face was blotchy, and her eyes still shone with tears, and she took deep shuddering breaths.

"Mum . . ." she began.

"No, Kaz, it was my fault. Your father and I knew you'd pledge, but," she drew a ragged breath, "we – I – just didn't want to lose you so soon. I was so *angry* when you left, and it took a long time for that anger to subside." She looked at Francon, who took one of her hands in his much larger one, squeezing it comfortingly.

"But it did subside at last," he smiled, "although not before we'd gone through months – and I do mean months – of moods and grumpiness."

Liselt looked embarrassed, blushing slightly, to Kazari's surprise.

"My behaviour was inexcusable," she said. "And you know why?" She drew Kazari over to the kitchen table and sat down with her as Francon began to make a pot of tea. Kazari shook her head, wondering. She'd grown up with a feisty mother, who didn't hesitate to make her displeasure known, but it sounded as if her mother had been . . . sulking? "It was because I knew you were right to go when you did, and that I was wrong to want to hold you back. My only excuse is that you're *my* little girl, and I didn't want you to go away."

"Little girl?" Kazari's eyes nearly popped out of her head.

"Just a figure of speech, Kaz," said her father, handing her a teacup. "It's hard for a parent to realise that their children are growing up. Although your mother is taking most of the blame here, I didn't speak up for you, and I should have." He looked momentarily embarrassed, but as he handed a cup to Javon, the older Hunter rested a hand on his arm.

"Francon, Liselt, this is not an unusual occurrence. The Lady understands how difficult it is for parents to allow their children to follow their own way. It is what she must do with each of us. The Writings tell us that: 'Each person must use their own free will to decide their way.'"

Both Liselt and Franco looked at Javon, surprised, while Kazari mused on her mentor's words. Her task as Hunter seemed even more important. And more difficult than she'd ever imagined. Perhaps it wasn't just the physical threat of gorgones that a Hunter fought.

"Mum, Dad," said Kazari. "I love you both, nothing can ever change that. And I'm just so glad to be here." She paused, because her throat had closed, and she wasn't certain she could get the words out without bursting into tears all over again. She took a breath, feeling the tightness ease, and went on. "And you're safe, which is all that matters."

She heard an indrawn breath from her mother, and realised she'd said more than she should have, and looked uncomfortably towards Javon.

Javon shook her head slightly, and tapped her chest very briefly with one finger. Kazari took that to mean she was to stop talking and let Javon handle things, but she had a feeling that the other Hunter might have a few things to say to her in private later and sighed inwardly.

"Kazari has been having nightmares," said the Hunter. "Nightmares in which the two of you figured. The Abbot felt it appropriate that she should return to her home village on a brief visit to reassure herself that you are well, which is why we're here a little ahead of schedule."

Well, all of that was true, thought Kazari, impressed with Javon's prevarication. Initiates did return to their home towns, but not usually until they were well trained, and she *had* been having nightmares.

"Nightmares?" said Liselt, surprised. "What kind of night-mares, Kaz?"

Kazari squirmed uncomfortably. "Just horrible ones, you know? And you and Dad are in them, and you're always in trouble, and I can't get to you to help you." And all of that was true as well. Except she'd omitted the bits that featured the unseen gorgone torturing them, or killing them, and she hadn't mentioned her brothers at all.

"Kaz, darling, why?" asked her father.

Kazari wriggled again and shrugged her shoulders, but Javon spoke again. "We've been concerned that Kazari's difficult leave-taking left her unduly anxious, and as you can imagine, a Hunter must be very focused on her craft. We wished to set her mind at ease."

Kazari nodded as Javon spoke.

"Of course," replied Liselt, "But I have one more question. What happened to her face?"

Kazari froze momentarily, uncertain of how to answer, but Javon went on without missing a beat.

"Once our initiates reach a certain level of skill, they go into the field. That scar was caused by a sucker."

"A sucker!" exclaimed Francon. "You've already fought a sucker, Kaz?" He looked horrified.

Kazari nodded again, unwilling to speak lest she say something else out of turn. Like mentioning exactly where she'd got the scar. The Abbot had impressed upon them all the need to keep the specific details of Suborden quiet, so that the Hunters and Navigators still in the field would be able to follow up any leads from people who appeared to have more information than was publicly available.

"But, a sucker!" Liselt was aghast. "They're dangerous!"

Javon nodded. "All gorgones are dangerous, Liselt – as the Lady reminds us in her Writings – however, to a Hunter, they are the least of our foes. Kazari may have a scar on her face, but she has already dispatched a number of suckers. You can be very proud of her."

"You have?" asked Francon. "A number of suckers?"

"Yes, several," replied Kazari, trying to keep her answers short. "I really should have been more careful with this one, though." She touched the scar, forcing herself to keep her hand steady. Her mother leaned forward and peered at it, tracing it with a gentle fingertip.

"It seems well healed, and it will fade with time, I suppose." But her face was troubled, and Kazari wished there was some way she could reassure her mother that nothing worse would happen to her.

"Careful?" her father snorted. "I'd be running in the other direction, not being 'careful.'" He looked at his daughter again, and this time Kazari could tell he was seeing her differently. "You've changed, love." He stepped quickly over, and placed a firm hand on her shoulder and gave it a quick squeeze. "You've muscled up, and you look – confident?"

"I spend a lot of time exercising now, Dad," Kazari said, glad to be off the subject of suckers. She sipped her tea and went on. "I have to run a lot, and I've learned to ride a horse."

Francon snorted with laughter. "Run? Really? Since when?"

"Since I joined the Hunters, Dad. I nearly died the first week!"

Her father laughed and the mood in the room lightened, as Javon elaborated on what was expected of a new Hunter. Liselt called the boys back down again, and from the rapidity with which they appeared, Kazari figured they'd been listening from the top of the stairs. Still, it was nice to be home again, and the evening progressed nicely. But later, as Kazari walked back to the chapel with Javon, she couldn't shake the memory of her mother's troubled face. Despite the warmth of her reunion with Liselt, she knew her mother would remember that her daughter was a Hunter for the Lady, not a Grower, or a Healer, or even a Judicar, and would thereafter spend her life worrying that she was on the front line of the battle against the gorgones.

Chapter Eighteen: Old Friends

Secure in the knowledge that her parents still loved her, Kazari slept without nightmares for the first time in months. She awoke refreshed, bright, and hungry, just after dawn. It was early, and the incumbent's house was still dark and quiet. Kazari washed and dressed quickly, not wanting to disturb her companions, and let herself outside.

She stretched in the early light, breathing deeply, and letting the comfort of Athos seep into her bones. She fed the horses and shovelled out their stalls, and then decided to walk for a while and take a look around the village. As she paced the old cobblestones, she felt as if she was rediscovering her old life – over *there* she'd tripped and fallen when she and Dari had been up to mischief, and it was on *that* corner she'd first seen the Lady's Hunter. She smiled as she remembered how she'd snuck around behind him. Fascinated, she'd thought him intimidating and had tried to stay hidden, now, she suspected he'd known precisely where she was the whole time.

The scent of baking bread rolled over her, and she turned towards it eagerly. Kareen, the baker, lived down the next street. She felt in her pocket. She had enough coins to purchase fresh bread for the morning meal. It would be a nice surprise for the others. The woman was just propping up her awning as Kazari rounded the last turn.

"Welcome, Hunter," she said, and then did a double take. "Kazari?"

"Yes, it's me," smiled Kazari. She placed her coins on the counter. "Do you have any of your seed loaves?"

"Of course I do!" replied the baker, cheerily. She turned towards the cooling racks and flipped a large loaf expertly into a cloth bag. "Ask Zarchess or Jenex to return the bag later, if you would. Nice to see you home again, Kaz. We were very proud when we heard you'd gone to the Hunters."

"Thank you," replied Kazari, somewhat awkwardly. Her village was proud of her? "Is it still three dins?" She pushed the coins forward on the wooden bench.

"Yes it is, but it's nothing today." Kareen pushed the coins back. "Take the loaf as a welcome gift from me."

"Oh, I couldn't," stammered Kazari.

"Of course you can," replied the baker, smiling, as she placed the coins back into Kazari's hand and closed her fingers around them. "We're proud of you. We need our Hunters!" She smiled again, and then turned to attend to another early morning customer.

"Morning, Hunter," said the new customer. It was a young man Kazari couldn't identify on sight. She looked at him curiously for a moment, as strangers in Athos were rare, but then shrugged mentally and smiled.

"Good morning, sir." She made a mental note to ask her parents who he was. For some reason he seemed vaguely familiar, yet she knew he wasn't of Athos.

Kareen's words warmed her as she walked back to the chapel, the bag with the bread clutched in one hand. She'd had no idea her village thought so much of the Lady's servants. Still, it was nice, and such a contrast to her leave-taking. Yet, even as she walked through the beauty of the early morning, Kazari's thoughts turned towards the gorgone presence now so clearly within Albatar. She wondered how long it had been since a team had been sent into the Outer World, and how much the Abbot, or the secular rulers of Albatar, knew about the happenings there.

Perhaps one day, she'd be in a position to know, but now, as only a trainee, she was at the bottom of the knowledge chain. Although, on reflection, perhaps she wasn't quite at the bottom. As a Hunter, and one newly come from Suborden, it was likely she knew a lot more detail than some of her fellow initiates.

Over breakfast, Andiss cautioned Kazari about her return home. "Although your family are happy to see you, they still need time to come to grips with your responsibilities and duties as a Hunter. The scar on your face will be a reminder of the dangers you will face for the Lady. Most people here will have met Hunters only occasionally, so you'll be an oddity – fascinating. Remember that The Book of Hunters tells us that the Lady says *All of My servants stand equal in my sight. My Hunters stand between the gorgone threat and My people, but they are no more, or less, than any of My servants.*"

Kazari nodded, sobered. When she remembered her own awe at meeting a Hunter, she could imagine how easy it might be to grow proud of her status.

"Javon and I will be scouting the villages nearby today. Sendar, you'll stay with Kazari. Kaz, you can spend time visiting friends and lunching with your family, but both of you should keep your ears open. Look out for anything unusual."

"What are we looking for?" Sendar asked.

"Anything that seems off – Kaz knows Athos and its people. Kaz, you're looking for oddities – comments, things that aren't in character – anything unusual." Javon passed a small bag across the table to Sendar. "There's a bit of extra money in there. Buy grain for the horses, and food for the kitchen here. Kaz, wander around, get your bearings and visit as many shops as possible. Both of you, spend more time listening than talking."

Kazari suddenly remembered the man at the bakery.

"There was someone at the baker's this morning," she said, frowning. "He's new. I'll ask Mum and Dad about him." Andiss nodded approvingly.

After waving Javon and Andiss off, Kazari and Sendar walked into the village to purchase what was needed. Buoyed by her parents' acceptance, Kazari was almost jigging with eagerness to show Sendar her old home.

Striding along, dressed in their Hunter's blacks, amethyst pendants evident on their chests, Kazari and Sendar drew stares, waves and some awed glances. After a while, Kazari began to feel a bit uncomfortable. These people had known her her whole life. Despite her clothing, Kazari knew that at her core she was the same person she'd always been – just a bit older, and with a wider perspective on life than the one she'd left with.

Kazari caught Sendar giving her a sidelong glance. "What?"

He wiggled his eyebrows at her. "Watching you try and get used to people's reactions to you being a Hunter is funny!"

"I bet *you* weren't any different," retorted Kazari, making a face at him, just as several people passed on the opposite side of the road.

"I reckon you just put paid to about half the Hunter reputation with that face, Kaz!" snickered Sendar.

After arranging for the grain to be delivered to the chapel stables, they moved on to the butcher and then the market stalls in the square. Kazari couldn't help looking around to where Quisil's stall had been. Now in the Grower's sept, the woman had, for many years, sold vegetables in the square.

"That was Quisil's spot," she said, waving a hand as she and Sendar strolled from stall to stall, looking for the vegetables Andiss had requested.

"She seems very happy with the Growers," replied Sendar. "She was old for an initiate, though."

"I suppose some of us take time to respond to the Lady's call," said Kazari, shrugging, and picking up a cauliflower and handing over the coins to pay for it. "Thank you Sanges."

The vendor smiled at her. "Anytime, Hunters."

They moved on, exchanging small talk with the stall holders, and adding to their collection of fruits and vegetables. The mood in the market was positive, thought Kazari, full of the normal chatter and bustle of a market in full swing, and she spent a happy morning chatting to old friends and acquaintances.

Eager to introduce Sendar to her parents, she hurried him into the village after they'd delivered the fresh goods to the chapel. Halfway there, Kazari saw the man from the bakery again. He was hurrying away from the tinsmith's, carrying a hessian bag.

"That's him, Sendar."

Her friend looked at the man and raised his eyebrows. "He looks pretty normal, Kaz."

"I've never seen him before," she replied. "And Athos isn't that big."

"Doesn't really mean anything," replied Sendar. "He's probably just new." It was true, Kazari thought. People did occasionally move to Athos. Still, she looked after the man curiously. Strangers were rare in Athos, and she wondered what had brought the man into the village.

Lunch with her family was a lighthearted affair, with her brothers and her parents chattering away to Sendar, and herself.

Finally, Liselt shushed the boys, as Francon began to make a pot of tea. "Go on, boys, leave your sister alone for a while."

"So, Sendar, your town is beholden to Seraph?" asked Francon, putting a mug of tea down in front of him.

"Yes, Chator," replied Sendar, picking up his mug and sipping appreciatively. "This is delicious."

"And you're about a year ahead of Kaz?" asked Liselt.

"Yes, still learning though."

Liselt fiddled with her own mug, frowning reflectively. "How long does it usually take?"

Kazari looked at Sendar, doubtfully, but the young man answered easily. "Three to four years, usually, but training finishes when it finishes. It depends on the initiate. Some of us learn faster than others." He shrugged.

"And it's pretty physical then, I mean, you think of the Lady's servants in their robes and with their Writings, but I hadn't really thought about how a Hunter trains," said Francon, looking at his wife.

Liselt nodded. "We were talking about it last night," she flashed a smile at Kazari. "You've come home with muscles, Kaz!"

"You mean I didn't have any when I left home?" asked Kazari indignantly.

Her father laughed. "Of course not – well, not like you do now, I suppose. "

"Believe me, Dad, I've got a long way to go. And there's a lot of book learning to do as well. We spend a chunk of time every day learning about the Writings, and the things the Lady teaches her servants," replied Kazari. "And being a Hunter is much more than just the physical stuff," she went on, "It's essential we understand the Lady's words, and know how to apply them. But if you're wondering, I don't generally pace around wearing a robe and waving my copy of the Writings."

Her mother smiled, but looked very thoughtful, nodding into her mug, and Kazari realised just how much she'd changed over the last months. She would never have imagined that she would have considered that being a Hunter was more than just fighting gorgones. Now she knew – to her very core – how important it was to be grounded in the truths of the Writings and within her own sense of self, and the learning in her other lessons had given her a much wider appreciation of greater Albatar – as had her travels.

With a start, she realised she'd been tracing the scar on her face, and surreptitiously pulled her hand down, placing it into her lap, hoping that her mother hadn't noticed.

Francon came to stand at her side, gently turning her face towards the light streaming in through the kitchen window. He traced the edges of the scar with a fingertip, and Kazari saw the sadness in his eyes and in the set of his mouth. He didn't speak, and the silence grew in stark contrast to the jovial mood over lunch, until a shadow of last night's awkwardness hung over the room like a cloud.

"We all have scars," said Sendar, breaking the silence. Kazari looked at him, startled, but he went on. "None of us escape unscathed in the fight against the gorgones. It's just that some of our scars are less visible than the one on Kaz's face." He looked uncomfortable, but went on. "Being a Hunter is dangerous, but we are well trained. In our sept, scars are badges of honour, because each scar is the sign of a gorgone that will no longer threaten Albatar. When you look at your daughter – when you see that scar – remember that it means that she has dispatched a deadly threat to Albatar's peace."

Kazari blushed and looked down. Sendar's words were welcome, and much more mature than she could have managed, but they were embarrassing as well. Still, perhaps they were the words her family needed to hear.

Francon nodded uncertainly, but dropped his hand from his daughter's face, looking thoughtful. "I suppose I hadn't considered that. We only focus on what is dear to us. Perhaps we should consider things more widely than we have." He raised his eyebrows at Liselt.

"Jenex often urges us to focus on the greater things, but the smaller things – our own personal lives – are so much easier to comprehend," she replied. "And so much more immediate."

Kazari stared into her mug. Before she'd left for the Abbey, her entire world had revolved around her family and the doings of Athos. She supposed that for most people, that was exactly how they lived their lives – caught up in only the local things, giving little consideration to other things outside their experience. Communication was slow across Albatar, so news seeped slowly through communities, and was sometimes many weeks out of date. She finished the dregs of her tea, and looked up at Sendar. The day was wearing on, and they still had much to do, no matter how much she'd just like to sit with her family and talk.

"We'd best be about our jobs, now, I'm afraid," Sendar continued. "Many thanks for our meal, Liselt, Francon, and – May the Lady's grace rest upon this house."

Kazari looked up, startled. She'd never heard him use the formal thanks before. But of course, he'd been a guest in her family's house, and the words were appropriate.

She stood and hugged her parents, and then departed with a backward wave.

"I'll try and pop in tomorrow, but I'm not sure what Andiss has in store for us," she said as they turned onto the cobble-stoned street. Liselt smiled back at her.

"Whenever you're able."

They walked back towards the chapel, nodding to passers-by, and halfway there, Kazari realised she hadn't asked her parents who the stranger was and let out a huff.

"What?" Sendar asked.

"I forgot to ask them about the man – the newcomer."

"Well, people must come and go here, Kaz. They do in Chator – they do everywhere."

"I suppose so," she replied. "But Andiss said to look out for anything out of the ordinary, and I think that man counts."

"Perhaps," said Sendar, "Maybe Jenex or Zarchess might know. Come on." He tugged at her hand, and pulled her along at a jog. They ran easily, and Kazari enjoyed the exertion. It was nice to be on her feet and off a horse, no matter how much she loved Stumpy.

"KAZ!"

The word, bellowed loudly, yanked Kazari to a sudden halt. "Dari?"

"Kaz! You're back!" Kazari looked around, trying to see where her friend's voice was coming from. Leaves shook in one of the trees near the schoolhouse, and then Dari dropped from its branches to land softly on the grass, grinning from ear to ear. She sprinted over to Kazari, and collided with her in a hug. Warmth spread through Kazari. Now she was truly home.

Chapter Nineteen:
Dari

Kazari smiled up at her friend. Dari seemed to have grown taller again, while she had stayed the same height. Always a bit shorter than her friend, Kazari now realised that Dari could be called 'tall.' In fact, as Sendar strolled over to them, she realised her friend was almost as tall as he was.

"You grew!" she exclaimed.

"You didn't," Dari giggled.

"Well, no, I'm just the right height for me – any more of me and the world might be overwhelmed. What did your parents do – make you stand in a paddock full of sheep poo?"

"Ooh! Good one, Kaz!"

For years, the two of them had practiced what they liked to refer to as 'witty repartee', imagining that one day, they might be somewhere other than Athos, where they could use it to good effect. In the meantime, it had kept them entertained.

"Kaz!" said Sendar, looking slightly aghast.

"It's all right," replied Dari, "This is normal." She looked Sendar up and down – rather appreciatively, Kazari noticed with a start. When had Dari ever shown interest in the opposite sex? "Who's your friend, Kaz?"

"Oops, sorry, this is Sendar. He's a Hunter trainee, like me, but a bit further along," said Kazari, waving an introductory hand at Sendar. "And this is Dari – Sendar – the one with the sheep farm I was telling you about."

"She's been itching to see you, Dari," replied Sendar, smiling. "In fact, she's been looking around every corner hoping you'd be there."

"You missed me?" asked Dari, turning back to Kazari.

"I did." Impulsively, Kazari hugged her friend again, and then held her back for another look. Dari's blonde hair was tied back as always, but her clothing was different – nicer somehow. "What's with the clothes?" She deliberately avoided mentioning the missing letters.

For a moment, Dari looked slightly embarrassed, but then she shrugged. "I gave in to Mum."

"You *what?*" Kazari was astounded. Her friend had always been a keen wearer of what she referred to as 'comfy' clothing. But as Kazari ran her eyes down Dari's trim form, she realised that Dari's clothes were still a lot like her old ones, just made of finer fabric and artfully tailored to show off her burgeoning curves. For a moment, Kazari's own muscular stockiness felt ungainly next to Dari's budding grace, then she shook her head and the feeling left her. She was strong, fitter than she'd ever been, and her body served her well. She was comfortable in her own skin, much more than she'd ever been before, truth be told.

"You know Mum," her friend said. "She nagged until I caved. But you can see she only won a little bit. There was no way she was getting me into a dress!"

"Now that *would* have been weird," replied Kazari. "How on earth could you wrestle sheep in a dress?"

"I couldn't," said Dari. "Mum thinks that if I dress – as she puts it – 'well,' then a husband will pop up from nowhere and whisk me off to a life of luxury."

Kazari did a double take. "A husband? But Dari, we're only . . . we're sixteen! I forgot about my birthday!"

Sendar turned to her with a surprised expression. "When was it?"

Kazari blushed. Her birthday had been shortly after their return from Suborden, but the momentous events had wiped the date's significance clean out of her mind.

"Two days after we got back to the Abbey from the training trip."

He put his hands on his hips and frowned at her. "Why didn't you say?"

"I forgot?" she replied. "We'd been a bit . . . busy . . . remember? And the day came and went before I realised it."

He nodded slowly. He knew what she meant. She'd woken all of them many times with her nightmares. And of course, it had taken many weeks for his leg wound to recover enough that he knew he wouldn't be crippled for life. There had been other things on everyone's minds. More important things than birthdays. Gorgones, Suborden, the changed, and Sendar's recovery for instance.

"Yes, I can see why you forgot." He turned to Dari, who was staring at them, hands on her hips, curiosity evident in every line of her body. "A new Hunter has many things to learn, and they work us hard – particularly in the first year. It's not surprising Kaz forgot what day it was."

"Anyway, what's this about husbands? Are you seeing someone?" Kazari was curious.

Dari made a face. "Of course not! Mum just thinks I should be, so she's trying to turn me into a 'young lady,' as she puts it. *You* know I'm going to run the farm eventually. Enda's gone, so there's only me, and I like the sheep. Speaking of which, will you be able to visit?" She looked over at Sendar, and raised her eyebrows.

"It'll depend on Andiss and Javon. Even though we're here for Kaz to visit her family, we've still got training to do," he said. "But it's quite possible we'll be left with Jenex and Zarchess for a day or two, to learn the work of an incumbent."

"What, you'd be teaching us? At school?" asked Dari, slightly sceptically. "No disrespect, but Kaz has only been at the Abbey for six months, and you don't look much older than we are."

Sendar smiled. "Of course not. You're correct to say that I'm not a *lot* older – I'm eighteen actually, as I deferred for a year. But we're not to be teachers, except perhaps one day when we're older – and then only for other Hunters. Not many Hunters become incumbents." He looked at Dari, and Kazari had a feeling he wasn't sure he was liking her friend's attitude. He went on. "Having said that, you might be surprised at how much Kazari's learned in the months she's been away." His voice had grown firmer and Kazari looked at him in surprise. It was almost as if he was challenging Dari.

The other girl looked slightly discomfited. "Of course, I didn't mean to imply otherwise. I suppose it's been mostly the Writings?"

"Mostly," Sendar said, "but also mathematics, philosophy, history, and of course, all the things a Hunter needs to know in order to defeat a gorgone." He put his hands on his hips, pushing back his jacket slightly, and Kazari saw Dari's eyes drop to the well-worn leather belt hung with sheaths. Kazari knew exactly how many knives Sendar had secreted around his person. The three sheaths in plain view were only the tip of the iceberg.

For some reason, Sendar was deliberately reminding Dari that Kazari's life had changed irrevocably. She lifted her own eyes to look into Dari's and realised that her friend's expression had changed to one she struggled to read, and for a moment everything was uncomfortable, as if Dari and Sendar had stretched a string to breaking point between them. Kazari looked from one to the other, discomfited.

Dari changed the subject abruptly. "Can you come and visit?"

"I hope so, Dari," Kazari said. "I'll check tonight and send word. Are you heading home now?"

Dari smiled again, back to her old self, and Kazari wondered if she'd imagined the brief awkwardness.

"I am. I'm not back in for school for two days, so if you're looking for me, I'll be on the farm. In my other clothes." She grinned, and she was back to the old Dari of six months ago, and Kazari was worrying about how to tell her parents she was choosing the Lady.

Kazari smiled back, but in the recesses of her mind, she was wondering about the conversation. She hugged her friend again. "I'll look forward to seeing those clothes. And the dirt."

Dari laughed, and trotted off, turning to wave when she reached the chapel gates.

As they walked up to the chapel, Kazari shot another glance at Sendar. She ran the day's events through her mind. He'd spoken up in her parents' house too. Not in the markets, or at the butcher, or even the grain merchant, but definitely when she'd been with her nearest and dearest. Was he trying to alienate her from them? Certainly not her parents; there, he'd just given her a way of explaining things to them as simply and truthfully as she was able, but his interaction with Dari had seemed a bit more edged. Kazari ran the conversation over in her mind again before mentally shrugging. Maybe she was imagining it.

"So, what do you think they've been up to?" she asked.

"They?" replied Sendar, "Oh, you mean Javon and Andiss – I suppose we'll know when they tell us." He changed the subject. "If we check the horses now, we'll know if they're back. If they're not, at least their stalls will be ready for when they are."

The stable was empty of Andiss and Javon's horses, so they prepared the evening feeds, and groomed Stumpy and Jumper. Afterward, Sendar turned to Kazari.

"Is there anywhere we can train? Somewhere quiet, where no-one's likely to come upon us?"

Kazari squinted at the sun and thought for a few moments.

"There's a clearing behind the schoolhouse, in the bush at the back, not far from here. If we wait another half hour, it should be empty. Dari and I found it a few years ago. It should be big enough. What kind of training?"

"Katas mostly, and perhaps some sparring? I need to keep working on my leg, and we both need to work on technique, or Alexando'll be disappointed."

He seemed quiet, and Kazari sensed that his mind was distant, somewhere else once again. Training seemed like a good idea. She felt the need to immerse herself in movement, to feel the sweat of honest exertion, and bury her rather confused feelings in activity.

The chapel house was empty, so Sendar left a note on the kitchen table, and Kazari scribbled a mud map on the back of it. It wasn't far to the clearing, and as Kazari had hoped, it was deserted. The trees were closely packed around it, with only a narrow path between them. Thick undergrowth, now sprouting fresh green shoots, and early blooms, hid the clearing from the casual observer.

Kazari had often wondered how such a space had come to be. Stumps on its periphery said that it had been deliberately cleared, and the thick grass that clothed the ground was clear of encroaching weeds. Someone cared for it, but she'd never seen anyone else there. Kazari stepped into the clearing, gesturing for Sendar to follow.

Occasionally, during the year before she'd decided to declare for the Lady, Kazari had snuck out of her house during the long summer evenings and made her way to the clearing to sit in the grass and think. She'd found peace in the little glade, and determination and strength enough to decide to stick to her chosen path. It had become something of a haven for her.

Although she and Dari had found the clearing together, the evening trips were hers alone. Hers and the Lady's, she realised. Not something that could be shared even with her best friend. As the light slanted through the trees, it echoed those summer evenings, and drawing in a deep breath, full of the scents of growing things, Kazari found a hint of the peace she'd sought so desperately and then found in the little glade. She felt her amethyst warm on her chest.

She raised a hand to it, touching its warmth, soaking in the sensation of the Lady's closeness.

"This is a special place," said Sendar quietly. "And it was made, not grown."

"I used to come here," Kazari replied. "When I was deciding to declare. It was my thinking place."

"I can see why. You said you found it with Dari? Did she come too?" he asked.

"Not when I was thinking. I needed to be alone, then," she said slowly. "Dari and I came here about once a week when we wanted to talk privately at school. We'd slip off during the lunch hour. I came alone some evenings."

He grunted. "Shall we?" He removed his jacket, hanging it from a convenient tree limb, and began to stretch, his long, dark-skinned limbs, limber and lithe.

Kazari followed suit, feeling the cool air hum across her skin. She shivered slightly in the chill, but as they began to move in the familiar patterns, her body warmed, and her arms and legs began to move easily in measured rhythms. They finished one pattern, and began the next, moving smoothly from stance to stance, gradually increasing their speed as the degree of difficulty edged upwards.

Part of Kazari marvelled that she could do this so easily, while the other half reminded her of the sweat, aches and pains it had taken to get her to this point. Now, here in her home village, in her safe place, she realised just how different she was to the nervous young woman who'd left home in emotional turmoil, all those months ago.

Of course, she was still in emotional turmoil, but the turmoil was of a different type now. Her breath came quickly as they moved faster, and a sheen of sweat began to coat her exposed arms, but even now, Kazari knew she was nowhere near her physical capacity. The pace with which she moved was much faster than her first stumbling attempts as a newly initiated

Hunter trainee. But it was still nowhere near the contained power that Javon and Andiss demonstrated when they did the katas. She'd watched them, awed by their strength and grace, and the sheer speed with which they moved.

Sendar showed the same promise, to her inexperienced eyes. Now, she knew enough to know how far she'd come, but also enough to know how far she had yet to go, despite her gifting from the Lady, and her growing skills. They finished the second pattern and moved onto the third.

It was a whirl of leaping and twisting, designed to prepare the Hunter for a fast-paced battle. Kazari and Sendar finished it in a lather of sweat, both breathing heavily. She followed Sendar, as he began the salutation kata, one designed not so much for physical training, but for that of the mind and the spirit. Each movement was a phrase of the Writings, performed as a prayer. As Kazari moved her arms up and outwards at the end, she breathed deeply, closing her eyes, and allowed her spirit to rejoice in the words her body had spoken. Once again, her amethyst warmed, and she could see the soft purple glow through her closed eyelids.

She opened her eyes, wondering, to see Sendar's similarly lit.

"Thank you, Lady," he breathed softly, and she echoed him, completely unselfconsciously.

"Shall we spar, Kaz?" asked Sendar as he stepped out of the final stance position.

"Yes," replied Kazari, "let's."

They separated, bowed, and began to work through the basic moves, taking turns to block, duck and weave against the other's attacks, before moving onto grappling techniques.

Kazari was still very much a beginner with grappling, and was inclined to end up tangled in her own limbs. Her compact shape struggled to encompass Sendar's longer arms and legs.

"Just take your time, Kaz," he said, patiently demonstrating again. "Yes, you're short, but you're fast. I'm bigger and stronger, but I can't match your speed – or your flexibility.

Remember that with a larger opponent, you have to play to your strengths. You can't let them take control or you're sunk. So go for the vulnerable bits, and make sure your technique is flawless."

He showed her again, encouraging her to escape his grasp, and she almost made it, but then she slowed down in her elation, just long enough for him to snake an arm out and grab her ankle. She hit the soft grass with a thud, and then Sendar was on her, and she was stuck, trapped in a vice-like grip. She wriggled as she'd been taught, but he was stronger, so eventually she tapped him on the leg, and he let her go.

"Got me again," she sighed as she extricated herself.

Sendar stayed on the ground, smiling up at her, long muscled limbs shining with sweat where the late afternoon light struck them. He wagged a finger at her.

"Don't celebrate before you're safe!"

"Thought I'd made it that time." She smiled at him. "Oh well. At least it was nearly, instead of not at all."

"We'd better get back," he said. "If Andiss isn't back, we'll have to cook, and I need to get clean. I smell." He waved a hand at her, and Kazari hauled him to his feet. He towered over her. "Thanks, Kaz." She looked down. She hadn't let go of his hand. She did so, blushing.

"Sorry." He smiled, and made a face at her, and she bobbed her head, trying to hide a second blush.

Chapter Twenty:
Sadness and Secrets

Andiss and Javon rode in late. Kazari set a serving dish on the table as they walked into the dining room where Zarchess and Jenex were already seated.

"Sendar, they're back!" she called into the kitchen. He appeared with another dish, and set it down next to the first one.

"You're just in time," Jenex said, "your trainees have more skills than expected." He gestured appreciatively to the dishes. Steam rose as Sendar lifted the lids, and savoury smells coloured the air. Kazari had been hard pressed to stop herself from 'tasting' the dish too many times during the cooking. It was one of her father's recipes, and after exercising so vigorously, she was starving. Sendar had concocted the vegetable dish, and it looked to be a fine accompaniment to her beef.

With a weary sigh, Javon shed her saddlebags in a corner and pulled out a chair, waving a hand at Andiss who nodded and sat beside her.

"Many thanks, Sendar, Kaz, we've had a long ride, and there's a lot to discuss. But later, after we eat." He stretched and then bowed his head, praying a short thanks to the Lady for her bounty, then the six of them tucked in, and for a time, there was silence, broken only by the sounds of cutlery clinking against crockery.

"I see you've shown Sendar our grove, Kazari," said Jenex as he pushed his plate away with a sigh of satisfaction. "And my compliments to the cooks, that was delicious!"

"*Your* grove?" said Kazari, surprised.

"Yes," replied Zarchess, "our grove. It was created by the Intercessors for the same reason you Hunters have one at the Abbey. It's our place to meditate on the Writings, and seek the Lady's will."

"But how come I never saw you there?" asked Kazari. "I went there a lot before I left at the Day of the Choosing."

Jenex smiled. "We saw you, Kaz, but you needed to be alone, so we didn't intrude. Some things can only be decided between you and the Lady."

Kazari nodded. The Intercessor was right – she had needed to be alone. "Was it all right for us to use it today?"

"Of course," replied Zarchess. "Any of the Lady's servants, or indeed, anyone at all who needs the solitude, is welcome to spend time there."

Andiss pushed his own plate to one side, pushing his chair back. "We'll need the two of you tomorrow." He waved a hand at Sendar and Kazari. "Today left us with a lot of questions." He sighed, and ran his hands through his hair, leaving some of the dark strands sticking up.

Kazari exchanged a curious glance with Sendar.

Javon pushed her chair back, and gathered the plates into a pile. "I'll make tea, and then we can talk."

Kazari looked at Sendar again, raising her eyebrows. He shrugged, and then they both moved to clear the table of the dirty dishes.

"Let us," said Zarchess, touching Kazari's arm. "It's rare that we have someone cook for us."

"Thank you," replied Kazari, surprised, putting the plate down. She hurried over and began to help Javon with the tea, carrying mugs over to the table as Javon filled the pot.

A few minutes later, Kazari tucked her hands around her mug, warming them, and eating the last of the sweet biscuit Zarchess had brought to the table.

Finally, Andiss stirred, put his mug down and leaned forward to where Javon was unfolding a map on the table, holding the corners down with the salt and pepper bowls. He pulled a pencil from a pocket and began to draw small crosses on it.

"Each cross represents a place we visited today where things didn't seem quite right." He took a deep breath and placed his pencil on the map again. "And the circles represent towns and hamlets where everything seemed quite normal." He pushed the map across the table, and Kazari and Sendar leaned forward. Circles and crosses were in equal numbers on the map, but it was clear that there was a pattern developing. Crosses proliferated to the east of Athos. And the closer they were to Seraph, the more there were. To the south and west, there were more circles.

Sendar looked up. "You did do a lot of riding today. Did you find any malmetal?"

Javon shook her head and pulled another chair closer and put her booted feet up on it with a weary sigh. "None."

"And although we know some had to have ended up in Chator, we didn't find any in clear sight there – not that we expected to, really." She sighed. "We've been following rumours. Fortunately, some people will always talk to Hunters. There have been several trading caravans from the border towns recently, and the local Judicars and Intercessors tell us that unrest and minor crime has slowly begun to escalate in their wake. It's suggestive to say the least. With luck, Abel and Elliam, and Sendar's family, via Alexando, will add to the picture."

"So you think that increasing crime might relate to the presence of hidden malmetal?" asked Kazari slowly.

Javon nodded, and Andiss tapped the map with his pencil. "It's possible, that given what we found at Suborden, we might encounter more of the 'changed'."

Cold struck through Kazari's bones. The 'changed' still haunted her dreams. They'd exploited her ability to heal by torturing her. She found her hand lifting to her mouth, touching the scar that marred her face. They hadn't inflicted that wound, but the unseen gorgone who'd touched her with its power during the fight against the suckers was most likely the 'Master' to whom the old woman had repeatedly referred during that endless night.

She shot a look at Sendar. His normally deep brown skin had paled as much as she'd ever seen, and his hand was gripping his thigh. Without Kazari's ability to heal, the torture inflicted upon him had nearly left him crippled. Kazari reached across, covering his hand with her own, feeling the tension in the curve of his fingers.

"You really think there might be more 'changed'?" Kazari asked. She was pleased that her voice had remained steady, but she'd had to work hard to stop her own hand clenching atop Sendar's.

"We don't *know* anything," replied Andiss, "but it does seem logical. The malmetal ploy nearly succeeded at Suborden – who's to say it wouldn't work here? Or Chator? Or Seraph? Suborden is a prosperous village, for all its isolation, but some of the villages we visited today were not so prosperous, and the closer they were to Seraph, the poorer they became." His lips thinned. Kazari frowned slightly at his tone.

There was a clear implication there was something wrong in Seraph, and possibly the surrounding villages, which backed up what they'd learned in Chator. But what if Andiss was wrong, and the source of the trouble was elsewhere? What if it was here, where her own family lived? Suddenly she wondered how long there had been problems nearby. Or . . . in the town.

"What do you think we should do?" asked Sendar.

"We'll need Kazari to cover as much ground as possible," said Andiss. "She's our best hope of discovering any gorgones, but we can't leave her to roam the countryside alone – or even just with you, Sendar. The last time we left the two of you alone, you had to take down a greater gorgone." A hint of a twinkle lightened Andiss' expression as Zarchess gasped, and Jenex put his hand over his mouth to strangle a startled yelp.

"They what?" he managed at last.

"It was a fire gorgone. They buried it in snow until it succumbed," replied Javon. It had been quite a bit more than that, thought Kazari, but she was glad that Javon was downplaying the drama in front of the Intercessors.

"But a fire gorgone – there was one within Albatar? Why hasn't a general alert gone out?" asked Zarchess, frowning.

"The Abbot decided we needed more information," Andiss said. "We will be alerting every incumbent we meet in our travels, Zarchess – just as we've alerted you. Not necessarily about fire gorgones, but most definitely about the malmetal and the changed."

Jenex nodded slowly. "The reach of gorgones is long, or so our history tells us. Even the seemingly incorruptible are not beyond them. And the Writings caution even the Lady's servants about arrogance, pride and fear. Every sept has stories of her servants who have believed in their own humanity rather than trusting the Lady's power – to their detriment. Despite hearing Her voice more clearly than others, some of Her servants still choose to try and live by their own strength at times." He sighed, sadly, it seemed to Kazari, and went on. "The lesson learned can be very hard, and in some cases, fatal."

"You mean they fall away?" asked Sendar, sounding surprised.

Javon looked uncomfortable. "They don't fall away as such, but their effectiveness is limited. They are committed now and forever to the Lady, but without allowing her to work through them, they act only as human beings, without any of the Lady's Gifts."

Kazari's brow creased as she thought through the implications of Javon's words.

"Could this happen to any of us?" she asked, suddenly concerned. Was it happening to *her*? How would she know?

"Kaz, it happens to all of us at some point," Andiss told her. He smiled at her look of alarm and went on. "We've talked before about being fallible human beings. The degree of reliance on the Lady is the key. When you're immersed in her Writings, and surrounded by her people, it's difficult to fall so far away from Her that you don't hear her voice. But anyone can choose to shut Her out. You will find that sometimes you will feel as if the Lady walks every moment of the day with you, while at other times, you feel as if she has moved far from you. The truth is that *She* never moves. It is us alone. And sometimes it's just our own perceptions." He smiled. "It's complicated."

He waved a hand at Javon, who continued, as Kazari felt slightly panicked.

"And then there are the Gifts conferred by our enemies."

"But . . ." The import of what she was hearing dawned on Kazari.

"You mean that the gorgones confer Gifts?" exclaimed Sendar.

"Then anyone – anyone at all – could have the same Gifts as ourselves? And the changed? They could have Gifts like ours also?"

Jenex looked at Andiss with his eyebrows raised, and Andiss nodded.

"What you're about to hear is usually part of the final training imparted before your novice period is over, but circumstances have changed, and we believe it is possible we may encounter those with powers granted by the gorgones."

"But –" Sendar began, to be stopped by Jenex

"Hear me out, Sendar. It's a thing of legend, and only occurs – as far as we know – as part of a greater incursion. It means that at least part of the Outer World has sunk so far under the gorgone yoke, that open gifting is possible, and open rule by the gorgone-horde is only a step away."

For a moment, Kazari didn't understand what Jenex was saying, and then slowly, the words began to make sense.

"You mean that gorgones don't rule openly in the Outer World?" she asked, surprised. Her mind had always pictured the Outer World as a cesspit of corrupted states, ruled openly by monstrous creatures, who revelled in the destruction of humankind.

"No. Not at all," replied Jenex. "Did you really think human beings would allow that? They work much more subtly, usually. It's only when some of the lands or nations under their control have descended to such a depth of corruption that such a thing is possible. And even then, the neighbouring nations will sometimes take matters into their own hands and destroy their neighbours. You see, open rule is not generally the gorgone way. They prefer deception, subtle corruption, and slow degradation. They delight in pulling the upright down, and grinding the weak into submission And if they can force human beings to do those things for them, then they feed off the despair with great delight – the more despair the better. And nothing makes human beings despair more than uncertainty and evil within their own kind."

Kazari squeezed her eyes shut, trying to reconcile her naive beliefs with what was apparently reality. "But," and this time Jenex let her continue, "that's not what we're taught!"

Jenex smiled. "It is, you know. Think, Kaz. Think back to what you've learned."

Kazari cast her mind back, somewhat rebelliously, running the legends and stories she'd been taught through her mind. They did mention some gorgones – Greater ones – by name. They frequently mentioned places in the Outer World that she'd seen on maps. They talked about rulers, particularly the second king, by name, and they described the chaos that had taken the world at the First Incursion from Beyond, that had allowed the gorgones into this one. Nowhere did the stories suggest that gorgones ruled in their own forms – except when they invaded Albatar.

"But everyone *believes* they rule openly in the Outer World," said Sendar quietly, and Kazari knew no-one would miss the accusation in his tone.

"People will believe what they wish," replied Zarchess, "even when it flies in the face of what they've been told."

"Isn't it deception, though?" asked Kazari uncomfortably. "Aren't we meant to be better than that?"

"Some might call it so," replied Andiss with a sigh. "In fact some have said that it is, and still we debate it within the Order. But the fact remains that it is only the assumptions that are wrong, not our teachings."

"But isn't it lying by omission?" persisted Sendar, a frown creasing his forehead.

"Some have said so. Rest assured, that if any of us are asked directly, then we always reply with the truth. But it seems that most people are more comfortable believing a fiction, and few ask. And remember that although we are the Lady's servants, we are *not* the rulers of this land." Andiss' words were spoken without expression. He was right – he was not a lord, or a king or queen of Albatar. Isolated in her rural town, the highest authority figure Kazari had ever met was the Mayor of Athos. And the Abbot of the Abbey. Of course, the Lord of Seraph had been a feature of their discussions for some time now, but she'd rarely given much thought to the rest of the rulers of Albatar.

The local Lady of the region pretty well left the Mayor of Athos to get on with things, staying put in her own city. Kazari had never seen her. The Mayor simply mentioned her by name at town meetings, and Kazari knew he visited her in her city every quarter, but as the crow flew, Seraph was actually much closer than the provincial city of Chester that officially 'ruled' Athos. Well, really, the Mayor and the council ruled Athos, if 'rule' was actually the right word for such a collaborative process.

She frowned at her empty mug, while Sendar continued to argue the point.

At last Javon held her hand up to stop him.

"Sendar, if someone asks you, answer as you feel you should. It is the secular rulers of Albatar who have chosen this path. As the Lady's servants we will always answer a question truthfully, and we will always teach the stories and the Writings as they are. Know that the Abbot discusses this very point with the Queen each time they meet in the Council of Abbots. Our Advisers encourage her to consider a more straightforward approach to the issue, but for many years, the rulers of Albatar have chosen to allow perception and assumption to take the place of fact."

Kazari felt dismay colour her thoughts. She'd never considered that what she 'knew' wasn't necessarily exactly . . . true. Or even completely correct. Or that those she respected might have a hand in allowing certain things to be believed, even if they weren't exactly as people believed they were. The taste of disappointment was bitter and spreading. She looked up at the others, seeing her discomfort mirrored in Sendar's downcast eyes, and Javon's flushed cheeks.

At least she knew that the Abbot, and by extension, the Order, didn't agree with the secular authorities. Then she began to wonder what else they might disagree about. A hot twist of anxiety began to churn in her stomach.

Chapter Twenty-one:
Differences

In the end, Andiss had Kazari and Sendar continue in Athos the following day, while he and Javon roved towards Seraph. Accordingly, they made their way down to the market again, once again shopping for supplies for the chapel house, and also to replenish those they'd used on their trek. Andiss had also given them permission to ride out to Dari's farm in the afternoon. "You can catch up on the local gossip," he'd said. "Friends will often know if anything's amiss, and you can sense there, Kaz." Unspoken were the words: *And you can reassure yourself that there are no gorgones close to your family.*

As they entered the market, Kazari smiled at the cheerful bustle, its very normality reassuring her.

"Come on, the cheese we need is over in that corner." She tugged at Sendar's arm and drew him towards the cheese seller. Rounds of hard and soft cheeses sat in neat rows on her stall, and there was a small plate in front of each cheese, offering samples to prospective buyers.

"Kazari!" The aproned woman bustled forward, wiping her hands on a clean rag.

"Hello, Mahsi! I told Sendar that you have the best cheeses," said Kazari, clasping the woman's hands.

Mahsi smiled, her eyes crinkling, and proffered one of the plates. "Here, try this one."

Kazari took a piece and handed it to Sendar, and then turned back to Mahsi. "We need cheese for the road, Mahsi – something that will keep for days in a saddle bag."

"Then you'll be wanting these – I've several different ones, and they're all waxed, so they'll travel well. Taste them first, and then make your selection."

Kazari chatted to Mahsi while they tasted the various offerings. The cheesemaker was full of the gossip of the town, and her cheeses were just as good as Kazari had remembered. She arranged for Mahsi to deliver a variety of the cheeses, waxed in small rounds, to the chapel house, and then they wandered the market making the rest of their purchases.

Savoury smells wafted from one end, where vendors filled flat bread with hot slivers of peppery meat and fried onions, and Kazari dragged Sendar over to them, holding two fingers up to the man cooking on the corner. He smiled and nodded.

"You have to try these, Sendar!" she urged, handing him one of the hot snacks. Then she licked her fingers as hot meat juices dripped from the bread, and took her own first bite. Savoury flavours burst on her tongue, and she smiled around her mouthful as Sendar murmured his own appreciation through a mouthful. As Kazari finished her last piece, she caught a glimpse of the stranger she'd seen at the bakery. He was leaving the tinsmith's stall, carrying another hessian bag. She elbowed Sendar. "Look! It's him!"

"Who?" asked Sendar, through a mouthful.

"The stranger," Kazari replied. "Over at the tinsmith's." He followed her head nod with a glance.

"And? He still looks pretty normal to me."

"Excuse me, Hendry, but who is the man at the tinsmith's?" asked Kazari politely. "I don't remember him."

The man looked up from his hot plate, raising an eyebrow. "He's an apprentice, come down from Seraph these last three months, Kaz. He delivers every day at this time. Why do you ask?"

"I just wondered," she replied. "I've never seen him before. What's his name?"

The man frowned. "I'm not rightly sure, Kaz. Perhaps ask Mahsi if you're popping by her stall again? She knows everything."

"I just might do that. I've seen him around a few times, and it seemed impolite not to address him by name, when he's greeted us. He's quite old for an apprentice, though, isn't he?"

"Well, old depends on your point of view," replied Hendry, cocking an eyebrow at her. "There are some who seem old to you, but are really just youngsters to the rest of us."

Kazari laughed.

They made their way back to the cheese seller's stall.

"His name?" Mahsi said. "Let me think. Ah yes – Sereth – I think that's it. He hasn't been around long. He's an apprentice tinsmith. Not much else to tell, really – he keeps to himself when he's not working. Not one for socialising, apparently." Then she smiled and handed Kazari a small bag. "Try this later. I think you'll like it – it's a new one."

They left the market to ready themselves for the trip to Dari's farm, but the image of the stranger – Sereth – wouldn't leave Kazari. "What do you think he's doing here?" she asked.

"Who?"

"That man – Sereth," replied Kazari.

"Being an apprentice, apparently," said Sendar. "Come on, Kaz, he has every right to be in Athos."

"But we were told to pick up on anything out of the ordinary, and that's what he is – out of the ordinary!"

"I think you're reading too much into it, Kaz. You've been gone for months, so to you he's out of the ordinary, but to everyone else, he isn't. Look, of course we'll mention it to the others, but I reckon they'll think the same as me," he replied. "Besides, you didn't sense anything, did you?"

Kazari made a face. "No, but promise me we'll mention it – properly?"

Sendar sighed. "I promise, but like I said – he has every reason to be in Athos. I'm sure there were people who came and went before you left."

Kazari nodded, he was right, but she'd still mention him to the others. For some reason the man irked her, and Sendar's dismissal irked her, and she didn't like being irked. She hefted her bags of produce onto her shoulder, and they made their way back to the chapel house in silence, Kazari's grumpiness putting a damper on the conversation.

Still, once they were on the road to Dari's farm, the mood lightened. Kazari was glad to be back on Stumpy, sitting easily in her saddle. She relaxed into Stumpy's rhythmic stride, enjoying the sun of the early spring air.

The barred gate at the farm sat neatly on its hinges, the hand painted sign proclaiming 'Settler's Run' – a name handed down by Dari's family over the generations – was as tidy and fresh as ever. Kazari edged Stumpy sideways, and he obligingly allowed her to open and close the gate without having to dismount.

"How far to the house, Kaz?" asked Sendar, standing in his stirrups and shading his face with his hand.

"It's behind the stand of trees over there, but I expect Dari'll be out with the sheep somewhere. We'll check and see if anyone's in the house before we head out into the paddocks."

As they neared the house, Kazari sniffed appreciatively – she could smell something savoury wafting on the breeze. A moment later, she heard the sound of barking, then two black and white dogs appeared at a run.

"Jinny, Splash," called Kazari as they hurtled towards them, "Stop!" Stumpy bounced restlessly, and Sendar's mount snorted as the two dogs came closer. Kazari whistled, and then called the dogs' names again. "Jinny, Splash! Stop!" Uncertainly, the dogs halted, noses in the air, sniffing, and tails held straight out behind them. Kazari dismounted hastily, and handed her reins to Sendar, before walking forward with one hand extended, speaking the dogs' names again.

At last they recognised her, wagging their tails and greeting her with gentle nose touches to her hand. "I should have thought about the dogs," Kazari said, "They're not accustomed to visitors on horses."

"Are they safe now?" asked Sendar, hesitantly.

"They were probably never unsafe," replied Kazari. She patted Splash, so named because she was fond of swimming and sticking her feet in her water bucket. The two dogs ran on ahead as they headed towards the farmhouse. The familiar surroundings were like a second homecoming. She and Dari had been almost inseparable as children, and she'd never forget Gweda and Farin standing in as support to her when she'd declared for the Lady.

"Kaz?" A familiar voice called a greeting.

"Farin?" Kazari turned her head towards the sound of the voice. Farin came striding across the grass at the front of the house, arms outstretched in welcome. She ran into them. Dari's father had been more like a favourite uncle than a friend's father. He smelled faintly of sheep, but more strongly of cooking.

"Welcome, Kaz," he said and then held her back, looking at her. She saw his eyes pause on her scar, and then deliberately move on. "Dari told us you were home, and that you hoped to pop out and visit. Gweda will be very happy to see you, but I suppose you'll be wanting Dari?" She nodded and he went on. "They're both out in the top paddock. Leave your horses with me, and walk on out. They're bringing in the wethers for shearing before it warms too much more. Take Splash with you – you haven't forgotten how to work her?"

"Of course not! And thank you, Farin. Oh, and this is Sendar – he's a year ahead of me in training." She handed Stumpy's reins to Farin, who nodded to Sendar as he took them.

"Pleased to meet you, Sendar," he said, and then flicked his head in the direction of the top paddock. "Go on, off with you. When you catch up with them, tell Dari and Gweda there'll be roast for dinner tonight." He led the horses towards the small house paddock. "And you're both welcome to eat with us."

"Thank you, Farin, we'd like that," Sendar replied. Andiss and Javon had given their dispensation already.

As they walked to the paddock, Kazari entertained Sendar with tales of her childhood escapades with Dari on the farm. The top paddock finally came into sight, and Kazari could see two human figures huddled over the fallen form of a sheep.

"Something's wrong," said Kazari, swinging into a jog. Sendar followed, and Splash bounded ahead, to be joined by two more of the black and white dogs. Kazari recognised Flinn and China as she drew near.

"Kaz! Something's been at the sheep!" said Dari as Kazari jogged up to her friend. "This is the second one we've found."

"Hello, Gweda," said Kazari. "This is Sendar. What do you think did it?" she asked, her attention drawn back to the sheep on the ground. Whatever had attacked the sheep had mauled it dreadfully before eating the soft under parts. Judging by the churned up ground, there had been more than one attacker, and the sheep looked as if it might not have been completely dead while its assailant had gnawed at it, judging by the marks in the soft earth. She looked more closely at the ground, hoping to see tracks, but then acridity stung her nostrils, and she jerked her head up and looked at Sendar.

He met her eyes, one eyebrow raised, and she nodded, just once, before looking back at the ground, surreptitiously sniffing the air. Yes, she was right. The faint stench of sucker lingered, lending a haze of corruption to the once pristine air.

"It could have been a dingo, perhaps, or maybe a rock creeper." Gweda frowned. "But they don't usually maul like this, and they eat more. There was another one further up the paddock. It's already buried. At least we've extra hands for this one. Kaz, would you look for a good spot?"

"Send Sendar when you've found a hollow, and then we'll drag the sheep over," said Dari. "If we leave it, it'll attract scavengers."

Kazari nodded, and gestured for Sendar to follow her as she walked towards a stand of trees.

"Sucker?" he asked quietly.

She nodded. "I'm fairly certain." And to her surprise, she was. Perhaps the understanding of sensing was in the repeated doing. But her blood ran cold – a sucker, on her friend's farm – and maybe more than one.

"We'd better find a spot and help them bury the carcass, and then get the rest of the sheep in, before we send a message to the chapel. We'll have to go hunting."

Sendar nodded in turn. There was no question of them leaving Settler's Run without at least trying to locate the sucker – or suckers.

"We can't tell them, though, not until we're sure, and the suckers are dead," said Sendar, meaning Dari and Gweda.

"We'll tell them that we'll see if we can find whatever's killed the sheep," said Kazari. "It's true, and we don't have to explain any further than that it's our job." She kicked at the ground near a clump of bushes, just beyond the treeline. "This looks like a good spot. It's not too hard, and there aren't any rocks."

Sendar nodded, and vanished back towards the others.

With Sendar gone Kazari hunted around in the undergrowth, looking for a decent sized stick with which to begin digging. By the time the others had dragged the carcass over, she'd made a good start on loosening the soil in the hollow.

Once the remains had been buried and the ground weighted with fallen branches, Kazari straightened up, brushing her hands over her trouser legs.

"We'll scout around for whatever killed the sheep, Gweda," she said casually. "If you're fine with that?"

"It would be very helpful," replied Gweda. "We need to get the rest of them down to the sheds, and if you don't mind, it would take a weight off my mind. It's been a while since we had a dingo or rock creeper, and we really don't want another one. Are you sure you'll be all right?" She darted a look at Kazari uncertainly.

Sendar smiled, however. "Of course, Gweda. We Hunters are known for our resourcefulness." He rested his hands on his belt, and the three knives in their well-used sheaths.

Kazari choked down the indignation and hasty words that had risen to her lips. She was a Hunter, not a child living at home with her parents, but perhaps Gweda still saw her as the girl she'd been when she'd left Athos. Kazari knew that Gweda tended to view her as an extension of Dari, who was still living at home. And despite her Hunter's garb, and the knives on her belt, it appeared Gweda hadn't yet seen Kazari as more than the teenager she'd known for so many years.

"You'll be back for dinner?" asked Dari. "There's so much we haven't talked about yet, Kaz."

Kazari nodded. "Your Dad said it's roast. Smelled delicious when we rode in." Although a wave of distaste almost obscured the remembered smell as she recalled the butchered sheep.

They waved Gweda and Dari off with promises to return for dinner, and then they began to cast about, searching for any hints of suckers. Kazari paused near the scuffed earth, still spattered with gore in places, and drew in a slow breath. The acrid smell of gorgone tainted the cool air, but it was now faint, and it was difficult for her to determine a definitive direction. She walked slowly in circles around the area, and then widened her radius.

"Anything?" asked Sendar. She was about to shake her head when the stench sharpened slightly, so she gestured to him, and he joined her. She drew in another breath, questing, took a few steps hesitantly, and then more confidently followed the taint as it wound among the rocks and shrubs on the edge of the trees. Slowly it grew stronger, and she loosened her long knife in its sheath, knowing without any doubt at all, that Sendar was doing the same thing.

Chapter Twenty-two:
Suckers

The afternoon air seemed to still as the smell of suckers grew stronger. How she knew it was only suckers, and not something larger, like the viper gorgone, Kazari didn't know. Somehow, she also knew there was more than one. She held up a hand as Sendar trailed her, and they paused while she oriented herself. She and Dari had played in these trees many times, and the terrain was familiar, but at that moment, the familiar was overlaid with a sense of decay, as if one of her childhood dreams had been smeared with mould, leaving a patina of corruption on its previously pristine surface.

She shook off the feeling, and concentrated on her surroundings, wishing she had half the skills of a Navigator. The stench grew stronger as they crested the hill and began to descend into closely growing trees. The undergrowth grew more densely as well, and it became more difficult to force their way through. At last, when the stench felt as if it was singeing the inside of Kazari's nostrils, she motioned Sendar closer.

"There's a small clearing at the bottom. I think they're there," she whispered. "More than one, but no idea how many."

He nodded. "Then we watch first. Wait for my signal to attack. If there are too many, one of us will have to go for help while the other one waits and watches." He motioned her forward, and she resumed her steady movement, placing each foot with care, and peering around the larger trees before moving into the cover of the next.

At last, they paused behind the bole of one of the larger trees that Kazari knew bounded the edge of the clearing. She inched her head around it, and felt her breath catch in her throat. Three times she'd seen suckers, and three times she'd fought them. This was the first time she'd deliberately stalked them. Four of them clustered in the middle of the clearing, tentacles sliding over each other, and stalked eyes focused on something at the centre of their group.

Decay ringed them, as if their very presence damaged the grass beneath their limbs, and the stench of them beat at Kazari's nose with an intensity that seemed almost physical. She glanced back and held up four fingers to Sendar, who nodded, and eased his long knife from its sheath. She followed suit, checked her throwing stars, and discovered that it seemed to be harder to deliberately attack the suckers than it had been to react to an attack from them.

"Ready?" Sendar whispered. "Back to back if possible, but we've both killed four at once alone, so this should be well within our capabilities."

Kazari nodded, noting he'd neglected to mention the dozens they'd killed in Suborden before they'd faced down the fire gorgone together. She felt her breath come more quickly, and stilled a tremble in the hand holding her knife.

"On my count." He held up three fingers and dropped them one by one.

Together they leaped from concealment into the clearing. Kazari felt herself flow automatically into the forms that Javon and Andiss had drilled into her, and felt the moment when she began to dance with the suckers, Sendar at her back. Almost at once, she felt the assault on her mind. Despite the flailing tentacles with their edged teeth, the suckers' strongest weapon was their ability to suck the hope from a person, leaving them defenceless and defeated before the fight had even begun.

Stalked eyes swayed and attempted to mesmerise, and an image of Kazari as a cosseted baby caused a momentary hesitation in her dance. The sucker had somehow divined her consternation at Gweda's unthinking comment and elaborated upon it. A tentacle swung towards Kazari's unprotected left side, and she moved sluggishly, fallen from her Dance. Too slowly she moved her knife hand to block it, knowing it would strike her left arm.

Sendar's thrown knife took the sucker between the eyes, and Kazari jerked herself back into movement, shame bringing a burst of heat to her face, and felt the sucker die, the image fading from her mind. It was as if her feet had suddenly been released from the clutch of muddy ground. She flowed back into the Dance, forcing herself to concentrate, to focus on the here and the now.

She *knew* what suckers did. She *knew* they drew the emotions of hope and good and happiness from their victims and focused their fears, yet still she felt them beat at her, as if it were for the first time. Fortunately the movements drilled into her by her teachers, Javon, Andiss, the Abbot, and most recently Alexando, had sunk deeply into her body, and even as her mind quailed, she continued to Dance, even if the joy of the movement seemed somehow lacking. Her knives struck true, and the throwing stars were unneeded in the end as the last sucker fell dead at her feet.

She lowered her arm, breathing fast, sweat slicking her face.

"I'm sorry, Sendar," she said. "I underestimated it." She paused, and then spoke more truthfully. "I – I hesitated because it . . . it distracted me with an image."

Sendar stopped and wiped his blade on a patch of clean grass, watching it wither and die as the sucker gore contaminated it, and shook his head. "No damage done, Kaz."

"Only thanks to you," she replied contritely.

"One day you'll do the same for me. Forget about it – they're horrible things. I hate them." He shuddered and motioned to her blade, and she bent to clean it before sheathing it again, while Sendar plucked his throwing knife from another sucker corpse.

The stench of them was still strong in Kazari's nostrils as she scrubbed her blade on the grass. She frowned. Why could she still smell them? They were dead. She prodded one with a booted toe. Nothing. Then the other three.

"Sendar, I can still smell sucker," she whispered uncertainly, crouching with her knife held defensively before her.

He spun and tucked himself into a fighting crouch, newly cleaned knife whispering into his hand smoothly. "Where?"

Heart pounding, Kazari concentrated. It was hard, with the tangled corpses lying at her feet, begging her to investigate them again in case one was only pretending to be dead. There was a tiny scuffling sound behind her, and she whirled, just in time to see a tentacle vanish into a shadow behind a rock.

"Over there." She spoke as she moved, automatically raising her knife, following the hint of movement with her eyes and the stench with her nose. It faded as they moved, and she wondered just how fast a sucker could move. There was a hole beneath the pile of rocks, with the beginning of a tunnel beneath. It was surprisingly small – much too small for a human being, but not for a sucker, with their rubbery bodies and compressible tentacles.

"Can you still smell it, Kaz?" asked Sendar. His back, against hers, was firm with tension, but rock steady, affirming and trusting.

"It's fading," she replied. "What do we do now? We can't follow it, and I can't sense through rock and earth." She felt him relax somewhat and move away slightly, but she noticed he hadn't sheathed his knife. He frowned, thinking, and kicked at the pile of rocks above the tunnel.

"Maybe we can collapse this on the hole?"

Kazari looked at the rocks. Like many in the area, it was a tumbled pile of granite boulders, piled up haphazardly as if they'd fallen from a sack carried by a passing giant.

"How?" she asked quizzically.

"Maybe I can pick one up with my Gift," he said. "Apparently it's possible, and there are records of others doing it, but I haven't tried it yet."

Kazari rolled her eyes at him, sceptically. "And you think now's a good time to try it for the first time?"

"Well it's that, or levers, or one of us staying here alone while the other goes for help."

She sighed and nodded, shuddering at the thought of either of them waiting alone by a gaping hole, into which at least one sucker had vanished. "Do your worst then. What do you want me to do?"

"Maybe just say a few words to the Lady on my behalf," he said, seriously, and she blushed, ashamed not to have thought of that herself. "Just give me a moment while I think about how to do this."

He frowned again, while she thought a quick prayer to the Lady, clutching her amethyst on its thong, and then watched as sweat broke out on his forehead and the topmost boulder gave a wobble. Sendar's gift was usually used to pick up another person and fly them around. Indeed, he'd picked her up twice at Suborden. Once when they'd been scaling a cliff, and again during the fight with the fire gorgone. She shivered in remembrance, not because she was frightened of Sendar's Gift, but because some of the memories still haunted her.

More sweat beaded Sendar's brow, and his face reddened, almost as if he was physically trying to lift one of the rocks. The topmost one began to rock rhythmically, and Kazari found herself urging it on. Then it toppled, knocking several others in the process until the whole pile destabilised, collapsing in a heap on top of the hole in the ground.

Dust rose from it and drifted across the clearing, highlighted by the shafts of light slanting through the canopy above them. There was a soft thud, and Kazari turned to see Sendar had dropped to his knees, swaying slightly. She dropped to her own knees and placed an arm around him to steady him. He raised an unsteady hand to his forehead and wiped a runnel of sweat away.

"Sendar?" Kazari queried.

"That was hard," he replied. "Just give me a moment."

Kazari looked at his ashen face and shook her head.

"You rest. I'll drag those into the undergrowth, and then we can head back to the farmhouse." She waved a hand at the dead suckers. Flies were beginning to settle on the corpses. "You decide what we're going to say to Gweda and Farin." Sendar dropped from his knees to sit on the ground, bending his knees up to rest his forehead and arms on them and waved a grateful hand at her.

Moving the suckers into the undergrowth was an unpleasant job. The bodies were already beginning to decay. It seemed that once suckers perished, their fleshy bodies began to disintegrate rapidly, unlike those of the greater gorgones. Fortunately, despite the length of their tentacles, sucker bodies were relatively small, and not overly heavy. As she piled branches on top of the last one, Kazari wondered at the sheer malevolence contained in such a small package. The damage a sucker could do as it undermined a human being's sense of self-worth was terrifying, and the thought that there had been more than one on the farm where her friend lived, was a nightmare.

How and why were they there? What had drawn them to Settler's Run? She supposed that it was a fair way out of Athos, which was one probability, and this paddock was one of the less frequently used ones, bordering as it did on the bushland that ran uncleared, other than the occasional small hamlet or farmstead, between Athos and Seraph. But where did those suckers sit in the greater picture?

Her home was under threat. Her friends and her family were under threat. The reality of a gorgone incursion was more immediate than ever, and she wanted desperately to run and blurt it all out, and urge them all to take precautions, to run away to where it was safe.

But where was that? Where was safety? Athos was not on the edge of Albatar, it was well inside the borders. What motivated a human being, raised in Albatar, the *haven* against the gorgone threat, well versed in the stories about the dangers of gorgone corruption, to invite those same gorgones into Albatar?

"Kaz? Are you all right?" It was Sendar, his voice worried and tired, and she could hear him pushing himself to his feet in the clearing, so she hurried back to help him. He'd managed to stand, but he was clearly still very tired, wobbling slightly.

"I'm fine, just frustrated," she replied, slipping an arm around him, and belatedly remembered the little cheese Mahsi had given her. "Here, eat this. It might help." She dug a nail into the wax and pulled it off, carefully shelling the cheese from its casing, and then handed it to Sendar.

He looked at it doubtfully. "Didn't Mahsi say it was a new variety?"

"Go on, we've still got to walk back to the farmhouse, and I can't carry you," Kazari urged. Indeed, her own mouth was watering – Mahsi's cheeses were wonderful, and it was considered an honour to be given a new variety to try. He shrugged and took a tentative bite. Kazari smiled as his eyes opened wide in appreciation. He waved it at her, but she shook her head and told him to eat it. The colour returned to his face slowly.

"I feel better," he announced after swallowing the last bite. "And we need to buy some of that before we leave! Come on, I think I'll make it back now." He took a couple of steps without wobbling, to Kazari's relief. "We'll go slowly, and we can sort out our story on the way."

Chapter Twenty-three:
Why?

Dinner at the farmhouse was a pleasant affair. There were no questions when Sendar explained that they'd tracked what looked like a pack of dingoes into the trees, but had then lost them over a large area of granite slope on the far side of the hill.

"You remember it, Dari – the one we used to slide down?" asked Kazari.

Dari nodded, smiling. "It's pretty steep, isn't it? Do you remember the day after the rain? When the moss was super slippery?"

Kazari laughed. The grazes both had sustained when the combination of damp moss and water on the rocks had slid them twice as fast as normal, had stung dreadfully, and the ensuing explanations about ripped trousers had resulted in both sets of parents banning them from seeing each other for a week. She felt guilty about not telling them about the suckers, but what were they to say that wouldn't alarm the family unreasonably, particularly now that the den had been dealt with and the tunnel closed? The scent of sucker had vanished, and Kazari was confident that there were no more in the immediate vicinity.

Still, the need to return to Andiss and Javon to let them know of the encounter was urgent in her mind. But to leave immediately after dinner when she hadn't spent any time with

Dari, would be completely out of character. Particularly when they all knew that the Hunters could move along at any time.

"How are your parents, Kaz?" asked Gweda, offering Kazari another bread roll.

"It's been good to see them," replied Kazari, "and things are much better than they were."

Gweda nodded and smiled. Her own daughter, Enda, was with the Healer's Sept, and she and Farin had stood with Kazari on the Day of the Choosing, when her own parents had failed to show.

"I know they were distraught when you left, and desperately saddened when they realised that they'd lost their chance to farewell you . . ." She broke off, but Kazari could hear the unspoken words that would have followed. *As a result of their own stubbornness.*

She ducked her head, slightly embarrassed, and there was silence at the table for an uncomfortable moment, until Dari spoke.

"Well that's all sorted now, isn't it?" Grateful for her friend's interruption, even if she seemed to have missed the unspoken words, Kazari nodded.

"Yes, it's good now, Dari." She went on, changing the subject without missing a beat. "And you've got Dari into nice clothes, Gweda? How'd you do that?"

Farin snorted. "Well, nic-*er*, I think is the word. You know Dari!"

The rest of the dinner passed without any more uncomfortable moments, and after dessert, Dari and Kazari retired to Dari's bedroom to talk by themselves, while Sendar offered to pass on the news of wider Albatar to Farin and Gweda.

"He's nice, isn't he?" said Dari, perching herself on the bed, while Kazari took the chair near the window. Dari's room was large. It had once been an attic full of junk, but Dari had commandeered it as soon as she'd been able to talk her parents into it.

"Who, Sendar?" said Kazari, surprised.

"Of course, Sendar, who else would I be referring to?" asked Dari, somewhat ungrammatically.

"I didn't think the two of you were getting on particularly well, that's all, so you surprised me," replied Kazari, slightly uncomfortably. She hadn't forgotten the tension in Dari and Sendar's first meeting.

"I can't imagine why you'd think that?"

"I must have been mistaken, then. And yes, he is nice." Kazari changed the subject. "Now, tell me about everything – especially the clothes." She'd noticed that even on the farm, Dari's work clothes were nicer than strictly necessary.

They gossiped for some time, with Kazari laughing hilariously, as Dari described her mother's machinations involving the new clothing, and updated her on the whereabouts of her school friends. After the Day of the Choosing, some had finished at school and slotted into apprenticeships, while a few had continued on with their learning. With her eyes now opened to the wider world, Kazari realised just how much tradition had played a part in her friends' choices, and indeed just how much tradition limited those choices.

Tradition was certainly part of what had limited Sendar's family's ability to survive, and she wondered how much tradition drove much of what happened in Albatar. On the whole, she reflected, although the traditions of Athos seemed predictable, they weren't harmful – unlike some of what she'd seen in Chator.

Even in her short time as a Servant of the Lady, Kazari knew that her worldview had widened well beyond what it might have been had she remained in Athos. And she knew that she was the better for it. She was still somewhat naive at times, yet she was much more thoughtful than the girl who'd left Athos all those months ago.

Despite her protestations, Dari didn't seem particularly disappointed by her new clothes, and Kazari noticed that she'd rearranged the way she sat and stood, the better to show off her new figure. As her friend chattered away, she found herself slightly disturbed. Dari had changed in ways she didn't really understand.

It was disconcerting – the idea that someone might wish to marry her friend, or that Dari herself might even think about marrying. She was much too young. Kazari had never really thought that far herself. Once she'd decided to declare for the Lady, her future had in some respects been settled – or so she'd thought. But then she recalled the moments with Sendar, when she'd felt more perhaps than what she should have.

She smiled as Dari showed off one of her new jackets. It was artfully tailored, and cleverly constructed to be functional, while showing off more of Dari's figure.

As a Hunter, Kazari would wear Hunter garb for the rest of her life. There were variations in it – her travelling and training and fighting clothes were different to her ceremonial clothes, and to those she wore when training was over for the day. She'd even seen armour, for desperate times, but she'd not yet worn any.

Even the clothing she wore to relax in at the end of a long day had sheaths sewn into the sleeves, and hidden pockets for necessities. Wearing her weapons was now routine – as much a part of getting dressed as it was for her to pull on her underwear. The gorgone threat could occur anywhere and at any time.

Yet, as she pondered on it, while listening with half an ear to Dari's commentary about her new clothing, she knew that she was glad she'd made the choice she had. She'd done a lot of growing up since she'd left Athos, and listening to her friend prattle on about clothing and sheep emphasised it even more. Still, she didn't begrudge Dari her new fascination. Kazari realised that she'd been able to find new friends, new companions, and enormous fulfilment in her new life, despite the dangers and uncertainties, while Dari had lost a constant companion, and at this point, hadn't yet discovered another friend to fill the gap.

Perhaps that was the reason for her sudden interest in what Kazari now considered the trivia of life. As far as Kazari was concerned, as long as her clothes were comfortable, she was happy.

Eventually, Dari wound down and sat back down on her bed, crossing her legs, and propping her elbows on her knees. Her hair shone in the lamplight, its golden tones contrasting with Kazari's dark fuzz, and even darker clothing. Slightly self-consciously, Kazari reorganised herself in the chair, stretching out her legs and loosening her jacket slightly.

"So, Kaz, what's it like, really? Being a Hunter I mean," said Dari.

Kazari pondered for a few moments, wondering exactly what to say. Much of what she'd learned was for Hunter's ears alone, and she certainly wasn't going to tell Dari about Suborden; of being tortured, the fire gorgone, or the shadowy threats made against her family.

Eventually, as Dari wriggled impatiently, she leaned forward. "It's more than I could ever imagine, Dari. I mean, I didn't ever imagine becoming a Hunter to begin with. Who does, really?" She said, half musing to herself while she arranged her thoughts.

"But a Hunter," said Dari, "You're a *Hunter*, Kaz. Well, *almost* a Hunter, anyway. You're carrying a knife, and you have a horse!"

Kazari smiled.

"His name is Stumpy, Dari, and he's great, but he's really only a pony. And we all carry a knife – all Hunters that is. It's part of what we do."

"But Kaz, if you carry one, surely they're teaching you to use one," her friend said, craning her neck and tilting her head. "Tell me, what's it like?"

"Ha! It's hard work, that's what it is," she replied. "I had to get fit first. And the first few weeks nearly killed me!" She elaborated on her fitness training, skating over the fighting and the weapons, and avoiding her initiation or any mention of greater gorgones and Gifts.

"And what's with the scar," said Dari at last. "You haven't mentioned it, but it's pretty obvious."

Javon had been quite open about telling Kazari's parents that her scar had come from a sucker, so she supposed that it wouldn't hurt to mention it to Dari.

"It was a sucker. We train on suckers." She shrugged.

"Seriously, Kaz? You train on *suckers?*" Dari's eyes were wide. "What's that like?"

Kazari shrugged. "Different. Dangerous." She touched her scar absently.

"What do you mean, different?"

"Suckers, Dari, they're not . . . fun."

Her friend looked at her, an expression Kazari couldn't read on her face.

"Look, there has to be more than that to it."

"It's not something I can tell you about, really. It's a Hunter thing."

"But I'm your best friend," wheedled Dari, "surely you can tell me a little bit extra." She looked pleadingly at Kazari, who shook her head regretfully.

"Look, Dari, there is some stuff that I just can't share with you. It's the rules." As soon as she'd said the last bit she wished she hadn't. "You know as much as Mum and Dad now. We train on suckers, because there's more of them than any other kind of gorgone. And we learn about all the others, and hope we never have to battle one. You've been taught about some of them – you know what I mean." She stood up, suddenly uncomfortable with the tack the conversation was taking. "I'd better get back to Sendar, it's getting late and we may be off early tomorrow." It was an excuse, and she knew it, but it was also the truth. Somehow, her relationship with her best friend had changed more than she'd realised, and something had just gone slightly sour.

Dari unfolded herself from the bed and tossed her hair over her shoulder. It was out, Kazari realised, not tied back as it had been out in the paddock, and shining in the lamplight, the ends curling slightly.

"Well, if that's how it is, then I suppose that's it," Dari said, her voice tight. "I only wanted to know because I wanted you to know it doesn't make any difference to me."

"What doesn't make any difference?" asked Kazari puzzled. Her training? How could it make any difference? Dari had known more about her determination to become the Lady's servant than anyone else, even Kazari's parents.

"The scar." Dari waved a casual hand at Kazari's face. "I mean, it's not pretty, but I'm still your friend."

The words fell like stones in the sudden silence, and Kazari felt each one like a knife to the heart. She couldn't believe that Dari had actually said them. Why had she said them? It had no bearing on their friendship. If Dari had turned up with a scar, then she'd have wanted to know why, and how, but she wouldn't have qualified their friendship – or felt the need to – by demanding answers she clearly couldn't give about a physical blemish.

Without speaking, Kazari did her jacket up, checked her boot laces, and nodded to Dari. Her friend knew she'd said the wrong thing, and Kazari could tell she understood why it was the wrong thing, but there was no apology, just a stubborn set to Dari's chin. She could understand Dari's curiosity, but she *couldn't* understand the words that had just come from her friend's mouth.

She felt sick, betrayed, and saddened. Could Dari have changed so much in six months? Were the clothes an outward sign of something that had changed so fundamentally within her friend that she was unable to understand it? Part of her wanted to rationalise the words away and make excuses for her friend, but they'd shared so much over the years that it was beyond comprehension that Dari had just said what she'd said. If she'd left off the qualifier – the 'I'm still your friend' bit –

then things would have been fine. She could have tossed it off with a joke and Kazari would have appreciated it, knowing that *of course* Dari was still her friend. But that qualifier – something didn't ring true. Something had changed in the months she'd been gone. Something that went further than the changes in clothing. She was still 'Dari' but there was now a distance between them that Kazari didn't like.

She shrugged her shoulders to settle her jacket properly, automatically checking the hang of the sleeves with the knives in their hidden sheaths, even more conscious now of the differences between the two of them.

Perhaps it was her.

She stood up, paused, wanting to say something, but not knowing what. Finally, she simply left Dari's room without speaking. What could she say without making things even worse? How could Dari have thought she'd think their friendship would be changed because of a scar? She could understand her mother's potential misgivings – Liselt was her mother, and she'd had hopes and dreams for Kazari, even if they weren't the same as Kazari's. And, yes, some of those dreams had involved young men. In Liselt's world, face and figure featured in the marriage market. But now Liselt knew that Kazari's life would be anything but the one she'd probably imagined, and despite her misgivings, she'd clearly decided to make the most of what there was.

But Kazari and Dari had never been focused on such things. They'd hoped and dreamed for different things – the Lady's Order, and Settler's Run – and they'd spent their time together joyfully, sharing those things, helping each other and encouraging each other when things were difficult. They'd been birds of a feather – friends who'd spent so much time together they were more like sisters. But now something had irrevocably changed between them.

Turmoil spun within her like a whirlwind. She even struggled to farewell Gweda and Farin appropriately, stumbling over the formal phrases, while Dari stood silently to one side.

Fortunately Sendar, clearly sensing her disquiet, covered for her admirably.

It wasn't until they were walking their horses back towards Athos under the moonlit sky, that he asked what had gone wrong.

Kazari shook her head, not knowing what to say. It seemed silly, and almost impossible to explain to someone else. Sendar would think she was an absolute idiot to be concerned with such an innocent phrase when Albatar's future might hang in the balance.

"Do you think there are other suckers, Sendar?" she asked, changing the subject.

"I'm sure there are," he replied. "That's one thing we know about suckers – there are always more."

They rode in silence for a few more moments, and Kazari busied herself by playing with Stumpy's mane, trying to distract herself from thoughts of suckers, her hesitation earlier in the day, and Dari's words. They echoed inside her mind.

"The thing is, Kaz," said Sendar, eyes glinting in the moonlight, "suckers are usually in built up areas – inside towns, or lurking on their outskirts, not in isolated paddocks. Generally suckers cluster where there's something to . . . well . . . suck."

Kazari nodded, she knew those things as well as Sendar. In Suborden, the suckers had been very close to the town, and the 'changed' had been within its very homes and businesses. What a tunnel was doing on her friends' farm was a mystery, and she wondered how, and why it was there. And if there was one lot of suckers near Athos – albeit in a paddock – how many more might there be nearby? It added to the whirl of emotions rolling around inside her head.

"Sendar," she said, "How bad exactly, do you think that a gorgone incursion would actually be? I mean, how many gorgones? What types – things like that? And, you know, the Mayor? What if there are more like him?" The words seemed to dim the clean moonlight as she spoke them, images of the gorgones she'd studied in the sept's texts floating in the gloom before her as she rode.

"I don't know, Kaz, and it's something I hope never happens," he said, "but I have to keep telling myself that Albatar has survived other incursions, and I'm sure the Abbot will have the Advisers briefing the Lords and the incumbents now. And maybe what we do here might make a difference. And the Mayor? That fire gorgone? I don't know – I have no idea how that happened, and when I asked, neither did the others."

He'd asked – why hadn't she thought to do that? Suddenly Kazari felt stupid. How had she been so wrapped up in her nightmares that she'd not thought to ask such a simple question? Maybe if she'd thought less about herself and more about the wider implications she'd have thought to ask the questions that were important.

"Do you think it'll come to that?" Kazari asked eventually.

"I hope not." Sender's tones were measured, as if he was trying very hard to keep his tones level. "But I'm worried that it will. There have been so many signs."

They rode on in silence after that, but Kazari's mind continued to dwell on the day's events, cycling Gweda's and Dari's words over and over, and repeating the moment when she'd frozen during battle. From a morning full of promise, it had become an evening of uncertainty tinged with shame. She also wished she was back in the Abbey, where she could burrow into the library, looking for information about previous incursions. She knew of them of course, but not a lot more than the dates and the heroes – mostly Hunters and Navigators – who had made their way into Albatar's histories.

Lady, she whispered inside her mind, *help me!* But she didn't really know what she meant when she thought those words.

Chapter Twenty-four:
Places

The discussion about the suckers at Settler's Run had continued late into the night. For some hours, Andiss and Javon had debated whether to leave, or to stay and investigate further, but eventually, the need to move on and explore using Kazari's Gift of Sensing, won. As Javon had said towards midnight, if there was one crèche of suckers, then it was possible there might be more, but Kazari had sensed nothing else in Athos, and the need to discover what might lie behind the proliferation of problems in the surrounding areas outweighed the need to hunt out what would most likely turn out to be nothing.

Kazari had lain awake for hours, the conversation with Dari replaying in her mind. Her homecoming had been surprising, saddening, exhilarating and disappointing all at the same time.

What had changed within Dari? Normally the two of them talked about anything that bothered them, and Kazari wondered why her friend's letters had mentioned nothing about her mother's clothing crusade. She should have shared the whole thing as a joke with Kazari. Of course Kazari now knew that Dari had *liked* the clothes. Perhaps that was the problem. Maybe she thought Kazari might have disapproved, or perhaps she'd been too embarrassed to admit it.

Certainly, she herself had only discussed the things of the Order in general details – but that was different – or so she told herself at least. There were things about the Lady's servants that were only for the Lady's servants to hear, and there were valid reasons for that. Even if some of them seemed . . . troubling to her.

Perhaps Dari had decided that a Hunter wouldn't be interested in Gweda and Farin's plans for their daughter. But even as she thought about it, the justifications for her friend's actions seemed hollow, and a touch of sadness followed her as they rode through sunlight the next morning towards their first village.

By her side, Sendar was yawning and looked tired. Perhaps she wasn't the only one who'd had a sleepless night. She wondered what it was that might have kept Sendar up. It certainly hadn't been nightmares, or if it had been, he hadn't followed Alexando's instructions and awoken her. Then she realised that she hadn't had a nightmare, either. For a moment, her worry about Dari was eclipsed by relief, then she began to worry about the *lack* of nightmares. Eventually she sighed and shook her head as they paused at an intersection.

Javon motioned to Kazari to ride beside her.

"Something's bothering you, Kaz."

Kazari shook her head, uncertain whether to tell Javon of her fears. She felt stupid in the light of day. It had been one sentence, and it shouldn't have rankled so much, even if it had felt like a betrayal of all she and Dari had seen and done together.

"It's nothing, Javon, just . . . suckers again. And on my friends' farm. It bothers me." What she'd said was true, but it wasn't all of the truth. She *was* worried about the suckers, and her hesitation, and the fact that the suckers were on Settler's Run, but at the bottom of all her fears, were Dari's words.

"You're right to be concerned, Kaz, We're all concerned about the suckers. The numbers we've seen in the last few years are unprecedented, and it's been many, many decades since a gorgone has approached the Abbey. And the fire gorgone, and a viper gorgone – the last one was over twenty years ago, and near the northern border."

Kazari was surprised to see that Javon's eyes were worried, full of concern, both for the situation in Albatar, and for Kazari herself.

She debated with herself, but at last she decided to come clean about her failure during the fight. Besides, she wasn't sure she could talk about Dari without bursting into tears.

"Javon, I froze yesterday," she said, finally. "During the fight with the suckers – one almost got me." She looked down. "Well, it would have, except for Sendar."

The older woman looked at her, swaying gently in her saddle as her horse negotiated a rough bit of road. "Kaz, everyone freezes at some point. Do you really think that suckers don't bother the rest of us?"

"B . . . but," began Kazari.

"We *all* feel the draw of the sucker – and we feel it every time we fight one. At some point, nearly all of us hesitate. We're human beings, not invulnerable super beings." She smiled gently at Kazari. "If we're alone, then it's extraordinarily dangerous, which is why we try to work in pairs. Size is not the only indicator of a gorgone's threat." Javon's eyes stared straight ahead, and Kazari had the feeling she was remembering something – and remembering whatever it was with sadness.

She was slightly reassured, although she couldn't imagine someone like Andiss, or the Abbot, being pulled by a sucker. It just didn't seem possible. Both seemed invulnerable, calm, and completely in control of themselves. Their sense of assurance was something Kazari craved. Perhaps if she survived to serve the Lady as long as they had, she might attain that kind of serenity. Maybe. If she survived. Surrounded by her gloomy thoughts, she rode on, trying not to notice the sidelong glances from Javon. Clearly, the talk hadn't completely convinced Javon that she'd addressed all of her concerns.

Eventually, the brightness of the spring day elevated her spirit despite her worries. After the long winter, Kazari basked in the colours of spring as they bloomed around her, trying to let them soothe her fears.

Several hours later, they approached a tiny hamlet that Kazari had visited on more than one occasion. It was well known for its groves of apple trees and the cider it produced. Now, in the early spring, the apple trees were loaded with young fruit. Their orderly rows bordered both sides of the road, and here and there, people were visible, tending the trees.

"Ho, Hunters!" called a cheerful voice from one side.

An older man stood by the road, leaning on a shovel, one hand raised. It was dirt stained and calloused, and his clothes were smeared with mud. He was smiling.

"What brings you to Cidertown?"

"Roving, as always," replied Andiss, cheerfully. "You'll see we have two youngsters with us." He waved a hand at Kazari and Sendar.

"Will you stop for a drink, then?" asked the man.

"We'd appreciate the stop to water our horses," replied Javon.

"There's a trough in the square. And if you pop into the inn, tell Adie that Sim sent you."

"Many thanks, Sim," Andiss told him.

The man smiled and shouldered his shovel, then vanished into the apple trees with a wave.

In the square, Sendar and Kazari watered the horses. It could barely be called a square, mused Kazari, looking around. She sniffed, but there was nothing but the faint smell of apples on the air. Andiss vanished into the inn as directed, and a few moments later, he returned with a woman carrying a tray. Four tankards sat upon it and Kazari's mouth watered.

She remembered drinking the cider years ago. It was delicious, sweet, and refreshing.

"Thank you for your service, Hunters," said the woman, proffering the tray, first to Andiss and Javon, and then to Sendar and Kazari.

"This Hunter thanks you for your thanks to the Lady," replied Andiss gravely, and Kazari joined the others in repeating the traditional phrase. The cider was as satisfying as Kazari remembered, and she saw Javon raise her eyebrows in appreciation.

"Delicious, Adie," said Andiss. "I must remember to tell our cooks – this is far superior to anything served at the Abbey."

The woman blushed, and nodded. "It would be our privilege, Hunter." She held the tray out for the empty tankards.

"Is there anything we might do for you, while we're here?" asked Javon, placing her tankard on the tray.

Adie shook her head, but then paused.

"Nothing here, Hunters, but we've . . . heard rumours. Perhaps you might follow them?"

"Rumours?" queried Andiss.

"It's probably nothing, but these last few months, several trader caravans have been through."

Kazari didn't think that was particularly unusual. Caravans passed through Athos regularly.

But the woman hurried on. "We have caravans, of course, but not at this time of year." At their obvious confusion, she hastened to explain. "It's too early for the apples, and too late for new cider. What we've left we sell locally, or drink ourselves. And these caravans have been . . . different."

Kazari looked curiously at the woman. Her face was flushed, and she seemed uncomfortable.

"What do you mean by different?" asked Javon.

"We didn't think much of the first one. They wanted the hard cider – the stuff we distill down over winter, and sell on for other use – cleaning, mostly, or as a base for perfumes. But the price they offered was too much. It's not fit to drink, that stuff. It gives us something to do when it's cold, and it makes a tidy profit at the end of winter." She shrugged. "That happens sometimes, and we just say no, even at this time of year, because it's likely they're out to sell under the table, so to speak, and we don't hold with that. But the second caravan stayed in the paddock there," she pointed, "for two days. They met with Sim, and with Zenda, and the price offered was twice what the previous caravan had offered. And there were sounds in the night." She shivered, and Kazari had the feeling she hadn't realised she'd done so. "Sim says that maybe I was imagining things, but I'm sure I wasn't."

"What type of sounds?" asked Javon, taking the woman by the arm, and gently leading her over to the wooden seat by the horse trough. Adie put the tray down on one end of the seat and sat down, heaving a sigh.

"It sounded like something crying. Or moaning, perhaps. And rattling. Like there was something trapped in a cage somewhere. And that wasn't the end of it. That caravan left and I began to think that Sim was right – that I had imagined it. But then the third caravan came."

"Did they offer more than the cider was worth?" asked Sendar curiously.

"No, young Hunter, they didn't. They offered only the normal price, but they *demanded* the cider. And only the hardest of the hard. When we wouldn't sell, they resorted to threats. Still, my Sim doesn't bow to threats, and after three days they left empty handed. But when they left, we found they'd fouled one of the wells, and a litter of pups had gone missing – and old Aron's cow."

"Three caravans? When did the last one leave?" Andiss asked, frowning.

"Only three days ago," said Adie. "We sent a message to Seraph. But it's too soon to hear back – I thought perhaps you might catch up with the last group? They were pulling heavy wagons, so they're slow. Only, old Aron needs his cow, and Sim had plans for those pups." She looked suddenly embarrassed. "And there are rumours, you see, coming out of Seraph, that the Lord has forgotten his duties, and I'm fearful we might never hear back. I mean, you're Hunters and all."

Javon's face was grave as she patted the woman's arm again.

"It would be our pleasure, and our duty, to see what we might find for you. The Lady's servants are honour bound to help her people, and gorgones are not the only threats to Her peace. Thank you for telling us, Adie."

The woman looked relieved that the Hunters had taken her fears seriously.

"Many thanks," she said. "You'll send word if you see or hear anything?"

Andiss nodded. "Word will come via Jenex and Zarchess at Athos most likely, or perhaps Alexando in Chator. Or perhaps we'll drop through again ourselves. We'll be making several trips for these two to find their feet. We'll keep our eyes out, and perhaps we'll catch up with the last caravan." He indicated Sendar and Kazari. "And now we must be off."

The Hunters followed the deep wheel ruts left by the caravan. The road wound through more apple orchards until at last they gave way to the normal bushland. Once again, the spring weather was perfect. Vegetation grew lushly on either side of the road, and the sounds of bellbirds echoed through the trees, their pure tones sweet and piercing. If they hadn't been searching for gorgones and caravans that stole livestock, it would have been one of the nicest rides Kazari had ever had. As it was, she was on edge again.

Javon had cautioned them about the caravan. "We can't automatically assume that there's anything sinister about the caravan. Sinister in the context of gorgones, I mean. They could simply be normal people who don't baulk at thievery." Then she'd shown Kazari and Sendar how to determine how long ago the wheel ruts had been made, explaining about weather, depth of tracks, how much the ground had dried out, and whether anything else had crossed the tracks since the wagons had rolled through.

Kazari had touched the tracks, looked at the paw prints and bird feet impressions, and tried to embed into her mind exactly what it all meant, eventually leaning back and regarding Javon with something akin to awe. The woman seemed to be able to read the ground like a book.

"It'll come Kaz," she said, smiling. "It took me a fair few years to get to this point, and even now, my skills pale into insignificance next to those of a Navigator."

Sometimes Kazari's mind boggled at all the things she needed to know as a Hunter. Every time she turned around there was something new to add to the list. Her book learning seemed easy in comparison – her memory was excellent, and she generally picked things up quickly, but the acquisition of new physical skills was a never-ending activity. Even now, when she was fitter than she'd ever been, she stood in awe of Javon and Andiss and their easy athleticism.

At least she wasn't having to walk everywhere. Stumpy's sturdy legs carried her and her gear much more easily over the damp ground than her own legs would have. And from what Javon had said, they'd probably be travelling about twice as fast as the caravan they were following.

She did the calculations in her head. They should catch up within a couple of days, assuming they didn't need to deviate from following the caravan. Kazari sniffed, inhaling deeply, reminding herself that their primary task was seeking gorgones, not necessarily following caravans.

And then that took Kazari on a whole new train of thought. She still didn't know how close she needed to be to sense different gorgones, or even whether the distance changed with the type of gorgone. She'd found the viper gorgone from quite a distance, when she thought about it, while for suckers it seemed she needed to be closer. But then she found herself wondering about the one at the Abbey. It was a greater gorgone, and she had no idea how far away it had been when she'd first detected it.

Of course, she hadn't known she was detecting a gorgone at the time, so perhaps that one didn't count. As they rode along, Kazari resolved to try to take more notice of things like distance, smell intensity, numbers, and type of gorgone.

Chapter Twenty-five:
Caravan

The following day wore on slowly. Towards midday, Javon began to check the caravan tracks more often. Even Kazari, with her rudimentary ability to understand what the tracks in the soft earth meant, could tell that they looked fresher. Finally, two hours after their midday stop, Javon signalled a halt and dropped to her haunches by a particularly deep rut. "They're ahead by only a few hours now," she said.

Andiss dismounted and joined her, peering at the soft earth. A pile of droppings had been partially mushed into the rut, but from Stumpy's back, Kazari could smell that the dung was fresh, and from a large horse. Possibly one of the wagon horses, she mused. She drew in another breath, questing for gorgone, but apart from the fresh manure, there was nothing but the warm scents of spring on the breeze.

Andiss squinted at the horizon. "The question is, do we want to catch that caravan today? Kaz, no sign of gorgones?"

Even though she'd just done it, Kazari took another deep breath through her nose before replying. "Nothing."

Javon rose from her crouch. "We've only about three hours until twilight." She pulled her map from her saddle bag and spread it open on a convenient rock. "We're about . . . here. There's another town about two hours down the road. I'd say they've stopped there for the night. It's what any caravan would do. In fact, there's a major crossroads there – the caravan has the option of continuing towards Scinde, or turning off and heading for Seraph." She tapped it thoughtfully. "I'd suggest that we take to the trees in about an hour, and approach the town without being seen. It's a pity we don't know where Elliam and Abel are. It'd be good to have a Navigator's skills beside us."

Andiss nodded his agreement, and an hour later, Javon took them off the road into the trees. She dismounted, and from then on, they led their horses. Kazari could sense nothing sinister on the air, but the thought of walking into the unknown chilled her, so she was hard pressed to stop herself sniffing with every step. 'Spiky wattle' clawed at her legs as she pushed her way through it behind Andiss, dropping golden pollen onto her black Hunter's clothing. Sometimes being short really annoyed her. His longer legs seemed to have no trouble dealing with the bushes. Fortunately, her Hunter garb offered some protection or she'd have been scratched to bits.

Stumpy didn't seem to mind at all. Rather, he seemed to appreciate the leafy foliage, occasionally tugging at the reins to nip a few of the leaves with his teeth. Eventually, Javon held up a hand to signal a halt. By that time, Kazari was scratched, speckled liberally with yellow, and felt as though she had bits of leaf and twig itching their way down her neck. She brushed a few bits out of her short curls with her free hand, noting that she'd need to trim it when she returned to the Abbey. She could see a small clearing, and what looked like the edge of the trees not far away. At least, she could see more blue sky in that direction than she'd seen since they'd left the road.

"We'll leave the horses here," said Andiss, "and set up camp. We'll be working our way into town when it's dark, so once you've got yourselves sorted, we'll eat." They hobbled the horses and set up two small tents, vestibule to vestibule. Javon showed them how to suspend a fine mesh above them which they then covered with dry vegetation. Kazari was surprised to see how well it disguised the tents – from a short distance she could barely see them at all. Certainly, someone coming from the village would only see them if they stumbled upon them accidentally.

After a quick meal of cheese and flatbread, the four Hunters perched themselves on the edge of the scrub, watching the village and what they could see of the road. Kazari checked her map in the late afternoon light, using her fingers to estimate distances. The village was named as Pleasance, and from her map, Kazari was surprised to see that Pleasance was as close to Seraph as Chator was, just in a different direction. She walked her fingers around her map a bit more, and realised that Athos was definitely a long way from its Lady's town, which explained why the local mayor loomed much larger in her mind than its Lady. In fact, she didn't think she could even recall her name.

She wondered why Athos hadn't come under Seraph's rule, rather than Chester's. Still, it probably didn't matter anyway, so she contented herself with studying the map, trying to make more sense of Albatar's geography than she currently had at her fingertips. Of course, on her travels, she'd been with Javon and Andiss, and they'd guided the journeys and given some basic instruction in navigation, but at the time it hadn't seemed as pressing as her regular training in fighting skills and the use of her Gifts.

As the sun sank lower, the warm spring air gave way to the chill of the evening, and Kazari added another layer to her clothing. Still, as the short twilight ended, and darkness enveloped them, she shivered slightly and wished she'd added yet another one. A moon rose slowly above the horizon, but the slight haze around it hinted of clouds to come as Kazari followed Javon out of the trees and across the paddocks on the edge of the village.

She stepped on a twig which snapped loudly underneath her foot and froze, convinced the sound must have startled the entire village.

"Move on, Kaz!" whispered Sendar, tapping her on the shoulder.

She almost let out a yell in surprise. He must have felt her start. "It wasn't that loud, but please try and look where you're going."

She rolled her eyes in the darkness – look where she was going? It was dark. Of course, that was the moment she realised that it wasn't really dark, and that her eyes had adjusted enough that she could make out forms and contours – even vague shadows of trees ahead and rocks on the ground, if the colour differential was enough.

She went to sigh, stifled it, and kept moving, trying to place her feet with care while keeping her eyes roving ahead. She wished there was more light, and then she didn't because light would have made them visible. She wished there was a Hunter's Gift that illuminated the dark for Hunters only, and almost fell over when she felt the impression of amusement and a faint warmth from her amethyst. She groped for it at her chest, but there was no glow. Of course, that would have made her visible too.

She almost fell over a rock she hadn't seen, and Kazari realised that she needed to stop thinking and concentrate on what she was actually doing. Her mind felt as if it was a litter of active puppies, thoughts darting here, there and everywhere, with no sense of control or focus. By the time they'd reached the village, she'd managed to focus herself on what might be ahead, so she didn't start when Javon reached back with a hand and drew her to her side.

"We'll make our way slightly west. There's a flat paddock there where caravans usually set camp."

Kazari nodded, realised Javon couldn't see her and whispered her assent. Then she reached back and passed the message to Sendar. A moment later, and they were on the move again. Here and there, lights shone from windows. Kazari quickly learned to keep her eyes averted, after she'd peered towards one and completely lost her night vision.

This village had a row of houses on this side, backing on to the southern border of the village. They passed a gate set between two of the houses, and when Kazari looked curiously between them, she saw a narrow alleyway that led onto a dimly lit street. She supposed that Pleasance was large enough to have street lamps and a lamp lighter to tend them.

She was warm from the exercise, and pleased now she hadn't added another layer or else she'd have been overheated. As they reached the western end of the row of dwellings, Javon slowed her pace just before her hand urged Kazari to a crouch.

"We'll take the north, and Sendar and Andiss the south. Follow me."

She moved off directly behind Javon, casting furtive glances through the darkness. The smell of woodsmoke hung in the air, gradually strengthening as she and Javon moved along the western boundary. It wasn't a square; the houses were more scattered, unlike the southern boundary. It seemed that Pleasance had gradually sprawled further west as it grew, so Kazari and Javon followed a meandering path, occasionally struggling through ditches and around trees. Or at least Kazari struggled, while Javon moved smoothly, or so it seemed to Kazari.

She had to remind herself to blink occasionally, but with the footing so uneven, Kazari found herself straining to pierce the darkness ahead. The moon was now fully risen, but clouds scudded across the sky, and the light was uncertain, sometimes changing from one moment to the next. Eventually, she spied a ruddy glow ahead. The smell of something savoury added itself to the woodsmoke, and her stomach grumbled. It wanted something hot, not just the bread and cheese.

The glow resolved into flickering flames, and the sound of conversation came faintly to her. There was the smell of horses not far away, and as the flames surged higher and embers fountained into the air, the shadowy shapes of wagons parked side by side on a small rise became visible. Javon drew Kazari down again, and they lay flat on the ground, looking up towards the wagons.

"We're going to move up behind the wagons, Kaz," whispered Javon. "We're too exposed here." She backtracked slightly before beginning to circle around the campsite, keeping the two of them clear of the edge of the village. Kazari felt her heart beating faster, and found that the palms of her hands had grown sweaty, despite the chill in the air.

Eventually, Javon paused a little way from the wagons, and Kazari saw that they were now just behind the rise where the wagons sat. Their high bases and large wheels left a gap beneath them so that Kazari and Javon could see some of what was happening by the fire. It was also unlikely that anyone looking up the hill towards the wagons would see them. She relaxed slightly.

As her eyes adapted, Kazari could see people sitting on low stools around the fire, plates and cups held on laps. Sparks fountained again, and she saw that someone had stirred the coals with a shovel and was piling fresh ones on top of several camp ovens.

"I guess we've found old Aron's cow," whispered Javon.

They'd found the cow, Kazari thought. Where? Just before realisation kicked in. The camp ovens and the savoury smell of roasting meat . . .

She strained her ears, trying to hear what the people around the fire were saying, but the voices were too quiet, apart from the odd word here or there. Kazari shivered slightly. The people looked warm, tucked around the fire, eating and drinking, and now that she was stationery, the chill in the air was making itself known. Javon touched her arm slightly and pulled her down behind the rise.

"We'll be here for a while, Kaz. You wait here and watch. I'm going to scout around further west, see if there's anything different there, and meet up with Andiss. I'll be back shortly. Keep your ears open." The woman slid back down the rise and moved off without making any discernible sound. Kazari wondered how long it would take for her to learn *that* skill. She crawled back up the rise and lifted her head cautiously, peering under the wagon again. She froze as the wagon rocked slightly, then she saw feet descending a small ladder at the front of it.

They obscured her view briefly, and then she was looking through the rungs – just as she had been the whole time, she realised.

The booted feet moved to the fire, joining the others around it, and then the savoury smell intensified and Kazari felt the wind rise slightly, brushing her cheeks with its chill. At the same time, a hint of acridity touched her nostrils, and she tensed – gorgones? It was there and then gone almost immediately, and for a moment she thought she'd imagined it. Then reason won over uncertainty. She'd smelled that exact same smell before – not gorgones – or not exactly – but the 'changed'. The smell was burned deep into her memory, along with the memory of pain, and the longest night she'd ever experienced.

She looked around to alert the others, then remembered she was alone. Alone and watching and listening, while somewhere nearby was a 'changed'. Or perhaps a changing. Kazari remembered the nightmare transformations all too well. They'd fed off her fear and her pain. Her mind raced – what should she do? Should she follow Javon? But no, she didn't really know exactly where the other Hunter was going, except to circle around the campsite. What if she decided to do an entire circle while Kazari chased her? They could end up going round and round without meeting.

Kazari forced her panic down, and made herself take notice of what was happening near the fire. She breathed in at the same time, widening her nostrils, trying to detect that elusive scent again. All that came on the breeze was the smell of beef stew. And something else. Something that wasn't 'changed', or gorgone, or stew, but still pungent, and oddly familiar.

Voices rose again, so she focused on trying to hear anything that might make sense.

With the wind rising slowly, the snatches of conversation came more clearly than they had previously, but the sentences were disjointed, their meanings unclear.

". . . From the old man at . . ."

". . . Underneath it – remember? When the messenger came, she gave us a description . . ."

". . . Infiltration is almost complete but there were a few . . ."

Frustrated, Kazari wished she could get closer, but with the firelight and the ground as it was, if she moved closer, she'd be clearly visible, even if she crawled under the wagon in front of her. The savoury smell intensified again as someone lifted the lid of one of the camp ovens using a tent peg. She squinted in the sudden flare of firelight. The familiar smell assailed her nostrils again, and at last she recognised it – apples – but only barely. The smell of apples was almost eclipsed by something stronger – the pungent smell of hard spirits. For some reason, they were heating it further, and doing something with it.

Kazari peered under the wagon again, trying to see anything that might be of use, all the time keeping her ears pricked for the fragments of conversation wafting on the wind. She started as a yelp sounded clearly on the wind, followed by frantic yapping. A door slammed at the front of the wagon next to the one Kazari was looking underneath, and the yelping escalated briefly, before a thud sounded and it subsided to whimpers.

Kazari's heart sank – Sim's puppies? She was fond of dogs herself, although her family hadn't had one of their own, and she'd enjoyed the company of Dari's sheep dogs. She craned her head to the right, trying to see if anyone was near the other caravan, wondering if she should somehow sneak into the caravan and rescue the puppies. Still, even if she could get into the caravan, how would she keep the pups quiet?

She looked to either side, hoping that Javon would appear out of the darkness, while the quiet whimpers kept distracting her from what she should really be doing. The wind blew more strongly, and the night seemed suddenly darker, and Kazari realised that clouds had now obscured the moonlight completely. She could hear quiet cursing coming from around the fire.

". . . Might be turning . . ."

". . . Finished that batch? . . ."

Something glinted brightly as the fire flared briefly again, and the smell of spirits, or something made from it, was suddenly chokingly strong. Kazari had to cover her nose and mouth to stop herself from coughing. Her eyes watered, and she blotted the tears quickly with her other hand, ducking below the ridge line into the fresher air.

She inhaled gratefully, wondering exactly what the caravaners were doing – even if the people of Cidertown hadn't sold them any of the hard cider, they'd obviously 'acquired' it from either Cidertown or somewhere else and were using it for something,

". . . Told you to keep it away from the dinner . . ."

". . . Your mouth, there's nothing in the stew, it's just the . . ."

Well, someone around the fire wasn't pleased with the stench either. Kazari risked a quick sniff above the ridge line and was pleased to discover that the smell had paled off to just a hint of its previous pungency. Firelight glinted redly off something that tinkled and clattered as one of the figures upended a pot onto a rug on the ground. Kazari narrowed her eyes – surely not? She'd seen things like that before – in Suborden.

A whisper at her side made her spin in place, reflexively drawing a knife from her boot. A heartbeat later she subsided with relief – it was Javon.

"Javon – I think there might be 'changed' here," she whispered urgently.

Chapter Twenty-six: Malmetal

"You're sure?" whispered Javon.

"Yes," Kazari whispered back. "And they've been doing something with alcohol at the fire, and I think the litter of pups is here as well."

Javon drew her down behind the rise, and then two of them moved further into the concealing darkness. The darkness was all encompassing at first, and after looking into the fire lit campsite, Kazari's night vision took some minutes to return, and she felt as if she might stumble and fall any moment as Javon moved them further away. At last the older woman stopped and tugged her into a squat behind what Kazari belatedly realised was a pile of debris, set in a cone for a bonfire.

"Now, tell me what you think you've seen and heard," Javon said quietly.

Kazari ran through her list – the smell of the 'changed', the pups, and whatever they'd been cooking up on the fire. Then she remembered the snatches of conversation.

"They said something about infiltration being 'almost complete.' But I couldn't hear anything that made any sense of that," she finished. There seemed to be so many things to recount, and Kazari had no idea what they should pursue first. The 'changed', maybe? Her mind raced.

Javon was silent beside her for a long time, and Kazari had to force herself not to fidget. The woman was clearly thinking over what Kazari had told her, and perhaps she had more to add from her own reconnaissance. At last, Javon spoke.

"That rise is our best spot for listening, so I want you to go back there. Don't do *anything* but listen – listen and remember *exactly* what's being said." In the faint light, Kazari saw Javon tilt her head to look at the sky. The dense clouds had scattered slightly again, but Kazari could see the clouds scudding quickly across the sky, and what light the moon emitted was intermittent. "I'll get the others. They might have a bit more information by now. Sendar was going to try and lift Andiss onto the top of a wagon."

"What?" exclaimed Kazari. Javon's hand covered her mouth, and Kazari shamefacedly realised that she'd spoken loudly. She looked about wildly, but they were downwind, so hopefully no-one at the fire had heard anything.

"Keep your voice down," hissed Javon, and for the first time since meeting her, she heard hints of irritation in the Hunter's voice.

"Sorry," whispered Kazari. "But . . . how? I mean, what if the top of the wagon collapses?"

In the darkness, Kazari felt, rather than saw Javon shrug. "It's necessary. Now, get back to the rise, and listen. Ignore the pups, they're the least of our worries right now. If this caravan is what I think it is, then we've bigger problems that we'd thought."

"Javon, what do you mean?"

"I suspect they're manufacturing malmetal charms and distributing them. And if they're talking about infiltration, then we need to know what's being infiltrated, and where and how. And if you think there are 'changed', then that complicates matters even more. We need information, which means we can't just wade in and dispatch them."

Kazari rocked back on her heels. What was Javon saying? That they'd let those changed go? Or capture one – or more? Or what? Her mind reeled. Javon's hand on her shoulder shocked her back into the present.

"Kaz!" Javon whispered. "I need to know you can do this!"

"Yes. I'll be fine, it's just . . ." Words failed her.

"There's more to our hunting than just fighting, Kaz," whispered Javon. "And this is part of it. Go on, we won't be long." She squeezed Kazari's shoulder and then vanished into the darkness. Kazari sat on her heels for another moment, drawing deep breaths, and then pushed herself off and moved back towards the wagons. She to emulate Javon's silent movement, but eventually settled for being as quiet as she could, relieved that the wind continued to blow towards her.

As she drew closer to the wagons, she slowed, dropped to her belly, and crawled the last few metres. She squinted beneath the wagons again. The firelight had dimmed slightly, and it was quiet around the fire, but the smell of the stew was strong on the strengthening breeze. Perhaps their mouths were all too full for much talking. Kazari inched slightly further up the rise.

There was a clank, and then the rattle of metal. A foul stench assaulted Kazari's nostrils once more. Somewhere, a 'changed', or perhaps more than one, was close by. The first drops of rain began to fall, just as words came clearly on the wind.

"Give them to me," rasped a voice. A misshapen foot appeared on the steps of the caravan Kazari was looking under. Scales glinted in the firelight, and the curve of dew claws bit into the wood at the back of the step. A second foot joined the first, and then one of the fireside figures moved forward, holding a basket that clinked as the woman stepped forward and bowed.

"As you command," she said, obsequiously. All Kazari could see after that was two pairs of legs, one set human, and the other set horribly not.

"Set the circle," rasped the voice again, and the woman's legs moved off towards the fire, while other figures around the fire pushed stools away and deposited plates in a pile on the ground. They spread out around the fire, spacing themselves evenly, and faced inward. A rattling clink sounded, and the stench from the 'changed' heightened. Kazari shivered, wondering what 'setting the circle' meant – it sounded ominous. Raindrops fell like tiny icicles on her face, but then the chanting began, and Kazari shivered. The words – if words they were – were indistinct, but each one sounded cold, and the firelight dimmed to a sullen glow.

Kazari felt her heart pound even as she shivered again, goosebumps rising underneath her sleeves. She felt her hands tremble, and clenched them into fists. *Lady!* Her mind shouted the plea soundlessly, as a fog of malevolence rolled from the fire lit circle towards the feet on the steps. It wasn't just a feeling, but a darkness she could see with her eyes. Warmth bloomed on Kazari's chest, and she slammed one hand over the amethyst on its chain, while the scar that tugged at her lip tingled strongly.

She fought a gasp down, feeling herself take strength from the warmth beneath her hand, repeating words over and over inside her head: *The Lady's Hunters hear her voice in the darkness.* She let the words roll through her, just as the figure on the steps joined the chant. The fog darkened to a blackness so intense, it was as if a hole had appeared in the fabric of reality. The words of the Writings rose as a shield in Kazari's mind, and she held them as a barrier between her and the darkness.

The rasping voice shouted something unintelligible, and suddenly the blackness coalesced into a dense sphere, hovering above the fire, and then it rose, out of Kazari's line of sight, but she knew instinctively that it had hurtled towards the basket. There was a metallic rattle, as if the things in the basket had taken sudden life, and were about to leap from the wicker container. The noise rose to a crescendo and then subsided with an echoing clang that Kazari felt reverberate through her chest.

There was a great gust as the air was sucked against the prevailing wind, and then her amethyst warmed once again and she was in a pocket of calm. A moment later, the wind began to blow strongly again, riffling her short hair. It was normal wind this time, and Kazari felt a wave of relief wash over her, despite the circle of figures still chanting around the fire.

"It is done," said the rasping voice, and the dew claws withdrew from the wood of the steps, and the feet thumped down onto the ground. The legs were misshapen as well, horny growths and scales where knees and skin should have been. As the figure drew closer to the fire, more and more of it was revealed in silhouette. It was tall, with overlong arms, and a fringe of slowly moving tentacles drifting around what would once have been its waist. Memories of those who'd been changed at Suborden intruded on her mind, and she found her hand rising to her scar once more.

At last the chanting ground to a halt, and the 'changed' raised the basket high in the light of the fire, as the human figures dropped to their knees.

"They are blessed! Take them out to the masses! Use them well! The Master has spoken. Albatar will fall as foreseen!" It lowered the basket to the ground and turned. For a moment, coals glinted on the face of the thing, and something tugged at Kazari's memory, but then the moment passed and the figure was striding back to the wagon, its features hidden by the light behind it. She drew in a shuddering breath and hunched down behind the rise, trusting to the darkness and the terrain to keep her hidden.

For a moment she huddled, stunned at what she'd witnessed. She was certain she'd seen malmetal charms imbued with whatever it was that made them so insidiously dangerous. She hoped desperately that Javon would return soon. But then her amethyst warmed slightly again, and she remembered that she was *never* truly alone, no matter how deep the darkness might seem. The Lady walked side by side with her Hunters, even when they had forgotten that she did. Slightly comforted, but still wanting the familiarity of other Hunters, Kazari steeled herself to look back over the rise again.

The figures were drifting back to the fire, collapsing tiredly on the stools they'd pushed away so hastily. Perhaps the thing they'd just done had drawn something from them? They were quiet, slumping, with elbows propped on knees and heads hanging.

"Food! Now!" said the rasping voice, and one of the men clambered tiredly to his feet and staggered to the adjoining wagon. There was the sound of scrabbling feet, several yaps, and then a wave of panicked puppies poured down the steps and scattered.

The man cursed, and his arms shot out and began to scoop wriggling, terrified bodies up as they ran in all directions. Another figure joined him, and together they wrestled armfuls of squirming fur back into the van, until only one was left in the first man's arms.

He walked towards the other wagon, and Kazari drew herself down again as his feet climbed the stairs. There was the sound of the wagon door, a terrified yelp from the puppy, suddenly cut off, and then the wagon door slammed and there was silence.

Kazari fought a sudden urge to vomit, and clutched her amethyst more tightly, shuddering.

Chapter Twenty-seven: Mud

It seemed like eons until Javon reappeared with Sendar and Andiss. There had been little to see or hear after 'the circle,' as the caravaners were obviously exhausted, one by one trailing off to their wagons. The rain had begun in earnest by the time the others joined her, and lightning flickered on the horizon, hinting of worse weather to come.

"Follow," said Javon as she reappeared silently by Kazari's side. "There's much to discuss."

Shivering with cold, she followed Javon through the rain and mud, feeling washed out and emotional, until she was slogging along in a kind of dream, simply placing one foot after the other.

Eventually they reached their hidden campsite, and Kazari crawled soggily into her tent to get her pack. Rain slashed down, and she was glad of the vestibule between the tents. Dripping, she removed her boots and socks in the lantern light, and shed her soaked exterior clothing. Then she dressed herself in dry clothes, sighing gratefully as she pulled dry socks on.

There was a rustle at the tent flap, and Andiss and Sendar crawled in. Both looked exhausted. Kazari shoved her pack back into the tent, then crawled across to the other tent and extracted the other two packs. She could see Javon assembling flat bread and cheese in the open flap of their tent. She hung the sodden clothing on one of the lines between the two tents as the two men changed. Javon pushed flatbread and cheese towards Sendar and Andiss, after they'd added their outer clothing to the line. With a sigh, Sendar folded his legs beneath him and sat next to her. He smelled of warm, damp, wool, which sent a tiny wave of homesickness rushing through her. It was crowded, and the hanging wet weather gear added soggy humidity to the chilly air, but the four bodies in the enclosed space at least provided some warmth.

"Never thought I'd see a malmetal forging," Andiss said, shaking his head. "Do you think that was the only 'changed', Kaz?"

"Not sure, Andiss, but probably."

The four of them discussed what they'd seen and heard. Sendar had managed to lift Andiss to the roof of one of the wagons, but only just, and he'd then had to use his gift to 'keep hold' of Andiss while he was there, or the stiffened canvas top would have collapsed under his weight. That, and the cold and wet, explained their exhaustion. From his elevated position, Andiss had been able to see much more than the others, and he spent some time describing it in detail.

Kazari had heard more, however, but not nearly enough to be certain of what 'infiltration' meant. Eventually, they came to the conclusion that they needed to keep following the caravan. They needed more information, not the scattered snippets that alarmed but didn't inform.

Andiss and Sendar returned to their own tent to don their wet weather gear and return to the caravan, and Kazari curled up in her bag with a sigh of relief. The rain continued unabated, and lightning flickered and flashed through the treated canvas walls of the tent. Her dreams for once, weren't the nightmares that stalked her, but a confused mishmash of family, friends, and the Abbey.

She awoke to more rain, with the daylight glowing dimly through the tent's walls.

"Still raining, I see," Javon remarked.

"I doubt they'll be moving along in this," said Andiss an hour later. "Those wagons are heavy, so until the roads dry out a bit they won't be going anywhere."

"Gives us more time to find out more," Sendar said. "And at least we won't have to pack up in this." As if to punctuate his words, thunder cracked overhead.

Still, the unrelenting rain didn't absolve them of horse care. Nor did it stop them from spending time in pairs huddled in the trees around the western side of the flat field. Both Andiss and Javon had been adamant that the caravan be kept under surveillance around the clock. It made for cold, wet, and boring duty. Kazari was beginning to wonder if she'd ever feel dry again. Her cloak was waterproof, but it didn't keep her face dry, or her boots, and every time she went in or out of her tent, another layer of damp followed her.

Eventually, halfway through the third night, the rain stopped and the moon slid out from behind the clouds, bathing the landscape in unexpected brightness. Kazari was tucked behind the rise once again, this time accompanied by Sendar. The sudden cessation of rain was a relief, at least until the temperature began to plummet. It was still only early spring, and Kazari realised that they were most likely in for a sudden frost. She huddled into her cloak and tucked her gloved hands into her armpits, wishing that she was tucked up in her bedding.

As dawn approached, she wriggled to ease a cramp, and ice crackled from her cloak. "Sendar," she whispered.

"Huh?"

"I'm all icy." She moved cautiously, and the cloak unfolded stiffly, making tiny creaking sounds.

"Me too. Hang on." There were surreptitious sounds of movement next to her, and inch by inch, both of them shed the ice that had formed on their cloaks. It sounded too loud in the early morning stillness. They'd become used to the constant patter of rain and intermittent rumbles of thunder, and now the sudden stillness seemed to emphasise every sound.

There was a sound from the wagon in front of them, and Kazari realised that without the cover of the weather, they'd be exposed if they stayed where they were. Moving slowly, they withdrew to the trees on the northern border of the field, and then worked their way around the edge. By the time they'd moved into the bush on their way back to their own campsite, it was clear that the caravaners were determined to be on the move as soon as possible, even if the roads were still boggy. Perhaps they thought that the frost might have frozen the mud enough for it to remain firm under their wheels. The camp was now a hive of activity, with more people than Kazari would have credited moving about.

They hurried back to their own campsite. Kazari grimaced as she cracked the ice on a puddle, splashing her boot into the freezing water. She shivered and increased her pace, longing for a hot drink, and something hot to eat. They'd had mostly trail rations during the rainy period. Perhaps they could light a fire at last.

To Kazari's delight, Andiss and Javon were brewing hot tea over a tiny fire when they arrived back at camp.

"They're packing up," said Sendar, crouching over the fire to warm his hands.

"In that case, we've plenty of time for a decent breakfast," replied Andiss. "They'll have more trouble moving than they think."

"I'd be waiting another day, myself," said Javon, balancing the edge of the billy on her boot to tip its steaming contents into four mugs. Kazari wrapped her hands gratefully around the warm mug. "They'll be bogged in the first hour." Andiss propped a frypan on the fire, and a few moments later, the smell of sizzling bacon made Kazari's stomach rumble. Her mouth watered at the thought of hot food.

"Won't they smell it?" she asked.

"Wind's in the wrong direction," replied Andiss, "and even if they did, so what? Someone's camped on the other side of town. Or maybe it's coming from inside town." He shrugged.

"Mind you, once we've eaten, we'll have to take turns watching to see when they leave. I'm not too concerned, though, it'll take them hours to be ready, and then they're going to be moving at a crawl."

"We can pick up some provisions on the way," replied Javon. "Once they've left, it won't matter if one or two of us are seen."

Kazari heaved a silent sigh of relief. She could eat a hot breakfast, perhaps even have a brief nap, and they'd still be ready to follow the caravan. The days and nights of watching in the rain had taken their toll. She was tired, cold, slightly grumpy, and the long hours of doing nothing after the intensity of watching malmetal charms being made in front of her had left her feeling emotionally void. She just wanted to roll herself up in her bedding after a good meal, and sleep as if nothing was going on and nothing was wrong.

"You two have a rest after breakfast," said Andiss. "We'll pack up one tent, and if you get your stuff sorted, you can get a few hours in before we move. Javon and I will keep watch this morning. It'll be after midday before they move – if they decide they can of course." Then he frowned. "They must have a pressing deadline if they're off so soon."

Kazari rolled herself in her blankets and was asleep almost before she'd dropped her head, and didn't wake until Javon called her name. She was still yawning when she mounted Stumpy and squinted at the sun. It was well past midday.

Once they were under way, Andiss peeled off into Pleasance while Kazari, Sendar and Javon rode down a sidetrack. He'd scouted the caravaners earlier, and determined their heading, and he and Javon had decided that one lone Hunter was of lesser note than all four of them together.

Andiss had explained that they should arrive at the next crossroads significantly in advance of the caravan, but that the sidetrack would be impassable by the wagons. As they rode off, Kazari mused that what Andiss had so optimistically called a 'track' was much more like an overgrown game path. Stumpy picked his way carefully through overgrown grass, pockmarked by puddles and clinging mud. Still, she thought, it was better than trying to negotiate a roadway that all too soon would be scored by deep ruts.

Their progress was slow, but steady, but by the time they reached the designated crossroads, they were all mud spattered. The sun was warm, and as Kazari looked down at the mud speckling her boots and legs, she discovered that it was already drying. Hopefully dry mud would be easier to brush out when they finally stopped for the day.

They came to a halt about ten metres before their track joined the crossroads.

"Off the road, now," Javon urged, and Sendar and Kazari followed her into the trees. She led them into a closely growing thicket and dismounted. "Hobble your horses. Kaz, you organise some food, and Sendar, I want you in the trees on the verge in an hour. In the meantime, see what you can do to cover our tracks."

Kazari checked Stumpy's feet, removed what seemed like vast quantities of sticky clay from his hooves (how had he kept his feet with all that on them?) and hobbled him, still saddled, as Javon had instructed, and then set about preparing food.

"Kaz, we'll need you by the roadside to see if you can sense anything."

A few moments later, Andiss appeared through the trees, followed by Sendar. The young Hunter was carefully hiding the signs of their passage.

"I reckon they'll be a couple more hours," said Andiss. Kazari noticed that he was covered in twigs and his sweating horse had mud part way up his belly. "Followed them out of the village before coming cross-country to here." Andiss slapped his horse's neck affectionately. "He's a champion, this one!" He dismounted, and loosened the girth, before hobbling his horse and setting him to graze.

"Once we know which road they take, we'll have a better idea what our next move should be."

Chapter Twenty-eight:
Seraph

As she crouched behind a rock at the crossroads, Kazari wondered how many years of her life as a Hunter she might end up spending waiting. She was stiff, and her knees were feeling creaky. It was late afternoon, and the caravan had yet to appear. They'd seen several travellers, all riding, over the last two hours. So far, there'd been no wagons. The mud had slowly begun to crust over, but Kazari knew that the thin dried crust covered a stickiness she had no desire to experience at close quarters.

She shifted slightly, distracted, as a butterfly wandered past then paused on a blossom next to her. She watched, fascinated, as it probed the depths of the flower, before settling in to drink the new nectar. All around her, bees buzzed, butterflies bobbed, and flowers blossomed. It was as if the days of rain had accelerated the growing process. It felt strange to be hiding, awaiting a caravan containing pure evil, while crouched among such beauty. A sharp crack rent the air, and she started, attention snapping back to the road.

"Wait," breathed Andiss, cautiously moving forward to peer carefully down the road towards Pleasance. "Yes, it's them. Just watch, Kaz, nothing else. Tell us what you sense as soon as you sense it."

Kazari nodded, crouched next to Sendar, and fought the urge to lean forward to see what was happening. To distract herself, she drew in a long breath. Hints of gorgone corrupted the fresh smells of spring.

"Changed," she whispered. "More than one." Her ability to sense seemed to be developing rapidly. Each time she sensed another gorgone, her brain catalogued and stored the information. She supposed she should be grateful, because it was becoming more useful, but the frequency of gorgone exposure was rather depressing.

Andiss nodded as the caravan came into view, moving slowly. The horses were labouring, sweat streaked and heavily muddied. She wondered at the imperative that drove them to move so soon after the rain. She sniffed again, feeling her stomach roil as the smell of 'changed' grew stronger with every step the caravan drew closer.

Then she stiffened. The smell wasn't completely localised to the oncoming caravan. She turned her head side to side, trying to inhale quietly. There was something in the trees directly opposite them.

"Andiss! There's another 'changed' across the road!"

"You're certain?"

She nodded. Andiss looked at Sendar and jerked his head. Sendar's long form moved silently off into the trees.

"You're certain it's not a full gorgone?"

"It's definitely another 'changed'." The smell was imprinted deeply into her memories. She shivered slightly.

The caravan came closer, and then slowed to a stop at the crossroads, and the horses stood, heads down, blowing, legs trembling. Kazari wished she could run over and liberate them from their heavy harnesses, so evident was their distress. One of the wagon drivers stepped down from his wagon, picking his way through the mud to the signpost in the centre of the crossroads. Several others dismounted from their seats, and fanned out around the crossroads and to either side of the wagons.

Kazari shrank down behind her screen of vegetation. There was a rustle, and the smell of the 'changed' intensified. She gripped Andiss' arm, and she felt him tense in response. A woman stepped out from the trees on the other side of the crossroads. She didn't *look* 'changed', but Kazari knew without a doubt, that she was. The man in the middle of the crossroads whistled, and then another man, bearing a small clinking sack, emerged from the lead wagon.

The woman from the bushes joined them in the middle of the crossroads, and the bag changed hands without words. Kazari was squinting, trying to see what differentiated her from the other human figures, when a butterfly meandered across the road and a prehensile tongue snapped from the woman's mouth, the butterfly vanishing in an instant. Kazari was so shocked, for a moment she forgot to breathe.

Faster than she could have believed, the caravan resumed its slow movement. It was obvious that the meeting with the woman had been pre-planned. How many more times would the deadly delivery be repeated in the next hours and days? She stayed crouched by Andiss as the caravan took the road towards Seraph.

A hand touched her shoulder, and she followed Andiss silently back to join Javon, mind awash with thoughts, fears, and what-ifs.

Javon was sitting on a rock with the horses grazing around her. It was a scene of tranquillity, so at odds with what they'd just witnessed that Kazari felt disoriented, as if she'd stepped through a door into another world.

"Changed," said Andiss, shortly. "They transferred malmetal charms. Sendar's following the one who picked them up. I wonder where Elliam and Abel are. We could do with a Navigator or two right now." He sighed heavily.

"And the caravan?" asked Javon.

"Heading to Seraph, it looks like," replied Andiss.

"We wait here for Sendar, then we'll follow the caravan. Hopefully he'll have more to report," Javon said. "We can afford to let the caravan get some hours ahead of us, or even wait here overnight if required – it's not going to be moving very fast."

"But we'll miss any other drop offs!" said Kazari.

"There's only four of us, Kaz," Andiss said patiently. "If we can send a message to Alexando, he can call for reinforcements. With a bit of luck, Elliam and Abel might still be around. They're better at following unseen than we are."

It made sense, Kazari reflected. If they all went haring off in different directions, they'd have no way of letting the others know what they'd found. How could Andiss and Javon know that their decision not to follow every delivery would be the right one? What if a malmetal charm corrupted an innocent?

She frowned. "But what if they're spreading the malmetal around? How many people might it infect?" she asked.

"Kaz, it takes a certain 'type' of person to desire such a thing. It's not as if people succumb to them by accident. Most people will feel their pull, but they'll be able to throw it off as an aberration, or a wrong thought. The work of a gorgone is usually subtle – open evil alerts people to their presence. Think of it like this: to be seduced by a malmetal charm, you must already have a leaning towards evil, some failings, some nastiness. Perhaps without the charm you might not have walked down a path so evil, but it's likely you would have strayed towards it anyway." Javon's voice was quiet, but her tone was intense.

"But – that could be anyone," replied Kazari.

"Of course it could," replied Andiss, "But there are few of us who truly desire to do actual evil. And of course even those who struggle with that desire can resist it, should they simply call upon the Lady, or even seek help from those around them. People do not 'accidentally' fall into wrongdoing; they actively choose it."

Kazari still felt troubled. The idea of malmetal charms being distributed around Albatar gave her the horrors. What if someone just toying with what they thought was a pretty bauble, was influenced down the wrong path? Could that happen? What did Andiss actually mean?

"Think of it this way, Kaz," said Javon. "Remember the discussion about puppets?"

Kazari nodded.

"We are *not* puppets – not at any point in our lives. A malmetal charm can be a powerful seducer, but it cannot *force* someone to perpetuate evil. We destroy them so that those who struggle with their desires are protected, but in the end, just as we choose to follow the Lady of our own free will, so do those who follow the gorgone path."

Kazari nodded uncomfortably. Were they saying that you already had to *be* evil to be affected by a malmetal charm? Or just have the tendency towards it? Given some of the things she'd felt within herself, recently, she could have been one of them! *Protect me, Lady!* She breathed silently. And then felt stupid. She'd pledged herself to the Lady. She had tangible evidence that the Lady protected her. Clearly it wasn't as simple as her brain kept wanting to make it. She resigned herself to trying to figure it out over time. Still, she couldn't help feeling uncomfortable. Could a malmetal charm seduce her friends or family? And who would even know?

The afternoon wore on into early evening without Sendar appearing. As the light dimmed, they set their tents up and risked a small fire, fed with dry kindling from Andiss' saddle bags to minimise the smoke. Javon showed Kazari how to dig a pit and surround it with stones to hide the flickers of light from any casual observer.

"It really doesn't matter at the moment, Kaz. The caravan is long gone, and Sendar needs to be able to find us," said Javon when she voiced her concerns. "And we need a hot meal, of course, but it's a good lesson anyway." Just then, Sendar jogged into view. He looked tired and was covered in mud.

"She went towards one of the smaller villages just north of Seraph," he said. "I left her when she turned onto the main road. No cover. Thank you." He took the mug Kazari had filled and sipped. "Didn't see anyone else. She gave me the creeps, though." His hand strayed unconsciously to his amethyst.

"We'll make for Seraph in the morning, then," said Andiss decisively. "We'll pay our respects to Lord Juster, and send messages from the Cathedral."

They followed the deep wheel ruts on the slowly drying road the next morning. The struggles of the draft horses were written plainly in the cloying clay. The road was pocked with holes, and at one point it was clear that one of the horses had gone down. Around each turn in the road, Kazari expected to see either a dead horse, or the wagon train struggling along, yet as the morning progressed, it appeared that the caravan must have kept moving through the night. There were marks on the roadside at one point, where it appeared that they'd changed the horses.

At last, as the sun indicated afternoon had arrived, Javon motioned them off into the trees on the side of the road.

"They're not very far ahead now," she said to Andiss. "And neither is Seraph."

An hour later, the trees gave way to prosperous looking paddocks, peppered here and there with farmhouses. Another hour, and the paddocks gave way to houses that grew closer and closer together until they sat up against a wide stone wall surrounding the largest town Kazari had ever seen. Accustomed to her own small village, she'd thought Chator was a huge, busy place, but it was nothing compared to Seraph.

A profusion of signposted roads scattered in every direction from the city gates. It *was* a city, Kazari realised, in the same way that Athos was really a village, and Chator really a town. Great iron-studded gates stood open at a gap in the wall, where carts, wagons, and people on foot and on horse, moved back and forth in a kind of surging river. Enterprising vendors had set up small stalls in the lee of the walls, hawking food and drink to travellers, while several uniformed guards wearing cloth patches on tabards waved people in and out of the gates.

Kazari noticed the weapons carried in clear sight on their belts, something she'd never seen anywhere except among the Hunters and Navigators of the Abbey. Of course there were more dangers in Albatar than gorgones, but as the resident of what she now knew to be a small village, Kazari hadn't seen much more than the town watchman. And the watchman's most visible weapon had been his baton, which was more of a badge of office than an actual weapon, and his bell, with which he summoned help if marauding wildlife proved too much for him alone.

Stumpy didn't even flick an ear as the sounds of the bustling city assaulted Kazari. Curious gazes tracked them, as always. It seemed days since they'd ridden so openly, and Kazari felt suddenly exposed. What if they came upon the caravan? Reason reasserted itself. The caravan had no idea they were following it, or even that they existed. Surely Hunters came and went from Seraph frequently.

Hunters travelled constantly, she knew, roving through Albatar on the Lady's business. Still, all those eyes were disconcerting. Here and there, a hand raised in greeting. Andiss and Javon gave each one a grave nod, and Kazari tried to follow suit. The Hunter legends held sway even in a city the size of Seraph. She expected Andiss to lead them directly after the caravan, or to the chapel in Seraph, but instead, he took a road that wound directly away from the chunks of mud that had all too clearly fallen from the wheel rims of a wagon, and instead meandered its way through the city, gradually winding upwards.

"Are we heading to the chapel?" she asked quietly.

"Unfortunately we need to pay our respects to Lord Juster first," replied Andiss. "It's expected. And here, it's not a chapel, Kaz, it's a cathedral." He sounded amused. "I sometimes forget you've never been anywhere."

"A, a cathedral?" she asked. "What do you mean?"

"I suppose you could call it a bigger chapel," he replied. "But let's just say that it's a bit bigger than anything you've seen previously."

Kazari frowned. Did he mean bigger than the Abbey? Surely not. "And pay our respects to Lord Juster?"

"It's expected in a city, Kaz. Where there are Lords, there are politics, and I'm the Abbot's second in the Hunter Sept. I'm known here, as is Javon, and so we, and you, as our trainees, must pay our respects to the city Lord on our arrival." He sighed. "It's a bother, but there are more reasons than just courtesy, given what we've heard and seen."

She nodded slowly in reply.

"And there is the matter of etiquette, of course. Just follow my lead."

"Etiquette?"

"Politeness, if you like. We present ourselves to Lord Juster, and he officially knows we're in town. He may wish to question me regarding the alerts sent by the Abbot, or not, but at the very least, he'll want to know why we're here. The answer, of course, is that we're on a training trip, which is completely true. Hunters are always on training trips when accompanied by new inductees."

He paused briefly and smiled. "But sometimes there are other reasons too."

The road ended at the highest point in Seraph. A huge building sat on the rise, surrounded by yet another wall. This one had narrow crenelations and was topped in spiked metal. Another open gate was flanked by spotlessly uniformed guards, each wearing a red belt studded with well-polished eyelets, from which hung a long sabre. They drew to attention as the Hunters approached, and a man stepped forward, bringing a hand smartly to salute.

"Welcome, Hunters. Lord Juster awaits you in the Grand Hall. It is an honour to host the Lady's servants." His words sounded sincere and heartfelt, and Kazari felt her face reddening. She was suddenly aware that her garb was travel stained and that her boots were muddy. She followed Andiss through the gate, and towards four waiting, liveried women. Dismounting, she followed his lead, handing Stumpy's reins to one of the women, with a word of thanks.

She rubbed surreptitiously at a mud stain on her trousers as she followed the older Hunters through imposing wooden doors, side by side with Sendar, and into the interior of the building. Andiss and Javon strode confidently through a tall entrance hall and up a short flight of steps to pause before yet another metal studded door.

"Stand tall, Kaz and Sendar. You're the Lady's servant, and she bows to no man. Stay silent unless asked a direct question, and stand to our left, half a pace behind. Take the third stance," said Andiss. Without further ado, he knocked firmly on the door, which opened smoothly, and strode through, Javon only a step behind him and slightly to his right, into a hall that took Kazari's breath away. For a moment she hesitated, then she remembered Andiss' words and tried to match his confident stride, Sendar beside her.

Their boots echoed loudly on the polished stone of the floor. Light streamed through windows so high above them, that if she'd wanted to look at them, Kazari would have had to crane her neck. Tall columns stood at measured intervals down either side of the hall, each one wound with polished copper and silver that spiralled in delicate patterns around the grey stone. Tapestries to either side depicted scenes picked out in coloured thread, and at the end of the hall, a polished wooden dais was set with several large chairs.

In the centre one, a richly clad, dark-haired man sat. To his right, sat a woman, just as richly clad, and to his left, a gold robed Adviser waited, his gold chained topaz clearly evident on his chest. Behind him, stood another gold robed Adviser, clasping a number of books. Several other figures stood at the foot of the dais, most wearing the red of the guards, but more richly decorated. Kazari decided they must be officers.

She felt out of place among the richness – a crow among songbirds. The hall was splendid, but felt hollow. Even the sound of their footfalls seemed to strike empty tones. It was intimidating, and clearly designed to be so, she realised with a sudden spurt of irritation. The irritation removed a chunk of her apprehension, and Kazari's steps firmed. *The Lady bows to no man.* She *was* the Lady's servant, and as such, her emissary, or representative, and in this situation, she should feel like one.

The hall seemed endless, and some of Kazari's confidence had retreated by the time they reached the dais, and as Andiss drew to a halt, she almost didn't stop in time. She hoped no-one noticed the slight shuffle as she shifted her feet into third stance. It was a posture of poised readiness, deceiving in its solidity. The man on the dais looked down at them.

"Hunter Andiss, welcome. Hunter Javon, welcome." His voice was deep and drawling. And the two words did not seem welcoming to Kazari. "And these are?" He waved a lazy hand towards Kazari and Sendar.

"Our newest trainees, Lord Juster. Sendar and Kazari."

"Hunter Sendar, Hunter Kazari, welcome," replied the Lord, looking down at them with a slightly raised eyebrow. His mind dismissed them, quite clearly, Kazari thought, with a flush of irritation, as he went on. "And what brings you to Seraph, this time, Andiss?"

"Training, my Lord," replied Andiss. "Teaching our newest the patrolling duties of a Hunter. Improving their riding skills, and taking them places they've never been." He seemed diffident, almost casual, Kazari thought. It was at odds with the urgency of their real mission, and it troubled her. Politics, Andiss had said. If that was an excuse, then she was angry. Her memories of the poverty in which Sendar's family lived stoked that anger. This man had the power to change those things. And he hadn't. In fact, it seemed possible that he'd reaped some personal gain from it, if the wealth on his person and within the hall was anything to go by.

"Nothing more than training, Andiss? The Abbot's second?" Juster turned his head and took another look at Kazari and Sendar. "There must be more to you than meets the eye, then."

Kazari's anger spiked suddenly. Who was this man to make such a comment? She choked a hot response back down, remembering Andiss' instructions to her, but she could feel her face reddening.

"And you're from?" Juster asked – looking directly at Kazari.

"From Athos, originally," she replied, forcing her tone to remain even. "My Lord," she added hastily.

His eyebrow lifted slightly again. "A tiny place, I understand," he said. "It's no surprise Andiss feels you need a bit of travel under your belt then."

Kazari nodded, rather than trusting herself to reply in a calm voice. Her dislike of Lord Juster was growing rapidly, despite only having spent two minutes in his presence.

"And you?" he asked, looking at Sendar.

"Chator, my Lord," replied Sendar.

"Ah, yes. You were the one who went to the Hunters a year ago." He looked at Sendar thoughtfully, "From the *edge* of town, if I remember rightly."

"Come now, my Lord," said the richly dressed woman. "Don't make assumptions just because she's from a small town and he was from the *edge*. Remember, Andiss came from humble beginnings himself, and look where he is now." Kazari turned her gaze on the woman, curiously. Her words were at odds with her tone – slime dressed as honey perhaps. "*Anyone* can rise within the Order."

"You are indeed correct, my Lady," replied the Adviser. He stepped forward, and Kazari looked up curiously. The man's voice was thin, and his step unsteady, and his assistant seemed poised on his toes, as if to support the old man.

The Adviser cleared his throat and spoke again, mild reproof colouring his tones. "Our Lady sees all as equal within her sight. Some may have been called to rule, while others farm, yet within the Lady's sanctuary, each fulfils an important role." Kazari found herself nodding. The man's voice may have been thin, but his words were wise and measured, and were spoken firmly.

"Of course," replied Juster, "Thank you, Eriad." He waved a hand at the Adviser. He went on. "Will you be joining us tonight, Hunters?"

Andiss shook his head. "Unfortunately, not tonight, my Lord. I have business from the Abbot to take to the Cathedral, and these two have much to learn. We may be here for some days, so perhaps another evening?"

"*Such* a disappointment," drawled Juster. He leaned to the left, propping an elbow on the arm of his elaborate chair and resting his chin on it. "I'll await your word. And don't disappear without dining with me. There is much to catch up on." He wagged a finger, and then, as if it had been an afterthought. "Bring your trainees when you come. I'm sure they'll find the experience enlightening. Don't you think so, my love?" He waved a hand at them as he turned to his wife, and Andiss dipped his head, motioning to Kazari and Sendar with one hand.

"Of course, Lord Juster."

Kazari matched Andiss' gesture, then followed him back down the length of the hall, confused, perturbed, and angry.

Her shoulder blades itched all the way, and she couldn't wait to get out of the building. It was all she could do not to break into a jog. Dine with Juster? She wanted to run at the very thought.

Chapter Twenty-nine:
Cathedral

It was only when they were back on their horses and riding away from the great house, that Kazari felt she could ask exactly what was going on.

Andiss settled himself more firmly in his saddle and checked one of the straps on a saddle bag before answering.

"Politics, Kaz. Politics."

"But . . ."

"We'll talk about it later. Not here." He gave Javon a look that Kazari couldn't interpret, and then turned his head firmly to the front and urged his horse to a trot, forcing the others to speed up as well. She looked at Sendar, who shrugged. Kazari narrowed her eyes. She knew her life prior to the Order had been sheltered, possibly more than most, given what she'd seen in Chator, and now Seraph, but for Lord Juster to imply that she was an uneducated country bumpkin rankled her more than she cared to admit.

The fact that she knew so little about politics irritated her even more. But then she bet Lord Juster couldn't carve leather the way she could, or even attach a buckle for that matter. He probably had someone to do that for him. Imagining him struggling with a leather belt made her feel a bit better.

And his wife? She'd seemed to ooze poison under her facade of sweetness. Kazari berated herself for not trying to sense in the hall, but surely her gift would have manifested without effort had there been something to find? That seemed to be how it worked most of the time. She discovered she was grinding her teeth, and relaxed her jaw in annoyance, then apologised to Stumpy, because she'd transmitted her own tension to her clutch on the reins and he'd tossed his head. She patted his neck contritely.

As they rounded a corner, she let out an involuntary gasp. The building at the end of the street was the most elaborate structure she'd ever seen. The stonework facade towered above the neighbouring buildings, yet still managed to blend into the trees clustered around the base of it. They formed a green buffer between it and the rest of Seraph. The tops of the towers that crowned it glistened in the late afternoon sunlight, one in each sept colour. A tiny portion of her brain wondered what made the colours pop so vividly, while the rest boggled at the sheer size of the thing.

Although the sprawling Abbey with its satellite buildings would still have dwarfed it, this was just one building. One. The seven towers formed a kind of crown on the top of the build-ing – six of them around the edges and the centre one (clad in gleaming white) housing a huge bell.

"Kaz!" Andiss called.

Kazari started, and realised she'd pulled Stumpy to a halt, and the others were well in front now. She squeezed him into a walk and followed the others again, her head swivelling from side to side, trying to comprehend why the building needed to be so big. She dismounted in a daze, her eyes dazzled by the carved stone at the cathedral entrance, which was gilded with gold and silver. Juster's hall may have been designed to awe, but this building . . . She wasn't sure whether to laugh or exclaim in horror.

"You can laugh if you want," said Andiss. "I did, the first time I saw it."

"But . . ." was all Kazari managed.

"It's not quite what you were expecting?" Javon asked, wryly.

"It's . . ." Once again words failed her, so she resorted to shaking her head.

"Not quite what you envisaged for the Servants of the Lady?" said Andiss.

She shook her head mutely. Of course the Abbey was quite grand, or at least in spots it was. The sanctuary for example. But this? It almost made her eyes hurt to look at it.

"It actually began life as a fortress," said Andiss. "But Juster's grandmother got to it about sixty years ago. She said – according to the records kept by the prior at the time – 'That the Lady deserved a place that reflected her glory.'"

"Her g . . . glory?" Kazari stuttered. Glory wasn't the word she'd have used.

"It appears that the Lady's servants and the old Lady of Seraph had differing ideas on the interpretation of that particular word," said Andiss. "Still, the beds are comfortable, and the grounds are marvellous. There's even a grove here. Back behind the main building. You'll probably be relieved to hear we're accommodated in something a little less grand?"

"Yes?" she replied, still bemused. She looked at Sendar. He was clearly amused, which suggested this was not the first time he'd been in the place.

"I'll give you the whole tour, later," said Andiss, grinning openly now. "You won't believe what the sanctuary's like."

"But . . ." stammered Kazari at last. "The Lady . . . surely she wouldn't want this?" She waved a hand at the gold and silver ornamentation. Andiss' face sobered.

"The Lady has more uses than decoration for gold and silver, but *politics* tells us that sometimes we must put up with things like this monstrosity to continue to pursue the greater good."

Just what Andiss meant, Kazari discovered later. Inside the building was more elaborate ornamentation, but when she queried the gold and silver figurines set in niches around the sanctuary, he led her over to one of them and showed her that the outer shell was a facade. "Over the years, one statue at a time, we've copied them, and the metal has been put to better use. It's a secret of the Order, now entrusted to you." Then he'd smiled. "But Juster doesn't know that."

Kazari was relieved to know that her Order had managed to maintain its integrity. "But . . . the people?" she queried.

Andiss shrugged. "Many people believe that the Lady should be worshipped among 'finery' worthy of her."

"But . . ." Kazari began again, but Javon shook her head.

"It's complicated, Kaz. In most places, people are just happy to live in Albatar, under the Lady's protection, and the protection of her Order. There are some, however, who equate outward displays of wealth with power. Sometimes a building like this is useful for such people. We'd prefer it wasn't so, but we use what we're given when we need to, even if that means displaying the *outward* trappings of wealth on occasion."

Kazari heard Sendar suppress a snort of laughter, and then followed him out of the sanctuary and to the quarters reserved for them. As Andiss had said, they were comfortable – probably the most comfortable she'd stayed in since leaving her own bed in the Abbey.

"You said you'd explain," said Kazari.

"And I will," replied Andiss, "But first, we need to train."

Two hours later, Kazari washed the sweat from her body in the lavish bathroom attached to their quarters and then followed the others into the cathedral dining hall. Andiss hadn't yet answered her questions, and she was almost seething with impatience. Hopefully once the dinner was over, he'd keep his promise. She was dressed in her last clean set of Hunter blacks, and at Andiss' instruction, she'd placed her dirty sets in a large bin for laundering. Relishing the feel of clean, dry clothing, she took a chair at one of the long tables set at right angles to the head table. The set-up mimicked that of the Abbey, and some of her irritation eased.

Not all the tables were set, but a good number were, and after a quick count, Kazari realised that Seraph must have quite a contingent of the Lady's servants there. Again, she felt a bit stupid. Of course it did. It was a city. The population was large. The Lady's Healers, Intercessors, Jurists, and Advisers would have a lot to do in a town this size.

A clattering in the hall outside heralded the arrival of what seemed like a crowd of the Lady's servants. Chairs scraped and clunked, and Kazari saw the familiar black of Hunter garb take the chairs opposite them. When she looked up, she recognised Mikel and Jern, clearly back from Suborden. She was about to speak to them when the prior stood and began to speak the blessing.

Suddenly cheered by the familiar, Kazari felt as if she'd come home. The words rolled over her like a wave, and she realised that she'd missed being with a large group more than she'd expected. It wasn't as if she didn't like journeying with Andiss, Javon, and Sendar; it was just that being among a large group of those who'd taken the same vows and made the same promises, lifted the experience to a whole new level.

When the food was passed around, she leaned in to listen to Andiss talk to Mikel and Jern.

"I have letters from the Abbot," Mikel said.

"For us specifically?" Andiss asked.

"One," replied Mikel, "and a general letter for any Hunter. I'll give you copies in case you meet any of our fellows on your travels." He looked around. "And I have news from Suborden. The Abbot sent a group to replace us. There'll be Hunters rotating in and out of course, but there's also three Intercessors, an Adviser, and two pairs of Navigators stationed there. It's better than it was, but it's still a sad place."

Kazari nodded, remembering. She wondered what Suborden looked like in spring. Her mind struggled to equate colour and exuberance with a town that would forever remind her of some of the darkest days of her life. She looked down at her plate, lost in the memories for a moment, until a warm hand on her shoulder brought her back into the warmth of the dining hall.

"You did well there, Kaz." It was Jern. Normally overshadowed by Mikel's forceful personality, she had a smile that warmed Kazari. Surprised, Kazari threw a quick smile back.

"Join us in our quarters after the meal," said Andiss. "We've much to discuss, and I'd like that letter as soon as possible."

The rest of the meal passed in normal chatter – stories from their travels, news from various places Kazari hadn't been to but the others had, and now and then, one or more of the Lady's other servants would stop by with a greeting for Andiss and Javon, and an introduction to Sendar and Kazari.

When they rose at the end of the meal, the sung response to the prior's words almost brought tears to Kazari's eyes. It was as if some of the weight of seeing and hearing evil in the flesh, had lifted from her shoulders. Once, she'd wondered why the Hunters returned so regularly to the Abbey. Now she understood. Time with others from the Order, no matter how brief, was like a long, refreshing drink, that poured calm on her soul.

Once inside their quarters, Mikel produced two letters, handing one to Andiss and Javon, and the other to Kazari and Sendar. Kazari opened the stiff folds and began to read:

My Hunters,

It appears that evil stalks our borders and has entered our towns. Our Lady's refuge, our beloved land of Albatar, is at risk. There has been an incursion in Suborden, and only by the Grace of the Lady was it discovered and overcome before it became a beachhead for the enemy. It is now a warning to us all.

The Lady has seen fit to grant the Gift of Sensing in this most dangerous of times. Its use is not yet well understood, but should you hear word of it in your travels, or find any reference to it within the libraries of Albatar, forward the information with all haste to the Abbey, or to Alexando in Chator. Should you encounter gorgones of any type, report them once you have dispatched them, via the usual methods.

The Hunter Sept is now on full alert status. You have your assigned duties. Be about them as soon as you receive this missive.

The Lady reminds us that we stand in the breach for Albatar. You walk with her all your days, and she will be with you always.

Signed by my hand: Injani of the Hunter Sept, Abbot of Austral Abbey and all Albatar, this tenth day of spring'

Kazari wondered what the 'assigned duties' meant. She supposed that had she been with the Order for longer, she'd know. As it was, it was yet another question she itched to ask. But Andiss was still head down with Javon over the other letter. She folded the stiff page again, placed it by Javon's hand, and waited silently for him to finish.

Mikel was, as was his habit, sharpening a knife, sitting cross-legged on the floor, while Jern had propped her long form in a chair next to the dresser. Sighing, Kazari copied Mikel. Andiss and Javon would speak when they would, and not before. At least sharpening her knives gave her something to do while she waited.

At last, Andiss put the paper down, looked at Javon with concern written across his face, and picked up the Abbot's more general missive. Then he ran a hand through his hair and sighed. "There are more worrying rumours from a number of towns. Kazari, Sendar – your dreams, have they changed?" Startled, Kazari exchanged a quick glance with Sendar and shook her head, and then after a few more moments thought, shook it again, more firmly.

"No, nothing different, just the same stuff."

"Dreams?" queried Jern, surprising Kazari by beating Mikel to the question.

Javon took a moment to explain, while Kazari watched the shock blossom on first Mikel, and then Jern's faces. Shame-facedly, she looked down at the knife she'd been sharpening.

"But this . . . is a wonderful opportunity," said Mikel, star-tling Kazari so much she nearly cut herself on the knife.

"What?" she blurted.

"Early warning!" exclaimed Jern. "If your dreams change, we might be able to get a jump on the next bit of nastiness."

Kazari coloured slightly. "They don't make a lot of sense, most of the time, and they're pretty well confined to horrible things happening to people I know and love. I'm not sure how much help that really is."

"But *any* kind of warning is better than none," Mikel said. He tucked his knife away and stretched out his legs, leaning back on his hands.

"The problem is, we don't know how far ahead the warning applies, or what it refers to," Andiss said.

"But there are three marked now," Jern said. "Surely if you compare dreams, there'll be something."

Sendar shrugged. "Not so far." Then he added. "But we write it all down, and it makes some of the nightmares a little more bearable."

Jern looked slightly ashamed. "I'm sorry, Sendar, I hadn't really thought about that."

There was silence for a moment or two, and then Andiss went on. "The Abbot sends word that a number of our Advisers have reported trouble with their nobles. And reports from incumbents speak of resistance to teaching among the young in some areas." He looked grave. "Albatar is indeed at risk should we not discover how the gorgones have penetrated this far into our haven."

"This far?" asked Mikel.

Andiss nodded. "We have encountered the 'changed' again. There is at least one here, within the city itself."

Mikel pulled another knife from his boot and began to sharpen it with long, steady strokes. "Then you may rest assured that Jern and I will assist in any way we are able. Our assigned duties have us here until the Abbot orders otherwise. Have you spoken with Eriad yet?"

"Not yet. Tomorrow perhaps," said Andiss. "And at some point, we have to dine with Juster." He made a face. "We were unable to avoid it."

Jern grimaced. "There's something wrong with that man." Then she looked questioningly at Kazari.

"Not that I could tell," she replied. "And yes, even after spending only a few moments in his company, that does surprise me."

Jern laughed, a wholesome sound that filled the whole room and warmed Kazari.

"The records warn us of many things," Andiss said. "And some of those things are human beings who remain human, despite their evil. They have no need to 'change' in order to bring destruction."

"Can you two focus on tracking down that caravan? I'm afraid, given Juster's interest, that the rest of us are a little too obvious. And I think we'd better get the dinner over and done with as soon as possible so he can get back to ignoring us. Politics." He shook his head in disgust.

"Politics – you keep saying that, and not explaining it," said Kazari, slightly exasperated.

"Politics is the art of saying one thing while meaning something completely different," said Andiss.

"And lying without lying," said Mikel.

"While smiling and sticking a knife into your back." Jern rolled her eyes. "Sometimes it's not that bad, but there are always meanings inside meanings. Does my head in."

"Then what really went on this afternoon?" Kazari asked.

Javon sighed heavily. "As you know, Albatar was founded as a refuge."

Kazari nodded impatiently.

"That was many, many years ago now, and many generations. Our towns were established one by one, each cared for by a noble appointed by the Order, under the guidance of the Lady. Eventually those appointments become hereditary, despite the Order's wishes, and the now royal family have overall control."

Kazari nodded again. She'd learned all that at school.

"Over the generations, we've experienced many incursions. All have been repulsed. The Order and the secular authorities stood in unity and strength against each one, and we have always prevailed. But it has been over a hundred years since the last incursion."

"But there have always been gorgones, here and there, even in Albatar." Kazari was confused.

"Wherever there is human selfishness there will be things such as suckers," Mikel said, "but greater gorgones? No, not in Albatar, or at least not in *central* Albatar. There are always occasional greater gorgones on the borders."

"But now, there *are* greater gorgones within Albatar," Kazari said.

"And now, for the first time in our history, we have a number of city nobles deliberately playing politics with the Order," Andiss said wearily. "Don't misunderstand me, there have always been politics – it's why we have Advisers – but these politics are different. They're not about squabbles, or disagreements between towns, or regions, this time they're about the very things upon which Albatar was founded."

"Some of the Lords and Ladies argue that the threat to Albatar is over, and some, here and there, have queried whether there was ever a threat," said Javon.

The words fell heavily into the room. Kazari was incredulous.

"But . . . but . . ." she gestured wordlessly. She'd *fought* gorgones, trained on suckers, and had seen how much horror and havoc they could wreak.

"You see, Kaz, in some ways we've done our job so well that the average person in Albatar has never encountered a gorgone, or even met someone who has. For many, they're the mythical monster hiding under the bed, used by pedants to frighten children into good behaviour."

"But our *history*!" she burst out.

"There are some – like Lord Juster – who accuse the Order of fabricating some of it. Or of overemphasising the dangers. Or suggest that our histories are just analogies – myths, if you like."

Kazari was wordless.

"And then there's the fact that within the Order, anyone might rise to become a sept leader, an abbot, or a prior. You heard the way Juster dismissed you at the beginning. To him, you were just an ignorant youngster from a provincial village, and Sendar comes from 'the wrong part' of Chator. Prior to your induction to the Order, you were able to be ignored from the lofty height of his Lordship – you didn't exist. But now, as Hunters, the two of you have significant social status under Albatar's laws – even as trainees."

Javon went on. "As Andiss said when we entered Juster's hall – the Lady bows for no man. She is above pettiness and politics, and we are Her servants. What we do is enshrined in Albatar's most ancient laws."

Andiss tapped the thick paper of the letters.

"Juster, and those like him, resent this. They believe that the Order exercises too much power within Albatar. In some ways I wish I had gone to meet him alone, but he would have heard exactly how many Hunters had entered the city, and it's best to be obvious in our dealings with such a man. Unfortunately, you'll now have to endure a state dinner and cope with the vile political manoeuvring so often found at such functions. And he's taken notice of both of you in a way I'd rather he hadn't."

"You see," Mikel elaborated. "Some of our nobles believe in their own superiority, choosing to think that due to the accident of birth, and their city location, they are more than those who are born otherwise."

"And that's what we're about to drop both of you into," said Andiss ruefully.

"Oh."

"And we really don't have the time."

Chapter Thirty:
Dinner

Kazari stared down at the array of cutlery on the pristine white tablecloth. She was seated on the right of Andiss at Lord Juster's high table. Andiss, in turn, sat to the right of Juster, with Ralen beyond Juster, and Eriad, the aged Adviser, to her left. Sendar and Javon were beyond Eriad. Inside her head, she recited Mikel's advice: "Start from the outside and work in."

Mikel had been surprisingly knowledgeable about cutlery, etiquette, and social occasions, to her surprise.

"Despite politics, or perhaps I should say *in spite* of politics, children of Albatar's rulers also make their choice," he'd said, and explained that he was one of eight children born into a ruling family in northern Albatar. He'd grown up attending formal dinners. "And don't forget to use the serviette, and always avoid the wine."

Kazari gave the array of glasses in front of her a dubious glance. Only one was full, and it certainly wasn't water as far as she could tell. To her right sat one of Juster's ranking soldiers – high ranking if the elaborate epaulets were anything to go by. She'd introduced herself only as Siap, before directing her attention to the man on her other side. Kazari felt left out, awkward, and uncomfortable. And she was certain the placing was deliberate, and intended to make her feel ill-at-ease.

The murmur of voices ceased abruptly as Juster rose, glass in hand.

"Welcome all, and a special welcome to our visitors; Andiss, second in the Hunter Sept of The Lady's Order, emissary of the Abbot, and defender of Albatar. Also welcome; Hunter Javon, and the new Hunter novices, Kazari and Sendar. Join me as we drink to our brave defenders." He raised his glass, and as one the hall stood, while Kazari shot a sideways glance at Andiss. The older Hunter sat stoically, hands resting on the table. He inclined his head just once as Juster went on, "To our defenders," and drank. Fortunately, Kazari hadn't picked up her own glass. She hastily followed Andiss' lead, inclining her head, even as her face reddened. She did not enjoy being the centre of attention, particularly the centre of attention at this particular dinner. Hopefully, that would be the extent of the attention from the Lord and Lady of Seraph for the evening.

"Be welcome, and at rest," said Juster, turning towards them. "My table is yours for tonight. Be sure to pass my greetings to the Abbot when you return to the Abbey. We welcome our brave defenders to Seraph. Eriad – will you speak the blessing?"

The old Adviser rose as Juster sat. Kazari bowed her head as Eriad spoke a simple blessing, and then more food than she'd ever seen in her life came dish by dish into the hall. There was a clatter of cutlery and crockery, and the dinner began. Course followed course, accompanied by wines, ales and other drinks Kazari had never heard of.

Once she'd figured out which was the water glass, she restricted herself to it alone, occasionally casting surreptitious glances at Andiss to be certain she had the right cutlery for each course. To her relief, she was largely ignored, until after the last course, a platter of fruit and cheese – mercifully simple after the rich dishes preceding it. She'd eaten a little of everything, but forewarned by Mikel, she'd restricted herself to small helpings, or eaten only part of each serving. Still, despite a healthy appetite, she felt stuffed, and was desperately wishing she could go back to the bed awaiting her in the cathedral. Or at least take a short walk in some fresh air.

The night seemed interminably long. She'd caught snatches of the conversation between Andiss, Javon, and Juster. Even those tiny snippets seemed guarded – on Andiss' part – or barbed – from Juster. She was glad he'd left her alone. She looked across at Sendar. He was composed, but there was resignation in his expression as he replied to a comment from the man to his left.

The woman on Kazari's right had continued to pay all her attention to the dinner companion on her other side, so Kazari had spent most of her time eating her food in tiny bites, while looking around the hall, unable to avoid noticing its gaudy grandeur. For a Lord whose surrounding villages demonstrated poverty, he certainly lived in style. She didn't understand how he countenanced it, but then, she suspected that he didn't actually care, if what she'd observed was anything to go by.

The hall was full. Men and women wearing elaborately embroidered clothing made of rich cloth, and adorned with gems and precious metal, sat in rows. They chattered like flocks of the colourful lorikeets that fed from Albatar's wildflowers. In fact, as Kazari watched them, she was hard pressed not to snigger. She could imagine them squabbling, as the lorikeets so often did, over the choicest morsels. Idly, she picked a strawberry off the plate in front of her, regarding its deep colours with appreciation. When she bit into it, it was as delicious as she'd imagined. Perhaps Juster had a greenhouse, where such things grew this early in the spring.

"Kazari," said a smooth voice from behind her right elbow. Kazari started and looked up. It was Ralen, Juster's wife. The woman was wearing a long tabard embroidered with gold thread that shimmered in the light of the multitude of lamps set around the hall.

"M . . . my Lady?"

Ralen made a gesture and the woman next to Kazari stood up and vacated her seat and to Kazari's horror, Ralen sat down next to her.

"So, what did you think of our little dinner, young Hunter?"

"It was delicious, my Lady," replied Kazari, carefully keeping the irritation from her voice. Young Hunter indeed. By her side, she felt rather than saw, Andiss move slightly. "My thanks for the invitation."

Ralen smiled at her, as if she was rewarding Kazari. Irritation flared again, but she squashed it vigorously and made herself smile back. She felt a little like a crow to Ralen's songbird. Her own Hunter garb was comfortable, but utilitarian, and Ralen was quite obviously dressed to impress. Still, the Lady's amethyst hung on its cord from Kazari's neck, and its rich hue meant more to her than all the gold thread in Albatar.

"You must join us again, Kazari. If you're in Seraph long enough, that is." An eyebrow rose inquiringly.

"That will depend on Andiss and Javon, my Lady."

"Oh, of course it will. Do you know what you'll be doing within our city?"

"I'm not sure, my Lady, it depends on many things, and how fast we learn."

"Such a pity Andiss and Javon will be so occupied while you're here," mused Ralen. "We've known each other for years, have we not, Andiss?"

Surprised, Kazari looked at Andiss, who'd now turned sideways in his chair. His expression was inscrutable.

"It is many years since our school days, my Lady."

"Many, Andiss?" she laughed, a light tinkling sound that somehow chilled Kazari to her core. "Many is perhaps not a word I might have used. *Some*, perhaps, but not *many*."

Icicles might have been warmer than the last word, and Kazari stammered the first thing that came into her mind, anxious to divert the woman's attention.

"It was a very elaborate dinner, my Lady." She waved a hand at what was left of the food.

"Nothing at all, really, just a trifle. Once the weather's warmer, we'll have much more to choose from." The woman dismissed the subject with a wave of a hand. "But Andiss, is it not delightful to catch up with old friends? Surely that is reason enough for us to dine in state?"

"My Lady, catching up with old friends is always delightful," replied Andiss. "But a state dinner is not usually the place to do the 'catching up.'"

"Well, perhaps you'll just have to 'catch up' with me at a less formal occasion? Perhaps tomorrow? In the gardens?"

"We'll be occupied tomorrow, I'm afraid, my Lady," replied Andiss.

Kazari felt as if there was a second conversation going on above her head, one with a subtle subtext.

"Ah yes, Kazari and Sendar." The woman turned her attention to back to Kazari as if she'd momentarily forgotten she'd existed. "The Hunter's garb suits you, young one. But whatever happened here?" The woman's hand had risen without Kazari realising, and was touching the side of her face, along the scar. Kazari flinched away from the woman's touch.

"A . . . a training accident, my Lady," she stammered. And then her own hand was tracing the scar. She snatched it down.

"A training accident?"

Andiss shrugged. "The Lady's Hunters train with edged weapons, my Lady. Sometimes accidents happen."

"But her face – it would have been so pretty without the scar. Surely your Healers could do something? I've seen some of the miracles they've wrought." Her words were smooth, but all of a sudden, Kazari could hear the question beneath them. She froze.

"When there are greater needs, a scar is a small thing. We Hunters regard scars as honourable badges. A tiny thing in our service to the Lady."

Kazari almost let out a sigh of relief, but the woman was resting her hand on her shoulder and might feel it. Andiss hadn't lied, but he certainly hadn't told the whole truth.

"But still," Ralen's hand wandered up to the scar again, and this time Kazari forced herself to stay still, "such a pretty face. What a shame."

Kazari wanted to slap the woman. She was much more than 'a pretty face.' If that was what drove this woman, then the sooner they left her company and the sooner they left Seraph, the better. But they couldn't – at least, not until they knew where the caravan had ended up.

"So, Kazari, would you like a tour of the manor? We have many wonderful historical paintings, and many from the Order come to study them," said Ralen. She let her hand drop. "Andiss, you stay here, and I'll show Kazari the sights." She pushed her chair back, and stood, beckoning Kazari to follow her. Kazari looked at Andiss, willing him to forbid her, but he nodded.

"That would be wonderful, my Lady. Be sure to show Kazari the murals on the second floor. Kaz, they're marvellous. Take note of the third one from the staircase." He clapped her on the shoulder, tightening his hand briefly, in what she took for a signal to be careful with her tongue, and turned back to Juster, who was now talking to Eriad and Javon.

Kazari stood resignedly and followed Ralen down the length of the high table. During the conversation, the hall had largely emptied out, and there were few people left at the long tables set at right angles to her own. Ralen was silent as she led Kazari from the room, and to the bottom of a grand staircase.

"I'm sure you've been told that the manor began life as a fortress?"

Kazari nodded.

"If you look closely, you'll see that the wood on the staircase covers the old stone base. This was the centre of the main keep. This staircase links each level. This was once a separate building, but it's been some centuries since our ancestors fled here, and each succeeding generation has built further out. Still, if you look to either side as you climb, you'll see the old arrow slits. Nowadays we mainly use them as decorative niches. They open out only onto other rooms now." She began to climb the stairs.

They were steeper than Kazari had realised, but the woman ascended them easily, moving with a trained grace. She was much fitter than her frivolous garb suggested. At the first-floor exit, she pointed out sleeping chambers, and small reception rooms. "For the family." They left the staircase on the second floor, and Kazari began to wonder why the woman wanted to show her around. Surely she had better things to do. Still, the information was interesting, and the reorganisation of the old keep into a grand house was fascinating, if rather at odds with the original purpose of the building. Kazari found herself picturing the original building in her mind, surrounded by the Lady's enemies. She shivered slightly.

"These are the murals Andiss mentioned," Ralen said. "They tell our history. Of course, that was a long time ago. Scholars from the Abbey often study them, but nowadays only those who have sworn their lives to the Lady seem to find these old things interesting." She drew Kazari down the hallway, gesturing to the murals. This part of the building had no covering of wood or cloth, and Kazari could see that the murals had been carved into the very stone of the keep itself. They must be ancient, she thought, stepping closer to examine one of them.

It was an image of the crossing into Albatar. She'd seen variations of it on the Abbey wall, and in the various texts she'd studied at the Abbey. This one appeared to have been modelled on one of the classics she'd seen represented in a textbook in the Abbey library. Then she did a double take. The stone of the keep was ancient, and she realised that it was more likely that the textbook image had been a reproduction of this original. As she looked more closely, she could see that the once vibrant colours had somehow been etched into the stone itself, and the mural was now chipped in some patches, faded in others.

Navigators led the column of refugees, clearly fleeing from a horde of ravening gorgones. At the rear of the column, Hunters stood ranked in rows, their amethysts gleaming from their chests, and Kazari saw that each of the stones was actually a real gemstone. She bent forward to examine the mural more closely. Each of the Servants of the Lady had a real gemstone set into the stone. Diamonds sparkled on the breasts of Intercessors, spaced around the sides of the fleeing people, while among them, flashes of ruby signalled the presence of Healers ministering to the injured and infirm.

Aquamarines glowed brightly on the Navigators at the forefront of the column. While Growers, bearing emeralds, kneeled on the edge of the chasm urging vines to span its width in a sturdy bridge. Advisers flanked the leaders of the people, golden topazes flaring with the urgency of their pleas, while the sapphires of the Judicial sept glinted deep blue as in turn, they attended the Abbot of the time, raised from their own sept, and carried small children.

It was a great work of art, every line carved in the stone wall radiating the urgency of the moment. The artist had depicted the Lady's rainbow of colour arching over the green bridge, and flaring into brightness that illuminated the Hunters fighting as the rear guard.

It took her breath away, and she stood transfixed, the scene brought to life in her mind. She could feel the strain and fatigue in the Hunters' stances. She could hear the cries and moans of the injured, and feel the urgency with which the Growers worked, while the Navigators, Judicars and Healers urged the people onward. In her mind's eye, she saw the Navigators fall back to join the Hunters as the first of the refugees set foot on the bridge. Arrows flew thick and fast, arcing into the gorgone-horde as it scuttled and scrambled towards the border.

She remembered the first time she'd heard the story – told by her father one night when she was a small child – and realised that it was then she'd first had an inkling of the Lady's call. And now, here in this building, she relived the moment from her history, so starkly portrayed in the stories, and now given life by a slowly fading mural in a building bastardised by a lord whose ethics seemed to stand against everything the Lady and her Order stood for.

She took a deep breath, closed her eyes briefly, and sent words of thanks winging silently to the Lady, for this timely reminder. Ralen's cultured voice, as she spoke, sounded almost like an ugly parody.

"What is it that you see, little Hunter?" she asked, curiously. "Each time one of you comes here, I see the same thing. You look, and for moments it's as if you're elsewhere."

"It's a stark reminder, my Lady, of what was, and what must never be again. This is the Lady's sanctuary, and we are her people," said Kazari, after a moment's reflection. She almost added more: *And you, and your husband stray far from her. Can you not see this, and look after her people as you are meant to?* But she thought better of it and squashed the words back down. But the thoughts stoked her anger, and she was hard pressed not to frown. *Little Hunter, indeed!*

"Of course," replied Ralen smoothly. "Such an important thing to remember. I see it every day, you see, so perhaps I see the details less clearly. Please, follow me, and you'll be able to see the rest of the murals." Kazari followed the woman from room to room, still wondering why the woman was spending so much time with her. Then the questions began, almost like an afterthought to a comment.

"If you'll look to your left now, Kazari, you'll see an image of the first Lord here – Kerigan, a Lady of the first wave. She's Juster's ancestor of course, many generations removed. And you're from Athos yourself? Such an old town, if small. Tell me more about it." A little later, the next question came.

"See here the family tree tapestry. We keep it updated – you'll see where the stitching is old and new. You can see many names from the first wave, of course. Which wave did your family come from?"

One by one the questions popped out, all related, or apparently related to the topic of the current artwork or a snippet of history. The woman was delving into Kazari's history, her family, and her background. She was also trying to find out more about the Abbey's inner workings, Kazari decided after they'd looked at a tapestry depicting a 'choosing' ceremony. Of course, the general populace knew about the Gifts of Healing, and those of Growing, perhaps not all the particulars, but at least in general. And Ralen at least, suspected there were more in other septs.

Why she wanted to know about them was another question. It could be idle curiosity, but Kazari discarded that thought almost immediately. The woman never asked anything directly, but alluded to things in a roundabout fashion, always keeping her queries general, but making them difficult to answer in anything but a specific fashion. By the end of the tour, Kazari was exhausted and wrung out from prevaricating, and was wishing for some of the eloquence of an Adviser. Some of the later queries had verged on Abbey policies, of which Kazari realised, she knew more than she'd thought. She had been hard pressed not to accidentally say more than she should.

When the door of the dining hall came into view again, she was so relieved she increased her pace without realising, and Ralen had had to hurry to keep up with her. As they entered, Andiss rose, beckoning to Javon and Sendar.

"Ah, they're back. We must be off, my Lord. There is much for us to do tomorrow." He tilted his head towards Juster slightly. "Training takes time, as I'm sure you can imagine, and Kazari is still very new to the Order, and Sendar also has much to learn. My thanks for your offer. We'll take advantage of it tomorrow afternoon. And my Lady Ralen, thank you for showing Kazari the manor house. There is much of interest here to one of the Lady's servants." With that they took their leave, and Kazari followed the older Hunters thankfully from the room.

This time she knew better than to discuss anything until they were well down the road. At last, when Andiss, who could clearly sense Kazari's growing discomfort, nodded, she nearly fainted with relief.

"She tried to find out everything there is about me, Andiss! And what the Abbot thinks about pretty well everything! And what we're *really* doing here!"

"I thought as much. Did you tell her much?" he replied.

"I don't think so," sighed Kazari. "Why did you let her take me alone?"

"Politics, Kaz. And I judged you were up for the task."

"Barely. Thank heavens I'm not an Adviser!" she sputtered. "And you're going to ask me exactly what she asked, aren't you?"

Andiss smiled at her, and nodded. "Of course I am, but not until we get back to the cathedral. And I'll tell you all what Juster tried to get out of me, and what I got out of him." He smiled in a self-satisfied manner and refused to say any more until they were back at the cathedral.

Chapter Thirty-one:
Spectacle

"Juster's taking a very unhealthy interest in the Abbey's affairs. He's also hinting that Eriad is too old, and should be replaced. But not replaced by an Adviser from the Abbey, but rather by one of his own sycophants." The words fell into an aghast silence in the sitting room allotted to the Hunters at the cathedral. Kazari had tucked herself up on one of the large chairs, sitting with her legs crossed and her hands wrapped around a large mug of tea. Exhausted by Ralen's questions, her eyelids had been drooping until Andiss' words penetrated.

"What?" exclaimed Mikel. "His own – that's not how the charter works!"

"That's impossible, isn't it?" asked Jern. "I mean, our laws . . ."

"Are not as watertight as we thought," replied Andiss. "They only say 'Adviser' not 'the Lady's Adviser.'"

"But . . ." spluttered Mikel.

"We need a legist to look at the exact wording of course, but I'm fairly certain he wouldn't have mentioned it unless he felt that the option was potentially valid."

"This is what the Abbot was afraid of," said Mikel. "When she asked us to keep our eyes and ears out." He sighed heavily. "We've all seen the signs of course. There have always been a few who believe that the gorgone threat is small, or past, or impossible, but now the numbers seem to be growing. It's not that they're evil, or corrupt even. They've simply decided not to believe, or that the threat is over. Complacency is the worst threat we have – particularly on what appears to be the eve of a major incursion." He thumped a frustrated fist into the arm of his chair, startling Kazari.

"We'll send word in the morning," said Andiss. "Kaz, you sensed nothing?"

Kazari shook her head and sipped her tea tiredly.

"And Ralen was digging into your background?"

"Among other things," Kazari replied. "She wanted to know which wave my family came in – that kind of thing. But also what I know about the Abbot's directions, and Abbey stuff. And I think she wanted to know about our Gifts."

"Our Gifts?" asked Sendar.

"She kept alluding to the Healers' Gifts, and the Growers', and she clearly knows something about the Advisers' Gifts." Kazari shrugged. "I suppose she's extrapolated that we have them too."

"What did you say?" Andiss' tone was urgent.

"Nothing, really. I sort of 'misunderstood' what she was asking, when it came up. I think she believed me, or at least thinks I don't know anything. And anyway, why do we keep them quiet?" That was something she'd always wondered about.

"To avoid frightening the general populace," replied Jern, easily. "I mean, you must know how they look at Hunters already. Think about how they'd look at us if they knew some of the other things."

It made sense, Kazari reflected. Still, the Abbey had kept the secrets for hundreds of years, quite successfully, it appeared, but Juster and Ralen couldn't be the only ones who wondered, given the Healers and the Growers. She was about to make the point, when Mikel spoke again.

"And over the years, people have suspected, or know about them, but most of the time they're people who can be persuaded to keep things quiet for the good of Albatar. And we always choose neither to confirm nor deny their presence." He shrugged. "People can be a bit funny about those of us who choose the Lady anyway. Usually they put our occasional oddities down to that. They expect us to be different – particularly the Hunters – but at the same time we're not obvious in the way Healers and Growers are. Except when we're fighting gorgones, of course, and the general populace doesn't usually see that, or if they do, they don't care how we get the job done."

Of course, he was right, reflected Kazari. She'd had no hints of Hunter Gifts until after she joined the Order.

"This 'wave' thing, though," said Jern with a frown. "We've heard it mentioned a few times since we left Suborden. It seems to be becoming a mark of social status. The earlier the wave, the more status."

"So that's why she was asking?" said Kazari.

"Probably. It's part of the general disaffection with the things of the Lady," replied Mikel.

"Some people feel a need to be more important than others," said Andiss, "so they invent reasons if they have to. In the end, anything like that is simply an accident of birth. It's a weakness of our system, that we've allowed for hereditary nobles, in my opinion. At least within the Order we've stayed true to the Lady's ideals."

He poured himself another cup of tea, and waved the pot at the others.

"Kaz, Sendar, we'll be training tomorrow. First in the grove, and then I'm going to run you ragged up at the manor. Juster offered some of his soldiers for sparring practice. I couldn't refuse, so we may as well take advantage of it, and you do need practice facing those who haven't trained as Hunters."

Kazari looked at him with horror. She was going to spar with soldiers? As relatively untrained as she was? She couldn't imagine anything worse. "What?" she said, stupidly, blood rushing to her face.

"Look, it's pretty good practice for the two of you. Of course you'll have to avoid using your Gifts while you do it. No use of Dance or Anticipation."

Kazari looked at Sendar. He looked as apprehensive as she felt.

"Jern, Mikel, you'll join us at dawn in the cathedral grove?" asked Andiss.

"Of course," replied Jern, "It will be good to greet the Lady with others of our sept."

The next morning dawned cool and clear, and surprisingly, Kazari had awoken feeling bright and alert, despite the late night. She was also nervous about the afternoon, but as they worked through the steps of the training katas, she found herself relaxing. The familiar movements were soothing, and she moved smoothly from stance to stance, feeling her body celebrate its strength and flexibility. They finished with a salutation to the Lady just as the sun rose above the treetops. Despite being in the centre of the city, the cathedral grove was still a place of peace.

Kazari felt better still after eating, and then another two hours work with Andiss and Javon on paired fighting, and fighting in groups. Of course she'd had no choice but to fight groups of suckers already, but suckers weren't people, she reminded herself. At least people didn't exude fear, or prey on emotions.

She rode through the manor gates beside Sendar, feeling apprehensive. She'd never sparred with anyone except other Hunters. It did cross her mind that for a soldier to defeat a Hunter, even one in training, would be regarded as a bit of a coup. The thought made her feel even more anxious. Given Juster's seeming fascinating with Hunters, could he have an ulterior motive? It was probably more politics, she supposed.

Still, Andiss had impressed upon both of them the value of what they'd be doing, even if it seemed wrong in many ways.

Once again, people were taking Stumpy's reins almost before she'd dismounted. She waved them off, choosing to loosen her horse's girth herself, before she released him into their care with a last pat.

"This way, Hunters," said the woman who'd sat next to Kazari the night before. And ignored her, she remembered with stab of anger. Siap? Yes, that was the woman's name.

"Thank you, Captain," replied Andiss.

They followed the woman into a spotlessly kept training yard, edged with raised seats, all of which were filled.

"We understood this was a private training session, Captain," said Andiss.

"Lord Juster indicated his wish to observe, Hunter Andiss," replied the woman smoothly. "And he wished a number of his court to accompany him."

Andiss paused in his stride and turned to look at Kazari and Sendar, with one eyebrow raised. She returned his look, hoping he could read the horror in her eyes, and hoping he'd find a way for them avoid having to perform in front of Juster. She shot a look at the assembled crowd. It seemed to have swelled even more in the brief moment they'd paused. Then she saw his mouth firm.

"Well, then, we'd better be about it. Kazari and Sendar – we'll begin with the first kata, and then work on unarmed technique during the sparring."

Kazari felt a shot of adrenaline surge through her body, but nodded as calmly as she could. Apparently Juster wanted a spectacle for some reason, and Andiss had decided that they should provide one. Suddenly, she was very glad of the peace she'd found in the grove. She drew on it as she settled her clothing and deposited her water bottles on a small table to one side of the arena. For that was what it was, she realised – an arena rather than a training ground.

They worked through the steps of the first kata, and Kazari felt her body relax again, despite the sudden silence of the watching audience. Then, slightly apprehensively, she took the centre of the arena with Andiss, Javon and Sendar, and watched as Captain Siap pointed to a mid-sized fellow to accompany her out to the middle of the arena.

"With your permission, Hunter Andiss, I have arranged for five bouts? Four single bouts each for your trainees, and one with multiple opponents?"

"All unarmed bouts," said Andiss firmly. "And both Kazari and Sendar will take the *arena* in the final bout."

Kazari noticed the emphasis he'd placed on *arena*. Siap coloured slightly, but then nodded.

"And fights will be to submission only," Andiss continued. "No deliberate injuries are to be countenanced, but reasonable contact is acceptable."

"Reasonable contact, yes," Siap nodded. "And no disabling blows. Of course, we wouldn't want a future Hunter injured *this* early in their career, would we?"

It was only then that Kazari realised that the woman expected her soldiers to win the bouts. She was suddenly furious in a cold, clear, way. Not the hot anger of unreasoned rage, but the glacial anger that recognised a set-up. For some reason, Juster wanted a Hunter defeated in full view of his court, and a trainee would do well enough for the purpose, no matter the possible damage done to the Order's reputation.

Andiss nodded to the guard captain. Then he took both Kazari and Sendar by an elbow and drew them towards him.

"You remember what we discussed?"

Kazari nodded. She wasn't to Dance, not here in front of a crowd, and she was to react exactly as if she was sparring with Sendar, or any other Hunter for that matter. He'd had further instructions for bouts with more than one assailant, but it was clear that he'd decided that if there were multiple assailants, there would be two Hunters.

"Then let's be about it. Remember, no disabling blows. And remove your weaponry, Kaz, Sendar."

Kazari nodded again. All Hunter bouts avoided disabling blows. The only times she'd ever fought to injure was when she'd been fighting for her life. The idea of injuring someone badly during training was anathema. And to injure another human being? A Hunter's Gifts were for the *defence* of humanity. She began to remove her collection of knives and stars. Sendar's pile was still larger, she realised with a small smile.

"Captain Siap? When you're ready." Andiss' voice was quiet, but its solid command cut across the arena and there was a sudden cessation of chatter.

Siap motioned to the soldier at her side, and then towards another woman, also clad in a uniform tabard. "Jessen will referee."

The woman stepped forward. "Bouts will alternate – Sendar, then Kazari. Standard rules apply. To submission only. No weapons, and no disabling blows."

Kazari watched as Sendar settled himself. She was glad she wasn't the first to spar, but hoped that her friend would put up a good show against the soldiers. Of course, he had more training than she had, so hopefully his skill would make up for her lack.

To Kazari's surprise, the fight was over almost before it began. The soldier Sendar faced was as tall as he was. But as he charged towards Sendar when Jessen signalled for the bout to begin, Kazari realised that the man had underestimated his young opponent. There was a brief flurry of movement, and then the man was on the ground with his leg locked in one of Sendar's. Sendar released him as he tapped out.

The referee beckoned to Kazari.

"This is Besan." She beckoned a soldier forward. "You'll begin on my whistle. If you need to ready yourselves, you have two minutes."

Kazari eyed Besan as he stripped down to his shirt and trousers. He wasn't huge, but he was well muscled and looked fit. Of course, not huge still meant bigger than she was. He was looking at her with one eyebrow raised, as if he'd expected something different, not the short, young woman facing him.

Her Hunter garb was designed for fighting. Comfortable, despite its close-fitting nature, it allowed excellent movement.

She'd already removed her knives, so she just shook her head and smiled at her opponent. It seemed to irritate him.

"On my mark."

Kazari relaxed into one of the stances her tutors had so painstakingly taught her, and poised herself, feeling apprehensive. Despite her regular sparring with the others, she was still only a beginner by Hunter standards, and she hoped she wouldn't make a fool of herself, or the Lady's Order.

"Begin," said Jessen. The soldier rolled his shoulders and cracked his neck to one side, then shifted into a fighter's stance and began to circle.

Kazari let herself move, focusing on her stance as she'd been taught, watching for any sign of Besan's next move. She feinted with one hesitant jab, watching the man sway easily out of her way. He smiled, an unpleasant sneer of a smile, and almost without warning, exploded into movement. He was quick, Kazari thought as she ducked under his arm, but not nearly as quick as the Hunters she'd practiced with, and apparently he hadn't had a lot of experience with shorter people. Or if he had, it hadn't occurred to him to think about what might happen if one of them ended up inside his guard.

As she ducked under his arm, Kazari tucked herself tightly into his body, grabbed the flailing arm, shifted her hips, and dumped him over her shoulder onto the ground and locked his elbow up. It happened almost before she'd thought about it. Just like that. He squirmed, but his elbow was at full lock, and as she tightened her grip, he grimaced and then tapped the ground. His face was ugly. Apparently, another thing he hadn't considered was losing.

Kazari released him and stepped back, feeling slightly surprised herself. It was a very basic move, one she'd mastered months before, and it had all happened so fast. She hadn't expected to win her first bout, and certainly hadn't expected a seasoned soldier to fall for something so simple.

The arena was still quiet, but then the sound of clapping came to her ears. And a voice.

"Well done, Kazari," Juster said, his voice ringing out across the arena. "Siap, I hope you've picked someone with a little more experience than Besan for our little Hunter's next opponent."

The guard captain looked annoyed, but nodded and waved a hand to the referee.

Sendar stepped forward. His opponent matched him in height, but not skill. Kazari could see that as soon as he took his stance. She sipped from her water bottle as Sendar's second fight took even less time than hers had. Her friend's graceful movements made his opponent's look untutored, barely a beginner.

When Siap gestured to Kazari, there was a jerkiness to her movement that suggested irritation. Kazari's new sparring partner was a woman. She walked forward, and from her demeanour, she was happy to be chosen. A woman in her thirties, she looked shrewd, fit, and calculating. Kazari wondered if she looked as worried as she felt. This woman was seasoned. This fight would be different.

Except that it wasn't. The woman was clearly experienced, clever, and thoughtful. But her fighting style was slow, despite its power, and Kazari was fast. Sendar had always said she was fast, but she now realised that even if she was still only fairly ordinary by Hunter standards, Hunter standards were extraordinary in comparison to everyone else.

Their third bouts went much the same way. Her opponent was short and fast, but his technique was unimaginative, and he wasn't flexible enough to counter some of Kazari's moves. Sendar's opponent was strong and skilled, but even his practiced strength wasn't enough to match up to Sendar's level of training. Sendar's fourth bout was longer, but barely enough to make him sweat.

By the time she stepped up to her own fourth bout, Kazari was sweating lightly in the spring sun. Her opponent was a large man, older by far than the others. Perhaps about to retire, she thought, and looked at him warily. There was a lack of expression on his face that chilled her. His legs were like tree trunks, and his biceps appeared bigger around than her thighs, and she knew with a thrill of fear, that his sheer size and strength would be a counter to her flexibility and speed. If she got in too close, he'd have her, no matter what Hunter trick she used. It was something she'd been warned about repeatedly.

When the whistle blew, she circled warily, keeping her stance low, and her body centred. He was lighter on his feet than she'd expected. He circled as well, waiting, watching her, sizing her up. And he'd had time to study the earlier bouts. He knew a lot more about her than she did about him. If the rule about disabling blows had been waived, she knew she could have beaten him. But it hadn't been, so somehow she had to try and make him submit, and she knew holding him in an elbow lock or a leg lock was going to be almost impossible.

He feinted a punch, and she swayed away from it as she circled, and almost didn't see him change direction, trying to close with her. She inhaled sharply and slipped sideways, just avoiding the bear hug, and then scrambled backward. There was a murmur from the crowd, as if they'd drawn a sharp breath all at once.

She kept circling, hands up, and then changed direction herself. He followed suit easily, his eyes watching her intently. A long arm jabbed forward, and she ducked it, and ended up with his other fist darting for her body. She leaped backward, but not before it had caught her a blow on her ribs. She felt something snap painfully and nearly doubled over. She waited for Jessen to signal a disabling blow and stop the bout, but the huge man came straight at her, and she had to move rapidly again to avoid his fists. He aimed for the same place he'd just hit.

Kazari felt anger spike her body with adrenaline. Her broken rib healed, the pain ebbing slowly as she moved warily around the man. Somewhere in the back of her brain she could hear Andiss and Javon speaking loudly. But there was no whistle. She looked up at her opponent and knew that he'd been sent out to deliberately hurt or injure her. It made her blood run cold.

Help me, Lady. Preserve me for the real battle. The words leaped from her mind without conscious intent. She knew she could Dance and defeat the man, but she was a Hunter and she'd promised Andiss. Of course, the man had no idea that her rib had healed.

She felt her teeth clench as she bit down on a smile. Then, as he jabbed towards her again, let his leading hand crunch into her ribs. She didn't need to fake the pain, it hurt every bit as much as the preceding blow, and this time she felt two distinct snaps. Instead of dancing away, she let herself hobble, partially doubled over, and heard him step closer. She looked up through her eyelashes, feeling her ribs heal again, and allowed herself to topple into a roll, right under his swinging arms, and when she regained her feet, she was behind him.

Kazari fastened herself like a leech to the man's back, wrapping her legs around his chest, and throwing an arm around his throat. She locked it in as tight as she could, and held on for all she was worth. He roared and grabbed for her forearm, his fingernails scrabbling at her skin. His chin got in the way. Taken by surprise he'd not tucked his chin down, and her arm was around his short neck, taking up all the available space, and making it difficult for him to gain purchase.

Each time he tried to pull it away, he was forced to lift his chin to try to get his hands around her forearm. And that was a self-defeating move. He changed his attacks to her legs, wrapped around his chest like she wrapped them around Stumpy when Andiss made her ride bareback. His fists felt as if they were made of wood, and he targeted her shins and knees, and each blow felt as if it might break her bones. Still there was no whistle, no call for the bout to end, and she could hear both Andiss and Javon shouting furiously above the roar of the watching crowd.

The sweat on Kazari's wrist lubricated her grip, and she tightened her fingers frantically while the huge man heaved and flailed, but eventually, she began to feel his struggles weaken. It became a race between her sliding hands and his staggering steps. Moment by moment, she hoped that he'd tap out, but eventually, her vice grip on his throat cut his air supply enough that he dropped to his knees and then toppled forward onto his face and her legs and arms.

Her arms felt as if they'd locked solidly in place. Faintly, she could hear pounding footsteps, followed by Javon's furious voice. "Kaz, are you all right?" She unlocked her arms at last, and rolled tiredly off to one side, drawing gasping breaths.

"Bruised, more than anything." Her voice wobbled slightly.

"Your ribs?" she asked.

"Think they're springier than they look," she replied, conscious of the listening ears around them. She saw relief flood Javon's face. She knew exactly what Kazari meant. She could feel the bruises on her legs beginning to settle as well, but she suspected she'd still be a bit sore later. She might be a Healer but, however her Gift worked, somehow it seemed to know when to 'heal' her quickly, versus leaving minor things to settle more slowly. It was an oddity that she shrugged off as a reasonable compromise. She could imagine that if she just assumed that everything that happened to her would heal immediately, she'd probably end up dying as the result of some sudden rashness.

Sendar reached down and helped her to her feet, eyes anxious.

"Can you manage the final bout?" asked Andiss. "I can call it off. No-one will argue after that display."

Kazari took a deep breath, trying to steady herself. She didn't want another bout, here in front of Juster and his lackeys, but unfortunately, she thought, she was beginning to understand what 'politics' meant. And politics sometimes meant you had to throw off good sense and take risks.

"I think so. How many of them?" She meant the soldiers, of course, not the crowd.

"Siap wants five."

"Five?" she almost squeaked. She was tired. The last fight had pushed her hard. She was sweating, shaking from reaction, and slightly wobbly. Her ribs were healed, but the soft tissues around them were sensitive. Then she cleared her throat, muttered '*politics*' under her breath, which she realised Andiss had heard when she saw his eyebrows lift, and nodded.

"All right," she said. "They wanted a display, so let's give them one." Then she stopped talking for a second. "But . . . um . . . how?"

Andiss didn't speak for a moment, just looked at her, and then smiled faintly. "Back to back, but remember the third kata."

"What?"

"The third kata. And when you're done, the salutation." He turned away, signalling to Siap before she could say anything else, and five soldiers moved forward. There was no doubt that these were seasoned fighters. She could see it in the easy way they moved, and the ripple of muscle that showed in the sleeveless jerkins they wore. Two women, three men. And all of a sudden, Kazari wondered how they'd attained their seasoning. She shelved the question as too distracting for the moment.

Jessen motioned them to join her in the centre of the arena. "Same rules – no disabling blows, and to submission only."

Kazari felt her face darken, and bit back a sharp retort. She wiped a drop of sweat off her brow and rubbed her hands through her hair, forcing herself to nod evenly.

"You'll begin on my signal." Jessen waved the whistle.

Sendar bowed, hands together, in the formal manner Kazari had been taught at the Abbey. She took her cue from him, placed her hands together, and bowed as well. The soldiers nodded, almost in unison, each head inclined just enough to avoid insult, but only barely. Jessen bowed back, and waved them to opposite sides of the arena.

"They'll want to surround us, Kaz," murmured Sendar, "and today we'll let them. On the signal, straight to the middle

– Juster wanted a show, and he's going to get one. Third kata once the first one rushes."

Kazari nodded uncertainly. Sendar's instructions flew in the face of everything she'd been taught. She'd fought multiple suckers – while dancing. Every lecture she'd had at the Abbey though, had emphasised the futility of fighting multiple opponents on multiple fronts. Generally strategy discussions had gone something like – 'just don't, but if you have to, get to somewhere they can only come at you one at a time.' Still, she was certain that Sendar had a plan, and knew what he was about, so she shrugged her shoulders and nodded, and then waited for Jessen's signal.

When it came, she sprinted for the centre, Sendar at her side. By the time they were back-to-back, she could see that it wasn't what the others had expected, and that they were happy about it. She could see the glee on their faces.

Sendar and Kazari had done exactly what they knew to be the wrong thing, or a move of last resort.

"Ready, Kaz. *Lady, for you.*"

Kazari echoed his last words, and breathed out, deliberately preparing herself for the rapid movements of the kata. The last time she'd practiced it with Sendar it had ended slightly awkwardly. Unbidden, her face reddened, and she wrenched her thoughts away from the moment and into the present, eyeing the three soldiers she could see from her position, slowly closing in on them.

From the corner of her left eye, she saw the man on her left take three rapid steps towards them, and spun straight into the third kata. Sendar moved at exactly the same time, and then she was into the rhythm of it, feeling for the first time, the purpose behind its fast, complex moves. She'd been taught that it prepared a Hunter for speed, but now, she could feel and see that it prepared a Hunter for much more than that. Her momentum took her towards the left, and at the end of her first move, the leap and spin at the end let her foot slam heavily into the rushing soldier's chest. She pulled the kick slightly, leaving him winded rather than fracturing his ribs, and then let the kata take her back towards the woman in the centre. Clearly caught off guard by the speed with which Kazari was moving, she almost stumbled as Kazari changed direction.

In the kata, the movement was a forward roll, and the Hunter would then regain her feet, before letting her momentum carry her to the right. Kazari used the roll to cannon into the woman's legs, dropping her to the ground, heavily, before leaping to her feet and to the right. Her arms moved into the patterns of their own volition, her right hand colliding with the third soldier's head, and her left, his armpit, her hand hooking up into the soft parts. His arm dropped of its own volition, and Kazari knew it would be numb and tingling.

She moved again, circling inexorably towards the man who'd been the recipient of Sendar's first kick. He was staggering drunkenly towards her to his credit, but she let the kata take her in its measured steps into a leap that resulted with her legs around his neck and his body on the ground, one arm trembling the tap out. She rolled off him, coming to her feet in a swift movement, to where Sendar's second victim was still moaning softly as she dragged herself off the ground. Kazari stopped short beside her, gathering the woman's arm into a lock, improvising, and the woman dropped back to her knees again, signalling with one hand.

Kazari dropped her like a hot potato, took the final half dozen steps of the kata, and looked across to where Sendar had submitted the final man, still holding his numb arm. He beckoned, and she joined him where they'd started the third kata. As one, they began the salutation to the Lady. This time, Kazari's thanks were heartfelt. Her amethyst was warm on her chest, and the sun warm on her head. The arena was silent.

When they finished, Andiss nodded to Juster, Javon gathered their water bottles, and they left without a word, to the sound of absolutely nothing.

Chapter Thirty-two:
The Inn

"Politics!" spat Kazari. "I didn't understand what you meant until today, but now I do. Andiss, is it going to be like this the whole time?"

Her mentor's eyes crinkled momentarily, but then sobered.

"Not always, but enough." Then he sighed heavily. "Juster's never been a friend to the Abbey, but now he's definitely an enemy."

"And Ralen," replied Kazari.

"Yes, and Ralen. And Siap, and all those soldiers, sadly." He looked up from the cup of tea he was cradling in his hands. "I'm sorry to have dumped the two of you in it but . . ."

"I know, politics," she replied, sipping from her own cup. They were back at the cathedral, in their quarters. "But what do we do now?" She was angry, her side was still twinging, and she was frustrated – again. It seemed that every time they had a lead on a gorgone infestation, the trail trickled away. So far they'd had to waste time on a useless dinner, and a stupid series of fights, just to prove to a dodgy 'Lord' that The Lady's Hunters were not the pushovers he'd wanted them to be. "He did that to try and undermine us, didn't he?"

Javon nodded slowly, and put her cup back onto its saucer, refilling it from the pot on the side table.

"As the Lady's servants, we are her body here in Albatar. Hunters, it has been said, are her armour and her weapons – but in more ways than one. We're the visible reminder that there are things beyond our borders that threaten our very existence. If we are weak, or proved weak, then the Abbey is seen as weak, and by extension, the Lady. Or seen as limited in scope, at the very least. That's why we kept on, even though it was obvious that Juster had set us up. And you were well able for the task, even though you didn't realise it until the end. And, of course, it was valuable experience. You won't only be fighting gorgones, you know. You've met the 'changed', and seen the worshippers, and of course, the Mayor of Suborden, who was unable to be sensed, even by yourself, until he had revealed himself. Which is troubling. It makes me wonder how many like him there are in Albatar."

Andiss sighed heavily and reached for his own teacup, and they drank their tea for a while in a silence that was thick with frustration.

"Mikel and Jern may bring more information today," Andiss said, finally. "In the meantime, I'm assuming you've healed adequately?"

Kazari nodded.

"In that case; you, I, and Sendar are going to make ourselves visible, 'training.'"

"Training?"

"It's our excuse to be here, remember. So today, that's what we'll do. You'll follow me around while I point out the sites of interest, the Cathedral's suppliers, and we'll also visit Eriad. That's a normal part of the training for a new Hunter."

Kazari, Sendar and Andiss spent the rest of the day being conspicuous. Bathed, and dressed in clean blacks, they followed Andiss up and down Seraph's streets from monument to monument. As the day wore on, Kazari realised the value of what she was seeing, and that it wasn't a waste of time. Seraph was one of the older towns, and its history was long and illustrious. Many of the early battles to secure Albatar had taken place there. The city was a maze of streets lined with plaques and statues. Some of her Hunter and Navigator heroes rated their own statues.

It made her uncomfortable, to see someone in Hunter garb immortalised in marble, or bronze, or in one case gilded in gold. Although she revered them, those early Hunters were very much simple men and women, and in her training at the Abbey, she'd been made aware of just how human they were – the Hunter archives were unadulterated, and more frank about the great ones of the Order than Kazari could have believed. As she looked up at the gilded statue of Felia, she remembered the words she'd read: *Although a mighty fighter, Felia's untamed temper sometimes led her into rashness. She was a prickly woman, with a heart of gold, and an abiding love for the Lady. She also snored so loudly she had her own room.*

Kazari almost snorted as loudly as Felia might have snored, when Andiss grinned at her after they'd read the plaque at the base of the woman's effigy. *One of our Lady's greatest. She gathered the children under her wings, and sheltered them within her grace, and with the strength of her steel. She is remembered with love for her abiding gentleness.*

Well, perhaps she was gentle – with children – thought Kazari, because a second comment had been: Felia trained our novices for many years. She was a hard master, and outspoken about the level of effort a trainee put in. She was well known for making her trainees scrub the archway at the grove with a toothbrush if she felt the day's effort was inadequate.

Still, as they moved from place to place within Seraph, Kazari began to get a feel for the town. People pointed and waved, as they had all across Albatar, but here, the people were subdued, despite their outward smiles. There was a heaviness to the town that Kazari found frighteningly similar to that of Suborden. The people had no intimate knowledge of many of their neighbours, so the heaviness seemed less personal, but more generally oppressive – and even more menacing for that generality.

Eriad turned out to be delightful, and very skilled. Kazari realised that his grasp of the politics he negotiated daily was all encompassing. He and Andiss had discussed the ramifications of Juster's recalcitrance, and the staged 'training' that morning quite frankly, while Sendar and Kazari sat and listened. In the end, Eriad promised he'd do what he could, but urged Andiss to ask the Abbot to send another, senior, Adviser to assist.

"I might be old, but my wits are not dim – as Juster has implied – but this place is perilous, and the populace downtrodden. A set of fresh eyes and a strong will would be of great assistance. We might yet salvage the situation." It was then that Kazari realised there was more to 'politics' than pettiness.

She patted Stumpy reflectively as they rode back to the cathedral for the evening meal. She was tired, and couldn't wait to eat and then turn in for the night, but her mind buzzed with the implications of what Eriad and Andiss had discussed, and the idea that not everyone in Albatar followed the Lady with as much reverence as those in her little hometown. Or at least had appeared to follow. The idea that some people might feign their reverence was quite upsetting. She shook her head as she rode, trying to get her head around the idea that people she'd known all her life might have been putting on a show. Surely not.

Her desire for rest wasn't to be however, because halfway through the meal, Mikel signalled from the doorway of the dining hall. Javon left her meal, and then, a few moments later, signalled the others with a jerk of her head. Kazari gave a regretful look at her plate – whoever did the cooking at the cathedral was a genius – and followed the others out of the hall.

"I have a lead on the caravan. It was unloaded in one of the upper districts. Apparently the caravaners are housed at an inn nearby. I also found this in one of the market stalls nearby." He proffered a handkerchief wrapped object, and Andiss unwrapped it carefully. A malmetal charm gleamed dully in the light. Kazari shivered slightly, despite the spring warmth.

"Have a local smith melt it down in front of you," said Andiss. "One we trust."

Mikel nodded and rewrapped the thing, tucking it away in his clothing with a look of distaste.

"Kaz, Sendar, go and ready yourself. The six of us will take a wander through that district tonight. Kaz and I will go openly, but Mikel, you and Jern need something to cover your Hunter clothing. Javon, you and Sendar visit the residence. Make some pretence – the mural, perhaps."

It was a quiet trip through Seraph, with the spring evening already darkening around them. Kazari was surprised to see that the streets had much less bustle than she'd expected, but already, slowly gathering fog was drifting down the streets, and the atmosphere smelled like rain. A lamplighter lit the street-lamp in front of them as they walked through the dusk, and the fog around it glowed yellow. Kazari shivered and tucked her hands under her armpits to warm them. Then pulled them out. She was a Hunter. She tried to copy Andiss' relaxed gait.

Andiss paused at an intersection, and loudly pointed out the different streets. "If you take this road, you'll end up back at the manor, and of course the one behind us leads directly to the cathedral. Tonight, we're going to explore these two. I want you to memorise the streets over the next hour or so, and tomorrow evening you'll be tested on your knowledge." He winked at her, and she nodded.

"Yes, Andiss."

"This leads to the upper districts. The roads here grew around existing dwellings, unlike those in the lower districts which were planned. It can be a maze at times, but as you know, a Hunter needs to be able to find her way anywhere. *This* road loops around the upper districts, and eventually joins this one behind the manor. We'll be exploring everything in between them."

He turned onto the upper districts' road, and Kazari followed him into the thickening mist. She couldn't help think-ing that it was going to make everything more difficult. Several passers-by gave her sympathetic looks. She tried her best to return them with a smile and a nod of thanks. Still, she couldn't help feeling a little guilty that they weren't telling the whole truth. Then she realised that she actually did need to memorise where she was going in case she and Andiss became separated. She felt like smacking her forehead with a palm.

Still, the fog was thickening, and Seraph began to take on an eerie cast. Kazari couldn't help glancing at the dark shadows in the alley ways, feeling a small shiver wander up and down her spine. The morning had demonstrated her martial skills, and she was with Andiss, one of the sept's premier fighters, but there was something primal inside her mind that kept the adrenaline trickling through her bloodstream, and her body on a hair trigger.

The streets wandered in a way that differed from those in the lower districts, and shortly, Kazari was too involved trying to memorise their twists, turns and intersections. The true value of what had started as a ruse, was making itself known. At last, Andiss paused in the shadow of a large building, its imposing facade wreathed in misty tendrils. A short distance away, the 'inn' that Mikel had mentioned shone warm light onto the street, and well-dressed patrons came and went through the double doors opening onto the street. Music wafted from it, but rather than the folksy tunes favoured by players at the various inns Kazari had stayed in on her travels, strains from what sounded like a string quartet came clearly through the fog.

Kazari raised an eyebrow at Andiss.

"It's an inn – of a type. More a 'salon' if you like. A high-class residence for itinerants. But one where patrons of the arts gather to eat, drink and listen to the latest compositions." Every time she turned around, Kazari seemed to learn something new about Albatar. Patrons of the arts? A 'salon?'

"Are we going in?" she asked apprehensively.

"Oh yes," replied Andiss, to her consternation. "We of the Abbey are known to have a keen appreciation of the creative arts."

"We are?"

"Our Abbey houses some of the most marvellous musicians and artists in all of Albatar. Javon told you of her early ambitions?" Kazari nodded. "Most of us have hobbies of some sort, Kaz. Javon still paints, you know. And you've heard the choir."

"But when does anyone get the time to practice a hobby?" she asked. Her own days had been filled from dawn to dusk.

Andiss laughed. "It won't always be as intense as when you're learning, Kaz. Once you're trained, you'll have a few leisure hours here and there. As long as there's no incursions to stymie, of course." He sobered abruptly. "I'm a fair musician myself, which gives us a good reason for going into the inn. Keep your eyes and ears open and follow my lead."

She followed him to the door, and they stepped into the warmth and light. For a moment they were the centre of attention, curious eyes drawn immediately to their black Hunter garb, and then, as Andiss drew Kazari deeper into the room, the eyes gradually returned to watching what was indeed a string quartet, perched on a small stage. They really were exceptional, Kazari thought as Andiss steered her to a table in a dim corner of the room, where they could sit with their backs to the wall, then held up two fingers to a waiter.

The man nodded, vanished briefly, before returning with two steaming cups which he deposited on the table in front of them. Kazari settled back in her chair to watch the room, sipping the hot drink appreciatively. It was a large room, well-lit with lanterns and a monumental structure hanging from the centre of the high ceiling. It was covered in reflective crystals and stacked with huge candles. The rest of the room was furnished with comfortable chairs and tables, and the polished wooden floor reflected the light.

The musicians on the stage were playing with an intensity that awed Kazari. It was a piece that spoke of grandeur, and deeds of heroism, and she was swept into the music. When the piece finished, it was almost as if it left an emotional void. She sat back slightly breathless, while Andiss smiled at her.

"You liked that, Kaz?"

"It was . . ." words failed her.

"Juster has a conservatorium here – a place for training musicians. These will be some of the more accomplished students. That piece is the story of Felia. But without the snoring."

Kazari had to struggle not to snort with laughter.

There was a commotion at the door as the quartet began again, and Juster and Ralen entered the room. Both were elaborately dressed in rich hues glittering with brocade, and studded with gems. Kazari pulled herself further back into the dimness of her corner, hoping neither of them would notice the two Hunters.

The quartet played on as conversation in the room ceased briefly, as it had when the Hunters had walked in, and then resumed once more. This time, though, a servitor hurried forward and ushered the two to a vacant table with a prime view of the performers. Juster's gaze swept past them, and then returned to the Hunters in the corner, and his mouth tightened, while Ralen's eyes stopped immediately, and Kazari felt her heart rate accelerate as the woman held her eyes briefly. That woman made her skin crawl.

Then the moment was over, and the rulers took their seats, turning their attention immediately to the performers at the front of the room. Kazari noticed several of the courtiers who'd attended both the dinner and the training ground exhibition entering and taking up stations at adjacent tables.

"We'll need to stay for at least two more pieces, Kaz," said Andiss quietly as if he'd read her mind. "Politics."

She sat back, grinding her teeth, trying to think through the implications of what he'd said. If they left immediately the rulers of Seraph entered, then politics would say that the Hunters had something against Juster and Ralen. If they left too soon, the same thing would be said. Or that the Hunters were afraid, perhaps. If they didn't leave, that also sent a message. She frowned. Even two days ago she wouldn't have understood that.

So she sat back, sipped her tea, barely tasting it, and tried to concentrate on the music

"Strength, Kaz, there's more here than meets the eye. This is our best chance to figure out what's going on. Sometimes a Hunter must stalk her prey with stealth and knowledge, not only strength of limb," said Andiss. He picked up his own cup, eyes roving over the crowd in the inn. "Watch, see who speaks to whom, and for how long. Watch who comes and goes. And listen to the music, or at least pretend to." He smiled slightly, and she took a tremulous breath, and smiled uncertainly back.

For several minutes, Kazari's intense dislike of Ralen interrupted her observations, and then, slowly, she began to see why Andiss had urged her to watch. There was a kind of patten to the movements in the room – almost like a dance. After several minutes she realised that there were two types of people visiting Juster and Ralen – those who spoke to Juster, and those who spoke to Ralen. She puzzled over it for a while, trying to understand what was going on, absently sipping from her mug.

The musicians finished, and moved off the stage, and another group took their places, wheeling huge wooden instruments onto the stage, and positioning mallets between their fingers – two in each hand, in fact. The first sounds took Kazari by surprise; softly ringing, mellow tones rang forth, mesmerising in their complexity. In fact, so mesmerising, that Kazari stopped watching the people and just listened, spellbound. The parts overlapped and interwove so completely that Kazari couldn't identify which musician was playing what. She'd never heard anything like it in her life.

As the piece finished, she realised she'd leaned forward, completely entranced by the music and had completely forgotten the politics going on in the room. Sighing, she returned her attention to the central table and the ebb and flow of humanity around it. Both men and women attended Juster and Ralen, but some paused longer than others, and more than once, Kazari saw a piece of paper passed between the attendee and Ralen. The woman pocketed them quickly, without reading them, and then the person would nod and back away – sometimes almost fearfully.

The musicians rolled their wooden instruments away, and another performer took the stage. There was a hush, and a sudden air of anticipation pervaded the room. Kazari looked curiously at the woman. She was accompanied by a harpist. She was tall, and dressed in a ruby red dress that brushed the floor as she walked. Kazari looked around – the audience seemed to be holding its breath – as the harpist sent a ripple of sound floating through the inn.

Then the woman opened her mouth and began to sing. Her voice was astounding, and if Kazari had thought the percussionists were mesmerising, they had nothing on this woman. The music . . . beguiled . . . was the only word Kazari thought. Beguiled, beckoned, and pulled at the emotions. Harp and voice interwove to drag the listener into the song. It was deeply unsettling.

Fear tugged at Kazari's heart, and she found herself with her hand over the amethyst where it sat on her chest. Warmth spread from it into her hand and she looked at Andiss. His hand was similarly placed, and he met her eyes grimly, gesturing with his other hand.

The audience sat rapt, eyes fixated on the woman as she sang, Ralen and Juster no less enthralled, and Kazari heard and felt what she was singing. She sang greed and despair, and fear and hurt, but overlaid it with the honey of pride and self-satisfaction. The whole was enticing – at least to a large chunk of the audience. Here and there, Kazari could see unsettled faces, and people shifting uneasily in their seats, even as they were fascinated by the music, but a large proportion of the audience drew it in avidly. A hint of gold on the woman's gown piqued Kazari's attention.

She looked again – there wasn't anything obvious – and then she saw it again, a tiny flicker of gold centred on a bulge that strained the fabric of the dress just above the woman's left breast. It was as if she was wearing a brooch, Kazari thought, but a brooch *inside* her dress.

"Andiss!" she hissed. "I think she's wearing a malmetal brooch inside her dress."

The other Hunter nodded. "She is. That's what's helping her keep them in thrall." He tapped his amethyst with one finger tip. "*Lady, bring your light to this place.*"

Kazari hadn't realised he'd said the last words out loud until he pushed his chair out with a discordant scrape and stood, marching to the stage. Against the woman's voice, his footsteps sounded out of time, and his voice squawked like a crow's. She followed him belatedly, uncertain of Andiss' intent, but certain that whatever it was, it was right and proper. Her amethyst glowed brighter as she hurried after Andiss, ignoring the annoyed looks around her. The woman sung on, fixing Andiss with her gaze, but he ploughed through the tables unerringly, even as the vocals intensified, throwing out a wall of sound like a thick fog.

Kazari felt her feet struggle against the sound, but she grasped her amethyst tighter, and pushed forward, following Andiss. He drew his sword, and as shouts of outrage began, lunged towards the woman and sliced the fabric of the woman's dress in a move so fast Kazari had trouble following it with her eyes. A golden brooch hit the stage floor, and the woman's spell broke, and Kazari stumbled and almost fell. Darker red trickled from the woman's chest, staining the dress. Andiss had cut her skin as well as the fabric. He stooped and picked up the brooch on the point of his sword, turning to face the room.

"Malmetal." His voice was flat, its tones still harsh against the memories of the now stilled music. "Juster – how long has this corruption gone unchecked in Seraph?"

Chapter Thirty-three: Music

There was a shocked silence, followed by a babble of sound and a scraping of chairs.

"Malmetal?"

"What?"

"Hunter, what are you saying?"

"Silence!" The voice belonged to Ralen, and its ringing tones cut through the air like a knife. "Hunter, your accusations are serious. What evidence do you have?"

Kazari stared at the woman, gobsmacked. Was she seriously suggesting that Andiss was lying? Andiss turned his head towards Ralen for a moment and then deliberately turned it back to Juster. "Juster, what have you to say?" He lifted the tip of his sword where the malmetal charm glinted in the light, beguiling in its delicate beauty. To Kazari's eyes, the air around it shimmered, as if it was surrounded by its own tiny heat haze. The brooch was there in front of them all. How could Ralen question it?

The moment hung in the air like a falling glass on its way to the ground, waiting for the hand to catch it and place it back whole on the bench, or to plummet, eventually shattering on the floor. It was as if every person in the place were holding their breath in a moment outside time. Then the woman on the stage let out a strangled sob, and fled from the room, one hand pressed to her breast.

Kazari took off after her almost before Andiss' hand signal told her to, but even as she ran, she felt the glass plummet and the spell break, and a wave of sound began to rise above Juster's protestations, and she knew that somehow, what might have been a decisive moment in the war against the gorgone incursion had lost its momentum. The word 'politics' floated in the back of her mind, but she banished it for later thought and continued after the woman.

For someone in an elaborate dress, she was moving very fast. Kazari followed her through the stage door, through a room full of musicians and instruments, all looking dazedly up at her as she ran past, and into a hallway. She paused, checking right and left, before seeing a flutter of red cloth vanishing around a corner to the right.

She sprinted after the woman again, and just around the corner, saw a wall hanging rippling as if someone had just passed through it – even though it looked as if the wall was solid. Kazari slunk to the hanging, wary of nasty surprises, and lifted it cautiously by one edge. Instead of the blank wall she expected, there was a stairwell leading down into darkness. She paused at the top of the stairwell, sliding one hand onto the polished wooden banister, and crouched to listen. Muffled voices drifted upwards. In the dim light, she could see that the stairwell took a turn half-a-dozen stairs below the top, so she crept down them, hoping to hear more clearly. The voices grew louder as she descended, one of them clearly female, but then began to fade away again.

"There was a Hunter behind me . . ." trailed in the air. It was the woman's voice, and Kazari paused for a moment. Clearly the woman wasn't alone, but she couldn't hear the end of the sentence.

Realising that the stairs twisted around a central column, and that every time she rounded one turn the speakers had also moved around the corner yet again, Kazari ducked down another turn, heart pounding and breath coming quickly. Another fragment of a sentence drifted upwards.

"Think I lost her . . ."

"You can't be sure." It was another voice, male.

Then the clatter of feet resumed, this time moving more quickly. More fragments of conversation floated upwards.

"Juster's ripe . . ."

"Only a few pieces . . ."

"Now we've lost one . . ."

"Not safe."

She took another few steps, craning her neck unconsciously, trying to glean whatever it was that the unseen speakers were saying. She strained to listen, stepping quietly down and down as she did so, and then a thought struck her. She'd descended a long way. Much further than a basement would account for. More sounds floated up the stairwell, making the voices even harder to distinguish, and then the first hint of acridity hit Kazari's nostrils, and her blood ran cold.

Gorgone.

It wasn't strong, and it didn't seem close, or fresh, more as if it had been there, rather than *was* there. How she knew that, Kazari was uncertain, but still, she paused, undecided. If there were gorgones beneath the inn, then they needed to know. But should she keep descending? That there was more than one person below her, was obvious, but a gorgone?

Kazari inhaled slowly, trying to make her indrawn breath silent, and trying to discern exactly what she was sensing. It wasn't suckers, she was certain about that. And definitely not close – perhaps somewhere in the distance? It didn't smell like either the fire gorgone or the viper, but she had to admit that she'd encountered only a few of the many varieties of gorgone she'd read about. And in none of the histories were descriptions of how they'd smelled.

Again she hesitated. The voices echoed ahead again. The stench was fading slowly, as if whatever might have been there was receding into the distance. But how could something be getting further away? In a wine cellar or basement beneath Seraph?

Once again, Kazari paused, undecided about her course of action. *Lady, what should I do?* She pleaded, hand reaching automatically for her amethyst, but it remained cool under her seeking fingertips. Should she return to Andiss, or follow the sounds? He'd sent her after the woman, but she could be running into some kind of trap. There was now no doubt in her mind that there were, or at least had been a gorgone below, and the slowly fading stench finally decided her.

Kazari was skilled, at least compared to the rest of Albatar's population – Juster's little 'demonstration' had shown her that – but she had no idea what she might meet below. The woman was lost to them now, at least for the moment, so with slightly shaking legs, Kazari began to climb back up the stairwell. Her neck crawled, and her hand dropped to one of the knives in her belt, suddenly realising that someone might be ahead of her on the stairs, or following her, and she'd have no idea if they were. She shook her sleeves slightly, feeling the comforting weights of the extra knives and the throwing stars she'd secreted there.

By the time she arrived at the top of the stairwell, Kazari knew that the pounding of her heart was only partially the result of the physical activity. The rest was fear. She lifted a corner of the wall hanging cautiously and then re-entered the hallway. Noise from the performance room rolled down it and she jogged back towards it, a mixture of feelings rolling around inside her. Gorgones, malmetal charms and politics. It was like a maze with no clear entry or exit.

As she stepped back through the musicians' room, she knew immediately that something was wrong. They were clustered around the open stage door, all their attention on whatever was happening inside the performance room.

"Excuse me," she said, and then "Excuse me," again in firmer tones. Several faces looked back at her, irritation slowly subsiding to a mixture of deference and resignation, and then they parted to let her through. Andiss, Juster and Ralen still stood in the same positions, and the room's inhabitants were sitting wide-eyed, murmuring to each other.

"She's gone," Kazari said, keeping her tone even, while signalling as subtly as she knew how, that she had more information for Andiss' private ears. She saw the acknowledgment of her unspoken warning in Andiss' eyes, before Juster's voice cut in.

"Of course she has. Divi is an artist of the highest rank. Your accusations hold no sway here, Hunter. And woe betide you if your churlish behaviour has injured her delicate sensibilities. Malmetal indeed. A children's tale."

"It is no children's tale," said Andiss, "This charm is dangerous beyond belief, and your scoffing changes that not one little bit. If there are more of them in Seraph, then your city is in great danger, Juster." He swept his eyes around the room, and Kazari saw fear on some faces, awe on others, and open derision on still more. How much more malmetal might be in this very room?

"I say it's a children's tale," replied Juster. "And perhaps it's time for the Abbey to hold less sway in Albatar. Our history is long and your Order has been revered, but things have changed more than you realise."

Ralen laughed. A tiny silvery laugh that sent chills down Kazari's spine.

"Sequestered away as the Abbey is, how could they know that greater Albatar is moving on, Juster? Or rather, *has* moved on. Our people of Seraph have no need of the fairy stories told by the Order. *Our* people know that times have changed and that the power of the Order is waning." She tinkled her tiny, silvery laugh again, and several in the room joined her. Kazari was horrified. Nowhere else had the Lady's people been challenged so obviously, and so blatantly.

"Believing something, or saying something does not make it so, Juster. This *is* malmetal. The woman you call 'an artist' is no more nor less than an agent of darkness, tainted by the gorgone evil. You," and his gaze swept around the room,

including all the people within it, "might wish to believe otherwise, but that does not change the facts. The Lady can bring
light into darkness, except the darkness that you deliberately
wrap around yourself. Heed my words. I will dispose of this
thing. The Lady's servants are forewarned and forearmed. You
may choose to believe, or not, as you wish. Our fight is not
with the people of Albatar, but with the evil that at times besets
it." At that, Andiss flicked the charm off the end of his
weapon and into the fire burning on the hearth. A flare of
smoke erupted, and the heat haze around it winked out as the
metals warped in the heat of the embers.

Andiss jerked his head at Kazari and she followed him out
of the inn into the cold night air. Dead silence followed them.
The chill in the air had nothing to do with the goosebumps
that climbed her arms and walked up the back of her neck. She
opened her mouth to tell Andiss about the gorgone she'd
sensed, but Andiss shook his head and drew her towards a side
alley. The mist had thickened while they were inside the inn,
and it swirled in fanciful figures as they strode through it.
Kazari caught her breath as two figures appeared from the
depths of the alley, dropping a knife from her sleeve into her
hand. Then, slightly embarrassed as she recognised Mikel and
Jern, put it away again.

"Malmetal on a singer in the inn. And open derision from
Juster and Ralen against the Order," said Andiss resignedly.

"Anything more?" asked Mikel.

Even in the darkness and the swirling mist, Kazari saw the
frown on Andiss face.

"There are too many things leading to this one place."

"Andiss, I couldn't tell you inside, but the singer went down
a hidden stair in the inn. And there was, or at least had been,"
she corrected herself, "a gorgone somewhere down there. And
there were other people, so I didn't follow all the way – did I
do the wrong thing?"

"No, you did the right thing, Kaz. It's not the kind of place
even a full Hunter should venture alone. We do need to find

out what's down there, and I need to notify the Abbot that Juster and Ralen are openly hostile. Mikel, you and Jern stay here and scout around some more. Kaz, you'll stay with them and see what you can sense." Then he sighed. "And perhaps tomorrow Javon and Sendar may have more information."

A few moments later, Andiss vanished in a swirl of mist, and Kazari was left with Mikel and Jern.

"We'll quarter the area," said Mikel. "Kaz, let us know if you sense anything. Don't worry about anything except trying to sense – Jern and I will do everything else."

And for the rest of an extremely long night, they walked the streets of Seraph, keeping to the shadows, while Kazari did her best to sense gorgone. Here and there she found hints – a touch of acridity here, and a smidgen of corruption there – but there was nothing overt, or new. Outside a jeweller's near a market square, Kazari sensed a lingering haze of foulness, and Jern marked it as a place to revisit the following day. Several of the other stalls held hints of gorgone – a grocer, a wine merchant, and a tinsmith. She began to wonder how gorgones were able to wander Seraph's streets undetected. Eventually, Mikel directed them back towards the cathedral, and weary step by step, they made their way through the mist and back to their beds.

Kazari was barely able to keep her eyes open long enough to remove her boots and damp clothing, before she toppled into bed. But even in bed, despite her exhaustion, nightmares awaited.

Chapter Thirty-four:
The Market

Kazari reached for her notebook and began to write feverishly, trying to banish the nightmare images from her mind with the force of her words. Sendar in anguish. Dari, surrounded by gorgones, her blond hair glinting in the light of many lanterns. Tears on her mother's face. Anguish on Alexando's. She wrote, panting, until she'd poured the dreams onto the paper in front of her, then she lay back, wearily wiping sweat from her forehead. She looked over at Sendar, still slumbering peacefully, and decided not to wake him.

Her fingers lingered on the scar on her face, tracing it lightly to the corner of her mouth. It was uncomfortable in a way it hadn't been for many months. Remembering Alexando's instructions, she gathered the notebook to her chest, and tucked herself up cross-legged on her bed.

She stilled her mind, grasped her amethyst, and tried to meditate, letting her eyes track the words on the pages. She read them through, feeling tears start to her eyes, and rubbed them away furiously.

It had only been a dream. It wasn't real. She closed her eyes again and stilled her breathing, reminding herself of the nightmare images of her family that had turned out to be lies, and after some minutes managed to bring her emotions under a semblance of control. Then she pulled her Book of Hunters from the bedside table and turned to a page towards the back.

Even though the darkness stalks them, my Hunters will walk in my light. Though the earth fail, and all about is death, they are mine forever, she read. She focused on the words, allowing them to seep into her soul. When she looked up, she discovered she'd fallen asleep again, dawn had long gone, someone had draped a blanket over her, and the others were nowhere to be seen.

Yawning and still tired, she washed, dressed, and made her way downstairs to the dining hall, wondering if the other Hunters were even still in the building.

"Kazari!" called a familiar voice as she lifted the teapot.

"Abel?"

"And Elliam, of course," said her friend. They were seated at one end of a long line of tables.

"Have you seen the others? Or Mikel and Jern?" she asked.

"They left you a note," replied Elliam, handing her a folded piece of paper. "We rode in this morning with pigeons from Alexando to restock the lofts here." Kazari sat down and deposited her teacup on the table, ignoring the growling sounds from her stomach.

Rest up today, Kaz, we'll be about Hunter business tonight. I'm expecting a message from Alexando in the next few hours. When it arrives, bring it to me at the manor house. I'll be with Eriad.

Andiss.

She put the note in her pocket, and yawned again. "Do you know if there's been a pigeon for Andiss?"

Elliam shook his head.

"It's only mid-morning, Kazari, in fact, the others only left an hour ago. I'd suggest you get some breakfast into you, so that if one arrives, you'll be ready to get the message to wherever it needs to go."

Kazari yawned again, waving one hand apologetically, and went to get some food.

One of the Cathedral's Growers bustled up with a message tube in her hand just as Kazari had filled her mouth.

"For Andiss," she said, looking doubtfully at Kazari, and then back at Elliam. He motioned wordlessly to Kazari, and the woman blushed and handed the tube to her. "Will there be a reply, Hunter?"

Kazari shook her head uncertainly, swallowing to clear her mouth. "I'll ask Andiss when I give this to him." She took another, hurried, bite of her breakfast, and began to stand.

"Wait, Kazari. Finish your breakfast. If Andiss needs you after you deliver that, you'll be all the better for a full stomach," said Elliam. "Won't she, Abel?" He raised an eyebrow at his novice.

"Yes, Elliam. Um, I was in a hurry one day, and then sort of skipped breakfast, and, and . . . it wasn't a good choice."

"What he means to say, Kaz, is that he slept in, and tried to make up the time by skipping breakfast before a full day's trial of his Gift. We do like our trainees to learn to cope with a little deprivation, but only when we want them to. It's pretty hard to learn new things when the only thing you're thinking about is your stomach. And you tire faster, don't you Abel?"

Abel nodded, and made a face.

"It won't make much difference if you spend five minutes eating, Kaz. The bird's earlier than I expected, actually, given the distance." He looked slightly troubled.

Five minutes later, Kazari finished the last of her tea, and rose.

"I'd better get this to Andiss," she said. "Will you be here at dinner?"

"Yes," replied Elliam. "There are many things for a Navigator to learn in the wilderness, but sometimes a little city learning can be helpful too. Tell Andiss we'll stick around for a few days."

Kazari nodded, and then went to the stable for Stumpy. He smelled of home – the Abbey, now – and things that were good. As she trotted him briskly through the winding streets to the manor house the people of Seraph went about their daily business around her, unhurried and unperturbed, yet somewhere in their town, gorgones stalked. Somewhere in their town, sellers of malmetal charms lurked, purveying their corrupted wares with impunity. And in the manor house to which she rode, a Lord and his Lady, sworn to uphold the safety of Albatar, had abandoned that oath.

As she rode, with each of Stumpy's steps her unease grew. What was Andiss doing, consulting with Eriad when gorgones stalked Seraph? When Albatar was endangered! She drew Stumpy to a clattering halt at the manor, breathing an apology to him as she dismounted, and handed her reins off to one of the ever-present stablehands.

She entered the manor house, requesting Eriad's offices to the senior of the servants inside the imposing door, and followed the woman through the maze of rooms. When they at last arrived at Eriad's office, the woman paused and turned to her. "Not all of us agree with our Lord and Lady, Hunter." Her eyes darted from side to side, and her voice was soft. "Remember that, please." Her eyes were troubled, but before Kazari could question her further, she'd bustled away.

Troubled, she knocked on the door, pulling the note from her pocket. Eriad ushered her inside, his long face looking greyer than she remembered, and waved a hand at Andiss, seated in a chair near a polished wooden desk, a stack of papers in his hands.

"You've the message, Kaz?"

She handed it over, and then stood, waiting.

"Sit, Kazari," said Eriad, "If you wouldn't mind shifting your own chair, that would be helpful. These old limbs and lungs aren't up to the task nowadays, I'm afraid." In fact, he looked quite unwell, she realised as she dragged a heavy wooden chair over to join Andiss. Eriad sat in his own behind the desk with a sigh, breathing more heavily than a simple walk to open a door should have required. He rang a small bell on his desk, and a moment later, another gold robed figure entered. It was the young man who'd stood behind Eriad when they'd entered the great hall. "Beved, would you bring Kazari a drink and then join us please?"

The man nodded and vanished, returning only moments later with a tall jug of water and several glasses, and then pulled his own chair up on Eriad's left.

"Alexando has news of malmetal charms in Chator. And the Abbot has sent word that the Queen has summoned her to the capital. We're to proceed there when we're able." He looked up and spoke directly to Eriad. "There are gorgones in Seraph." There was a sharp intake of breath from Beved, quickly stilled, and Kazari felt her face colour and then blanche, the two things so close together she was hot and cold, all at the same time.

Eriad sat back with a sigh, his eyes closed and one hand cupped around the topaz on its golden chain.

"There are many things wrong here. Juster and Ralen stray far from the Lady's side, drawing many with them. We have struggled against the heresy they speak, but it gains sway day by day. And now a gorgone. Perhaps, more than one."

"Master," said Beved, hesitantly, "We know they lie – our Lords I mean. Could it be that they've brought gorgones to Seraph as well?"

Eriad opened his eyes wearily. "Perhaps, Beved. Perhaps. One thing is certain however, you will attend me at every meeting from now on, no matter whether Juster wishes it. We will use the excuse of my health, although," and he smiled faintly, "as we know, it's not really an excuse. You will need to know everything – just in case – for my successor. Would that you might step into my role – but you are yet too young and have too much to learn."

Kazari looked at her hands, feeling as if she was intruding on something private. Beved and Eriad were obviously close. In fact, she could see that the young man's eyes were suspiciously shiny as he nodded to his mentor. But then Eriad looked up and straightened his shoulders.

"Last night's message from the Abbot said that my replacement has been dispatched. Feruna will bring a novice to assist as well. One of the new inductees, in fact."

"Charla?" asked Kazari, surprised.

"I believe that is her name," replied Eriad, then looked directly at Beved. "Feruna brings what we lack, Beved, and Charla has Gifts that mirror both of ours. She will become partly your responsibility." The young man nodded, unsurprised, unlike Kazari.

"The Abbot will send Charla here? Into danger?"

All three of the Lady's servants turned their eyes towards her, and then she blushed. Charla had precisely the same amount of time within the Order as Kazari, and Kazari was here.

"Where better to learn her trade?" asked Eriad with raised eyebrows.

"I . . . I only meant . . . I mean it's dangerous here."

"Child," said the old Adviser with a hint of a smile. "It is dangerous *everywhere*. The only difference is that some danger is easier to see in the physical realm. Your friend is clearly ready if the Abbot is dispatching her." He turned back to Andiss. "So, Andiss – our next move?"

"We'll leave you to deal with the politics," said Andiss. "Are you well enough?"

"I shall have to be," replied Eriad. "Beved will help."

"In that case, Kazari and I will scout the market, with Javon and Sendar, while Mikel and Jern watch the inn. Fortuitously, Elliam and Abel arrived this morning, so we'll have a pair of Navigators as well. You'll speak to the Cathedral's prior?"

The old Adviser nodded. "They're Growers and Intercessors for the main part, but their choir is something *quite* special, should we require them."

Kazari's mind flew back to the gorgone attack on the Abbey, and the ranked Intercessors singing through the darkness generated by the greater gorgone, and a tiny flicker of hope blossomed. They were truly not alone.

"And of course they have several Healers, and two of the Judicial sept. It's quite a community here. And before you ask, no, the Healers have done what they might for me. Age is something that cannot be healed, and I have had longer than many."

"In that case, Kazari and I will take our leave." Andiss stood, and Kazari followed him out. They left their horses at the cathedral, and then Kazari and Andiss walked back to the market area. It was warm in the spring air, and the bright sunlight was at variance with the evil that Kazari knew lurked somewhere in Seraph. Once again their black garb drew stares, and Kazari wondered whether the simple fact of their presence would send the vendors she'd marked the night before scurrying away.

Andiss stopped just before the market, and motioned her towards a back alley. "Jern has left a few things for us." She followed him down the alleyway, stepping over and around piled garbage. A skinny dog bolted from their approach, leaving the pile it had been foraging within. Kazari wrinkled her nose. The alleyway stank, not of gorgone, but of the detritus of humanity. Andiss stopped near a rundown outhouse and stood on tiptoes to reach into the roof space. A moment later, he pulled a sack containing light overclothes from it.

Kazari frowned at the mismatched collection in the sack, and pulled a face as Andiss handed her a long over robe, in the style she'd seen some of the merchants wearing.

"Put it on," Andiss told her.

The robe covered her down to her feet, concealing her Hunter garb, and had a matching head wrap that hid her short hair. She felt like an idiot. Andiss wore a matching outfit.

"They're from Western Albatar," Andiss explained, "and further north than you've been." He tucked the long ends of his head covering away so that it sat turban-like on his head. "Leave yours long – most women wear them draped rather than tucked."

Kazari flung the long ends over her shoulders, leaving her arms free and bounced a little to make sure she could move easily, then followed Andiss back down the alleyway and into the market.

People bustled everywhere, chattering like a multicoloured flock of parrots squabbling in a tree. Everywhere Kazari looked there were people haggling over prices, adding items to baskets, or moving from stall to stall. At Andiss' nod, she led him on a meandering path to the jeweller's she'd marked the night before. The place looked so different in daylight, and was so full of people that she could have led him directly there without anyone taking any notice at all, she realised, still, when she mentioned it, Andiss commented that such habits were good for a Hunter to develop.

She looked around, letting her eyes trail over the people in the crowd. A tall woman and young man, whose robes matched theirs, waved. She did a double take. Sendar? Javon?

The others joined them.

"Nice dress, Kaz," said Sendar.

"Matches yours," she replied, suppressing a snigger despite the gravity of the situation.

"You two wander for a bit. Javon and I will be in the jeweller's," said Andiss. "Kaz, can you sense anything?"

Kazari inhaled deeply. Underlying the smell of fresh baked bread was a smidgen of gorgone – not as strong as the night before, but clearly there, and definitely leading to the jeweller.

"The jeweller, I'm pretty sure."

"You two check the other stalls you found last night. Don't do anything without us. Just sense, Kaz." He motioned to Javon, and the two of them stepped quickly over to the jeweller's store.

Chapter Thirty-five: Tinsmith

"**H**ow was the mural?" Kazari asked Sendar.

"It . . . was incredible," replied Sendar. "Although we didn't really find anything more at the manor house. It seems like such a waste of time except for that."

Kazari nodded.

"Have you seen anything here, yet?"

"Nothing, really. We've been wandering, waiting for Andiss and you. He told us about last night."

Kazari nodded. "It was awful. There's so much wrong with this place." She shivered, and looked across the market. Despite the brightness of the beautiful spring day, Kazari couldn't help but wonder how many people in Seraph had been beguiled by the gorgones. A thought struck her.

"Sendar, Jalax? Is she all right? Have you seen her?" Sendar's sister was apprenticed to the rope maker in Seraph, and Kazari was ashamed to realise she hadn't even thought about her.

"She's fine. We dropped past this morning," said Sendar. "I'll introduce you tomorrow. Assuming we have time." He sighed heavily and turned his gaze towards the rest of the market. "In the meantime, we'd better do what we were asked." He looked back to the jeweller, where Andiss and Javon had been ushered inside. Through the wide glass windows, Kazari could see the older Hunters bent over a tray held by a young man. She nodded, and followed Sendar into the crowd.

After being given such a wide berth while in her Hunter's garb, it was strange to be jostled in a crowd, and Kazari felt safely anonymous. She relaxed and let herself sense, drawing in the smells of market. Here and there were traces of gorgone. Nothing new, but hints of presence – rather like the tracks Javon had so painstakingly taught them to follow in the mud.

She drew Sendar along, following the strongest taint. It went past the grocer's, intensified a little at the wine merchant's and then, from the corner of her eye, Kazari saw something that seemed hauntingly familiar. She stopped dead, and Sendar cannoned into her.

"What?" he whispered. "And sorry."

She brushed him off impatiently, trying to figure out what it was that had drawn her attention. The taint of gorgone was no greater there. Slowly, Kazari turned her head, letting her eyes drift across the crowds and stalls. Up towards the tinsmith's stall, a faintly remembered figure ducked out of sight.

"That man – he was in Athos!" she said.

"What man?"

"He's gone now, but he was at the tinsmith's stall – the new tinsmith's apprentice in Athos," she replied. "Remember I said we needed to ask about him. I never did, because then we saw Dari, and I forgot. But I'm sure it's him!" She tugged on Sendar's arm, pulling him after her. The crowd seemed to surge around them, impeding her progress.

"Kaz, he's a tinsmith's apprentice, there's no reason he *shouldn't* be at another tinsmith's," hissed Sendar in her ear.

"But there was someone in Chator too," she replied, trying to step around a woman. For a moment they did a little back and forth dance. "At the tinsmith's one morning when I went for a walk to clear my head."

"What?" Sendar exclaimed. "Why didn't you say something then?"

"That was the morning Alexando told us about being marked. I forgot. Again." This was the third connection to a tinsmith. The same man in at least two places, she was sure. She hadn't been able to see who it was in Chator, but the memory of someone watching made her neck crawl again.

"Shall we get Javon and Andiss?" she asked, stopping dead again.

"Not yet," said Sendar. "We need to make sure it was really the same man. And you need to sense near the tinsmith's stall." Come on." He grabbed her hand and drew her through the crowd. Kazari followed, glad that his tall form was cutting a path for them. And despite the gravity of the situation, she couldn't help but enjoy the feel of his strong hand holding hers.

As they approached the tinsmith's, Sendar slowed, and drew her up beside him.

Kazari drew in a breath, sensing. The taint of gorgone was slightly stronger.

"What do we do now?" she asked. "There has been a gorgone here. But the smell's similar to the jeweller's." She looked back across the market square. She could see glimpses of the jeweller's but no sign of Andiss or Javon.

"I think we need a new pot," replied Sendar. "Don't we?" She looked stupidly at him for a moment, until he rolled his eyes and the dots connected.

"Oh. Yes. We do. For the road."

Sendar stepped up to the stall, making a show of browsing, still grasping her by the hand.

"What do you think of this one?" he asked, pointing to a large billy. It had a spout, Kazari saw. Which was a really good idea.

"That spout's a great idea," she said. "I wonder if there's a bigger one. Remember there's four of us." She picked the billy up, and while she pretended to examine it, tried to look past it to see if she could see the man from Athos again. The stall stretched quite a long way back from the edge of the market, wares displayed on long tables inside the ramshackle building.

There were several people browsing the front table, while staff patrolled the tables inside, presumably to prevent thefts. The darker interior of the building made it hard to make out faces.

An older woman came forward.

"May I help you?"

"Do you have a larger one like this?" Sendar asked, pointing to the pot Kazari held.

The woman frowned thoughtfully.

"I think there may be a larger one inside – if you'd follow me? And is there anything else you'd like to see?"

"Do you have any enamelled mugs?" Sendar asked.

"Of course." The woman smiled. "This way." She led them past two long tables to the back of the stall. "There's a stack of those right over here." She rounded a support beam, and gestured to pile of mugs on a table in a back corner. "And right next to them you'll see the billies."

Kazari stepped forward, pretending to examine the mugs, drawing Sendar after her. There was the tiniest hint of a breeze, and then something hit her on the head, and everything went black.

Chapter Thirty-six: Corruptor

Kazari groaned and rolled over. Her head ached and her body protested, but then the ache in her head began to recede. Her Healing had kicked in. When her Gift had finished she was left hungry and tired. She supposed that the energy had to come from somewhere.

As her head cleared, she realised with a surge of nausea that the stench of nearby gorgone permeated the air. And where was Sendar?

The floor was cold and hard, and uneven – most likely rock – she thought, as she wobbled to her hands and knees. Faintly, Kazari could see bars on one side – she was in some kind of cell. A dark lump lay on the ground several metres away, and she crawled over to it, touching the inert form hesitantly. The familiar texture of Hunter garb met her touch, and she rolled the form gently over, trying to see who it was.

"Sendar?" she whispered hesitantly into the dimness.

"Kaz? A moment." There was a groaning sound, and in the faint light, Kazari could see her friend was levering himself upright. "Where are we?"

"No idea. I just woke up. Are you all right?"

"My head aches," he said tiredly. "And Javon and Andiss are *not* going to be happy with us."

Kazari swallowed. They were not. Once again, she and Sendar were somewhere they shouldn't be. In retrospect, they should have gone straight back to the jeweller's.

She put a hand on Sendar's forehead. "Give me a moment." She summoned her Healing. *Lady, let me get this right.*

A moment later, Sendar sighed gratefully. "Thanks, Kaz. So, where are we?"

"I think we're underground," she replied. "Again. Which means we probably know how they're getting around Albatar, now."

"Yes," replied Sendar. "The suckers at the farm were our first hint – the tunnel. Then here we've found entrances – at least I'm pretty certain you were at the top of another one last night – to underground facilities. I suspect they join up."

"And Suborden!" said Kazari. "They were underground there! But the others didn't find any connections to elsewhere, did they?"

"Not at the time, no. But remember, they fought their way through those tunnels." She could hear the frown in Sendar's voice. "Perhaps Mikel might be able to shed more light on things."

He pushed himself to his feet, and then hauled her up. "Let's see where we are."

Where, appeared to be a cage. Somewhere underground. The bars were solid, and fixed into the stone floor. Sometime between being knocked out and waking up, their concealing robes had been removed, and both were now clad only in their Hunter's blacks, but their belts were empty of sheaths and weapons. Kazari checked her boots – empty. The sheaths sewn inside her sleeves however, had been missed. Whoever had searched her had been sloppy. She had her stars and several knives.

"Sendar, I've got . . ." A metallic jangle interrupted, and then the darkness around them lightened. Footsteps, and a dry slithering, echoed off the rocky walls. The stench of gorgone intensified and her stomach tried to empty itself.

"Gorgone," she gasped. "One I've not sensed before."

"Lady, be with us," said Sendar, quietly. Then the light brightened abruptly as a lantern on a pole swayed into view, toted by a human figure, with another following behind, also holding a lantern. The slithering became even louder, and a bulky shape followed the humans into the room. The human forms were concealed by the lights they held, but the gorgone with them was illuminated.

"Well, well, well," rasped a dry voice. "Two Hunters – scum followers of the witch."

One of the humans stepped forward, and hooked a lantern to a hook in the wall, shedding even more light on the monstrosity. Kazari gagged at the sight of the many limbed monster etched on her eyeballs. Encased in what looked like a crumbly crust, it had two enormous eyes on stalks that waved and bobbled nauseatingly, dripping ichor that splattered onto the gorgone's front parts.

'Corruptor,' had been the label on the drawing she'd studied back at the Abbey. She cupped one hand over her nose and mouth, futilely trying to block the stench from the creature. Unfortunately it didn't make any difference. She wished it had. The creature's stench was imprinted on her brain.

Kazari's stomach roiled and rebelled, and she was forced to swallow convulsively, breathing slowly in order to regain control.

"Nothing to say, Hunters?" the monster asked.

Kazari shot a look at Sendar. His face looked battered in the light, and she could see that one eye was partly closed by swelling.

The gorgone smiled. "And I can feel that you both bear the 'mark' of my own Master. *You* were at Suborden."

Kazari nearly threw up then and there, partly from fear, but more from the overpowering stench rising from the gorgone – like that of overripe fruit, combined with something that had been dead for days, sweet and repellent. She raised a trembling hand towards the scar on her face, and a jolt of fire ran through it. She gasped and clutched the side of her face, but the pain was gone as fast as it had arrived. Still, sweat dotted Kazari's forehead, and she found that her hands were trembling.

"Leave her alone, corruptor!" said Sendar. The creature spun away from Kazari, and she took a deep breath through a throat that was too tight, and crossed her arms protectively in front of her, bringing her hands closer to her hidden weapons. A tiny spark of hope illuminated the darkness in her mind.

"Leave her alone?" sputtered the gorgone. Ooze spattered from its eyes, dotting the floor of the tunnel. "You, who also bear my Master's mark, and who will barely stand when I've finished with you. You want me to leave *her* alone?"

Kazari heard the threat to her friend. Felt his fear. She'd seen how Sendar's recovery after Suborden had affected him. And then, by her side, Sendar doubled over, hands reaching for the scar beneath his trousers, as a strangled cry forced itself past his lips. Fire struck her face anew, but by strength of will alone, Kazari kept her own hands down. She grasped Sendar's arm, and put her hands over his, trying to lend comfort to her companion.

"You have no power over the Lady's servants," Kazari said defiantly. The words sounded much braver than she felt. He clearly had power enough to send them pain. But it was pain alone, she knew. There was no blood trickling down her face, nor soaking through Sendar's trousers.

"You, sitting in that cage, say I have no power? You, who are weak, and young, and barely tutored in the Hunter arts."

Kazari took a wobbly breath. "Yes, I'm weak, and I'm young, and barely trained, and I'm in a cage. To keep you safe from me, I assume. What must you feel when faced by a *full* Hunter?"

By her side, Sendar straightened, despite the pain she knew he was feeling, and then laughed. It was a wholesome sound, despite the effort evident in its tones. "Even our newest recruit has your measure, corruptor."

She felt the gorgone's miasma of rot intensify, yet as it did, she could tell that its ability to affect her was limited – almost as if there was something within her that acted like a repellent, and she felt a faint warmth on her chest from the amethyst beneath her shirt.

The pain in her face intensified again, but after Suborden and its hours of torment, momentary pain, though it left her gasping and her eyes tearing, was in the end, only pain and not damage – except to her psyche. Fear of the pain returning shook her more than the possibility of injury or deformity.

The sensation of rot intensified again, and Kazari was astounded that the very stones she was standing on hadn't crumbled with the force of it. There was a sudden surge of hatred, and something battered Kazari's mind – but it was weak in comparison to the suckers and the fire gorgone, or even the viper. She recalled the words of the text she'd read on the corruptor. Its presence was insidious to the mind, rather than abrupt, but its effects upon fertility, living things and crops were legendary. The text had made the point though – the powers of a corruptor took time to make themselves felt, but they were no less insidious because of that. And often they were longer lasting, burned deep into the psyche of the corrupted. But still, even those changes required, like all gorgones, the will of the person to accept the will of the beast.

Many things about Seraph began to settle into place inside Kazari's head. Malmetal. The corruptor gorgone. The insidious decline and falling away of the people of the town. They were all slow things, but they had penetrated the populace deeply. She wondered how long the corruptor had roamed the tunnels beneath the streets.

The monster snarled, an incoherent sound of rage, and struck the bars of their cell with a clatter of limbs.

"You lurk here beneath Seraph, spreading dissent and corruption, but we are already forewarned and forearmed. Wherever your type go within Albatar, they will be met by the Lady's servants," said Kazari, defiantly.

"And you underestimate the extent of our sway in Albatar, Hunter. The witch, that one that you call Lady, is weak, and her servants do not hold the respect they once did. Your time is short, and your hold upon this land tenuous."

Kazari's anger rose again. The words were despicable. "Our Lady stands between your hordes and Albatar. In fact, She stands wherever humanity resists your influence, not just Albatar. And not only her sworn servants revere her."

The gorgone spat a derisive laugh.

"Perhaps not, but *we* are many, and our adherents grow. Albatar tires of the yoke of the witch. Men and women of ambition seek more than life in this tiny land, and they know who can show them how to attain it. Our servants await only our signal to rise up and free themselves from its borders."

"And we, The Lady's Hunters, will resist you with all our strength, and all of hers as well," replied Sendar. He sounded so sure, and so certain, that Kazari's heart gave a bound within her chest.

"And when we take all that you love, and turn it to our will, what then?" the gorgone said.

Kazari felt a sudden pang. Her dreams – her fellow Hunters, caged. Her family, dead. This was what the gorgones threatened. Everything, and everyone, she loved.

"What then?" asked Sendar, "We are not puppets, monster. And no matter how far down the path of corruption someone might travel, there is always free will. Always a chance that someone will turn their back on what is evil, and return to seeking good. Even should all of Albatar be overturned, yet there will still be hope."

Kazari felt the power of the words as he spoke them, and they eased the ache within her a little. She'd made her pledge to stand with the Lady as long as her body still had breath within it, and while she had life there was always hope.

"Brave words, Hunter, but still only words." The gorgone turned towards the figures silhouetted against the light. "Bring her."

Bring who? Kazari wondered. A flurry of motion ensued, and then several suckers and a masked human walked forward. The human was surrounded by suckers, and at the corruptor's nod, removed her mask. Dari's golden hair, glinted in the lamp light.

Chapter Thirty-seven: Unmasked

Nightmares made real. Dari, surrounded by suckers. Did that mean the rest of them were real too? The gorgone laughed, an ugly sound, full of derision and hatred.

"Watching you watch your loved ones in pain provides great sport for our kind, and even for some of your own. For us, it is sustenance."

Kazari lunged at the bars, enraged by the beast's mockery.

"Kaz, stand down!" said Sendar, and she felt his hands on her shoulders.

Stand down? She wanted to rip the thing to bits, futile though that seemed right then. But it had Dari – her truest friend. The one who'd stood with her when her parents hadn't.

"Kaz," said Sendar again. "You'll only injure yourself."

Injure herself? The bars were sharp, she realised – sharpened, actually – but she'd heal, and now the pain seemed negligible. Of course Sendar knew she'd heal, he just wanted the gorgone to think she wouldn't. Or . . . something. She had no idea.

All she saw was Dari, surrounded by gorgones, golden hair glinting in the light, just as she'd seen her in her dream. How terrified must she be? And there was nothing Kazari could do to help, not here, not locked in the cage. Sendar's hands pulled her away from the bars, and she felt blood drip from her palms, then stop. She blotted them on her trousers, knowing that they'd heal, but let Sendar cradle them anyway. Going along with the subterfuge. She remembered what had happened in Suborden, when the 'changed' had realised she was a Healer.

"Dari . . . " she began.

"Kaz, I don't think . . ." began Sendar, but the gorgone interrupted.

"You recognise her, I see," the corruptor hissed. He slithered nearer, and his multiple limbs twitched and clicked. "That is good. Very good."

Sendar's arms tugged at Kazari, and dimly, she knew he was whispering something in her ear, but she was too distraught to listen. She pulled away and went to the bars again.

"Dari, I'm sorry! I'm so sorry!" Tears streaked her face, and she scrubbed at them, leaving bloody smears. "Somehow we'll get you out of this!" She almost put her hands on the bars again, but then tucked them into her armpits, hugging her arms around her body. She could feel her knives in her sleeves, perhaps somehow she could get one to her friend. And if she had knives, what might Sendar have?

Dari spoke. "But, Kaz, there's no need to be sorry."

"But Dari, it's my fault you're here." She raised a tear-stained face to her friend. "The others will find us, I'm sure."

The gorgone slithered closer to Dari, and Kazari couldn't help but admire the way her friend stood her ground in the face of its horror. She also seemed unaffected by the suckers surrounding her. Her hair glinted as she ducked her head, and Kazari could see that her face seemed . . . almost . . . serene.

"Well, in a way, Hunter, it *is* your fault," said the gorgone. His loathsome body hovered just behind Dari, and Kazari's skin crawled. "And now I think upon it, yes, definitely your fault. We'd never have looked for someone in such a backwater if *you* hadn't come from there."

Athos, a backwater? He was insulting her hometown? She almost laughed, despite her distress. "The tinsmith's apprentice," she said, regaining some composure.

"Among others," replied the gorgone, and the man she'd seen that morning stepped out of the darkness, holding a lantern. Kazari studied him as the gorgone went on. He was tall, well favoured, now she was looking at him properly, and his face held derision. "We were quite . . . surprised, I think is the word."

Others? Wondered Kazari. She couldn't imagine anyone from Athos following gorgones of their own free will, but her experience at Suborden had shown that corruption hid in surprising places. As it had in Seraph, and who knew where else across Albatar.

And her dreams *were* real – at least in some fashion. She had brought the gorgone threat to Athos. She'd brought it to her family, and to her friends. Those who loved and trusted her were in danger, and they were in danger only because *she* had chosen the Lady. Guilt wracked her, and her legs threatened to give way.

"Dari, somehow we'll get you out of here," she said, desperately hoping that her words were truth, and that somehow, one of the other Hunters would find them.

"Of course," said the gorgone, "there is something you might wish to consider, Hunter youngster." Its many legs skittered across the stone floor, and its eye stalks bobbled. Kazari leaned back unconsciously as it drew closer to the bars. "And that is whether your friend here *wants* to get out of here."

"What?" burst from Kazari's lips.

"What?" mocked the creature. "Ask her."

"Ask her what?" said Kazari, still confused.

"Ask her whether she'd like to leave."

"Of course she wants to leave!" replied Kazari. "Who in their right mind would prefer to stay as a captive of gorgones?"

"Kaz . . ." She barely heard Sendar's whisper. She looked at Dari. And this time, she looked properly. Her friend's hair hoarded the lamplight, glowing gold. It was neatly tied back, almost artfully arranged, and Dari's familiar figure was clad in the clothes her mother had talked her into. The tinsmith stood beside her. She was still admirably composed and Kazari felt a surge of pride at her friend's resilience.

"Dari, of course you want to leave," said Kazari. "When rescue comes, you'll be safe!"

"Safe?" said Dari, speaking at last. "I feel . . . quite safe, Kaz. Very safe, in fact." She twirled the end of her ponytail with one hand and inspected her nails. They were polished to a high gloss, Kazari noticed.

"Safe?! You're surrounded by suckers! You're probably not in your right mind."

Dari looked up, and then, very deliberately, waved one hand. The suckers backed off.

Dari took the tinsmith's hand, and turned to face him, drawing one polished nail delicately down the man's face. Then she reached up, drew the man's head down to her, and kissed him deeply. Kazari watched, thunderstruck, horror and disbelief warring with her childhood memories. Dari was here of her own volition?

"No!"

"The better word would be 'Yes.'" Dari smirked. "It *was* you who brought me here, or at least to this point. All that prattling about the Lady. All that stuff about 'choosing' the right thing, and Mum and Dad going on and on and on about Enda. It made me sick!" She almost spat the words. "So when the opportunity arose, I sought my own path. And a very good path it is too."

She drew closer to the cage, hand still entwined in that of the man behind her. He looked at Kazari and Sendar, and his lips twisted into a sneer.

"Dari!" The words were torn from Kazari's lips. "But your family . . . our friends in Athos . . . *you* helped *me* know I was right to choose the Lady!" Her mind refused to process the idea that her best friend – the one who'd stood by her on the Day of Choosing, and with whom she'd lived her entire life – could now be so diametrically opposed to everything Kazari had believed about her.

"Friends!" scoffed Dari. "Family? *Athos?* When there's so much more in the world? When our entire lives are fenced around by the boundaries of one tiny land? When I could be somewhere else doing more than herding sheep forever?"

"But you love the sheep!"

"Love the sheep?" Dari spat the words. "I *hate* the sheep. I will not be bound by expectations. You should know this better than anyone else. I *will* have what *I* want!"

Kazari had no words. The person standing in front of her seemed so removed from the Dari she knew, it was almost as if she were a different person. Faintly, she could hear murmured words and feel Sendar's hands on her shoulders, but it all seemed meaningless in the wreck of all that she'd thought she'd known. She was lost, staggering around in a whiteout of emotion so strong that it blanked out everything else.

The corruptor laughed, its stench intensifying so much Kazari almost lifted her hands to ward it off.

"Your foulness holds no sway with The Lady's Hunters." Sendar's voice broke through Kazari's anguish. She had no idea whether he was talking to the corruptor or Dari. He steadied her with his hands as well as his voice, and she clung to his tall strength as if she were drowning.

She tried once more. "Dari – this isn't you. It can't be! You're *good,* and kind, and Settler's Run has always been your life! How can you say that it isn't? You *couldn't* have lived a lie! We did so much together. I *know* you!"

Her friend smiled, and Kazari's heart skipped a beat, cold dread coursing through her limbs. It was as if a second mask had lifted from Dari's face. Her physical features remained the same, but malice looked from her eyes, and bitterness twisted her mouth.

"I'm afraid you really don't know me at all, Kazari."

Hearing her name spoken fully finally loosened her frozen mind, and Kazari felt tears start from her eyes.

"You've never called me that before."

"You weren't a Servant of the Witch, when we were children together," replied Dari. "I rather think your companion knows me better than you do." Dari looked over Kazari's head and Kazari knew that she was looking at Sendar.

"Sendar?" Kazari turned to her fellow Hunter.

Sendar's face was grim, and saddened. "I'm afraid Dari has walked further away from our Lady than either of us had ever imagined," he replied, and closed his eyes briefly.

"And now it's time for me to show you exactly how much I've changed. There are things you know that we need." Dari's eyes were like black holes in her head.

The man by her side stroked her shoulder.

"Perhaps you could give him a matching scar, my love? He seems to like her a lot."

Dari turned back to the tinsmith.

"What a lovely idea, Sereth. And if, by any chance, you two survive the night, every time you look at him, you'll see my mark and remember, so that you *know*," she mocked Kazari's emotional outcry from a few moments before, "who owns you both." She gestured to the suckers, and they surrounded her again, but now Kazari could see what they truly were an honour guard, and drew closer to the cage.

Kazari could feel the suckers; they were seething with anticipation. They were trying to fuel her fear, her despair and her confusion. She took a step backward, and felt Sendar's hand pulling her towards him.

"No-one owns another human being, Dari," he said, sadness permeating his voice. "No external marks can ever define what's inside another's soul. Only the owner of that soul can do that. You might talk of *ownership*, in one voice, and prate of your own freedom in the next, yet fail to see how you've sold your own soul into slavery. The Lady offers release from such slavery."

"You – *you*, talk of freedom, yet call yourself servants of the Witch?" snarled Dari. "You, who have sold yourselves into lives of endless servitude? And who now stand as prisoners in a cell? You have no idea, do you? No idea at all." She shook her head. "With your permission, my lord," she bowed to the corruptor, "Sereth and I will break these for you. Before our Master comes in power, there is much to do."

The corruptor turned towards Dari. "Your eagerness is praiseworthy," The monster's voice was that of a proud father.

He gestured, and a swarm of suckers came forward to join their fellows. There seemed to be hundreds of them. A small group of humans joined them, some with the scales of the 'changed' evident in the lamplight. Several produced crossbows, and pointed them at the two caged Hunters. Kazari's heart sank. She knew even her concealed weapons and skill would be no match for the numbers or the bows.

Sereth drew a key from a chain around his neck, and unlocked the cage door.

"Move apart." Neither Sendar nor Kazari moved. He flicked a finger, and a crossbow bolt brushed Kazari's ear, drawing blood. She exchanged a look with Sendar and stepped to one side. Four of the humans entered the cage. A man and a woman took Kazari's arms, holding them behind her, while the other two held Sendar. Without the crossbows and the suckers, Kazari now knew she and Sendar could have evaded them and escaped, but the gorgone had planned too well.

"Bring him," said Dari, pointing with one fingertip. The two men holding Sendar hustled him from the cage. Kazari watched with anguish, while he was forced to his knees in front of Dari.

With casual cruelty, Sereth slapped Sendar across the face. Kazari flinched, helpless to assist her companion. Then Dari drew a knife from her belt. Shocked, Kazari recognised it. It was her own, her original knife, taken from her below Suborden. She'd never thought to see it again.

"You recognise this, Kazari? It was a present to me from my Master." Dari let the blade catch the light. "Bring her closer."

Kazari's handlers wrestled her closer to the cage bars.

"Ah yes. Now, hold her head. A little more into the light."

With horror, still paired with disbelief, Kazari realised that Dari was measuring the scar that marred Kazari's face. Then with slow cruelty, Dari drew Kazari's first Hunters's knife slowly down the side of Sendar's face to his mouth. Blood welled, and began to pour in a steady stream from the cut.

Sendar's tall form shook, but he made no sound.

"Sereth, tell me. Is it right? Or have I missed the curve a little?" asked Dari. Tears poured down Kazari's face. The damage to Sendar's face, or the ruin of Dari's soul – she had no idea which one drove the tears more. She struggled against her captors, and Dari laughed.

"Be still, old friend," she sneered. "Or I'll put another on the other side. Now, what is it that you know of our presence in Seraph? Tell me, or I'll add to this."

The bloody tip of the knife described tiny circles over the wound marring Sendar's smooth skin, and Kazari stared, sickened, at the young woman she no longer knew.

Sereth stepped into the cage. "Let me try," he said, when neither Kazari nor Sendar spoke. Dari looked up from Sendar's face, eyes avid as Sereth approached Kazari. Kazari heard Sendar make a small sound, and then she buckled over from the punch the man had sunk into her mid-section. His ascending knee bit into her face, and she felt her nose break and bleed. Kazari gasped, more tears pouring down her face.

"Tell us!"

The torture in Suborden had been pointless – pain for pain's sake. This time there was much more at stake. Kazari gritted her teeth, knowing that her nose would heal, but that didn't mean it didn't hurt every time Sereth struck her.

"Tell us," Dari repeated.

Kazari hung heavily from the two holding her, letting them absorb her weight while she regained her breath. Sendar's face was bleeding heavily, and Dari had poised the knife at the corner of Sendar's other eye.

"Tell us," Dari said again as Sereth drew his fist back again.

Kazari tensed, anticipating more pain.

The sound of running feet interrupted them both, and a panting figure dropped to its knees before the corrupter.

"The jeweller's – Hunters!" she gasped.

The corruptor sighed and motioned to Dari. "Put your toys away. Prepare to block the upper levels then join me back here."

Dari looked petulant. "But we've only just begun, Master."

"My love. It will be all the better for waiting," Sereth said. "We shall do our Master's bidding, and then we shall take our time." He smiled at Kazari, and then wet his lip with the tip of his tongue. He left the cage, and motioned for Sendar's holders to throw him back in. The four left, and the cage was relocked under the watchful gaze of the crossbowmen. And then Dari gathered her suckers around her and Sereth like a cloak, and left down a side passage. Kazari choked back a sob, staggering over to Sendar, cradling his bloody face in her hands, as the corruptor watched her from the other side of the bars.

Chapter Thirty-eight:
Fight

"You see how deeply our power has penetrated Albatar?" the corrupter said. "That one has been ours for years. Once she knew you'd leave and abandon her to the dreariness of a tiny village and a nowhere farm, she sought out a different life for herself. *You* were the one who sowed the seeds in her heart, Hunter novice, and we thank you for it."

"Don't listen to it, Kaz," said Sendar. "Dari's actions are the responsibility of no-one but herself."

"Says one who is fearful," scoffed the monster, scuttling closer on its multiple legs. "Once she's been about her business she'll be back to break you properly. She has learned well, and I think she'll find much inspiration in having the two of you here. She and Sereth are a well-matched pair."

Kazari felt her hatred for the monster rise, momentarily eclipsing the despair and horror she'd felt for her friend. Her hands sought her sleeves, and her throwing stars dropped into her hands, and without pausing, she threw as the monster turned to leave. Her stars flew true, and corruptor roared and spun faster than Kazari would have believed possible.

Her stars hadn't appeared to affect corruptor more than mosquito bites would have affected her. By her side, Kazari felt Sendar stiffen. Then he moved. He pulled her away from the bars, and she felt him tense with concentration. Frost covered the bars of the cage door, glinting in the lantern light. At the same, Kazari's amethyst burst into purple light, and an arrow clothed in blue light struck the gorgone. It didn't kill it, or even immobilise it. Instead, the gorgone seemed energised and enraged, and even seemed to grow in stature. It roared, and another arrow slapped into its flank. Ichor spattered the walls as it thrashed its head, and then more arrows flew, even as four figures in black appeared from the tunnel, blades flashing. Jern and Andiss ducked and wove about the beast, while Mikel and Javon stood at their backs, holding off a barrage of suckers, not only with their blades, but with their Gifts of Force. More arrows flew, too many for one person, and Kazari's heart quailed as she realised that somewhere, Abel was standing with Elliam.

The corruptor was large, and it wasn't as physically dangerous as many other gorgones, but the suckers around it were dangerous in their very number. There seemed to be many more than even in Suborden.

"With me, Kaz. When I say, hit the door with your shoulder!" shouted Sendar. The frost on the bars thickened. "Ready – now."

They struck the cage door with their combined weight, and the cold-brittled bars broke, and they tumbled out into the fight. Kazari pulled her small knives from her sleeves, and began to Dance with more focus than she'd ever attained before.

More suckers poured in, and the flight of arrows faltered, and the four Hunters, skilled as they were, were clearly beleaguered by their foes. The corruptor flailed, slashing with its legs, and Jern leaped them without breaking her stride or rhythm, while Andiss darted in and buried his sword deeply into the beast's flank. Stinking ichor poured from the wound, making the footing slippery. Mikel slid as his weapons flickered like serpents' tongues among the suckers. Somehow, he kept his attackers at bay as he tumbled, but Kazari could see he was tiring. Javon ducked and wove, Forcing more suckers back.

Beside her, she saw Sendar reaching into his own sleeves. With a knife in each hand, they fell into rhythm with each other, forging a ring of flashing steel between them. As a fresh wave of suckers poured into the fight, Kazari danced faster. With her memory of the fight with Juster's guards firmly in mind, she allowed the Hunter katas to guide her steps, rather than trying to think too much in advance. Even then, it was hard. The confined space made things much more difficult. She could tell that Sendar had engaged both of his Gifts, as suckers flailed through the air and his rhythm matched hers perfectly – as if the two of them were almost extensions of the other. His rhythm was a steady counterpoint to her flickering motion.

The drag of the suckers, beating at their minds, seemed relentless, and the stench of the corruptor rose above and beyond that of the suckers. Kazari felt a tentacle slap a line of edged barbs into her arm. She heard Sendar grunt in pain. Dimly, she could see Mikel and Javon being slowly forced backward, and she could hear Andiss and Jern panting.

She ducked and wove, dancing, dancing, dancing. Each sucker she dispatched was one less to harass her friends. And then, in her mind, she could see the pattern of the fight. It took her Dance to a new level, and she drew Sendar with her as she moved the two of them through the fight to Javon and Mikel.

She drew them with her, weaving them into her Dance, and the four of them formed a square around Andiss and Jern, who grimly focussed on the corruptor. The huge monster had marked them both, Kazari saw. Andiss was streaked with blood, but determined. While Jern had a cut on her forehead that dripped blood into her eyes, and only her Anticipation kept her out of the reach of corruptor's limbs. Around the others, a ring of suckers closed in.

They had to hold on, Kazari knew. If they could dispatch the corruptor, then a huge weight would be removed from Seraph, and perhaps the gorgone menace in the city would be tempered. Sweat stung her eyes, and she panted, arms and legs slowly tiring. Dancer she might be, and strong and fit, but dancing sucked energy from her body like nothing else.

Just when it seemed as if the sweating, slimy, bleeding fight was about to crush them by numbers alone, a sound of pure delight spun like a sunbeam into the heart of the dungeon. The sound stopped the suckers in their tracks and renewed Kazari's strength in a burst of joy. She danced through the creatures before her like an avenging angel. For a moment, she had enough space to look up, and in that moment, she saw Andiss sink a final blow deeply into the corruptor, Jern duck a flailing sucker tentacle, and Mikel throw a knife behind him. Javon leaped into the air, hurdling the suckers in front of her and dropped the two that menaced Elliam and Abel. And then the first of the Cathedral's Intercessors strode into view, light shining from her body.

She was followed by another ten in quick succession, all singing, their harmonies perfect. The fog of despair generated by the suckers vanished, the corruptor fell, to lie oozing and motionless, and the suckers began to scurry into crevices and cracks, desperate to escape. Kazari dropped her hands, feeling her limbs tremble.

The last of the suckers vanished, and then there were only humans left in the dungeon, among a multitude of dead suckers, and the huge corpse of corruptor gorgone, all framed by the gleaming counterpoint of the Intercessors' song.

"Andiss," gasped Kazari. "My friend – Dari – she and the tinsmith's apprentice. They went that way!"

Mikel and Jern followed Kazari's pointing fingertip and vanished down the passageway Dari had taken. At a nod from Andiss; Elliam, Abel, and half the Intercessors followed. Kazari tried to join them, but was stopped by Sendar's arm.

"No, Kaz. That pursuit isn't for you." She tried to shrug him off, but he shook his head again. "Don't. What would you do if you caught her?"

"I'd . . . I'd . . . " Kazari stopped. What would she do? She had no idea. She didn't even know where she was right now. And neither did Sendar. Who even knew how extensive the tunnel network was? To hare off after Dari who had a significant head start, tired and anguished, was not a good plan. For a moment she was furious with Sendar for stopping her, then she was almost overcome with despair for Dari.

What had her friend done? What had brought her to that point?

"Andiss, Dari's . . . " Words failed her.

"We heard the end of it, Kaz. Sendar's right. There's nothing here for you to do right now. We need to discover the extent of this nest, and we'll need help to do so. Take Sendar and leave this place. There's a Healer above. She'll take care of Sendar's injuries better than either you or I. When you're back at the cathedral, send a message to the Abbey, to Ailani, for me. Ask her to send a Hunter contingent – she'll know what I mean – and four Navigators. Sign it using my name. And copy it to Alexando. Can you do that?" He tipped her chin up with one finger, looking into her eyes, searching them.

"Yes," she replied at last.

"Javon and I will return later," said Andiss. The other Hunter nodded.

"Kaz, you and Sendar have done enough today." She fore-stalled Kazari's reply with a lifted finger. "And yes, I know you feel as if you're abandoning your friend. But you're not, Kaz. It's she who has abandoned you. We'll talk more, later. Your responsibility is to Sendar now."

And as Kazari turned to her fellow Hunter, she realised that indeed it was. Sendar had propped himself on the wall, and even in the lamplight Kazari could see that his normally dark skin was several shades lighter, and his face was drawn with pain. The slice Dari had carved into him was still bleeding, and the wound was gaping in places.

She moved quickly to support him, remorseful that she'd allowed herself to be so caught up in her own anguish that she'd momentarily forgotten Sendar's injuries. She had nothing to staunch the bleeding except her shirt. She'd just begun to pull it out of her trousers when one of the Intercessors hastened over and handed her a clean cloth.

"Here, Kazari. When you're ready, I'll lead you out." The man's face was kind, and his eyes concerned. "I have little skill with wounds of the body, but perhaps I can help in other ways." He sang a short phrase, perfectly pitched, tones round and easy, and the darkness around them seemed to lift a little, and to Kazari's eyes, Sendar's face relaxed slightly. She folded the cloth into a long length, and then used a second one, proffered by the Intercessor, to tie it firmly around Sendar's face.

"Thanks, Kaz. And?" Sendar whispered.

"Jame."

"Thank you, Jame."

"Can you walk, Sendar?" asked Kazari. He nodded, and they began to make their slow way out, following Jame, whose diamond pendant shone with its own light. It was as if the Lady's light forged a path through the darkness, and Kazari was grateful for the reminder.

Yet, still, as they slowly made their way towards Seraph above, Kazari couldn't help but mourn the loss of the Dari she'd known and loved so dearly. How could something like jealousy or ambition, or rebellion, or whatever it was, turn a friend into the embodiment of evil? And how would she ever tell Gweda and Farin what had happened to their daughter – or worse, what she'd done?

Chapter Thirty-nine:
Respite

By the time they reached the exit, Kazari was glad Jame was with them. She was more exhausted than she'd realised, and Sendar was both exhausted and injured. The way out was the stairwell Kazari had discovered the night of the concert in the salon. It wasn't particularly far, but it was steep, and they had to climb multiple flights of stairs. She began to flag after the first few, and Sendar struggled even more. Jame had tucked himself under Sendar's shoulder, but by the end of the climb, Kazari had needed to add her support to the other side.

By the time they climbed into the now deserted building, it was dark, and blood had soaked the bandage around Sendar's face. Kazari and Jame helped Sendar into the wagon with the Healer for the ride back to the Cathedral, and then Jame had vanished back down the stairs, his diamond still blazing brightly.

The street outside was mostly deserted, except for two blue clad Judicars who nodded at Kazari, but continued to erect a barrier around the front of the building. As the wagon rolled away, out of the corner of her eye, Kazari saw a figure clad in Juster's livery vanish into one of the alleyways. No doubt to report to Juster and Ralen. Seraph had been corrupted, but only time would tell how deeply Seraph's rulers were implicated. Sometimes things seemed incredibly complicated.

She sent the missives to Alexando and the Abbot, fastening the messages to the pigeons with trembling hands. Then she visited Sendar in the cathedral's small infirmary, His face was pale, but clean. The dried blood had been removed, and the long wound had closed, and now looked as if it was months old. He was asleep. Kazari tucked a limp hand into hers, and sat in a chair, looking at him, feeling despair settle like a stone inside her.

It was twice now that he'd been injured in the last year – and this time it was because of her. She recalled the Abbot's face on the morning she'd awoken knowing she'd become a Hunter. There had been sadness then, and now that she'd been in the sept for a while, Kazari realised she was beginning to understand why. The sheltered life she'd left when she'd made her choice, now seemed precious beyond belief. The idea that someone might choose to destroy that way of life for others for personal gain – or what they thought would be personal gain – seemed madness. Her heart was so heavy with sorrow that she felt as if something within her might break.

She dropped her face onto the bed, hugging Sendar's warm hand to her cheek for comfort, and finally fell asleep in that position, face still damp from the tears that had leaked in exhausted trails from her closed lids.

When she awoke, it was to daylight, and she was cramped and uncomfortable. Sendar's hand was still in hers, but as she stirred, she felt his warm fingers move. His hand moved to stroke her cheek, and she jerked upright, to see his tired eyes watching her.

"Sendar! Are you all right?"

He smiled. "I'm fine – now. The Healers have done a great job." But Kazari could still see the shadows in his eyes that spoke of wounds beyond the physical ones. But then the shadows receded to be replaced by concern. "Kaz . . . Dari . . . I'm so sorry." He broke off.

Kazari's chest cramped as if it was caught between the jaws of a vice. Dari. Her friend. Her *best* friend. Her – she almost

couldn't think the words – her *enemy*. Or at least on a path at
such a radical angle to Kazari's own that it was almost beyond
believing. In fact, if she hadn't heard the words from Dari's
own mouth, she wouldn't have believed them. She shook her
head, eyes flooding with tears, and mind burning with pain and
anger so intertwined that she couldn't figure out where one
ended and the other one began.

Her throat was so tight she couldn't speak, or sob, or even
groan, her body a ball of emotional agony so powerful that she
felt as if every muscle was about to snap. Sendar's hands
gripped her own, and the strength of that grip made her lift
her eyes to his again. In them, she saw sadness, pain, the
shadows of the last year, and a compassion so deep that she
imagined she could feel it pouring from his hands into her
own.

She squeezed back, her hands thawing, until a single sound,
half sob, half groan, escaped her spasmed throat. It was as if
something within her had burst, and she clung to Sendar's
warm hands as if they were the only thing secure in a world
that had suddenly turned into the heart of a storm. Her body
heaved with dry sobs, and the tears that she hoped might fall
to ease her pain, dried. Eventually, the dry sobs ceased, and her
body uncurled, and she realised that Sendar had bent forward
to tuck himself around her as if to take her pain upon himself.

Her muscles relaxed, and she was empty except for the
comfort of his tall frame curled around hers. They sat like that
until one of the Healers came in with a tray of breakfast for
them both.

"Andiss wishes you to breakfast and then join him and
Javon once you've bathed and changed your clothing,
Hunters," she said. "They'll be in the grove. No-one will disturb
you there."

After bathing, and donning clean clothing, Kazari felt
physically better, even if her mind was still reeling from Dari's
betrayal and the encounter with the corruptor. As she waited
for Sendar, Kazari couldn't help but feel that her childhood

was now only a distant memory. Her innocence was lost, and her memories of Dari would now always be stained with the patina of malice that had marred her friend's voice. The violence she'd done to Sendar – and apparently relished – was so at odds with the generosity and warmth of the years Kazari had spent with her, that it seemed as if it must have been done by someone else.

Had her years of friendship with Dari been only a facade? Had there always been something else beneath the surface?

She closed her eyes and drew a wobbling breath, willing her shoulder muscles to relax, and her body to release its tension, and then turned with a wobbly smile to Sendar as he moved slightly stiffly to her side. In silence they walked to the cathedral's grove, and stepped within its calm boundaries.

Kazari breathed in deeply, smelling the scent of growing things around her, and followed Sendar over to where Andiss and Javon, with Jern and Mikel, waited, weariness evident in all of them. Andiss motioned to the ground, and they joined the others cross-legged on the spongy grass. As in many of the Lady's special places, calm surrounded them, and for a moment there was silence.

"The tunnel network was extensive. We found and killed many suckers, and of course, the corruptor is now gone. But we did not find Dari and Sereth, Kaz. And there were signs of many more gorgones, and of long-term habitation. It seems that the gorgone presence in Seraph is more established than even our worst fears." He sighed tiredly. "Mikel and Jern were forced to turn back. They'd set some of the tunnels to collapse behind them, so we have no way of knowing exactly how far they extend, or where they originate. At least we now know how they've been infiltrating Albatar."

"But for how long?" asked Javon. It sounded as if she'd asked the question before, so that this time it was almost rhetorical. There was no answer.

"What does this mean, for us, and for Albatar?" asked Sendar.

"It means that this incursion is bigger than we feared, and more established, but it also means that some of the things that have puzzled us have partial answers," replied Mikel. "The gorgone at the Abbey, for example. The Abbot will be scouring the countryside by now, searching for tunnels. And the general apathy – the drift away from the Lady – may well be founded not simply in the tendency of people to become complacent, but because of the subtle influences of ones such as the corruptor."

"And us – now – what do we do?" asked Sendar, uncertainly. A soft breeze stirred the leaves in the branches above them, and the smell of open flowers drifted down, and Kazari felt comfort roll down with the scent. She looked up, surprised, as the wind stirred the branches even more, and a shaft of sunlight floated down, and came to rest upon Sendar's head. His dark skin gleamed in its light, the long line of the wound clearly evident on his skin, and the amethyst on his chest lit to a vivid violet. His eyes widened, and took on some of the amethyst's tone. Then he spoke. "Yes, Lady, I hear you."

Kazari bit off a startled exclamation.

Sendar took her hand in his left one, and she reached out blindly for Andiss. His calloused hand enclosed hers, and then they were all seeing what Sendar saw. Fire. Smoke. gorgones. And arrayed against them, Hunters, flanked by Navigators, and standing resolutely behind them, the other Septs of the Order, arrayed in their rainbow of colours. For a moment, Kazari thought the vision was symbolic in nature, but then the scent and smells of battle rolled over them and she knew that it was a foreshadowing of what might come.

"Remember that you do not stand alone in this fight," came the Lady's voice, warm and familiar. *"You are mine, and my Gifts will sustain you. And even now, you are much more than helpless against the gorgone-horde. Seek those who are still lost. You will find them everywhere, even in the halls of power. Search for those who look for me, and give them direction. This day's work will provide a brief time of respite. Use it wisely."*

The last words finished on almost a whisper, and the pool of sunlight faded from Sendar's form. Slowly, his eyes lost their violet tone, but Kazari could feel her amethyst warm upon her chest. She looked down, to see it glowing on its leather thong and for a moment was lost in the sensation of the Lady's love. When she returned to herself, her pain, although still present, had less of a sharp edge. It was still right to feel it, because what *she'd* treasured about Dari had been real, even if her friend had lived a lie, at least for a time.

"Is it right to still feel hope?" she asked, hesitantly, "For Dari, I mean."

"It is never wrong to feel hope," replied Andiss. "The Lady forgives when you or I would walk away."

Then Kazari was embarrassed. The Lady had provided a vision, and all she could do was think about her lost friendship. She turned to Sendar. His tall form was sitting so still he might have been an ebon statue. The last of the violet tone drained from his eyes, and he lifted a trembling hand to his amethyst and bowed his head.

"Thank you, Lady," he breathed. Then he looked up. "You saw?"

Andiss nodded gravely. "It has been long since we've had such clear direction from the Lady. You and Kazari will go to the Abbey and consult with Ailani. She may have insights we lack, and the overall direction of the Order is at her discretion. She must hear first hand of this revelation." He paused as a rustle sounded outside the grove.

"Your pardon, Andiss, but word has come for you." One of the Growers moved forward, a note in hand.

"Thank you," replied Andiss, and took it and read. He paused. "From Ailani. We are to go to the capital. She will join us there. We must consult with the rulers of Albatar. The Queen calls on us to inform her parliament of the things we have found here, and also in Suborden. She wishes to hear them firsthand from all of us." He looked up at the Grower. "Please ask if we might have provisions prepared so that we may leave tomorrow."

The Grower nodded and withdrew, green robes rustling like leaves. Kazari noticed absently that the creepers twined around the grove's pillars drifted slightly towards her as she passed between them.

Uneasily, she contemplated the future. Tunnels beneath Albatar – and who knew how many, or even where they might be? Or lead? How many of her friends and family were in danger that very moment? Her reunion with her family now seemed such a fragile thing. And she was going to the capital – to meet with the Queen? She looked up at Javon and Andiss.

"More politics?" she asked. Javon sighed heavily, and Andiss nodded grimly.

"Yes, more politics. And probably worse. And we have the Lady's command as well. 'Seek those who are still lost. You will find them everywhere, even in the halls of power. Search for those who look for me, and give them direction. This day's work will provide a brief time of respite. Use it wisely.'"

"It seems we have a small space to regather, and to find those who truly seek the Lady," said Javon. "And then to do . . . what?"

"How many underground nests might there be in Albatar?" wondered Jern. She looked at Andiss. "Mikel and I will wait here until the Hunter contingent arrives. Then we'll make haste to join you in Eyrie. Mikel, do you think Arilin will be happy to see you?"

"Now that's the question, isn't it? It can be a bit . . . awkward at times," said Mikel. Kazari knew that Mikel had come from one of Albatar's ruling families, but he knew the Queen? And things were awkward? "She's my cousin," he said shrugging. "We know each other pretty well, but I'm the black sheep. The family had other plans, which I messed up by becoming a Hunter."

Mikel was the cousin of the Queen? The day was getting stranger by the minute.

Chapter Forty: Never Wrong

They'd stayed in the grove for some time, discussing the events of the night before, and sharing their knowledge of exactly what had led to each decision and each moment. It was painful, but at the same time, cathartic. Kazari knew there were things she might never reconcile, but the process helped her to categorise some of her feelings and thoughts.

They'd then spent time doing the most familiar of Hunter things – working their way through the katas. By the time they'd finished, Kazari felt more relaxed, despite her sadness. The movements themselves spoke of the Lady's love, and were like soothing balm to her battered soul.

"The rest of the day is yours," said Andiss. "Javon and I have politics to do at the manor house." He smiled briefly. "This time we'll leave you out of it. You'll have enough politics in Eyrie."

Javon nodded, sighed, and then told them to eat well, use the hot baths at the cathedral, and pack for departure in the morning. The four older Hunters departed the grove, but as Kazari stood up to leave, Sendar placed a hand on her arm.

"A moment, Kaz," he said. "Just for us."

"It'll probably be the last one for a while," she replied, nodding her agreement, and turning to face him. She looked sadly at the scar on his face. It would always be there, a reminder of the pain her friendship with Dari had brought him. A pang of guilt struck her, but she took a deep breath, and reminded herself of what Javon had said the day before. Dari's actions belonged to no-one but Dari.

"Kaz," said Sendar. "We . . . we haven't really spoken . . . but . . ." He paused, and Kazari thought he was blushing.

"Spoken?" she asked. The air around them was suddenly warmer than it had been, she thought. He moved a step closer, and she could smell the clean smell of his soap. He took her hand, and his hand was warmer than she could have imagined, all lean strength and gentleness at the same time.

"I mean – talked about – about us." He stammered, his words at odds with his grip. He *was* blushing she realised, and so was she. He was talking about this . . . thing. The thing she knew had been growing but that neither of them had named for what it was.

"Um . . . yes. I mean, no," she replied. "No, we haven't." He pulled her closer, and her breath caught in her throat.

"It doesn't seem right, and the timing is off, but . . . I care for you, Kaz," he said, awkwardly, stumbling over the sentence. "I – I just want to know if you . . . care for me too. I mean, in the same way."

Kazari looked up at him, suddenly shy to meet his eyes, but when she did, it was as if a part of her that had been frozen suddenly thawed.

Wordlessly, she nodded, using the strength in his hands to draw herself even closer. And then Sendar bent his head and kissed her, and for a moment, the world stopped, and the struggles of the last weeks and months faded to nothing. It was a moment of peace, and rightness, that eclipsed all the pain she'd been feeling so that Kazari wanted to live only in that moment forever. And it was such a contrast to Dari's actions in the depths below Seraph that she could feel how inherently *good* it was.

Of their own volition, her arms went around him, holding him even closer, and his mirrored hers, so that when their lips parted, Sendar was able to tuck Kazari into his chest. She rested her head there, his heart beating strongly under her ear, and the firm muscle of his frame a familiar, comfortable support. There was nothing demanding about their embrace, but it was a moment of care – of love – that made Kazari realise that together they might find moments of happiness, whatever might come in the future, and however uncertain that future seemed to be.

Eventually, Sendar sighed, his arms loosening reluctantly. He looked down at Kazari, and she saw her thoughts mirrored in his eyes.

"Is it right?" she asked. "To feel like this when everything else is falling apart?"

"It can't be wrong," he replied. "Love could never be wrong."

Kazari smiled at him, the first smile in what seemed like days, and the movement of her lips seemed to send warmth and life flooding through her entire body.

"It might be complicated, Kaz, maybe even unwise, but I couldn't go on without knowing if you felt the same way. Not now, not if . . . " He broke off.

"Not if something happened? To one of us, I mean," she said.

Sendar nodded, and his arms tightened around her again.

"Nothing's the same, is it?"

He shook his head slowly. "No, nothing's the same, and maybe never will be. It wasn't the same after Suborden really, but now I think we're at a crossroads. Albatar is in more danger now, than at any time since the Founding, and I think it has been for a long time. Those tunnels didn't happen in a day, or a week, or even a month. This must have been many long years in the planning."

"Then we should be on our way again," replied Kazari. "Even if all I want to do is stand here like this, forever."

Together they turned their faces towards the future.

Thank you for reading DARK DAYS. We hope you enjoyed it.

If you would like to be kept informed of further releases by Leonie Rogers, or other new books from Hague Publishing, why not subscribe to our newsletter at:

www.HaguePublishing.com/subscribe.php

And if you loved the book and have a moment to spare we would really appreciate a short review. Your help in spreading the word is gratefully received.

About the Author

Originally from Western Australia, Leonie now lives in NSW in the Upper Hunter. She is the author of the Frontier Trilogy, published by Hague Publishing, and also works part time as a physiotherapist. *Amethyst Pledge*, Book 1 of the *Chronicles of Albatar*, and a new fantasy, was launched in 2020. She has a past life as a volunteer firefighter and SES member, and once trekked almost six hundred kilometres with eight camels and several other human beings. She is married with two adult children, two dogs and three cats, one of whom frequently handicaps her ability to use a laptop computer.

Hague

Publishing

www.HaguePublishing.com

PO Box 451 Bassendean
Western Australia 6934

www.ingramcontent.com/pod-product-compliance
Lightning Source LLC
Chambersburg PA
CBHW070044120726
47909CB00002B/286